2/2

A
Dark-Adapted
Eye

A
Dark-Adapted
Eye

Barbara Vine

BANTAM BOOKS
TORONTO · NEW YORK · LONDON · SYDNEY · AUCKLAND

A DARK-ADAPTED EYE

A Bantam Book / July 1986

*Grateful acknowledgment is made for permission to reprint the
definition of dark adaptation from* A Dictionary of Psychology
*by James Drever (Penguin Books, 1952). Copyright © 1952 by
James Drever. Reprinted by permission of Penguin Books Ltd.*

Library of Congress Cataloging-in-Publication Data

Rendell, Ruth, 1930–
   A dark-adapted eye.

   I. Title.
PR6068.E63D3   1986   823'.914   85-48231
ISBN 0-553-05143-1

*Bantam Books are published by Bantam Books, Inc. Its trade-
mark, consisting of the words "Bantam Books" and the por-
trayal of a rooster, is Registered in U.S. Patent and Trademark
Office and in other countries. Marca Registrada. Bantam
Books, Inc., 666 Fifth Avenue, New York, New York 10103.*

PRINTED IN THE UNITED STATES OF AMERICA

DH   0 9 8 7 6 5 4 3 2 1

DARK ADAPTATION: *a condition of vision brought about progressively by remaining in complete darkness for a considerable period, and characterized by progressive increase in retinal sensitivity. A* dark-adapted eye *is an eye in which dark adaptation has taken place.*

—James Drever, *A Dictionary of Psychology*

I

ON THE MORNING Vera died I woke up very early. The birds had started, more of them and singing more loudly in our leafy suburb than in the country. They never sang like that outside Vera's windows in the Vale of Dedham. I lay there listening to something repeating itself monotonously. A thrush, it must have been, doing what Browning said it did and singing each song twice over. It was a Thursday in August, a hundred years ago. Not much more than a third of that, of course. It only feels so long.

In these circumstances alone one knows when someone is going to die. All other deaths can be predicted, conjectured, even anticipated with some certainty, but not to the hour, the minute, with no room for hope. Vera would die at eight o'clock and that was that. I began to feel sick. I lay there exaggeratedly still, listening for some sound from the next room. If I was awake my father would be. About my mother I was less sure. She had never made a secret of her dislike of both his sisters. It was one of the things which had made a rift between them, though there they were together in the next room, in the same bed still. People did not break a marriage, leave each other, so lightly in those days.

I thought of getting up but first I wanted to make sure where my father was. There was something terrible in the idea of encountering him in the passage, both of us dressing-gowned, thick-eyed with sleeplessness, each seeking the bathroom and each politely giving way to the other. Before I saw him I needed to be washed and brushed and dressed, my loins girded. I could hear nothing but that thrush uttering its idiot phrase five or six times over, not twice.

To work he would go as usual, I was sure of that. And Vera's name would not be mentioned. None of it had been spoken about at all in our house since the last time my father went to see Vera. There was one crumb of comfort for him. No one knew. A man may be very close to his sister, his twin, without anyone knowing of the relationship, and none of our neighbors knew he was Vera Hillyard's brother. None of the bank's clients knew. If today the head cashier remarked upon Vera's death, as he very likely might, as people would by reason of her sex among other things, I knew my father would present to him a bland, mildly interested face and utter some suitable platitude. He had, after all, to survive.

A floorboard creaked in the passage. I heard the bedroom door close and then the door of the bathroom, so I got up and looked at the day. A clean white still morning, and no sun and no blue in the sky, a morning that seemed to me to be waiting because I was. Six-thirty. There was an angle you could stand at looking out of this window where you could see no other house, so plentiful were the trees and shrubs, so thick their foliage. It was like looking into a clearing in a rather elaborate wood. Vera used to sneer at where my parents lived, saying it was neither town nor country.

My mother was up now. We were all stupidly early, as if we were going away on holiday. When I used to go to Sindon I was sometimes up as early as this, excited and looking forward to it. How could I have looked forward to the society of Vera, an unreasonable carping scold when on her own with me, and when Eden was there the two of them closing ranks to exclude anyone who might try to penetrate their alliance? I hoped, I suppose. Each time I was older, and because of this she might change. She never did—until almost the end. And by then she was too desperate for an ally to be choosy.

I went to the bathroom. It was always possible to tell if my father had finished in the bathroom. He used an old-fashioned cutthroat razor and wiped the blade after each stroke on a small square of newspaper. The newspaper and the jug of hot water he fetched himself, but the remains were always left for my mother to clear away, the square of paper with its load of shaving soap full of stubble, the empty jug. I washed in cold water. In summer, we only lit the boiler once a week for baths. Vera and Eden bathed every day, and that was one of the things I *had* liked about Sindon, my daily bath, though Vera's attitude always was that I would have escaped it if I could.

The paper had come. It was tomorrow the announcement would appear, of course, a few bald lines. Today there was nothing about Vera. She was stale, forgotten, until this morning, when, in a brief flare-up, the whole country would talk of her, those who deplored and those who said it served her right. My father sat at the dining table, reading the paper. It was the *Daily Telegraph,* than which no other daily paper was ever read in our family. The crossword puzzle he would save for the evening, just as Vera had done, once only in all the years phoning my father for the solution to a clue that was driving her crazy. When Eden had a home of her own and was rich, she often rang him up and got him to finish the puzzle for her over the phone. She had never been as good at it as they.

He looked up and nodded to me. He didn't smile. The table had yesterday's cloth on it, yellow check not to show the egg stains. Food was still rationed, meat being very scarce, and we ate eggs all the time, laid by my mother's chickens. Hence the crowing cockerels in our garden suburb, the fowl runs concealed behind hedges of lonicera and laurel. We had no eggs that morning, though. No cornflakes either. My mother would have considered cornflakes frivolous, in their white-and-orange packet. She had disliked Vera, had no patience with my father's intense family love, but she had a strong sense of occasion, of what was fitting. Without a word, she brought us toast that, while hot, had been thinly spread with margarine, a jar of marrow and ginger jam, a pot of tea.

I knew I shouldn't be able to eat. He ate. Business was to be as usual with him, I could tell that. It was over, wiped away, a monstrous effort made, if not to forget, at least to behave as if all was forgotten. The silence was broken by his voice, harsh and stagy, reading aloud. It was something about the war in Korea. He read on and on, columns of it, and it became embarrassing to listen because no one reads like that without introduction, explanation, excuse. It must have gone on for ten minutes. He read to the foot of the page, to where presumably you were told the story was continued inside. He didn't turn over. He broke off in mid-sentence. "In the Far," he said, never getting to "East" but laying the paper down, aligning the pages, folding it once, twice, and once more, so that it was back in the shape it had been when the boy pushed it through the letterbox.

"In the Far" hung in the air, taking on a curious significance, quite different from what the writer had intended. He took another piece of toast but got no further towards eating it. My mother watched him. I think she had been tender with him once but he had had no time for it or room for it and so her tenderness had withered for want of encouragement. I did not expect her to go to him and take his hand or put her arms round him. Would I have done so myself if she had not been there? Perhaps. That family's mutual love had not usually found its expression in outward show. In other words, there had not been embraces. The twins, for instance, did not kiss each other, though the women pecked the air around each other's faces.

It was a quarter to eight now. I kept repeating over and over to myself (like the thrush, now silent), "In the far, in the far." When first it happened, when he was told, he went into paroxysms of rage, of disbelief, of impotent protest.

"Murdered, murdered!" he kept shouting, like someone in an Elizabethan tragedy, like someone who bursts into a castle hall with dreadful news. And then, "My sister!" and "My poor sister!" and "My little sister!"

But silence and concealment fell like a shutter. It was lifted briefly, after Vera was dead, when, sitting in a closed room after dark, like conspirators, he and I heard from Josie what happened that April day. He never spoke of it again. His twin was erased from his mind and he even made himself—incredibly—into an only child. Once I heard him tell someone that he had never regretted having no brothers or sisters.

It was only when he was ill and not far from death himself that he resurrected memories of his sisters. And the stroke he had had, as if by some physiological action stripping away layers of reserve and inhibition, making him laugh sometimes and just as often cry, released an unrestrained gabbling about how he had felt that summer. His former love for Vera the repressive years had turned to repulsion and fear, his illusions broken as much by the tug-of-war and Eden's immorality—his word, not mine—as by the murder itself. My mother might have said, though she did not, that at last he was seeing his sisters as they really were.

He left the table, his tea half-drunk, his second piece of toast lying squarely in the middle of his plate, the *Telegraph* folded and lying with its edges compulsively lined up to the table corner. No word was spoken to my mother and me. He went upstairs, he came down, the front door closed behind him. He would walk the leafy roads, I thought, making detours, turning the half-mile to the station into two miles, hiding from the time in places where there were no clocks. It was then that I noticed he had left his watch on the table. I picked up the paper and there was the watch underneath.

"We should have gone away somewhere," I said.

My mother said fiercely, "Why should we? She hardly ever came here. Why should we let her drive us away?"

"Well, we haven't," I said.

I wondered which was right, the clock on the wall that said five to eight or my father's watch that said three minutes to. My own watch was upstairs. Time passes so slowly over such points in it. There still seemed an aeon to wait. My mother loaded the tray and took it into the kitchen, making a noise about it, banging cups, a way of showing that it was no fault of hers. Innocent herself, she had been dragged into this family by marriage, all unknowing. It was another matter for me, who was of their blood.

I went upstairs. My watch was on the bedside table. It was new, a present bestowed by my parents for getting my degree. That, because of what had happened, it was a less good degree than everyone had expected, no one had commented upon. The watch face was small, not much larger than the cluster of little diamonds in my engagement ring that lay beside it, and you had to get close up to it to read the hands. I thought: In a moment the heavens will fall, there will be a great bolt of thunder. Nature could not simply ignore. There was nothing. Only the birds had become silent, which they would do anyway at this time, their territorial claims being made, their trees settled on, the business of their day begun. What would the business of my day be? One thing I thought I would do. I would phone Helen, I would talk to Helen. Symbolic of my attitude to my engagement, my future marriage, this was, that it was to Helen I meant to fly for comfort, not the man who had given me the ring with a diamond cluster as big as a watch face.

I walked over to the bedside table, stagily, self-consciously, like a bad actress in an amateur production. The director would have halted me and told me to do it again, to walk away and do it again. I nearly did walk away so as not to see the time. But I picked up the watch and looked and had a long, rolling, falling feeling through my body as I saw that I had missed the moment. It was all over now and she was dead. The hands of the watch stood at five past eight.

The only kind of death that can be accurately predicted to the minute had taken place, the death that takes its victim,

> . . . feet foremost through the floor,
> Into an empty space.

2

THREE TIMES IN the past thirty-five years I had seen her name in print. Once was in a newspaper headline over one of the parts in a series on women hanged in England this century. I was sitting in a train and I looked sideways at the tabloid page the man next to me was reading. The letters in her name leapt out at me, bold, black, upright, making me jump. At the next stop I got out. I longed in one way to see that evening paper, *The Star* in those days, but in another I dreaded it and dread won. Before that she had been in *The Times* when the abolition of capital punishment was the big issue of the day. An MP mentioned her in debate and it got into the parliamentary report. But first I had seen her name in a library book.

VERA HILLYARD was printed on the book's spine along with RUTH ELLIS, EDITH THOMPSON, and two or three others. I took it cautiously from the shelf, looking about me to make sure no one was watching. I held it in my hands and felt the weight and shape of it, but to take it out of the library, to open it and read—that seemed too big a step. I would wait, I would prepare myself, I would get into a relaxed, objective frame of mind. Two days later I went back and the book had been taken out. By the time I finally borrowed it, I had succeeded in putting aside fears and prohibitions and had worked myself into a state of excitement. I longed by then to know what some outside observer might have to say about my aunt.

It was a disappointment—more than that. The author had got it all wrong. He had mishandled the atmosphere, reproduced not at all the *flavor* of our family, and above all, he had missed the point. Indignant and annoyed, I was determined to write to him, for a whole day I was set on writing to him to point out that Vera wasn't a jealous virago, Eden a browbeaten innocent. But I no more wrote than I finished reading the book, for I understood that those chapters had served a purpose for me. A kind of catharsis had taken place, an exorcism, making me look things in the face and tell myself: She was only your aunt, it touches you only at a remove, you can think of it without real pain. And I found that I could. I was not involved, blood and bone, love and hate, as were those others so much closer to her. I even thought of writing something myself, an insider's account of Vera and of what led up to it all.

But there was Jamie to think of. That was before I had met him and talked to him by Landor's grave. The author of the account I had read wrote of him as a pawn who could know neither love nor pain, a wooden figure rather than a child, a puppet who was unimportant because he had not actually witnessed the murder but been snatched away in the nick of time and carried from the room. I had scarcely thought of him during the years in which he must have been growing up—incredible that I had once wistfully hoped to be made his godmother. But after I had read the piece in the library book, the piece that was so inaccurate and false that it might have been some other family the writer described, after that I began to think of him. I understood that he had become an embarrassment to certain family members. He was the catalyst who had brought it all about. It must have seemed to them that it would have been better if he had not been born—better for him too, and that is a dreadful thought. The wisest course, from his point of view and that of others, was to tuck him away. I thought then vaguely, unclearly, that one day when I was in Italy I would try to see him.

It was he in part, his existence, the fact that he had been born and was a man now capable of continued suffering, which stopped me writing anything myself. Besides, I doubted my own abilities to reconstruct Vera's life. Memories I had, and many of them, but what of the great gaps, the spaces in the past? There were those years when I scarcely went to Sindon, stretches of time all-important in the fatal convergence of things, the winter for instance when Vera was ill, and the following year when she and Jamie escaped and fled like refugees from an oppressor.

Chad could have done it. He was a journalist, he knew how it should be done, and God knows he had seen as much of the unfolding and the fulfilled destinies as I had—more than I had, for he was always at Laurel Cottage, unable to keep away, fixated on a place, a house, as lovers are for whom bricks and mortar can soak up the essence of the beloved the way that nursery floor soaked up blood.

But did I, after all, particularly want a Vera book to be written? I had succeeded quite well at the business of forgetting her. My children were almost grown-up before they knew Vera Hillyard was their great-aunt—no, let me put that differently, before they knew that a woman who was their mother's aunt had been hanged for murder. The name of Vera Hillyard they had never heard. And when they knew, they weren't shocked, of course they weren't, only curious and rather excited. My husband and I never mentioned her. I don't think I heard my own mother, for the rest of her life, ever name her. Vera, in all that time, made herself known to me only in occasional dreams, when I would be a child again, and coming back from Anne's to Laurel Cottage on a warm summer evening, be reproached for my lateness or asked in Vera's peculiarly brisk querulous way how I ever thought I would be fit to do my schoolwork in the morning. Or I open a dream door into a dream room and Vera is sitting there, Madonna-like, tranquil and splendid, her breasts bare and the suckling Jamie in her arms. The baby never looks at me, he turns his face away or covers it with his arm. But he is Jamie and all roads always lead back to him.

We were staying in an hotel in the Via Cavour. Later on, Jamie told me it was the one in which Francis had stayed when first they met after twenty years apart. In Francis's room were two pictures, ugly abstracts in raucous colors, and pretentious too. He got two narrow strips of white adhesive paper, wrote on one in Italian *Section Through a Blackhead* and on the other *Contents of a Drain in the Borgo Pinti,* and carefully attached each onto a picture. Jamie asked me to try to get into Room 36 and take a look if I could. I did and the stickers were still there, *Contenuto d'un Canale dal Borgo Pinti* and the other which I don't remember the Italian for. No chambermaid or bellboy had ever spotted them, and if guests had seen and marveled, they had never mentioned their discovery to the management. How typical of Francis this was! Jamie took a gleeful delight in it, in this aspect of Francis, laughing in his shrill hiccuping way at the very thought of Francis's teases and practical jokes. They had become friends of a kind, those two, the last thing one would have expected.

It was more than twenty years since I had seen Jamie, nearer twenty-five. Of course I knew he lived in Italy, had felt a special affinity with Italy since spending his school holidays with the Contessa who had a house somewhere near Verona. After school came to an end he stayed for a while in London with another Pearmain relative and then Tony sent him to the University of Bologna. Always, you see, he had to be kept out of sight, for he was an embarrassment and a reminder. In all this time I don't think Tony saw him but communicated with him through solicitors, like people in Victorian novels, turning him into a remittance man, but one who in this case had committed no offense. But this may not be so, or not quite so, or different in detail. Jamie's life has been and still is a mystery, his very existence a mystery.

Patricia it was who told me he was a journalist, a war correspondent who had been in Vietnam. Helen believed otherwise. In her version, Jamie worked at the Biblioteca Nazionale and had been one of those concerned in the salvaging of precious books when the Arno overflowed in the great library in November 1966. Francis might have told us the truth, but none of us, not even Helen regularly, kept in touch with Francis, except Gerald, his father. And Gerald, Helen said, must have been "going strange" even then, for he averred Francis had told him Jamie was a cook.

All these beliefs contained something of the truth, as such beliefs usually do. I went to Florence without any idea of looking Jamie up, for this was the third or fourth time I had been there, and without doing more than reflect that for a few days we would be in the same city, he and I. But at Pisa, where, having just missed the Florence train, we had time to kill, we bought a newspaper, *La Nazione,* and on an inside page I found Jamie's name: James Ricardo. His byline (as journalists call it, as years and years ago Chad Hamner first taught me to call it) was under a heading which, translated, means "delicious crust" and over an article on how to make *pâte sablée.* Jamie *was* a journalist, he *was* a cook, and later on I heard from his own lips that it was true he had helped in the book rescue.

When we got to Florence I looked him up in the phone book.

There were a lot of Ricardos but only one James. I was nervous about phoning him. People can put the phone down but all they can do with a letter is not answer it. I wrote him a note. This was before he went to live in the gardens of the Orcellari—the Otello restaurant is on the corner at the top—and the address was a street off the Viale Gramsci, up near where the Porta à Pinti once stood. Jamie wrote back by return. He had heard of me, Francis had mentioned the existence of a cousin and said we knew each other when he was a child, but of that he had no recollection. Perhaps we should meet. Would I meet him in the English Cemetery when it opened at three on the following afternoon?

"Why can't he ask you to his house or come here like a civilized person?" said my husband.

I said that since his life and his origins were so shrouded in the mysterious, perhaps he enjoyed keeping up the mystery. He must like the arcane.

"I'm not sure *I* like the idea of my wife having assignations in cemeteries with strange cookery columnists," he said. "At any rate, you'd better look out for yourself crossing the piazza, the way the traffic sweeps round."

But he wouldn't come with me, fearing Jamie might have turned out like Francis. He went off to buy a pair of shoes.

The Cimitero Protestante di Porta à Pinti, known as the "English Cemetery," though there are Americans and Poles and plenty of Swiss buried there too, stands like a hilly green island in the middle of the Piazza Donatello. And the traffic, as my husband said, rushes round and past it as a millrace might sweep past just such an island. It was a beautiful day, clear and sunny, blue-skied, hot by our standards though not by those of the Florentines, who by the end of September, having endured months of true heat, were already wearing their winter leather and wool. The iron gates were closed but the custodian, seeing me, came out and unlocked them and showed me the way through the archway in the gatehouse into the graveyard on the other side.

It was not silent in the cemetery—how could it be with that traffic not a hundred yards away?—but it had an *air* of silence, an air of endeavoring to be silent, brought about by the ranks of pale, bright gray stones and the thin cypress trees. At first I didn't see Jamie. The cemetery appeared to be empty. I walked slowly up the path towards the Emperor Frederick William's marble column, past Elizabeth

Barrett's tomb, looking rather cautiously from side to side, feeling exposed now, feeling watched. But Jamie wasn't watching me or even watching for me. I found him when I turned back, seated on the grave of Walter Savage Landor and reading, perhaps not too surprisingly, Brillat-Savarin's celebrated work on gastronomy, *La Physiologie du Goût*.

I hadn't known Landor was in there. Chad had quoted him on Eden's wedding day, standing by the lake in the garden at Walbrooks: "There are no voices . . . that are not soon mute, however tuneful; there is no name, with whatever emphasis of passionate love repeated, of which the echo is not faint at last." The echo of Eden's name was faint by then. I had forgotten what Chad's voice sounded like, though his face I remembered and Hadrian's ears. Jamie looked up at me and then he got up.

"Yes," he said, "you look like a Longley. I would have recognized you as a Longley—from photographs, of course."

I held out my hand to him. We shook hands.

"I mostly come here in the afternoons," he said. "It's peaceful without being quiet if you know what I mean. People don't come much. People are frightened of cemeteries." And for the first time I heard that curious neighing laugh of his. "I suppose you would have preferred to be invited to my apartment?"

The American term sounded strange in Jamie's voice, which is English-public-school with overtones of Italian, especially about the R's. They are a bit too liquid, his R's, pronounced too high up in the mouth. I said I didn't mind, it was nice to be able to sit outside. We couldn't do much of that in England.

"I haven't been back there for fourteen years," he said. "I don't suppose I shall ever go now. The thought of England fills me with horror."

It is disconcerting, the way he laughs after he has said something not at all laughable, in just the same way as he laughs when he has expressed pleasure or amusement. The laughter died and he stared at me. Suddenly he made a flicking movement with his right hand towards his left shoulder, caught me looking and drew his hand away, laughing again. He is a thick-set, going-to-seed, not very tall man who looks older than he is. He also looks Italian with his round, full-featured, sallow face, his red lips, and his dark curly hair. And this is very much what one would expect, all things considered. Though fair-haired as a child he always had olive skin. His eyes, which in those days the grown-ups looked at curiously, surreptitiously, watching for the color to stay or to change, are a dark velvety glowing brown, animal eyes but feral, not meek. That time in the English Cemetery he reminded me a little of Chad, which is absurd. There was no real physical resemblance and Jamie was too young to have creases on his earlobes. Perhaps what they had in common was a look of desire unsatisfied, of lives spoiled and incomplete.

I sat down facing him and he asked me hesitatingly, as if curiosity was overcoming his better judgment, to tell him about our family—his family too, of course, as much as mine. So I talked, going carefully, for I had rehearsed this on my long walk along Cavour. It wouldn't do, I felt, to mention Goodney Hall or the name of his mother or the men who had made themselves his enemies through no fault of his but because of his very existence and because of jealousy and resentment and hurt pride. My mother was still alive then, so I spoke about my parents, and about Helen and her children and her granddaughter.

"I called myself Richardson because of Aunt Helen," he said. "Pearmain didn't care. He wouldn't have cared what I called myself." He neighed with laughter and I shuddered at the way he called Tony Pearmain with such disgusted vehemence. His right hand came up again, flicking from his shoulder invisible contamination. "Zia Francesca used to tell me how much he loved children. It was her way of making me feel all right about staying with her instead of being with him. He was too busy for me but he really loved children. Did you know he was a bigshot in the Save the Children fund? He loved all the children in the world but me. Tough on him, wasn't it?" Jamie paused, staring into the sunlight, the thin parallel black shadows the cypresses made, like the bars of a cage. "Aunt Helen used to tell me what wonderful people her grandparents were. I hadn't known many wonderful people, you see, so when Pearmain said—very stiff and shy about it, Pearmain was—that now I was going to prep school I mustn't be called by my surname anymore and how about James Smith? I said not Smith but Richardson, and it was all one to him. So I called myself Richardson and later on I had it changed to Ricardo. Have you ever heard an Eye-tie pronounce 'Richardson'?"

He is practically Italian himself yet he calls Italians Eye-ties in a grinning cockney way each time he mentions them. His charmlessness suddenly clarified itself before me. It seemed to underline the absurdity of our meeting in a cemetery. The noble stones, the cypresses, the blue sky, the terra-cotta-roofed gatehouse, all these should have formed the backdrop for someone tall, handsome, and Byronic, a gracious man of character. And that was the way, I thought, Jamie had promised to grow up when last I had seen him and he was five. But the terrible things that had happened were already waiting for him, crowding at the gate, had been gathering there even before he was born.

"I don't remember anything that happened before I was six," he said. "The first thing I can remember is the summer when I was six and always being with two women I didn't like."

"Mrs. King and your nanny," I said.

"I suppose so. Pearmain used to come and look at me sometimes, the way you'd go and look at a dog you'd had put in quarantine."

I wanted to speak Vera's name then but I was afraid. The picture of the little boy—such an articulate, lively, *good* little boy he had been—alone at Goodney Hall with his two paid guardians upset me disproportionately. After all, it was long ago, it was lost in the past. Afraid and distressed, I wanted to say something about missing his mother, about my own feelings of sympathy for that, but I couldn't, and not only because of the effects of emotion. As much as that, doubt prevented my speaking, a doubt of how to phrase this expression of pity and of what terms to use. He came to my rescue.

"Would you like to go somewhere for a coffee?"

I shook my head. One of the few things I dislike about Italy is the coffee. *Cappuccino* is out for me because I don't drink milk. *Espresso* would be fine if you could have half a pint of it and not a teaspoonful.

Jamie said: "Next time you come I'll cook for you."

I realized I was honored. In this country of *haute cuisine* he, an Englishman, had made a name for himself as a cook and adviser of cooks. In that moment Vera came into my mind and I remembered her excellence in that sole aspect of culinary skill Englishwomen are best at—baking. I saw her with the puff pastry buttered and turned on the veined gray marble slab, the wood-handled marble rolling pin in her hands, and I seemed to taste again her lemon-curd tarts, her Victoria sponges, and all the rest of the panoply laid out for tea.

Jamie shocked me. "My mother was a good cook," he said.

The feeling I had was like what we have when we are in the presence of someone known to be mentally disturbed but whose manner and way of speaking are so rational that we forget the psychosis, the schizophrenia, until we are sharply and suddenly reminded of it by a remark he makes on the other side of sanity, out there in the region only the mad inhabit. Not that Jamie was anything but sane, remarkably normal really. It was more that what he said opened a door into the incredible and one's reaction was first to be horribly startled, then to feel the pity one has for those who take comfort from delusion.

His eyes that are like the eyes of a bear came back to meet mine. He jumped up, gave his shoulder a brisk brushing with his hand.

"Come on," he said. "I'll show you the graves. I'll show you Isa Blagden and Mrs. Holman Hunt."

After that he walked back with me quite a long way down the Borgo Pinti. It was then that he told me about Francis and the paintings and asked me to check if the titles Francis had given them were still there. We were shaking hands again, about to part, when he said to me, and for the first time he seemed embarrassed:

"If anyone ever wants to write about all that—you know what I mean—if they do and they approach you, I mean they're just as likely to approach you as anyone, if they do, I wouldn't mind. I don't know about Francis but I wouldn't mind. As a matter of fact I'd welcome it to put the record straight, I'd like to see the *truth*."

"But you say you don't remember," I said.

His laughter echoed in that narrow street and people turned round to look. He said good-bye to me and walked away and I never saw him again.

I couldn't agree with Jamie that any potential biographer of Vera would be as likely to approach me as anyone. For one thing, I wouldn't have expected such a biographer to find me, for I have twice changed my name since Vera died. And for another I was a mere niece, while she has a son and a husband and a sister living. Helen has reached an age when life itself has become fragile, when each day must be an only half-expected gift, when she knows there can be no future to talk about. Her memory for contemporary things is gone but her memory of the distant past is bright, and as for her mental grasp of things, I know no one sounder of any age. Yet when she told me to expect a letter and a request, I hardly took her seriously. This writer, this man called Daniel Stewart, might well have a Vera-book in mind as a project, might have asked Helen for information, but me, I was sure, he would ignore. And Helen, moreover, swore my name had not been given him by her. By Jamie then?

Stewart is a common-enough name. I must have met many Stewarts and Stuarts in those intervening years, yet when I see it at the end of this letter, I am reminded of Mary Stuart, whose life we acted out, Anne and I, and that Goodney Hall was designed by Steuart, a fact that Eden and Tony always made much of. The letter accompanies a book: *Peter Starr, the Misunderstood Murderer,* by Daniel Stewart, published by Heinemann at nine pounds ninety-five.

It is a London address on the headed paper, not too far from us on the other side of the Cromwell Road.

"Dear Mrs. Severn," he begins. "By now you may have heard from others of the project I have in mind, a biographical reappraisal of the Vera Hillyard case. Your name and address were given me by your cousin Dr. Frank Loder Hills, who does not, however, personally wish to contribute a memoir. . . ."

Francis, of course. Purely to cause trouble, I suppose, and then, as my husband suggests, to sue me and Stewart if we defame him. Stewart goes on to say he feels Vera has been in some ways misjudged. Apparently he has made a specialty of reassessing murder cases, looking at them afresh and from the viewpoint of what he calls the perpetrator.

"Mr. James Ricardo, of the Via Orti Orcellari, Florence, has undertaken to write something for me about his early memories. Mr. Anthony Pearmain is at present in the Far East but . . ."

In the Far, in the Far . . . This geographical commonplace in newspapers and on radio and television I have never been able to see or hear without remembering my father on the morning of Vera's execution reading aloud in the toneless senseless voice of a mynah bird. "In the Far . . ." he said and stopped and folded up the paper and sat there silent.

"Mrs. Helen Chatteriss has already contributed a memoir and Mr. Chad Hamner has promised to jot down for me some of his own impressions. His own intention to write a biography of Vera Hillyard he has now abandoned due to ill health.

"If you would be kind enough to read my book on Peter Starr, and if you feel satisfied with my abilities at this kind of *reportage,* I would like to send you a copy of my draft first and second chapter, my first being an account of the murder itself. I realize that since you were not present at Goodney Hall at the time you will be unable to judge the accuracy of this. Of those who were present, only Mrs. June Stoddard is still alive and her memory of events, as she herself admits, is confused.

"My second chapter, however, purports to give some family history, beginning at the time of your own great-grandfather, William Longley. Your confirmation of this account would be invaluable to me, as would any corrections you may like to make. You will see that I have drawn heavily on correspondence in the possession of Mrs. Chatteriss and the Hubbard family, as well as, to some extent, on information given in the Vera Hillyard section in Mary Gough-Williams's book *Women and Capital Punishment*."

His letter stops quite abruptly. It is as if he realizes he is beginning to write on the assumption that I shall approve, I shall want to contribute. But how very much I dislike having to read a book for some set purpose. The days when I had to do that are so many years behind me, and then, at that time, the time of the murder at Goodney Hall, the books I had to read seemed to me worthwhile, they were literature, the best that had been written. What a judgment I am making on Stewart's work! And it is not a bad book, not bad at all, clear and simply written in plain language without contrived sensationalism. There was enough sensationalism in Starr's life without exaggerating it, as there was in Vera's. I shan't finish it, though; I don't need to, for I know already that I shall write back and tell him yes. I have read enough to tell—to hope—he will be sensitive, he will not be too harsh, he will understand the terrible pressures of love.

She has come back into my life after an absence that extends over more than a third of a century. Helen and Daniel Stewart have brought her to me and she is here in the house, the awkward guest she always was when she stayed in the homes of other people. I almost fancy that I can see her—not the Vera of the photographs in "the box," young, fair, earnest-eyed, but my thin, nervous, pernickety, often absurd aunt, performing that strange, uniquely characteristic action of hers, as unconscious as a tic, as unconscious as Jamie's flick of the hand, of pressing her palms together and bearing down on her clasped hands as if in some inner anguish. Time and time again these past days she has driven me to our unused littlest bedroom, where "the box" is, and made me lift the lid and turn over the contents, pausing to look at a picture or read a line from a letter, or simply staring in a daydream of nostalgia at the memorabilia of his sisters my father left behind him.

What would poor Vera make of the moral climate of the present day? I can imagine her look of mulish incredulity. A sexual revolution took place and the world was changed. What happened to her and Eden could not have happened today. The motive and the murder were of their time, rooted in their time, not only impossible in these days but beyond the comprehension of the young unless that moral code is carefully explained to them. Because Vera is with me, is in my house like the sort of ghost that is visible to only one person, the one with the interest, I have tried to tell my daughter something of it, I have tried to elucidate.

"But why didn't she . . . ?" is the way her interjections begin. "Why didn't she tell him? Why didn't she just live with him? Why did she want to marry him if he felt like that?" And, "But what could anyone have done to her?"

All I can say, lamely, is, "It was different then."

It was different. Does Stewart, also young, know how different it was? And if he doesn't, will he take my word? Or will I find myself, as I begin to think most likely, giving him the bare facts, correcting his obvious howlers, reminiscing a little, but keeping the real book that is Vera's life recorded on a tape run only in my own consciousness?

3

THE DEED IS done and they have pinioned Vera and taken the knife from her, the knife she wanted to turn on herself, and they have tied her hands. In the nick of time Jamie has been carried from the room. Was he crying by then? Did he cry out or call to his mother? No one has ever spoken of that, as if it had been a passive stunned little creature Mrs. King snatched up in her arms—and perhaps it was. Stewart has got it right, all of it, even to the clothes Vera was wearing, clothes contrived from cot blankets and prewar remnants, even to the nursery wallpaper, even to the flying blood that splashed onto the blue and white and the shining fireguard.

As far as I know. As he says, I wasn't there.

The nucleus of this mystery I see he has handled in the conventional way, repeating the accepted version. Can he be left to these innocent assumptions of his? Or shall I tell him there is a huge question still left unanswered?

Jamie knows the answer. Or so he tells me in the letter I have had from him today. This belief of his I began to have some inkling of when we met in the English Cemetery, but since he must be the most injured and most vulnerable actor in this drama, he can hardly be deemed an impartial judge. That, of course, is the last thing he would want to be, but what then of his claim that he remembers nothing before he was six? His conviction, surely, is based solely on an inclination of the heart, on nostalgia for an adored and adoring presence that he sees in dreams but of which he has no waking recollection.

In Stewart's second chapter, the history of our family, Jamie has no place. Perhaps Stewart shirked it because he did not quite know where to put him.

The Victorian villa (Stewart writes) in the village of Great Sindon in Essex had been lived in by Longleys for less than thirty years. It was in no sense a family home. Arthur Longley bought it with the money from a small inheritance which came to his wife coincidentally with his enforced retirement from the Prudential Insurance Company. Before that, if the Longleys had roots, they were in the busy town of Colchester. There, since the early part of the nineteenth century, they had been shoemakers in a cottage with a shopfront almost under the shadow of the castle.

Colchester is England's oldest recorded town. The Romans called it Camulodunum and there Queen Boadicea fought them. To the Saxons it was Colneceaste, its river being the Colne to this day. The castle is Romanesque, its keep built in 1080, and if you stand and look at its towers and pantiled roofs on a sunny day you might fancy yourself in Tuscany. Today Colchester is approached by dual carriageways, ringed with "experimental" double roundabouts, and has a bypass often more congested than the way through the town itself. It has multistory car parks inside red brick facades designed, not altogether happily, to resemble medieval fortifications, a relentless one-way-street system and, just inside the old Roman walls, a labyrinth of ancient houses that has become a precinct of walking streets.

There in very different days, in a more peaceful and tranquil atmosphere, William Longley made and mended shoes, and later, as he grew more prosperous, employed three men to sit at work in the room behind the shop. William's shop is still there, in a cul-de-sac off Short Wyre Street, the offices now of a firm of accountants. The door between shop and workroom still remains and there too is the circular pane of glass, two inches in diameter, inserted in the oak for William to spy through and check his men plying their needles.

William had married in 1859 Amelia Jackman of Layer-de-la-Haye. Three daughters were born to them and later a son. The boy was baptized Arthur William, was given a considerably superior education to that his father had enjoyed, but nevertheless was destined to follow him in the family business. Young Arthur was a promising and popular pupil at the Grammar School Henry the Eighth had founded in 1539, and he had other ideas. The lure of middle-classdom, so tempting to the Victorian workingman of that particular stamp, the leaning towards what we today call the "upwardly mobile," had ensnared him, and his father put up no opposition. William Longley took his daughter Amelia's husband into the cobbler's shop and Arthur joined the Prudential as an insurance agent. He began humbly enough, working his district on a bicycle and living at home with his parents and his unmarried sisters.

In spite of his ambitions, Arthur never earned much money. His district was not a prosperous one, so his commissions were small. What affluence he later enjoyed came to him through his marriage. His first wife was the daughter and only child of a gentleman, a landowner of substantial means called Abel Richardson. Arthur met her in a traditionally romantic way. Maud was out riding and her horse threw her just as Arthur happened to be passing through the outskirts of Stoke-by-Nayland on his bicycle. She had sprained her ankle and Arthur, who was strong, young, and ardent, carried her the half-mile home to Walbrooks. In the weeks that followed, it was only natural for the young man to call and inquire after Maud, and natural, too, for Maud to arrange it, via a sympathetic parlormaid, that next time he came he might choose a time when Papa was with the hounds (he was the local Master of Foxhounds), and Mamma out paying calls.

There is evidence that Abel Richardson strenuously opposed his daughter's intention to marry a more or less penniless and socially unacceptable insurance agent. After a year, however, he yielded to Maud's entreaties. Yielded sufficiently, in fact, not to withhold the fortune of five thousand pounds which in the past, before the advent of Arthur Longley into their lives, he had promised he would give with his daughter.

Five thousand pounds was a considerable sum in 1890, equivalent to perhaps twenty times that today. Arthur and Maud took one of the villas that were being built out on the Layer Road and settled down to live there very comfortably. To live, indeed, rather above their income, though this was augmented by frequent monetary gifts from Arthur's father-in-law. Maud kept her own carriage. Their household consisted of a cook and housemaid, a nurse for the child, a charwoman who came in to "do the rough," and a coachman-cum-gardener.

Maud's daughter, Mrs. Helen Chatteriss, now an old lady approaching ninety, has written this account of the household:

"I was only five when it all came to an end. My memories will therefore be hazy and incomplete. I remember being driven out with my mother in a very smart carriage drawn by a chestnut horse. My mother used to leave calling cards but I believe that many houses of the local gentry were closed to us on account of my father not being a gentleman.

"The only housework my mother ever did was to arrange the flowers and wash the best china. She lay down to rest every afternoon with white cotton gloves on to preserve her hands. My nurse was called Beatie. She was sixteen, the daughter of one of my grandfather Richardson's tenant farmer's laborers, and she used to take me to see her parents, who lived in a one-room cottage with a brick floor. My mother found out and dismissed her.

"I was told that my father had an important position in business but I remember him as usually being at home. He had a study where he would shut himself up for the morning. Now, looking back, I think he spent his time there reading novels. When he went out collecting insurance business, he would ride the second horse we kept, a roan gelding. I don't remember parties, dinners, that sort of thing, only my Richardson grandparents calling quite often and my Longley grandparents and aunts less often. I think my mother may have been ashamed of them."

This life-style came to an abrupt end in 1901 when Helen's mother died in childbirth. The baby, a boy, also died. Maud Longley's fortune, or what remained of it, was settled on her daughter, a careful provision insisted upon prior to the marriage by Abel Richardson, and by his wife's death Arthur Longley was left a poor man. He gave up his house, carriage, horses, and moved into what was hardly more than a cottage on the western outskirts of the town, dismissing his staff and keeping only a maid-of-all-work.

Also dismissed was his daughter. At any rate, she was parted from her father and sent to live with Abel and May Richardson in Stoke-by-Nayland. It was a separation that still rankles with Mrs. Chatteriss after more than eighty years, in spite of the happy childhood, sheltered, indulged, and luxurious, she enjoyed with her grand-parents at Walbrooks.

"I suppose he thought I should be too much of a responsibility," she says, "and it may be, too, that my grandfather and grandmother persuaded him. I would have minded more except that my grand-mother was so marvelous and I came to love her more than I had my mother. I seldom saw my father after my mother died."

In 1906 he married again. The first Mrs. Chatteriss knew of this second marriage was as a result of an unexpected encounter in Col-chester, near St. Botolph's. It was there that she attended a private school, being driven from Stoke and back in a pony carriage. Two years were yet to go before Abel Richardson made himself a pioneer in the neighborhood by buying a Rolls-Royce sedan, its hide uphol-stery buttoned in ebony and its dashboard of rosewood. One after-noon, after school, she found her father and a strange lady waiting for her at the gates. The lady was introduced to Helen as her "new mother" but thereafter no attempts were made to reinforce the rela-tionship. Her grandparents knew nothing of it for months and were angry when they found out, more from having been kept in the dark than from Arthur Longley's having remarried.

He was thirty-nine. In the twenty-two years he had worked for the Prudential he had received no promotion, and his fortunes having dwindled, he had returned to going about his meager business on a bicycle. His parents were dead, the business had passed to his brother-in-law, James Hubbard, and what very little money there was to his two unmarried sisters. Nor had his bride any money, though she was not without expectations. Ivy Naughton was twenty-eight when she married Arthur, having been governess in a family who were his clients. She had neither training nor qualification for this post, other than having attended school until the age of sixteen and being able to play the piano. But the people she worked for, known to the Richardsons, were seed merchants with pretensions, to whom the boast of having a governess for their three daughters satis-fied them independently of what educational benefit the girls might derive from it. . . . For this service Miss Naughton received her board and lodging and fifty pounds a year.

She and Arthur set up house together. Nine months after the wed-ding, in the spring of 1907, twin children were born to them. Ivy's aunt, Miss Priscilla Naughton, who had her own house and a small clientele as dressmaker, was one of the godparents and another was Arthur's daughter, Helen, who had been confirmed a month before. The twins, a boy and a girl, were christened John William and Vera Ivy. Like her husband, Ivy Longley was a great reader of novels—it was "talking about books" which had brought them together—and by coincidence, the heroine in each case of their favorite novel had the same Christian name.

"My father used to read Ouida," Helen Chatteriss writes, "and *Moths* was his favorite of her books. The heroine's name is Vera, as is the name of the heroine of Marion Crawford's novel *A Cigarette Maker's Romance.* According to my father, this was my stepmother's favorite book. And that was how they came to name Vera."

Vera Longley and her brother, being of opposite sexes, were not, of course, identical twins. They bore no more resemblance to each other than if they had been born at separate births, but both had the very fair hair and intensely blue eyes which were distinctive features of the second Longley family. . . . Arthur, his mother, and two of his sisters were fair-haired, and his second wife was a blond with extremely fair skin and light eyes. Ivy Longley's forebears were fisher-folk from the coast of Norfolk and it was said that one of her grandfathers, a seafaring man, had brought home a wife from the Faroe Islands. John was a handsome boy, Vera a plain child whose looks underwent a transformation as she grew older. A photograph shows her at fourteen as a pretty, sharp-featured girl with a mass of nearly white-blond hair, large eyes, and a serious, rather severe expression.

Four years before that picture was taken, her father had been pensioned off by the Prudential, a medical examination having shown him to have a weak heart. He was fifty and the Great War in its third year. That war was not to touch the immediate Longley family directly, although Amelia's son, William Hubbard, lost his life in it at Vimy Ridge. Soon after Arthur's enforced retirement, Priscilla Naughton died, leaving her house and five hundred pounds to her niece, Ivy. The Longleys moved out into the country and by the spring of 1919 were settled in Great Sindon, a village some ten miles from Colchester in the Vale of Dedham.

It was in no sense a "gentleman's house," which is how Arthur's villa on the Layer Road—now vanished to make way for a block of flats—might have been categorized. The agents through whom Arthur bought it described it as a cottage. Today we should consider this to diminish its status. Paul and Rosemary Oliver, who now own the house, have changed its name from "Laurel Cottage" to "Finches" and undertaken structural alterations to the ground floor so that the dining room and kitchen have been converted into one large living room, the dairy has become the kitchen and the drawing room the dining area. But in the Longleys' day, and subsequently in Vera's, there were four rooms on the ground floor with the staircase running up through the center of the house. When Arthur and Ivy moved in with their two children, there were four bedrooms. The smallest of these Arthur had converted into a bathroom, leaving the principal bedroom for his wife and himself and a room each for the son and daughter.

Externally, Laurel Cottage was built of the iron-free brick, yellowish gray in color, that is known as "white brick," with facings of cream-painted plaster, and roofed in slate. It is a symmetrical house, the front door in the center, a sash window on each side and three above. Similarly, the front garden is accurately bisected by a path which runs straight to the front door, or doors, for there are two, an outer of paneled wood and an inner of glass. The garden at the rear is large, containing, by the gate in the rear fence, an outbuilding that was apparently once a disused cottage in which the Longley children played on wet days, now converted by the Olivers into a garage.

What kind of childhood did Vera Longley have in Colchester and later in Great Sindon? What, if anything, happened to traumatize her? Two days after her twelfth birthday we find her writing to her half-sister, Helen:

Dear Helen,
    Thank you very much for the postal order. I am going to put it towards buying a tennis racket. Tomorrow I am going on holiday to Cromer in Norfolk. I hope it will be fine, as it is by the sea.

                        With love from,
                        Vera

And in the summer of the same year, 1919:

Dear Helen,
    Daddy showed me your letter. I should very much like to be your bridesmaid. I hope you will be very happy married to

Captain Chatteriss. Thank you for asking me to be your bridesmaid. It will be nice to meet soon and I am looking forward to it.

> With love from,
> Vera

The marriage took place in the autumn. Helen had met Victor Chatteriss of the Indian Army, then aged twenty-eight, when he was home on leave. In Helen's wedding photographs, Vera stands half a head taller than the other girl attendants, gawky, thin, with big, serious eyes, wearing a calf-length dress of some glossy material with inset lace panels. She seems to have been a favorite with her father, who wrote to his sister, Clara:

> . . . My little Vera is turning out a fine-looking girl, prettier than one could have hoped. She puts me in mind of you at that age, she has that same true gold hair that shows no sign of darkening. I think her brain superior to her brother's, which I can't help being sorry about in one way, though proud in another. Her school reports are really excellent. She came top of her class in English and history last term. I am giving in to her and letting her have tennis coaching, an added expense I should prefer not to have but she is doing so well I did not like to say no. It is a good social advantage too, don't you think? I believe in providing the best in that way for one's girl. But she will tell you all about it when she comes to you next week. . . .

Clara, five years Arthur's senior, had married late in life and gone to live with her husband in Cromer, where Vera spent occasional holidays. Her childless aunt made much of her and we have Vera writing to Helen in India that "Auntie Clo" bought her two dress lengths to be made up by Clara's own dressmaker and had taken her to a photographer to have a studio portrait done. As well as the tennis, Vera attended classes in ballroom dancing. She received a school prize for perfect attendance in 1921 and another, a calf-bound copy of Ruskin's *Sesame and Lilies,* for coming top in handwork three terms in succession. On the face of it, this was a happy and successful girlhood.

In 1922 Ivy Longley, aged forty-four, gave birth to another child. It was a girl whom the parents, admirers of Galsworthy's novels, intended to call Irene but were deterred by fears of the name being pronounced "I-reen." Instead the baby was christened Edith. Ivy had written to her aunt Priscilla Naughton in 1908 when the twins were babies that she dreaded having more children. After their birth she had been ill for months. The birth itself had been difficult and protracted, leaving her with a partial prolapse of the womb. To Miss Naughton she had written:

"I am still only thirty and could certainly have several more children—dreadful prospect! They say you forget the details of birth, the pain, etc., but I have not. Also there are twins in the family, as you know, not only mine but my mother had twin sisters who died as babies. I wonder sometimes if at forty I shall have a whole unwelcome brood. . . ."

Ivy's second daughter came at a time when she may have believed the danger past. According to all evidence and precedent, the new baby should have been an encumbrance. Its father was an elderly man with a weak heart, its mother menopausal and avowedly "not fond of children," its siblings adolescents with established niches in the family. John, like his father before him, a pupil at Colchester Grammar School, was at an age when boys feel deep embarrassment in the society of their fellows at any evidence of sexuality on the part of their parents. And what stronger evidence could there be than a new baby? Besides, his parents were so old, his father twenty years older than most of his contemporaries' fathers. As for Vera, on the face of it we should need to look no further for a cause of personality damage. Here was a new child and of the same sex as herself come to oust her from her place in her parents' affections.

But none of this seems to have been the case. From the first, Edith—soon to rename herself Eden—was generally loved. "Adored" might not be too strong a word, at any rate by her father, her brother, and her sister. Mrs. Longley's attitude towards the child remains a mystery. She was an infrequent letter writer, seems to have written to no one between the time of the death of her aunt and the removal of her elder daughter to India. No photographs survive of her with Eden, if any existed. In one snapshot only do they appear together, and Arthur Longley, John, Vera, and Clara Dawson are also in the photograph. It was taken on the beach at Cromer and shows Vera with the three-year-old Eden on her lap, Ivy very much in the background, sitting in a deck chair, her face shaded by a broad-brimmed hat.

Vera wrote to Helen Chatteriss in 1924:

I wish you could see my dear little sister. She is the most beautiful child that ever was and her photos don't at all do her justice. I will tell you something. When I take her out, holding her hand and walking with her or pushing her in her pushcart, I hope people will think she is my baby and I am her mother. Do you think that very silly and fanciful? Of course I am not really old enough to be her mother but people tell me I look eighteen. Last week someone Mother knows who had not met me before asked if I was twenty-four!! Mother was not too pleased, as you may guess, for it made her seem even older than she is.

We all call Edith Eden now because that is what she called herself before she could pronounce "th." It is rather a lovely name, I think. "Edith" sounds like someone's old aunt. I can't think why Mother and Dad chose it. Her hair is the most brilliant pure gold. I do hope it won't darken. Mine has not, of course, but then mine was white when I was her age. . . .

On leaving school, John Longley obtained a post with the Midland Bank. At the opportunity of working at a branch in the City of London he hesitated no more than a day before accepting and at the same time becoming a paying guest in the home of his mother's cousin and her husband. Elizabeth Whitestreet had been a Naughton before her marriage. She and her husband and their two children lived at Wanstead, which is in Essex but on the eastern outskirts of London. While living in their house, John met a young half-Swiss girl, Vranni Breuer, who also lodged there and who, though untrained, had some kind of job in the local orphanage as a children's nurse. Vranni's father died in the influenza epidemic of 1918, her mother seven years later. She, too, had been a children's nurse, or rather nanny, employed by a family in Zurich, which was where she met Johann Breuer. Vranni was two years older than John Longley, having been born in Zurich in 1905, and it was partly her seniority which led to his parents' disapproval of his choice when she and the twenty-one-year-old John were married in 1928. A greater cause of dismay to Arthur and Ivy was Vranni's provenance. In the 1920's, English people, notably English country people, still retained a deep distrust of foreigners. It would be no exaggeration to say that Ivy Longley, in 1928, felt much the same about her son's choice of a bride as today a woman of her background might feel about her son's marrying a black African. If it were true that Ivy had a Faroese grandmother whose genes were responsible for much of her own and her daughters' beauty, she had conveniently forgotten it now. According to Mrs. Chatteriss, her refusal to attend the wedding—though Arthur Longley did so, accompanied by the six-year-old Eden—was the cause of a permanent estrangement between herself and her daughter-in-law, and when John went to visit his mother, whom he adored, he was obliged to do so alone.

What Vera thought of John's departure from tradition is not known. She also was not present at his wedding, for by this time she was in India and had herself been married for two years. When she was eighteen, an invitation came to her from her half-sister asking Vera to come out to Rawalpindi. Helen Chatteriss offered to put up half the cost of the sea trip. Vera went to India in the late summer of 1925, arriving at Bombay just as the rainy season came to an end. As speedily as her twin brother was to settle himself, Vera, in the first week of her arrival at Captain (now Major) and Mrs. Chatteriss's bungalow, had met and been attracted by a young subaltern in Victor Chatteriss's regiment, Gerald Loder Hillyard.

Socially—and these things were still of great importance in 1925—Gerald Hillyard was a cut above Vera, several cuts above in fact, though by a quirk of fate (and the unpaternal attitude of Arthur Longley) belonging in the same class as Helen Chatteriss. He was the third and youngest son of a Somerset squire, a small landowner of good birth and very little money. There was a family tradition of younger sons entering the Indian Army and Gerald Hillyard had a forebear who had distinguished himself for gallantry in the First Afghan War of 1839–42 and a great-uncle who was with Sir Henry Havelock in the Mutiny when he broke through to relieve the residency at Lucknow. Gerald Hillyard was an old Harrovian and had been to Sandhurst. Physically, he bore a strong resemblance to George Orwell, or that is the impression his photographs give. He was very tall, over six-feet-three, thin to emaciation though perfectly healthy, with brown hair and a square dark mustache. His younger sister, Mrs. Catherine Clarke, writes:

> I did not meet Vera until about seven years after they were married. They came home on leave in 1930 and 1933 but I was away at school the first time. My father was dead by 1933. I think my mother felt that Gerald had married beneath him, and that he had been deceived into marrying beneath him partly by his own inexperience and partly the fact that Vera was staying with the Chatterisses as Mrs. Chatteriss's sister.

You could say that, because she was with them in that way, she partook of their social position, but really this would be a false impression. Of course, it is all nonsense, but it wasn't then. My mother only spoke to me about it once. I remember that she said that Vera was ladylike in the wrong way.

The marriage took place in Rawalpindi in March 1926 when Vera was nineteen years old and Gerald Hillyard twenty-two. In the following year, their son, Francis Loder, was born. When he was six years old, Vera and Gerald came home on leave to England, bringing the child with them and leaving him behind at a prep school in Somerset not far from where his grandmother Hillyard was living. Two years afterwards, Vera returned alone. Her father was dying but she arrived in time only for the funeral, not to see him alive. She had been his favorite child and very much attached to him. It is unfortunate that none of the several hundred letters she wrote him from India survive.

Arthur Longley was dead and Ivy, his wife, had only a few months to live. It was 1935 and Ivy was only fifty-seven but she was suffering from an inoperable cancer of the uterus. Instead of returning to Gerald in India, Vera stayed with her mother, and when Ivy died in the spring of 1936 remained to take charge of her fourteen-year-old sister, Eden.

Helen Chatteriss writes:

> After the first year or two, Vera had not much cared for India. She was very fair, you see, very fair-skinned, and she found the sun unbearable. As far as I know there was nothing wrong with the marriage—this wasn't a separation because she and Gerald no longer got on. It was simply that she was happier and more comfortable in the English climate, and, of course, her son was in England. As I think I've told you, she was particularly fond of Eden and in fact it was the idea of separating herself from Eden that had made her hesitate about coming to India in the first place. I admit it, I invited Vera to come to us to find herself a good, suitable husband. And she did. It's hard to imagine now because things have changed so much, but in the twenties girls did want husbands more than anything else and the main business of their lives was to get them. An awful lot of young men who might have been potential husbands for girls like Vera had been killed in the War. But there were a lot of eligible young men in India. I've never

regretted inviting Vera and introducing her to Gerald; I don't think it was a mistake on my part. The marriage *was* happy, at least for years it was, and I still think it was the war, I mean the war of 1939 to 45, that spoiled things for them, as it spoiled things for so many of us.

Catherine Clarke writes:

My brother came home with his regiment in 1939. Victor Chatteriss had retired the year before with the rank of major general and he and his wife and children were living in the house she had inherited from her grandparents in Suffolk somewhere. What home life my brother had was spent in the house called Laurel Cottage at Great Sindon with Vera and her younger sister. The house didn't belong to them. It had been left between Vera, her brother, and this sister, each owning a third. When the war came, the regiment was sent up north—Yorkshire, I believe it was.

So in the early years of the Second World War we have Vera Hillyard living very quietly alone with her sister Eden in the house where Eden had been born, in a sleepy village that boasted one shop, a school, a typically enormous East Anglian "wool" church, and an infrequent bus service to Colchester. It is a truism to say of a mother and daughter who are close that they are like sisters. Vera Hillyard and Eden Longley, who *were* sisters, were perhaps more like mother and daughter. Vera in 1939 was thirty-two, Eden seventeen. In the school holidays they were joined by Vera's son, Francis. Occasionally there were visits from John and Vranni Longley and their daughter, Faith. And, of course, a few miles away in Stoke-by-Nayland, lived the Chatterisses, the General and his wife and their two teenage children, Patricia and Andrew. A Naughton cousin would sometimes come to tea. And there were village acquaintances, among them Thora Morrell, whose husband, Richard, was rector of the parish.

But the life led by the two sisters was a gentle and uneventful one, their recreations sewing, embroidery, baking, listening to the wireless. Yet already the drama that was to erupt in that house was slowly unfolding.

4

T HE DAY AFTER Vera appeared in the magistrates' court to be charged with murder, my father went about the house collecting up and concealing everything that might connect her with him. Destroying too, I have no doubt. This may sound callous. My father was not unfeeling, far from it, but respectability was very important to him, that and his probity, his need to be beyond reproach. People must not know Vera Hillyard was his sister, the bank and its clients particularly must not know. He sorrowed in silence, letting concealment feed upon him inwardly. The outer man conducted himself as if Vera had never been.

It was my mother who told me what happened that evening. I wasn't there, I was in Cambridge, stunned by what I had read in a newspaper. My father came home from the bank. He ate nothing, he had eaten nothing for two days. He said to my mother, and it seems a curious question for a bank manager to put to his wife:

"Haven't we got a strongbox somewhere?"

She told him where it was. He took the box up to the spare bedroom, that room where Eden had once spent a night and enraged my mother by dusting the furniture, and there out of her sight—he would not carry out this solemn, almost ritualistic task under her eyes—filled the box with his sisters' letters and with photographs of them. In the room where my mother was sitting, our living room, were two framed photographs, a portrait of Vera and one of Eden in her wedding dress. My father came in and removed these pictures from their frames. One was the kind where the back is in the form of a hinged door secured shut by clips, but the other was backed by a sheet of gummed paper and this he ripped away in a single movement, so anxious was he to rid the room of Vera and her baby son. He cut his finger on the corner of the thin sheet of glass, and the brown mark, circular and, unless one knows, unidentifiable, on the edge of the photograph, is his blood.

It was one of those that went into the box. After my parents were dead, I found the box in the back of their wardrobe. There was a picture hanging on the spare-bedroom wall that I had never liked, though the frame was pretty. The backing had been clumsily sealed with Scotch tape and when I pulled it away I discovered between the Millais print and the sheet of cardboard two snapshots of Eden as a child. This gave me ideas and all over the house I began finding mementos of my father's sisters. Not for him to follow Chesterton's precept that the best place to hide a leaf is in a tree. He knew that the best place to hide things is where no one will look, not in the family album—every photograph extracted from there, the blank spaces bearing witness—but between the pages of an annotated New Testament, among the end papers of *A Girl of the Limberlost,* slipped inside the embroidered cover someone (Vera? Eden?) had made for the album of Kensitas cigarettes silk-flower cards, between the plywood base of a drawer and the red oilcloth that lined it.

I put everything into the strongbox along with those mementos which had seemed most precious to my father, took the box home with me and hid it in the cupboard under the stairs. A friend who came to stay found the box when sent by my husband in search of rubber boots to wear on a walk. We lived in the country then. She spent the evening going through the photographs while I answered her questions with white lies and my husband sat silent, looking at me sometimes, saying not a word. But I, too, am a Longley, with my share of their need to be private and withdrawn. My friend found the portrait of Vera Great-aunt Clara had had taken of her in Cromer and passed over it with the comment only that she was a pretty girl, but when she came to the Colchester photograph of 1945, the one that was in all the papers, some chord in her memory was struck and she paused a long time, staring at it, and telling me she was sure she had seen it somewhere before, years ago, in connection, she thought, with something terrible.

When we moved here, I put the box in our littlest bedroom and covered it with a brown blanket stamped with the letters "M of D," for Ministry of Defense that someone had acquired (or stolen) during the war. If I asked why my father hadn't thrown away the contents of the box, I might equally ask: Why hadn't I? It is as well for Daniel Stewart that I haven't.

Alone in the house at three in the afternoon—it is not Helen's day nor our day for sitting alongside Gerald's wheelchair—I feel as though embarked upon some guilty exercise, and anticipating the flurry I should be in if surprised, I open the box and take out the pictures and letters I had only glanced at when I gathered them up from the bookshelves and drawers in my parents' house. My inquisitive friend hadn't, of course, looked at the letters, though I had been on tenterhooks that she would. She had withdrawn them, or some of them, from the large brown envelope that held them all and pushed them back again with a quick explanation that these must be family letters. But perhaps if she had read them they would have given her no real clue to the identities of the writers.

I unfold them. They have a stale, very faintly sulfurous smell. Vera and Eden invariably wrote to my father alone, not to my father and mother. Here, for example, is Vera thanking him for a wedding present, though it was certainly my mother who had chosen and bought and packed the damask tablecloth and the dozen napkins initialed VH. But Vera disapproved of my mother because she was not English and therefore for a long while felt it legitimate to behave as if no such person as her brother's wife existed. Two more letters from India come next; then, of greater significance, the one that announces Vera's intention to remain in England to "make a home for" Eden at Laurel Cottage. Yet it is a mystery why he decided to keep some and discard others, until I recall a factor that seems absurd in its arbitrariness today. Vera wrote often, at least once a month, and these letters my father would invariably read aloud to us at the breakfast table, thereby causing my mother intense irritation. The current letter, replaced in its envelope, would be stuck on the mantelpiece for a week, after which, if it was winter, thrown in the fire, if summer, stuffed into a drawer by my mother or crumpled up in my father's pocket. Therefore letters written between May and October tended to be kept and letters written between October and May burnt—it was as simple as that.

Here, then, is Vera writing in June:

> Dear John,
> I am very glad you see things as I do and feel that instead of selling the house and dividing the proceeds we should keep it, at least for a while, as a home for Eden. While she is still at school it would be upsetting for her to remove her from Sindon. Of course it has been very hard for her to lose both parents so young. She is wonderfully sensible and old for her age—I am not talking about her schoolwork, though this is quite good enough in my humble opinion—I mean her outlook on life and nice ways and manners. She is delighted that I am going to stay in England and that we shall both live in this house which has always been her home and where she was born. . . .

The first letter of Eden's that I look at gives me a jolt. I had seen it before (though it had never been read aloud), forgotten it over the years, recalling how long it had stayed rankling in my mind. I had been remiss and I deserved a reprimand, but quite like this?

"Dear John," she wrote when she was seventeen and I eleven, "I have to write and tell you that I think you might teach your child better manners. I have not had a word of thanks from her for the postal order I sent her for her birthday. Surely by the time someone is ten she ought to know it is the right thing to write a thank-you letter. Mother dinned this into me from the time I could hold a pencil and she must have done the same with you. It is not fair on Faith, apart from the rudeness to people who give her presents, to allow her . . ."

Why had he kept this one? Because at heart he approved of it? Because at heart, as my mother accused him, if he did not hold his sisters in greater affection than his wife and daughter, at any rate he admired them more? Or is it here in this collection only because it came in May when there was no fire burning?

As I pick up the envelope and put away the letters, Eden's beautiful face appears, arising from a neckline that stands up and curves outwards like an arum lily. She is in her wedding dress, her huge billowing veil tumbling as if it were made of some less substantial stuff than gauze, like a cascade of foam. She is as she was that morning when Francis held her in his arms and led her to the altar and Chad devoured her with his eyes. These are the pictures my father tore from their frames, Vera and Gerald newly married, outside a late-Victorian Gothic church with Gilbert Scott steeple, a banyan tree and a dome in the background, Vera and the infant Francis, my father's blood on her hair. And here is the photograph Stewart will surely want for his frontispiece. Eden's bright hair falls in the way the film star Veronica Lake made famous but she has modified the look and her eye is not covered by the fall of hair. Here are shown to advantage the high cheekbones, the ever so slightly aquiline nose, the short upper lip, round chin, well-defined angled jaw, that Eden had in common with Francis so that the two of them looked more like brother and sister than aunt and nephew. She wears a light-colored dress with a draped crossover neckline and in the V a pearl necklace. The soulful, not-quite-of-this-world look that was so typically Eden's is in her rather too-wide-open eyes and the parted lips which the photographer has told her to lick and thus catch a highlight on the fashionable dark coating of lipstick.

But I hardly suppose it is for me to give permission for the use of this picture. The copyright may belong to Tony—or to the photographer who took it. On the back is the name of a studio in Londonderry and that fits the hairstyle, the probable date, even the remote, mysterious, secretive look in Eden's eyes.

At the bottom of the pile is a snapshot taken for no purpose one can imagine unless to record how on a certain hot day in a certain summer a crowd of relations gathered together in a particular garden. I am in this picture, my mousy pigtail hanging over one shoulder, wearing the voile dress that was someone's castoff, standing between Francis and Patricia. Behind us are Eden in what the magazines called a "tub frock," Vera with her hair newly permed, my father and Helen and a bunch of Hubbard cousins. The General must have taken it, or Andrew. If he existed, Jamie would have been in the picture, so he was not yet born and the date must be before 1944. I had my hair cut short in 1943. Perhaps it is as early as 1940 and Andrew has not yet gone to fight the Battle of Britain or Eden joined the WRNS.

I replace the lid on the box and sit there looking at it. I find that I am crying. The tears are running down my face, a curious thing, for it was all so long ago and I had loved none of these people except my father and mother. Oh, and Chad of course, but that was something different.

◆

When I was young, to be fair-haired was to be beautiful. This statement is a slight exaggeration but broadly it is true. Gentlemen—and ladies and everyone—preferred blonds. Eden was so fair, such a dazzling golden blond, that she would have been accounted lovely even without the bonus of her features. The first time I went to Great Sindon on my own, Vera met me on the station platform at Colchester, and having lightly stung my cheek with her lips, held me at arm's length and pronounced:

"What a pity your hair has got so dark!"

The tone was accusing, the implication that I had carelessly allowed this darkening process, if not actually helped it along. I said nothing because I could think of no answer, a frequent reaction to remarks of Vera's. I smiled. I tried to seem polite while with a corner of my handkerchief trying to rub off the lipstick I knew Vera's mouth must have deposited on my cheek. Makeup for women in those years was powder on the nose and lipstick on the mouth, bright red lipstick and loose powder from a Coty orange-and-gold box patterned all over with powder puffs. Vera wouldn't have put her head outside her front door without lipstick on.

"I wouldn't have bothered to kiss you," she now said, "if I'd known you were going to make such a fuss about it."

I had not been surreptitious enough. I put the handkerchief away and we walked to the bus stop. No one that I knew had a car—well, no one among my family and friends. The parents of one or two girls at school did and there was one father, said to own a company and to be rich, who not only had a car but a white car, a daring departure from convention. I had expected to go to Great Sindon by bus, and by bus we went, Vera humping my suitcase along and complaining about its weight.

"I can carry it," I said.

Vera's response was to hang on to the case all the tighter, transferring it from her right hand to her left so that it wasn't between us.

"I don't know why you wanted to bring so many things. You must have brought your entire wardrobe. You're lucky to have so many clothes. Do you know that when Eden goes away, she plans what she's going to need so carefully that she can get it all into a small attaché case."

This conversation must have affected me quite deeply, it and other homilies on the subject of suitcases and packing and prudence and preparedness which were delivered in the weeks to come, for even to this day I feel guilty if I take too much luggage with me on holiday. But then, for the life of me, I couldn't see how a smaller or less full case would have done. I was to be here indefinitely, autumn was coming, and I would need both summer and winter clothes. However, Vera must be right. She was a grown-up and my father's sister, often held up to me along with Eden as examples of what women should be. The size and weight of the suitcase troubled me while we were on the bus and I asked myself why I had brought this or that and what was there I could have left out. Vera's reproach had started me off on the wrong foot, making me feel both feckless and given over to a shameful frivolity.

It was September 1939. Everyone was afraid of bombs. A few years before, I had listened to the wireless with my parents and heard of the bombing of Nanking. It frightened me so much I couldn't go on listening, but went away and hid in the downstairs lavatory where that voice couldn't penetrate. But at the start of this war, it was my parents who were afraid, not I. Nothing happened, it was the same as if war had not been declared a fortnight before. There were no plans to evacuate my school, which was fourteen miles outside the center of London. Term had begun and things went on as usual. My father panicked and sent me to Vera. I was eleven; I had taken the examination which would admit me to the Grammar School and passed it, so with that hurdle behind me he probably thought missing a term's schooling would do me no harm.

The weather was warm, summer still. Vera wore a cotton frock with a turned-down collar and cuffs on the short puff sleeves, a belt of the same white material patterned with mauve and yellow pansies, a fashion which returned without undergoing much change a few years ago. Her hair was the color of newly cleaned brass, not in the least yellow and not "brassy." It was rather tightly permed and set into deep, narrow waves and small round curls. Down grew on her upper lip, pale as thistleseed and visible only at certain angles, and her arms and bare legs bore a somewhat coarser growth that showed as a fair, gleaming sheen. A complexion so pale that time and the Indian sun had reddened it, especially about the nose. Vera's eyes, like mine and my father's, Eden's and Francis's, were the intense, glowing blue of the Wedgwood Ivanhoe plates Grandmother Longley had collected and which now hung on the dining-room walls at Laurel Cottage.

The bus took us through that countryside that somehow should be dull, unmemorable, without mountains or hills or rushing streams, moorland or lake or particular vegetation, yet is not dull at all but has its own quiet, deep beauty. The loveliest houses in England are there, churches big as cathedrals, meadows that Constable painted and which then had changed very little since that day, before they pulled the hedges up and made a prairie of the fields.

Daniel Stewart makes Laurel Cottage sound small and ugly. Perhaps it was. It is almost impossible to be objective about a house one has known when one was young. In our suburb, a long way from the center of London, we inhabited a house that my father had had built to an architect's design, a "suntrap" startlingly, daringly modern. It was art-deco and might have been lifted out of the environs of Los Angeles, a cream-colored box with a green stripe painted senselessly round it like a ribbon tying up a parcel, windows of curved glass, a flat roof, and a front door whose inset panel was a setting sun with rays of orange, yellow, and amber stained glass. My father was reacting against the villa on the road to Myland where he was born and the terrace on the "wrong" side of Wanstead Flats where he and my mother lived when first they were married. I was reacting against the suntrap, whose roof leaked because it was not designed for a rainy country and down whose Hollywood walls the water had run in gray rivulets.

I loved an old house; in such a one I thought I should have liked to live. Laurel Cottage was not, of course, old enough for me. I asked Vera why she thought my grandparents hadn't bought one of the thatched cottages, of which there were many. Her reply was no doubt prudent and accurate—the fire insurance was much higher on thatched cottages and the upkeep of ancient houses costly—but it seemed to me unromantic. Each time I had come to this house with my parents, or more often just my father, I had looked up at the earthenware plaque set between the upper bays, and reading the date 1862, had wished it older, if only by fifty years.

Vera was a scrupulous housekeeper. Laurel Cottage had its own smell, a mingling I suppose of various soaps and polishes, the same smell in Vera's as in my grandmother's day. House smells must be passed on through the female line, for when Eden came to have a home of her own, hers smelt just the same, though ours never did. My mother was rather slapdash, pooh-poohing an excessive attention to cleaning as unintelligent. But I liked the clean, fresh scent of Vera's house, the windows whose panes were never spotted, the waxed floors, the shining, unmarked surfaces, and the flowered chintz curtains I remember as always fluttering faintly in the breeze.

Francis had gone back to school. Eden, who was still at her day school and in the sixth form, would be home at four-thirty. An enormous spread of tea had been prepared in my honor. There was as yet no shortage of food and I was never to see in that house a lack of the kind of constituents that go to make cakes and pies and biscuits. Vera had no refrigerator. Few people did in 1939. Her Victoria sponge and gingerbread, lemon-curd tarts, Banbury cakes, drop scones, and almond slices were on the kitchen table covered with clean, ironed tea cloths to keep off the flies. Vera stayed always thin as a rail, though eating her fair share of that rich, sweet stuff. As we carried the cakes in, arranging them on the dining table, laying the plates on a cloth embroidered by Eden in lazy daisy and stem stitch, Vera (having adjured me not to drop anything, she hoped I wasn't a "butterfingers") apologized for the poor quality of the tea and the lack of variety.

"I expect your mother would have an iced cake as well. Grandma used to insist on two big cakes always and at least two kinds of biscuits."

I assured her that my mother would have provided no such thing. Tea would probably have been sandwiches and digestives or custard creams.

"Shop-bought biscuits?" Vera said, both shocked and pleased.

In my innocence I told her I didn't know any other kind existed. The effect on her was electric. Vera, even then, used to become disproportionately excited over trivial things. The point was that to her they were not trivial.

"What, and you've had tea in this house a dozen times to my knowledge! You didn't know the biscuits were homemade? My goodness, but Grandma would turn in her grave! I can see we were wasting our time making biscuits for you. Might as well have gone down to the grocer's and bought any old packet of Maries. I wonder what Eden would say to that. I don't suppose she's tasted a shop-bought biscuit in all her life. Well, I hope our humble, homemade stuff will suit you, I'm sure I do. We're not up to these sophisticated London ways and I can't see us changing now."

It was a way she had of stunning me. I was silenced by it and made to feel guilty while obscurely knowing the onslaught was unfair. The technique was to seize upon an innocent remark of mine, attribute to me certain sentiments which might derive from it (though I had not felt or uttered them), and then castigate me for the expressions she had put into my mouth. She would do the same, or attempt to do the same, with Francis, but he was having none of it and would give her back as good as or better than he got. But when I was a child, I knew no way of handling it but to accept and be silent. And Vera, of course, desired no reply. She expected and wanted no defense. She was simply giving vent to the strong feelings she had about many things and looking for a peg to hang her violent expressions and beliefs on. Deeply conservative, she harked back to the old ways and customs and no doubt she truly believed that to buy a packet of biscuits was to set foot on the slippery slope to decadence. Only Eden was immune from these attacks. But Eden was immune from every violent, unreasonable assault of Vera's. When she had made this one on me, repeating herself a good many times, and embroidering on her theme, she was satisfied. I said nothing, but went on helping to lay the table. But I think I was scarcely there for her as a person at that point. That her victim's *feelings* might be hurt, that one might have a sense of injury or outrage at being told that one's mother was hardly doing one a kindness by encouraging such tastes, that one was wrong to inflict one's refined London palate on country cousins, and that one's ideas had better undergo some sharp revisions, never occurred to her.

The table laid, the tea cloths once more shrouding all the plates, Vera's manner changed again and became kindly and interested. I was congratulated on my scholarship results, complimented on the whiteness of my teeth, the color of my eyes (the Longley blue which I could in no way have been accounted responsible for, any more than I could for my mother's purchase of biscuits), and the fact that I had no spots on my face. I must come to the window with her and watch out for Eden. Eden would get off the bus in the village street and we should see her when she turned the corner. Great Sindon is a pretty village, was prettier then before there were new buildings, traffic signs, cars parked all along the roads. It was sleepy and quiet. You could not believe there was a war on and, of course, there scarcely was yet. Someone came down the hill on horseback, strolling down if a horse can stroll. The swallows were gathering on the electric wires. I knelt on the window seat, Vera behind me craning her neck.

I was conscious of the tension that emanated from her body. It was as if her body could not contain so much, such compression, such screwing up, so that the stress overflowed into the air around her.

Can I really remember that? Probably I am projecting what certainly later I knew and felt onto that time. But it is true that always with Vera there could be no relaxing, of herself or those with her, because they were with her. Eden came round the corner suddenly—how could it be otherwise, how but suddenly?—and Vera cried out:

"There she is!"

My arm was not actually lifted by Vera to be waved but it would have been if I had been three or four years younger. I was merely told to wave at Eden and I obliged, though feeling that a smile alone would have come more naturally to me. I got down from the window seat and prepared to meet her.

Young girls change so much in adolescence. This is apparent not only to their seniors but also to children like me. It was a year since I had seen Eden and if I had met her in the street I would not have known her. She was beautiful and she was grown-up. The Veronica Lake hairdo was not yet in fashion and she wore her hair in that style too awful ever to have been revived, the front rolled up and back into a sausage, the back hanging loose. Eden's beauty could not be spoiled by it. To me it seemed wonderfully chic. She had a gymslip on, a plain, round-neck pinafore, not one of the old box-pleated kind, a dark red blazer with her school crest on the pocket, and hanging from one shoulder, her satchel. She kissed me and called me her little niece in a very kindly way, asked me how my parents were—Vera had forgotten to mention my mother, but Eden did not—and said she hoped the train journey had been pleasant. Then she went away to her room, emerging ten minutes afterwards with powder on her nose and lipstick on her lips, her school tunic changed for a skirt and blouse. She seemed even older. We sat down to Vera's enormous tea, working our way through sandwiches and cakes and buns, and tea was always to be the principle meal of the day, this first one being no festive exception. It seems strange to me now to think of those teas, the bread and butter and mountains of sweet food we ate, at least four rounds of bread each, at least one slice of cake, a series of small buns, slices, biscuits, cupcakes. None of us put on weight or came out in spots. And we ate like that every day as a matter of course at five o'clock, Vera encouraging Eden and now me to stuff ourselves, saying it was all good, wholesome, and homemade food. She seemed to have the idea that everything bought in a shop was bad for you and

everything made at home good for you, a widely held view responsible, no doubt, for many an untimely death.

Eden said she would teach me to make puff pastry.

"Will you?" I said, but perhaps in a doubtful tone.

"Wouldn't you like to learn?"

I didn't know. It was a subject on which I had no opinion. I was
not even clear about what puff pastry was and I believe I confused it
with the choux from which éclairs are made. My mother wasn't
much of a cook and both my parents disapproved of girls being
taught domestic science at school, my father, however, at the same
time believing such things would come naturally as, in his innocence, he thought they had to his sisters.

"What do you like to cook?" asked Eden.

When we are old, we know how to answer. We know how we
should have answered when we were children. I should have said:
I'm a little girl, and I've never so much as tried to toast a bit of bread
without having my mother say: Leave that, I'll do that. We had registered for food rationing though it was not to start until the following
January. I should have said that if predictions were right, in a little
while there wouldn't be anything to make puff pastry with. But that
would have been rude, even ruder than not thanking her for her
birthday present. . . .

"I can't," I said, taking another lemon-curd tart for support, "actually cook anything."

They both registered the kind of shock that is not altogether surprised. A barrage of questions began as to what I *could* do, and this
did not mean theorems and French verbs. Having elicited from me
that I could neither knit nor sew, crochet or embroider, Vera sighed
as heavily and looked as despondent as if I had said I could not master the alphabet or control my bodily functions. She said, incredibly:

"Well, I'm sure I don't know what kind of a wife you'll make."

But Eden, always apparently kinder, told me not to worry about it.
No doubt I had never had the opportunity to learn, but now I was at
Laurel Cottage—a place she made sound like an institute of good
housekeeping—there were all sorts of things she would teach me.
After that they ceased to give me their undivided attention, indeed
they gave me scarcely any more attention at all, and began a mysterious, diffused conversation about people who lived in the village
whom I had never heard of. One of the difficult things about my

Great Sindon relatives was their way of assuming you knew exactly
whom they meant when they referred to someone or other, and when
people called, that you would know who they were without being
introduced. This would have been all very well if they explained
when you confessed your ignorance, but instead they became very
scathing, at least Vera did, and told you that certainly you did know, of
course you knew, but due to some carelessness or forgetfulness well
within your control—simple indifference probably—the identity of
so-and-so had been allowed to slip your mind. And this assumption
that the rest of the world was completely *au fait* with their ways extended to custom and habits, so that without being told, one was
expected to know what time to get up, when to use the bathroom,
where the backdoor key hung, when the milkman came, who was
Eden's best friend, what subjects she was taking for her Higher
Schools Certificate, the vicar's name, and have by heart the timetable
of the Colchester bus.

I had expected great things of my stay with Vera, a stay of necessarily indeterminate length and governed by whether or not bombs
started falling on the northeastern suburbs of London. Homesickness
I had considered as a possibility, for I had never stayed away from my
parents before, but I thought this would be compensated for by my
enthusiastic reception into a kind of sisterhood with Vera and Eden, I
making a welcome third in their lonely sorority. My Uncle Gerald, I
knew, was away somewhere in the north of England with his regiment. Francis was at school. I was old for my age, people frequently
said so, and I thought my aunts, one only a few years my senior,
would treat me as another adult, another sister even. It was a vision
or dream I was never entirely to abandon, in spite of constant disillusionment. Desperately I wanted to belong. They had the power,
those two, of making their world—narrow, confined, and bourgeois,
as I now see it—an esoteric, intensely desirable place, rather like an
exclusive club with unimaginably strict conditions for membership
and with rules no outsider could live up to. Sitting at tea that first
day, not knowing what a weary haul was ahead of me, what attempts
to enter and qualify, what failures, I listened attentively, hoping,
though hoping in vain, for some inquiry to be put to me, asking my
opinion, instead of the kind of questions I finally got:

"Do you always eat with your right hand?"

I had never thought about it. I looked at Vera, holding aloft (in my
right hand) the last of the drop scones. "I don't know."

"Left hand for eating, right hand for drinking," said Vera, adjusting, as she spoke, the positions of my plate and my cup and saucer.

I helped her with the dishes. My mother had told me that while I was at Laurel Cottage I must try to be of some service to Vera, and at a loss to know what service, had suggested drying dishes. Conversation had come to a stop, for Eden had retreated to the living room with a book to read for homework, and talking was always easier when she was present. I think it was at this point that I was conscious of the homesickness beginning.

We joined Eden. We had the wireless on. At ten to eight Vera suggested that in ten minutes' time I go to bed. It had not crossed my mind I should go to bed before they did. Nine-thirty was my bedtime at home, and that only when I had to go to school in the morning. There would be no school here.

"I was always in bed before eight when I was your age," Eden told me. Her voice was sweet and low-pitched. It may be my imagination that makes me say it often had a vague note as if the speaker were not much interested in what she was saying or in the person to whom she was saying it.

"Children always make a fuss about bedtime," said Vera.

"You mean Francis. I'm sure I never did."

"No, I don't think you ever did, Eden. But you were different from other children in so many ways. Come along now, Faith. It's starting to get dark."

In two months' time it would start to get dark at five!

"Good night, little niece," said Eden. "You'll find you'll fall asleep as soon as your head touches the pillow."

Nothing could have made me feel more thoroughly excluded from the sisterhood.

I was to sleep in Francis's room, though on subsequent visits always in Eden's. There was nothing of his about, as far as I could see, nothing to show me that this was the bedroom of a boy of my own age. Artifacts made by Vera which proliferated about the house were not lacking here—embroidered cushion covers, seat covers in petit point, pictures made out of silver paper, a cross-stitch bell-pull, a rag rug. Perhaps Francis's own things had been put away in my honor. What had not was a round metal clock that stood on the mantelpiece.

I was aware as soon as I was inside the bedroom with the door closed, of the loud, metallic ticking this clock made. When Vera had brought me up here earlier with my suitcase, I had not noticed it.

I unpacked and put my clothes away, rather intimidated by the hangers in the wardrobe, all of which had covers on them of ruched satin in various colors, and each a lavender sachet attached to its hook. I put on my dressing gown and went to the bathroom, the sounds from downstairs making my homesickness return in a wave. Vera and Eden were chatting away in animated fashion and every now and then Eden laughed. It was quite unlike the way they had behaved while I was with them, lively and relaxed and somehow *cozy*, and the conclusion was inescapable that I had been sent early to bed because they could hardly wait to be rid of me.

The problem of the clock, too, began to loom large. I thought I shouldn't be able to sleep with that clock in the room and I quickly discovered that, short of breaking it, there is no way of stopping a clock of that sort once it has been wound up.

The book I had with me distracted me for a while, but then I became nervous lest Vera or Eden see the light under my door. Somehow, young as I was, I already knew that though they had sent me to bed because they were tired of my company, so could scarcely care whether I slept or sat up all night reading, provided I were out of the way, nevertheless they would not admit this, they never, never would, but would insist that the bedtime they had ordained was for my own health and well-being. Therefore they had better not see my light still on at nearly nine-thirty. Once it was out, the ticking seemed to grow much louder. The room was not dark, for the moon had come up, a glowing, yellow harvest moon. It afforded enough light for my purposes. . . . I got out of bed, set one of the cushions on the seat of the pale-blue-and-gilt Lloyd Loom chair, and stuck the clock on it, having first wrapped it up in my dressing gown.

The ticking was muffled but still audible. The awful feeling came over me that I should never be able to sleep and that this would not be for one night only but many, many nights, a hundred perhaps. I would be trapped in here with this clock, unable to escape it, sleeplessly suffering its tick like someone subjected to the Chinese water torture. With Hans Andersen's tale of the princess and the pea I was familiar, and it seemed to me that if the princess's discomfort had stemmed from an auditory rather than a tactile source, it would have made a better story. For a while I thought about this, turning over in my mind what sound might be as disturbing to a princess as a pea buried under the twenty mattresses she is lying on. But it was only a momentary distraction from the ticking of the clock which thumped away through the folds of my dressing gown.

Vera and Eden came up to bed. On the landing outside my room they kept their voices down so as not to wake me.

"Good night, darling."

"Good night, darling. Sleep well."

The landing light went out. I picked up the rag rug off the floor and wrapped it round my dressing gown, round the clock. The muted tick was rather worse. I had reached that desperate point—often to be experienced later in hotel bedrooms—when the only way to escape the noise seemed to be to leave the room. I was no more able to do this in Laurel Cottage than I was at the Plaza in New York when an all-night party was going on next door. At the Plaza I made frequent fruitless calls to Reception, who were polite, willing, but unhelpful. Here Reception was asleep and would not, I sensed, have in any case taken kindly to a complaint of this sort. I opened the window and looked out.

Moonlight flooded Vera's beautiful garden. It had never been much of a garden in my grandparents' time but Vera had remade it, replacing the flowering currants and sumacs with viburnums of esoteric varieties, with a *Cornus alba,* and a smoke bush and many herbs. Of course I was not to know that then, but its beauty I could appreciate, the refinement that had come to it by the substitution of these rarer plants for the common ones. The moonlight bathed whitely the leaves, brilliant gold at this season by day, of a delicate, fluttering, man-high liquidambar. The windowsill was a broad one, made of stone. I unwrapped the clock, placed it on the sill, and pulled down the sash.

Some momentary qualms came to me while I was doing this that Vera might come into the room in the morning with, say, a cup of tea. Or for some other, unknown reason. I felt she would be sure to notice the absence of the clock. But with luck, anyway, I should waken before this happened.

The peace was so beautiful that I tried to stay awake simply for the pleasure of listening to the silence. This, of course, had the effect of sending me to sleep. When I woke up in the morning at about seven-thirty, I remembered the clock and fetched it in, beaded all over with dew but still ticking. There was no reason, I thought, why I shouldn't do this every night. Rain might present problems but I would worry about that when the time came. I began to wish I knew the proper time to get up and if I went into the bathroom, would I be keeping Eden, who certainly had a prior claim, out of it? The house was silent. I debated what to do and after about ten minutes, having decided that Vera and Eden were still in bed, I got up and went into the bathroom to wash. Later on Vera was to ask me why I hadn't had a bath and to adjure me to take a daily bath and not be "lackadaisical" about it. There was still no sound in the house.

The clock back on the mantelpiece, wiped dry on my handkerchief, I made my way downstairs. The house was very neat, all the cushions in the living room plumped up. The dining room was empty. I pushed open the kitchen door, hardly knowing why since I was scarcely capable of making a cup of tea, still less my own breakfast. They were both in there, silently eating shredded wheat out of Woods Ware rectangular bowls. I jumped, a start observed by Vera, who seldom missed anything of that sort.

"My goodness, aren't you nervous! You shouldn't be like that at your age."

Eden said that I had nearly missed her. She had to leave at eight-fifteen. Her voice was full of reproach and the implication that to come down to breakfast at this hour was to show a lazy disposition. Vera, who had sprung up when I came in and was now tensely poised between larder and stove, asked me what I should like for breakfast. A variety of foods was reeled off at high speed: poached eggs, boiled eggs, fried eggs, bacon, cereal, toast. There was, however, no porridge. Porridge, she said, was too much trouble to make when neither she nor Eden was likely to eat it. I said I hated porridge.

"It's a pity to take that attitude about wholesome food," Vera said.

"But you said—" I began.

"I said, I said. I hope you're not going to take me up on every little thing I say, Faith. I don't suppose I am as logical as you and your mother. I don't have the time, for one thing. Now then, have you decided what you'd like for your breakfast or shall I sit down and finish my cereal while you think about it?"

I said I would have a boiled egg. Vera began moving about with overburdened resignation to get out a saucepan, an egg from the rack. Eden jumped up.

"Let me do it. I've finished. Sit down, darling, you're up and down like a jack-in-the-box."

Eden, in gymslip, her hair tied back with a black silk bow, bustled prettily about, buttering "soldiers" for me.

"Three minutes all right?"

"Could I have five, please?"

"Well, of course you *could*. But that will be a hard-boiled egg. Are you sure you're going to want to eat a hard-boiled egg?"

It wouldn't be, but this time I didn't make the mistake of arguing. Instead I said I would watch the egg and take it out of the water myself. Eden possibly thought this a good moment to begin the cooking lessons, but Vera demurred.

"She'll only drop it on the floor, Eden, and you know the mess an egg makes." Before I had time for indignant denials, Vera turned to me and said in a voice both scathing and reproachful, "I'm sorry you don't like Eden's little clock. Eden put that in your bedroom herself because she thought it would be just the thing for someone without a wristwatch."

"Don't you like it, Faith?" said Eden.

I could say nothing. Paralysis seized me.

"Well, she can't do. I mean very obviously she can't do. If she liked it she wouldn't put it outside the window, would she? Yes, I know, my dear, it is most extraordinary, but I assure you that's what she did. Your little clock was most definitely not a success. When I went down the garden first thing this morning, what did I see but your clock on Francis's windowsill outside the window. It was a mercy it didn't get rained on, that's all I can say."

If only it had been all she could say! She began describing the clock minutely, as if neither Eden nor I had seen it before, speculating about the cost of it, whether this had been five shillings and sixpence or as much as five shillings and elevenpence, whether Eden had bought it this year or last year, and whether the purchase had been made in Colchester or Sudbury. Eden interrupted to ask why I had put the clock outside the window.

"Was it just because you didn't like it, Faith?"

Did they think me completely mad?

"I didn't like it ticking," I said.

"You didn't like it ticking?" Eden spoke as if I had revealed an incomprehensible phobia. My egg was forgotten, boiling away audibly but screened from view by Eden leaning against the stove. "But clocks always do tick, except electric ones."

"I know they do." Does it sound absurd when I say that by now I was near to tears? "I don't like them ticking. I can't help it. I put the clock outside the window so I shouldn't hear it ticking."

"I never heard of anything like it," said Vera.

"Why didn't you come and tell us if you didn't like it ticking?"

"I didn't want to disturb you."

"Surely it would have been better to disturb me," said Eden very gently and reasonably, "than to have ruined my clock."

"I haven't ruined it. It's still going."

"There's no need to cry about it," Vera said. "Crying won't help. Now what's happening to that egg? That egg's been boiling away for at least ten minutes."

Eden fished it out and put it in my eggcup. "I said you wouldn't like it hard-boiled. My goodness, I must fly. Look at the time!"

I was left alone with Vera. She continued to talk for some minutes about clocks, the price of them, the inevitability of their ticking, digressing from her main theme to say what a pity it was I was so nervy at my age. I had never heard of projection then but now I recognize this as projection. My egg would be uneatable. I must let her do me another. Incapable herself of taking offense, she expected me to be unaffected by the drubbing I had received. I dried the dishes for her. When I went up to my bedroom I found that the clock had gone. Where it had disappeared to, I never discovered, but I did not see it again during the rest of my stay.

My visit was not destined to be a long one. The phony war soon showed itself to be phony, people talked of it all being over by Christmas, and my father came to Great Sindon and fetched me home after a fortnight. It was five months later, in the following March, that Eden sent me a five-shilling postal order for my birthday. Vera had come up to London for the day round about that time and presented me with two half-crowns, so I had been able to thank her in person.

The reason I didn't write to thank Eden was not because I was lazy or badly brought up or disliked writing letters or didn't like getting five shillings. I didn't write because I didn't know what to say. I could think of absolutely nothing to say to Eden beyond the bare thanks. My paramount feeling at that time for her and Vera equally was trepidation. One way and another they had humiliated me and beside them I felt humble, hopeless, unable in any way to match up. If I wrote, there would be something wrong with the letter. The grammar would be bad or the handwriting indecipherable or the mode of address wrong. Of course I had written to Eden before, always signing my letters "Love from." But would that be changed now we had spent so much time in each other's company and I had received so many lessons, practical and metaphysical, in the conduct of life? Should it be "Much love" or "Lots of love" or, because of her evident disappointment in me about the clock among many other matters, a cooler "Yours affectionately"? I didn't know so I did nothing. Eden's blast came to my father a month later.

It made him rather sad. I think it gave him a bad day.

"I wish you'd written to Eden," was all he said at first, but he said it several times, and then, "You will write to Eden now, won't you?"

I never did write. The incident upset me. Of course I should never be able to face Eden again or speak to her, and as for that inclusion in the sisterhood, it was out of the question. The letter distanced us and for a while seemed to double the six years that separated our ages. At that time I thought only that I must be at fault, I imperfect, seeing in the conduct of their lives only a standard almost unattainable by me.

I thought: Yes, it's true I thought about them a lot. In my fantasy they remained eternally the same, following the same quiet daily routine in the sweet-smelling, spotless house, eating the huge teas, stitching and embroidering, kissing each other good night, two fastidious women behaving as women should. One day, if I tried hard, I might catch up with them, be like them, be welcomed in.

5

S OME OF THIS I have written down for Daniel Stewart, a syn-
opsis of it really, for I have to bear in mind that it is not my story
he wants but Vera's. Which brings me to the family secret. Am I
going to tell him about it or not?

Of course it isn't really a secret. It is known, it is recorded and
documented somewhere. For instance there must be a police record
of it. I have no doubt the police keep records of this kind of thing for
the sixty years it has been, and probably for longer. The little girl's
family—or should I say her collateral descendants?—they know it,
and so do those surviving members of my own family. Or do they?
Francis must, for Francis always knew everything, almost before it
had happened sometimes. Neither Vera nor Eden ever spoke of it to
me. It was my mother, not my father, who told me. She was angry at
something Vera had said or done, and suddenly she said she had
something to tell me that showed how absurd it was of my father to
keep holding his sisters up as paragons of virtue. Poor man, he was
to be disillusioned soon enough.

Obviously Stewart doesn't know of it. If he did, he would hardly
have left it out of that biographical chapter of his. Rereading this
chapter, it seems to me that he has left out a lot of things I think
important, things essential to a true examination of Vera's character.
I suppose he doesn't know of them and I must tell him. An example
would be her illness at the age of fifteen, a few months after Eden was

born. For a while the doctors thought it was meningitis. Today they would be more likely to diagnose one of those viral infections that do such strange things to people. Vera lay in bed for weeks (my father once told me), at first with a high temperature and delirium, later with her temperature normal each day but rising steeply in the evening. One of her lungs collapsed. She lost a stone in weight. And then, quite suddenly, she was well again, with no aftereffects except perhaps that extreme thinness that never changed. My grandmother had nursed her devotedly, necessarily depriving the new baby of attention in order to do so, but once she was well, Vera took care of Eden more and more, becoming a second mother to her. And that brings me back to the secret again. It is possible that Vera's illness had nothing to do with a virus, and if it was psychosomatic, nothing to do with jealousy over the new baby but brought about instead by the Kathleen March business? By guilt or remorse, possibly, but more probably in my view by simple misery that she had been blamed and ostracized.

Nor does Stewart mention the storm. It was Eden who told me about it, for this was a story she was fond of repeating. The first time I heard it—it was to be told me again on her wedding day—we were in the garden at Walbrooks one summer in the middle of the war. Eden must have been home on leave. She was wearing a dress made out of two old ones which Vera had contrived for her. It had a pink-and-white floral skirt and a blue bodice with pink-and-white collar and cuffs. Her hair was rolled back from the forehead and pinned, while the rest of it hung down in a pageboy bob. On her right hand she wore her mother's wedding ring, Eden being the kind of girl who always does wear her dead mother's wedding ring.

Helen and Vera had gone into the house. Eden and I sat on the terrace in deck chairs. It was a sultry day with thunder rumbling and no doubt it was the sound of this which brought the story to Eden's mind.

"You see that hummock down there at the bottom of the lawn?"

I had sometimes wondered what it was, a swelling under the turf as if rocks were pushing through the soil, though there were no rocks in that countryside of gently undulating hills.

"There used to be a tree there, an enormous horse chestnut—you know, a conker tree. Well, when I was a baby in my pram . . . Has nobody really ever told you this, Faith?"

"I don't think so. I don't know what it is yet."

"You would if they'd told you. Naturally Vera wouldn't, but I should have thought your father . . . Aren't people peculiar? Anyway, as I said, I was a baby in my pram and the pram was under that tree. Helen was in India, of course. This was her grandparents' house then. I expect you knew that, didn't you?"

I wasn't sure but thought it wiser not to admit this.

"Mother and Dad and Vera and your father and me had all come over on our annual visit. They used to walk—can you imagine?—all the way from Myland. It must be six miles. Mother put me under the chestnut tree. It started to thunder and suddenly Vera had a sort of premonition of disaster. They were all eating their tea in the kitchen—trust those Richardsons to make them eat in the kitchen, they always looked down on Dad—and it had a window you could see the lawn from. Well, Mother was keeping an eye on me through the window, as you can imagine, more or less deciding to run out and get me if it started raining, and they all thought Vera had gone mad when she jumped up and dashed outside without a word. You know what perfect manners Vera has, so you can see it would have to be something exceptional to make her leave a table without asking her hostess's permission. She went tearing down the garden and snatched me out of my pram and started to come back again, when there was the most enormous flash of lightning like a bomb falling in the garden. That's what Mother said, though she hadn't really seen any bombs; I mean, they didn't in the first war, not like we have. Well, the lightning struck that tree and shattered it into thousands of bits. It knocked Vera over with me in her arms, but she wasn't hurt and I wasn't, apart from a few bruises. There was nothing left of the pram and nothing of the conker tree except that stump you can see under the grass and about two feet of trunk, but they kept on picking bits of tree up out of the flowerbeds for years. Still do, I expect."

"So Vera saved your life?"

"Oh yes, I owe her my life. I do wonder John didn't tell you, it's quite peculiar of him."

So if that illness of Vera's was psychosomatic (as now for the first time occurs to me it might have been), a way of diverting her mother's attention from the new baby to herself, a disease real enough in its physiological symptoms but brought on by jealousy, she was over that resentment within a few months. By then she loved her sister enough to risk her own life to save the baby's. She even loved her enough to forget her table manners.

I shall tell Stewart about the storm and I shall tell it as Eden told it to me so that he can use direct speech, a much more effective way, I should think, of writing a book like his. And I may also tell him about Vera finding old Mrs. Hislop dead, even though this may not be really relevant. Why were none of these stories ever told to Chad Hamner? Or were they told him but he didn't listen or quickly forgot what he had been told, his attention, as I later knew, being elsewhere?

Vera used to go about visiting old people, a kind of survival from the days of the gentry doing good works in the parish (though the Longleys could never have aspired to gentility) and forerunner of community service. One afternoon she went round to Mrs. Hislop's and found her dead. It must have been a bad shock for the girl who had arrived with a bundle of castoff clothing and the cakes she had just made. Vera told me about it one day when she was in a rare expansive mood.

We were out walking with Jamie in his pushchair, just she and I, Eden at this time being in London with old Lady Rogerson. I was doing the pushing and Jamie had fallen asleep, the way he always did the moment the pushchair started to move, so that he inevitably missed all the things you wanted to point out to him—horses in a meadow, a cat on a wall, a fire engine. I can see him now, his round peachlike cheek and the thick dark lashes lying on it, his hair the true Longley gold, as yet uncut because Vera couldn't bear the idea of cutting off his curls. We came back home a way I had never been before, though by then I had regularly been visiting Sindon every year for five or six years. This was a lane that led nowhere, that petered out after a hundred yards and became a footpath. Vera and I had been forced to take this path after finding the road we intended to use blocked by floodwater. It wound along the edge of a dreary meadow, past disused gravel workings, but this wasn't why Vera had shunned it so long. The cottage came in sight and she laughed a little to hide her embarrassment or perhaps some more powerful emotion.

"I never come this way if I can help it. It's silly after so long, but I can't seem to alter my feelings."

Today Mrs. Hislop's cottage has been smartened up, all the studwork exposed and the roof, which used to be tiled, thatched. A teacher at the University of Essex lives there with his wife and son. When I saw it that first time, just after the war, it was a tumbledown lump of lath and plaster, the windows patched with corrugated iron, the garden overgrown with nettles and an old black-and-green Morris Ten disintegrating among them. Vera said Mrs. Hislop used to collect all sorts of fungi in the fields and cook them for herself, and people warned her it would be the death of her, she would kill herself. And when Vera found her, tiptoeing fearfully into the silent cottage, calling out, knowing there was going to be something dreadful behind the bedroom door, the old woman's body was bloated and swollen up with what they used to call dropsy, though she had never shown signs of this in life.

It was summer and there had been no fungi in the woods or fields for months. Mrs. Hislop hadn't vomited or shown any of the usual signs of fungal poisoning, nor were there any cooked or uncooked fungi in the cottage. There was an inquest and the verdict was death from natural causes, though the village all knew she had poisoned herself, Vera said, if they didn't know how or what with. She hurried me past the cottage, not looking back. I think this shows her as a sensitive person, someone to whom place and atmosphere were evocative of painful memory, so why was she apparently indifferent to the spot where the little girl's body was found? For years she kept clear of Loom Lane and Mrs. Hislop's cottage, yet never attempted to avoid Church Meadow or the churchyard itself and when she went to church entered the churchyard as often by the lychgate as by the drive between the avenue of yews. An explanation could be that she felt some degree of guilt over Mrs. Hislop, for not calling on her the evening before as she had promised, for instance, or for failing to tell anyone what she, and perhaps she alone, very well knew, that Mrs. Hislop's eyes were shrouded with cataracts by then and she was too blind to tell one fungus from another. Guilt might account for her revulsion from the cottage, whereas she might feel no guilt over Kathleen March, being entirely blameless in that matter. But how could she be entirely blameless when the child had been in her care?

Stewart will want pointers in the early life of Vera to what came later, to the long, slow course of poisoning she embarked on and, when that failed, the sharp, savage finality. His postulation, I suppose, will be that murderers don't murder out of the blue. There must be something to lead up to it, a tendency to violence, an indifference to the value of the lives of others. But both Vera and Eden have descendants who have a better right than I to decide whether the secret should or should not be told, a better right even though they may not know the story. Rather than speak Kathleen March's name

to Stewart (who, with that to guide him, would begin his own research), I must find out how Jamie feels about it and perhaps how
Elizabeth and Giles feel. Writing to their father will be useless, as
Francis has never been known to answer letters from anyone in the
family.

The Battle of Britain, the few in conflict up there above the heads of
the many (in which Andrew took part), was what sent me back to
Sindon in August 1940. I wanted very much to go, though most
people would find that hard to believe after what I have said about
my previous visit. My reasons had nothing to do with Vera, or
rather, Vera as drawback was to be weighed off against the obvious
advantages, seeing Eden, sleeping in a bed in a bedroom—at home
we had an air-raid shelter in the house which I slept in, while my
parents' bed was in our living room—the countryside. It was this last
which had reconciled me to staying on last time. The rapturous pleasure some children, especially girls I think, take in a beautiful
countryside in summertime is passed over or forgotten altogether by
adults. Of course it is what Wordsworth is talking about in the *Immor-
tality* ode. Growing up destroys it. Meadow, grove, and stream, the
earth and every common sight lose the dream's glory and freshness in
adolescence, and after that one is just fond of country life. At least, so
it was with me. I took intense delight in the fields and woods of Sindon, the birds and butterflies, when I was eleven, the fruits borne on
trees that many would say bear no fruit—sycamores and field maples
and alders—the formation of leaves, the life cycles of small creatures,
a spider trundling its great white egg, a butterfly emerging from its
chrysalis, a string of toad spawn, a cinnabar moth alighting on a
ragwort flower. All gone now. I do not see these things, or if I do there
is no joy in them; I have no time to stand and stare. But then I did. I
found them, or some of them, in the open areas of our still-half-built-
up suburb where further development had been stopped by the war.
Even then I was very good at the art of half-closing my eyes and thus
not seeing what I did not want to see, in this case, houses, in others,
disquieting manifestations of the emotions. But at Great Sindon there
was no need to close one's eyes. Laurel Cottage was one of the last
houses to have been built there. It was all unspoilt pastoral glory.

And I wanted to be with Eden once more. It seems an eleven-year-
old must have a crush on someone. Separation nourished my hero
worship. I even began to see the letter as just. After all, it was a

reproach to my father, not me. Perhaps he should have taught me manners, had me taught to cook and sew and be womanly. Vera had once or twice said she could not see what good all those Latin declensions would do me, and although I would have taken very little notice of that, coming from where it did, Eden had smilingly agreed, telling us with Vera's very obvious approval how she herself had been so hopeless at Latin that she had stopped it after two terms. She was beautiful, elegant, poised, self-confident. Although a young girl, only eighteen, she was the sister, not the niece, of grown-ups and treated by them with the respect due to a contemporary. She had left school and got a job. On her I would model myself. Traveling down to Colchester on the train, I wondered if her hair were still as gold, and if it was, whether I could put peroxide on my own without anyone finding out.

Somewhere over Essex a dogfight was going on. A fighter with smoke streaming from it tumbled out of the sky, its motion like a leaf falling. The passengers crowded to the windows, peering out and up. There was no man floating down on a parachute. He was still inside, whoever he was, burning inside there. It was a Messerschmitt, the passengers said, not one of ours, not a Spitfire or Hurricane. The sky emptied and the sun went on shining. Vera was at the station to meet me, to kiss the air an inch away from my cheek, to pronounce on my increased height, to grumble afresh about the weight of my suitcase.

This time, though, I was to remain for many months. Air attacks on London began that September, and three months later, in one single night, there were 1,725 fires in the city. My father came down and saw the headmistress and got me into the school Eden had been to. By then I had made a friend in the village, a girl who also went there, so I was happy to have Anne to travel back and forth with and happy, as people of that age are, to conform. Meanwhile it was holiday time and Eden was waiting at Laurel Cottage. "Getting the tea," Vera said. That morning, in my honor, she had made a sponge as only Eden could make it, beating the eggs for no less than ten minutes.

At Laurel Cottage, too, though I had forgotten about this, was Francis.

Until Jamie came along, he was my only cousin, my mother's sister and brother both being childless. As small children we had sometimes met, played together no doubt, perhaps got on, I don't remember. He was about a year older than I. Of his presence in the house, Vera, being Vera of course, said nothing, no doubt expecting me to know he would be there, as perhaps I should have done. After all, it was school holidays for him as well as me, and where else would he be but at home? A good many other places, I was later to learn, but that was later too.

It is not hard to remember but it is hard to refeel the sensations I had when I walked into the house and there was Francis in the living room with Eden. A sinking of the heart, something not far from panic, an idea that now all would be spoiled. Why? Why did I mind so much? Why was I so certain in those first few seconds that he and I would dislike each other and, worse than that, that he would some-how always make me feel awkward, inept, and stupid? In those first seconds, too, I was afraid of him, in a defensive way, drawing all my soft parts in under my shell.

Vera's perfect manners did not extend to reintroducing us to each other. Nor did Eden's. And perhaps I was ridiculous to expect any-thing. We were cousins, we were family—what kind of paranoid little prig was I that I wanted to be told things about him, and him to be told things about me, for something we might have in common to be found, and for Vera or Eden, by means of a sympathy for others they conspicuously lacked, start us communicating? Instead I stood there silently, wondering—of all absurd speculations—where I was going to sleep. I knew I wasn't going to be able to bring myself to ask.

He was a handsome boy. If you want to know what he looked like, then get hold of some numbers of the old *Boys' Own Paper* or a late-nineteenth-century novel for boys with illustrations. Francis looked like the prototype of the young hero, the clean-limbed young Englishman, captain of the first eleven, head prefect, later on rugger Blue, kind to underlings and a stern putter-down of injustices, of blue blood but modest about it—in American parlance, the perfect WASP, a youthful Sir Henry Curtis. Nowadays we would say he most resembled the actor Anthony Andrews. He was blond, his fea-tures chiseled, the jawline cloven out of teak with a sharp knife, his eyes a piercing blue, the lips not narrow but generously full. Apart from all this, he looked a lot like Eden. In appearance they were nearer to twins than my father and Vera, for Francis at thirteen was already taller than Eden.

We all sat down to tea, Vera embarking at once on praise of the large circular cake, its top scattered all over with someone's whole week's sugar ration. Eden giggled. Though a year older, she seemed less grown-up, less dignified. I could see, too, that others were not inevitably excluded from the charmed circle of two composed of her and Vera. And yet . . . No, I am wrong there. Now it was Eden and Francis who were a pair, and Eden and Vera, but they were never a trio. Of Francis's behavior to his mother I will go into later, though even at that first meeting, in those initial hours it shocked and intrigued me. He and Eden together were strange. They mystified and in a way alarmed me. I didn't know why, I was too young. The glances they exchanged, Eden's way of giggling at what he said, the whispering that brought reproaches from Vera to him if not to her, the apparent intense pleasure they took in each other's company until Eden seemed to recollect herself and become once more Vera's partisan—all this was outside my understanding. It threatened me (as the psychotherapists say) in that corner of my being that yearned, and still yearns, to belong. It seemed to set before me a standard of grown-up conduct to which I could never, I was sure, aspire. Years were to pass before I could analyze and solve the mystery. It was that they behaved like secret lovers.

But that evening I was at sea, drifting in a open boat on the deepest and least charted Longley waters. Conversation at tea was devoted to Eden's new job, but since everyone expected me to know what I knew nothing of—the nature of the job, the means by which she had got it, the name of her employer, her starting date, and so on—I couldn't join in. Without much success I decided to listen and gather what I could. Eden, now school was behind her, wore heavy makeup, one of those tinted liquid foundations that had not long come on to the market—or under the counter, to be begged and queued for—bright scarlet lipstick, gingery brown pencil on her plucked eyebrows, and a daring streak of blue shadow on her eyelids. Her hairstyle was elaborate, a construction in which the metal grips were visible, which was no drawback to chic in 1940.

The question of whether I should still be sent to bed at eight o'clock was one that I had been anxious about. Francis's presence, though in so many ways upsetting, eased my mind a little. They could hardly send me to bed and let him stay up, and somehow the two of us being sent to bed in the same ignominious fashion would be preferable to my isolated banishment. But soon after tea, Francis disappeared.

I dried dishes. Vera and Eden continued to talk about Eden's job, which I had by then gathered was something in a solicitor's office, and she had got it through General Chatteriss, who had been at school with the senior partner. More emerged. Eden was secretary to this man's son, whose name was Noel Hodderson. I was relieved to have learned so much without asking. It meant that when the subject came up I should not have to show my ignorance and be castigated for it.

Francis, of course, was not expected to wash or dry dishes or make his bed or do anything around the house. Returning to the living room, I thought he would be where we had left him, lying in an armchair reading *Gone with the Wind*. Vera reacted violently (today we should say overreacted) to his absence. Her face grew red. She stopped in the doorway and said loudly to Eden:

"He's doing it again, you see!"

"Darling, it's only ten to seven." Eden, I had noticed, was coming to call Vera "darling" more and more often.

"He takes advantage of our being out of the way."

This interchange mystified me. Francis was free, it was early. Why shouldn't he go out about the village somewhere if he wished? No one said any more about it for the time being. Vera and Eden sat down to their usual evening occupations. They were like Victorian ladies with their "work." Their leisure they spent facing each other across a table or sitting in armchairs on either side of the fireplace, sewing or crocheting or doing embroidery. To their tasks they now settled, Eden rather an incongruous sight with her elaborate hairstyle and bright makeup busy at such a Goody Two-Shoes pursuit as drawn threadwork on a handkerchief hem. But to me at that time everything she did was admirable and worthy of being copied, and when she found me a crochet hook and ball of wool and set me to "making squares" to be sewn together for blankets, I happily complied. Vera was embroidering a design for a firescreen, a lady in bonnet and crinoline with a basket over her arm. Crinoline ladies had been a very popular subject for this kind of art in the thirties, and in Laurel Cottage they were all over the place on cushions and tea cozies and nightdress cases.

I should have preferred to be out in the garden and the fields. But I feared to go in the light of what had been said of Francis's disappearance. Besides, there was delicious pleasure in being at one with the grown-ups, performing a similar task to theirs and being helped by kind Eden, who from time to time adjusted my clumsy hands, checked a tendency on my part to make uneven stitches, and finally, when a square was complete, remarked:

"That's really quite good for a beginner!"

Vera had laid her embroidery aside to write a letter. Sneaking a look, I saw it was to her husband, for it began "Dear Gerry." Where he was stationed she didn't know—"somewhere in England" was all she was told, unless he could indicate the place by hints subtle enough to get past the censor. The time was coming up to eight and in defiance of it I began another square, but I underrated Eden, who heard the church clock chimes begin one minute before the hands of the living-room clock reached eight. She tucked her needle into the linen, folded it, laid it on the arm of the chair, sharp scissors on top, perfectly aligned, stood up, smiling at me.

"Well, little niece, you're going to share my room so I'd better show you where you're to sleep."

I followed her to the door, disappointed, but with compensation for my disappointment in that I should be sleeping in her room. Vera, however, suddenly jumped up, pushed past us, and ran up the stairs. I heard her running from room to room, banging doors. Eden hesitated. She didn't look at me. Then she opened the door and we stood at the foot of the stairs. Vera came running down them, her face flushed, that look about her eyes and mouth of anger boiling up.

"He's not in the house! I told you, he's doing it again."

She threw open the front door, ran down to the gate, which she hung over, calling, "Francis, Francis!" to the left, and then "Francis, Francis!" to the right.

We started up towards Eden's room. Vera's voice could be heard, calling Francis's name, first in the front, then in the back. His bedroom door was shut and Eden opened it to look inside, but of course he wasn't in there. I didn't ask and she didn't explain. Her own room was extremely neat and tidy, with lace mats for her hairbrush and various pots and jars to stand on, the predominating color pink, the pictures on the walls including a colored photograph of the statue of Peter Pan in Kensington Gardens. The beds were not side by side but placed at angles to each other and as far apart as the size of the room allowed. There was, I saw to my great relief, no clock.

My suitcase was already there waiting for me to unpack it. I was to hang my things in a certain allotted area of the wardrobe, Eden explained, and I could have the second drawer down in the chest.

Vera's feet pounded up the stairs. She threw open the door. Children are embarrassed by signs of strong emotion in adults, and Vera was showing strong emotion at that moment, her face bright red with tears lying on it, her mouth working, her body screwed up spring-like, her hands held up in clenched fists. Eden went up to her, laid a hand on her arm.

"Why get yourself in such a state, darling?"

"He does it on purpose!"

"Well, of course he does. You should take no notice." Eden remembered me, waiting awkwardly, wondering what had happened, what could have happened to bring about such intense, furious, hysterical misery.

"Good night, Faith dear. I won't disturb you when I come up. I'll get undressed in the dark."

She closed the door, shutting me on one side of it, herself and Vera and Vera's mysterious agony on the other. I wondered, as I unpacked, if she thought Francis had run away or even been kidnapped. Would the police be called? Was I in on the first scene of some dreadful family tragedy? I went out to the bathroom and saw his door wide open, the bed turned down—Vera turned everyone's bed down after tea, taking off and folding the counterpanes—the room empty. On the mantelpiece the noisy clock was ticking away. Downstairs Vera was crying. I lay in bed, bewildered by the mystery, certain that the house would soon be invaded by policemen, neighbors, searchers. Someone crept up the stairs and I was sure it was Eden coming, so I feigned sleep. But Eden didn't come for another half-hour and when she did and Vera with her, the noise they made would have awakened me anyway.

"He's there! Look at him. And the door wide open. He must have crept in behind our backs. I should like to kill him."

"Darling, you shouldn't distress yourself."

"Why does he do it? Why? What does he get out of it?"

Curiosity got the better of me. I got out of bed and opened the door and stood there. Vera didn't see me for a moment. Francis's door was still wide open, the clock ticked away with a metallic reverberation enough to keep awake the soundest sleeper, but it hadn't kept Francis awake. He lay sleeping, half-uncovered, his breathing heavy, regular, and deep.

"I could kill him," Vera said again.

"The more wrought-up you get, the more he's going to do it."

Vera saw me.

"Now what are you doing out of bed?"

I said I wanted a glass of water.

"You get it for her, will you, Eden?"

"I can get it myself."

"Yes, and leave the tap running. I don't know where you get this business of wanting water at night from. Your father and I and Eden never had that as children. I don't know why you were allowed to get into the way of it."

She was venting on me the anger his sleeping prevented her venting on Francis, though I did not, of course, know this. Nor did I then know, though I was soon to find out, that this behavior of Francis's was a nightly occurrence, part of the cruel and calculated mother-tease he embarked on at the start of his holidays. This particular feature of it consisted in his disappearing each evening at seven—originally probably to avoid the ignominy of being sent to bed—hiding within earshot of the loud rage and misery Vera was unable to control or inhibit when he couldn't be found, then, once she had begun sobbing in Eden's arms, creeping up the stairs to bed and leaving his door open to display himself as if to say, "Look, here I am. What's all the fuss about?" Vera never became accustomed to it, never took Eden's advice and ignored it. Each evening the same hysterical scene took place, terminating in the two of them standing on the threshold of Francis's room, looking in on him with wonder like courtiers at the *couchée* of some King of France.

Why did he do it? What made him enjoy so much the sight and sound of Vera's impotent anger? For this was only one of many provocations, among them his obeying of her dictum about eating with one's left hand and drinking with one's right, to the extent of holding knife and fork both in his left hand. Then there were his red days and his yellow days, times when he would consent to eat only red food at the three meals or only yellow food, in the latter case subjecting items such as lemon-curd tarts, saffron cake, a hard-boiled egg, to the careful analysis needed to establish whether they were yellow enough. Far too subtle and original to resort to conventional practical jokes of the salt-in-the-sugar-basin or apple-pie-bed kind, he preferred the bizarre, knowing only too well how especially this affronted Vera. One hot August day, he turned all the blue flowers in the garden green by carefully bending their heads over and dipping them in a jar with half an inch of ammonia in the bottom of it. The *Daily Tele-*

graph would arrive in the morning with the crossword-puzzle clues still there but the frame cut out. Vera complained to the paper shop and involved herself in exchanges of abuse with the paper boy for weeks on end before she found out Francis was responsible. Francis would go to incredible lengths to carry out his teases, and thought nothing of getting up at six to catch the newspaper and cut out the puzzle the moment it slipped through the door.

Eden asked him why he did it. I was in the room with them, but for a while I think they had forgotten my presence. Vera had just run upstairs, weeping. It was one of Francis's white days. Food shortages were making themselves felt by then and there was a general consensus that it was unpatriotic not to eat up everything on one's plate. Francis had been able to eat his cauliflower and the white meat of chicken but there had been brown gravy on the potatoes, which he had insisted on washing off under the tap. Vera—incredibly—went along with him in this food-colors stuff to ensure that he ate, presumably, for she thought him too thin, and quite gravely produced this insipid meal with rice pudding to follow. Her compliance was not what Francis wanted. After the first spoonful of rice, he clapped his hand to his forehead like someone who has remembered too late a certain important injunction.

"Is it Tuesday?"

"Of course it's Tuesday," Vera said.

"Then it should have been a green day. What a fool I am! It may not be too late to undo the evil, it may be that no harm is done. Quick—have we a tin of gooseberries in the house? An apple, only it must be a green one. A cucumber, even?"

Vera threw down her napkin and rushed upstairs. Francis laughed. With a sideways glance at him, neutral, not willing to commit herself, Eden said:

"You are awful. Why are you so awful?"

I had never before seen anyone eat a cucumber like a banana. He peeled it like a banana, though necessarily using the knife.

"When we lived in India," he said, "I had a nurse, an ayah, called Mumtaz."

"You've told me about her before."

"Okay, so I've told you about her before. You said she had a funny name. It was only the name of the woman they built the Taj Mahal for. But I suppose that doesn't mean anything to you."

"Don't be horrible, Francis," said Eden.

"I don't think I will tell you. She died, anyway. She got something awful, typhus, and she died."

"You had your mother," Eden said. "Not like me. My mother died with I was thirteen."

"And you had *my* mother. The point is, I didn't. And I wasn't thirteen, I was seven. She sent me to school the minute she could, she got rid of me the moment she could. Nice, wasn't it? I was to go to school because they were in India, but *she* wasn't in India for long, she was here. And you were here. So she chose you and sent me away to school."

Eden suddenly became very grown-up and lofty. She gave me a bright smile. "Faith will get a really awful impression from what you've been saying, you know. Of course you don't mean it. I hope you know he doesn't mean it, Faith."

I was a silent child, at that time without social grace, given to nods and shakes of the head. I nodded, which was about as ambiguous as you could get.

"Your mother did what was best for you, Francis. Or what she thought was best for you. Maybe *I* would have liked to go away to school, but I didn't get the chance, did I?"

"Don't be such a bloody prig, Eden."

Middle-class people did not say "bloody" much in 1940. To me "damn" was strong language enough, and I was shocked.

"You've made Faith blush." It was true, he had, but I would have preferred Eden not to have drawn attention to it. "She's bound to tell her father, you know. Every word you've said will get back to her father and of course you won't get the backlash. Vera will be blamed for the way she's brought you up."

"Good," said Francis, taking Vera's box of thumbtacks down from the shelf. First he pinned the lengths of cucumber peel together at their ends, then made a pattern of tacks like studwork so that the peel looked like a belt. He rolled it up, took the belt from the pocket of Vera's raincoat, and substituted for it the cucumber-and-thumbtack one.

I thought he was mad. I still think I may have been right and he was. It was all revenge, this behavior of his, in no way a means of drawing attention to himself and thereby hoping to recapture his mother's love. He hated her, and it was hatred, not something masquerading as hatred, but the real, vicious, luxuriating thing itself.

Eden maintained a subtle neutrality, giggling with Francis and sometimes seeming with her giggles to approve—she knew he would never
repeat to Vera anything she said, he was too proud—and with Vera,
doing no more than sighing, shaking her head, and telling Vera to
ignore it, he would grow out of it. She couldn't trust Vera not to go
rushing to Francis with a quote hot off her tongue: "Eden says you're
disgusting, she's never known anyone treat his mother like you treat
me!"

No one expected me to take sides. I was never appealed to. By this
time I had met Anne Cambus and we were spending all our days
together, much of them in her home, and this was good for me, not
just for the obvious social reasons but because it showed me a contrast; that not all the world was either like Vera and Eden's household
or aspiring to be so. Some people were easygoing and warm and
casual, much as my mother was, and it was Vera's home, not mine,
that was the exception. So for much of the daylight hours I was with
Anne, wandering the fields and woods, going cycling with her on an
old bicycle that had been Eden's, playing an involved, absorbing
game we called Mary, Queen of Scots, in which was simply enacted
over and over the events as we had been taught them in Mary's life,
each of us taking it in turn to play the queen, while the other took all
the other roles—Darnley, Rizzio, Bothwell, and Queen Elizabeth. In
wet weather, this took place in the tumbledown cottage at the end of
Vera's garden everyone called the "hovel." A lot of the houses in Sindon and the surrounding villages at that time had a small cottage or
the ruins of one in their gardens. The place must once have been a
warren of wattle-and-daub shacks, patched with brickwork, huddled
together for convenience of building and for warmth, honeycombs of
dirt and disease and discomfort. Vestiges of them remained, preserved as storeplaces or washhouses. Whether anyone had ever done
washing in the Laurel Cottage hovel I don't know. Certainly it contained an old copper with a bleached wooden lid and a space beneath
it, a kind of cave, to light a fire in. The floor was of bricks. As a child,
Eden once told me, she had been allowed to use the place as a kind of
Wendy house, and that accounted for its less-than-derelict appearance. The tattered remains of gingham curtains still hung at the
small window, there was a rug on the floor, an old gateleg table, a
couple of canvas deck chairs. Vera, being Vera, routinely gave it a
clean-up from time to time. Anne and I crowned Mary Stuart and
married her, betrayed her, and beheaded her over and over again in

the hovel that summer and autumn. One night, five years into the future, I was to see enacted there a stranger ritual, but that was distant, impossible for a child to foresee.

By night I shared Eden's room. True to her promise, she undressed and got into bed in the dark, but on moonlit nights it was not so very dark and sometimes I was still awake when she came to bed, though feigning sleep. Even with the light off, she undressed with extreme modesty, first taking off her dress or blouse, next pulling the nightgown over her head, then slipping quickly out of her underclothes. All Eden's nightdresses were of fine pink or white lawn, embroidered by her or Vera at the neck and wrists and sometimes at the hem as well. Nylon had been invented by then but it was to take a long time to reach us.

In the dark too, or in the half-light, Eden sat at the dressing table and "cleansed" her face in the way the women's magazines then (and for all I know, now) recommended to their readers, finally massaging in the skinfood. Her hair was wound up and pinned in sausage curls, this confection covered with a pink chiffon scarf. Eden, as Helen has told Stewart her own mother did, slept in white cotton gloves to keep her hands nice. Pretending to be asleep, even to the extent of maintaining a loud regular breathing, I watched the nightly procedure with admiration and, I'm afraid, with envy.

Sometimes, of course, as the autumn came on, it was too dark to see, for both her and me, and all this must have been performed in the bathroom. And later I was moved into Francis's room, for Francis had gone back to school, having ended his holidays with a mother-tease coup.

This was on the evening of the day he tried to put an end to that left-hand/right-hand business once and for all. He didn't succeed but I think what he said shook Vera, for though she continued to point to our hands across the tablecloth and push our plates to the left-hand side of us, I felt that her heart was no longer in it.

Francis asked her if she knew that Moslems always ate with their right hands because they used their left hands for performing personal hygiene after defecation. I have put that euphemistically, which wasn't at all what Francis said. He told her that they used their left hands to "wipe their bums after they'd shat" and that was why cutting off a Moslem's right hand by way of punishment for stealing, say, was an even more cruel mutilation than it seemed. The victim was likely to starve to death.

Vera screamed with shock. She shouted that he made her feel ill, he made her feel sick with disgust. Later she said that there were no Moslems here, thank God, so why did he think we should be interested in their revolting customs?

"It makes you see what bringing people up by these rigid rules can lead to," Francis said, and he was right there, in more ways than one.

A gloom seemed to settle on him as the day went on. He grew abstracted and silent, and though it was a yellow day—Vera, on his instructions, had truculently served him with pease pudding and an omelet for lunch—he forgot about eating only Madeira cake and lemon curd for tea but absentmindedly got through a slice of date bread before he remembered. He got up and left the table without a word. Vera, missing him as usual that evening, found a suicide note left by him on his pillow when she turned down his bed. She drew back the counterpane—hours earlier tucked by her under the pillow and then smoothed over it and under the bedhead—to find an envelope inserted there by fingers that had ever so slightly disturbed her handiwork, making a wrinkle in the folkweave that was the first thing she saw as she entered the room. "Mother" was printed on it in Francis's presently favorite mauve ink. (How *colorful* Francis was, how I remember him in colors, his mauve ink, his yellow days, his transformation of blue flowers into green.) The note told her he was so miserable he had decided to end it all.

Vera believed it. I certainly did, of course I did, I was aghast and afraid. Eden seemed to believe it, at any rate it was she who said Vera should get the police. The village constable came on his bicycle, later more policemen in a car. Vera went to get the note to show them but it had gone, Francis, of course, who was hiding in the house, having abstracted and destroyed it. When the fuss was at its height, three policemen in the house, the rector's wife—who had called about something to do with the Mother's Union—Vera crying, Eden pacing, Francis walked in quietly to ask what all the fuss was about. He denied writing any note, denied the existence of a note, and the result was that everyone started doubting Vera. I hadn't been shown it but Eden had and it was extraordinary how cagey she was about it, never affirming that she, too, had read it, never coming out quite on Vera's side, but rather adopting the pose of nurse, confidante, and general calmer-down, telling the police and Mrs. Morrell that she would take care of Vera, Vera would be fine in no time, she was overwrought, she would soon be better. You could see the police thought Vera was an hysteric and that they had been called out over nothing. But Francis got what he had aimed at and went off to bed well-satisfied with the success of his culminating tease.

That autumn, though, someone in Great Sindon really did commit suicide. I have often wondered how significant this death was in what came afterwards. In other words, how much it contributed to the events that led up to the murder.

6

T HE RECTOR OF the parish of Great Sindon was called the
Reverend Richard Morrell. I had spoken of him as the vicar, for
which I was roundly reproved by Vera and told not to be so silly, but
in my ignorance I thought all clergymen of the Church of England
were vicars, I thought of it as a generic term like "butcher." Vera
went to church most Sundays, usually to evensong. For some reason
never made clear to me, my father did not want me to be confirmed. I
suppose he had lost his faith or had ceased to accept formalized reli-
gion. At the time I rather resented missing this surely indispensable
part of my education. A large framed photograph, much admired by
me, of Eden in her white confirmation dress with a veil over her hair,
stood on the piano in the living room at Laurel Cottage. Though
lacking this positive *entrée* to the elect, or even the promise of it, I
sometimes went to church with Vera, especially on the evenings
when Eden came too. To walk along the village street with my two
aunts, each of us carrying a prayer book—for no reason that I can
fathom, since a copy was placed in front of every pew seat—helped
me towards that "belonging" for which I was ever striving. After
the service, we all shook hands with Mr. Morrell, big, heavy, and
unkempt-looking, with the reputation of keeping the communion
bread unwrapped in the pocket of his surplice. He was first cousin to
a very eminent man who had been the Master of Balliol. I called him
"a master at" Balliol because I thought I had misheard and if he was

head of a college he would have been called a headmaster, an error for which I again got the rough side of Vera's tongue.

The Morrells had a maidservant called Elsie. People still had live-in maids then, though they were soon to disappear into munitions or the Women's Land Army. Great Sindon rectory was an enormous house with eight bedrooms, and very old-fashioned. Elsie, who was sixteen, the daughter of a farm laborer living in a village three miles away, did all the rough work of the house, leaving dusting and bed-making and ironing and, of course, the cooking to Mrs. Morrell. I knew her by sight. Anne and I, coming home from school, used sometimes to meet her on her afternoon off walking home to visit her mother, but we never spoke. We were dreadful little snobs. Although we knew we were not gentry in the way that Mrs. Deliss at the Priory was, we considered ourselves several cuts above the village people. Elsie, moreover, came not only from laboring stock but was a servant. Vera expected her to call me Miss and address her as Madam. She was a thick-set, florid girl, her skin always looking pink and weatherbeaten, with very bright reddish-gold hair that I am sure was naturally that color. Mrs. Morrell used sometimes to call at Laurel Cottage and in conversation with Vera grumble about Elsie, calling her lazy and slatternly. I think they enjoyed talking about what they called "the servant problem."

"You are so lucky not having that to contend with," I heard Mrs. Morrell say. "What wouldn't I give for a house this size." She wouldn't have given much in fact. Secretly, she, who, Anne told me, had been an unqualified teacher in a private school in Ipswich, adored living in a Georgian mansion bigger than Great Sindon Priory.

Once or twice when I had been there with Vera, I came across Elsie, broom in hand or on hands and knees scrubbing a stone floor. Vera always spoke to her, which meant that poor Elsie had to get up and look respectful.

"I hope Mother and Father are well, Elsie."

"Yes, thank you, madam."

As far as I know, Vera was totally unacquainted with Elsie's parents. Certainly none of us knew her surname until it came out at the inquest.

On one of her afternoons off, Elsie disappeared. When she didn't come back that night and hadn't appeared in the morning, Mrs.

Morrell sent to her parents to find out what had happened. By "sent," I mean she got the boy who came in once a week to cut the grass or sweep up the leaves to go over on his bicycle. Elsie wasn't with them either and later that day a farmer found her drowned body in his well.

Real wells that people actually use don't exist anymore as far as I know, but a few still did then. Most of the cottages and some of the farmhouses had no main water and no electricity. Piped gas had never been brought to Great Sindon and has not to this day. This well was fed by a spring of fresh water and had very clean-looking weedlike streaming green hair growing in it. Some time afterwards, when the well had been emptied and cleansed, Anne and I went to look at it. It was no more than three feet in diameter but reputedly very deep—reputedly, no doubt, much deeper than it really was— with a coping round its edge of small old bricks. Every time Elsie walked that way she had to pass the farm where the well was, and in November, when the hedge was bare, it was visible to the passerby. It was Anne from whom I first learned what had happened.

"Something awful—Elsie at the rectory committed suicide. She's drowned herself. Mummy told me. She said I wasn't to talk about it, but you don't matter. I mean, she knows I'd tell you."

I was shocked and somehow overawed. We stood waiting for the school bus. It was a cold morning, the air, the wind, everything, the world, full of floating, blowing, falling leaves. Never before had I been in a place where the falling of leaves was so apparent, for the village heart was planted on the green and in divergent lanes with huge chestnuts, planes, sycamores, and beeches. All of them were shedding their foliage, helped by the driving wind, so that to this day when I see leaves falling in autumn I am reminded of Elsie and her death by water.

I asked Anne why. Why had she done it? Sixteen is not the contemporary of twelve, but sixteen is young still, not like twenty-six, say, which we considered well over the hill. How could anyone of sixteen want to die?

"Mummy said she could guess. I heard her say to Dad: I can guess the reason for that—but when I asked her, she wouldn't tell me."

"Well, I can't guess, can you?"

"Unless she was very miserable working for old Mrs. Morrell," said Anne. "But if she was, I don't see why she couldn't have left and gone into a factory."

Nothing was said about Elsie's death at Laurel Cottage. I mean *nothing*. It was not even mentioned with Anne's mother's warning not to discuss it with anyone. Secretiveness was an important feature in Longley family culture, even when there was no real reason for it. Information was not given and news was not told. One was expected to know it already or not to wish to know it. Often Vera and Eden seemed to have secrets for the sake of having them, to delight in the lowered voice, the over-the-shoulder glance, the whispering behind hands. I fancy there was rather more whispering than usual about the time of Elsie's death, more entering of rooms and closing the door on me with a "Just a moment, Faith." Certainly they must have known about it; there was no possibility they could have failed to have heard either from Mrs. Morrell or from reading the local paper. Besides, the village buzzed with it. The stray bomb, last of a stick dropped by a damaged Dornier, which fell on a field near Bures and killed a cow, had been entirely superseded as current gossip topic by the death of Elsie. Vera and Eden knew, and knew, too, the result of the inquest at which the reason for Elsie's suicide came out. Again, it was Anne who told me, though she was unable to say whether her mother's guess had been correct. We spent a great deal of time that winter speculating about Elsie, the whys and wherefores, and Elsie's state of mind.

Meanwhile London was being destroyed by German bombs. And not only London—Coventry, Bristol, Birmingham. Terrible fires raged in the City and there was little defense against night attacks. The fear of invasion apparently was still strong. It is said of the novels of Jane Austen how remarkable it is that while giving an accurate picture of the social life of her day she chose so thoroughly to ignore the war in which Britain for a greater part of her life was engaged, to omit entirely mention of the battles of Trafalgar and Waterloo. Anne and I could have understood. We were not involved. The war did not interest or affect us. It was a long way away, not audible, not even known about if one chose to be out of the room when the wireless was on. The torpedoing of Italian ships by British planes in Taranto harbor, the situation in East Africa, the German infiltration of Rumania—all this was as nothing to us compared to our fascination with the plight and wretched end of Elsie.

It may seem strange today, but then, when I was twelve, I had never actually *known* anyone not married to have a baby. To be married was the prerequisite of having a baby. Anne and I, though mystified by the emotions involved, could understand perfectly the disgrace of being a single girl and giving birth to a baby in England in 1940.

"She couldn't have had it, could she?" said Anne. "You can see that."

I could see that. What would she have done with it in practical terms? An unmarried Elsie pushing a pram along the village street was unimaginable. Mr. Morrell would surely have refused to christen it or else have had to do so under cover of darkness.

"What did she do it for?" I said.

By "do it" I meant engage in the sexual act that had led to her pregnancy. Anne couldn't tell me. The facts of sex were known to us more or less accurately, but of the emotions we knew nothing, we scarcely knew emotion would be involved. Sex was something we thought of as being entered into for the experience alone, for the sake of knowing what it was like. The identity of one's partner seemed unimportant, while we did not know of the existence of desire. Elsie's conduct was therefore baffling to us, for though we understood how someone might wish to "do it"—we had confided in each other that we would like to "do it" at any rate once in the course of life—we were mystified by anyone's taking so serious a step without due preparation and the forethought necessary to prevent conception.

The well was never used again. I don't know where the farmer got his drinking water from, for I am sure it was impossible to have a system linked to the mains in 1941. Perhaps there was a pump nearby. Anne and I squeezed through the hedge and trespassed on his land to peer down the deep green hole. I am sorry to say that for a while playing Elsie displaced our Mary Stuart game and we would enact Elsie's walking along the lane, seeing the well, and jumping down it. These actions we performed in Anne's garden, a pit that had once been an ice cave doing duty as the well. We were only twelve and that must be our excuse.

At school, just as on wet mornings at assembly, if "Summer Suns Are Glowing" was due to be sung, a more suitable hymn would be substituted for it, so a round we had enjoyed singing was abruptly removed from our repertoire.

London's burning, London's burning,
Fetch the engines, fetch the engines.
Fire, fire! Fire, fire!
Pour on water . . .

. . . would have constituted a serious breach of taste in January 1941.

I had been home for Christmas only, returning to Laurel Cottage for the start of the new term. In our suburb, after the all-clear had sounded, the children went about the streets collecting up the pieces of shell from antiaircraft fire. I had a fine collection of shrapnel to show Anne. My Uncle Gerald had been home on leave for Christmas, Francis had his fourteenth birthday, and Eden, to everyone's astonishment, announced her intention of joining the WRNS.

Vera had more or less come to terms with it and rallied by the time I saw her again. Or else she was putting on a good front for my benefit.

"Of course it's very much the most superior of the women's services," she said. "The Ats are the lowest and then the WAAF and the Wrens at the top. That's a well-known fact. Eden won't be doing any manual labor, that's quite out of the question."

But she wouldn't be able to live at Laurel Cottage, I thought.

"The uniform is very attractive. Just like a smart navy-blue costume really. And that saucy little hat."

A tear ran down the side of Vera's nose and splashed onto the magazine she was holding, right onto the photograph in fact of a Wren in uniform. Her tears embarrassed me. I was stunned and a little unnerved when she clutched my hand. I murmured that everything would be all right, the war would soon be over, while vistas of grownup grief opened in my mind's eye before me and I glimpsed for a moment how limitless and infinitely varied these might be. Vera released my hand, dried her eyes, and told me fiercely not to say a word to my father that she had "broken down," still less to Eden herself.

Before I went back to London in the summer my Uncle Gerald had been home on embarkation leave. Almost certainly his destination and that of his regiment was North Africa. It may be that Vera suffered as deeply over his departure as she had over Eden's, it may have been even worse for her, but if she did and if it was she had learned by then to keep her unhappiness totally concealed. It was a fine Saturday in June when he left quite early in the morning. After he had gone Vera took all the bedroom curtains down and washed them at the kitchen sink.

> 24a Llangollen Gdns.
> Notting Hill Gate
> London, W. 11
>
> March 12

Dear Faith,

It was good to hear from you though I wish it could have been about something else. There is no reason why you should know this but I was seventeen before anyone told me who my grandmother was and then it was a girl at school who told me. I think it has set up a sort of block about anything to do with her. I shy away from it, I absolutely hate even thinking about it, and although I know it is unhealthy to be so uptight, I can't help it, I have tried.

Daniel Stewart did write to me and I wrote back and said what is the absolute truth, that I don't know any more about Vera Hillyard than everybody knows. Less, probably, as I have never read any accounts of the trial, etc. He seemed to think I was called Hillyard and addressed the envelope like that. Some sort of sixth sense made me open it—that name always makes my hair stand on end—and for weeks afterwards I imagined that other people in this house must guess that Elizabeth Hills is Vera Hillyard's granddaughter. That was stupid, of course, because they don't, most of them are too young to have heard of her, but it will give you some idea of the state I get into about the whole thing.

I have never heard anything about this secret. The name Kathleen March doesn't mean anything to me and I'm sure you'll find it doesn't to Giles either. As far as I'm concerned, you can tell it to Stewart, who is in the market for any sort of dirt, as these people always are. I shouldn't dream of reading his book so it doesn't matter to me. The only interest I have in it is in seeing that he doesn't mention my name or give any indication of who I am or where I live.

Mother sends her regards and says do give her a ring sometime. She says she would love to see you again. Sorry if this letter seems negative but you must understand by now how I feel.

> Yours,
> Elizabeth

6 Blythe Place
London W. 14

March 18

Dear Faith Severn,

I'm afraid I can't remember if you and I have ever met. Daniel Stewart wrote to me but I didn't reply. As far as I am concerned my mother and Elizabeth are the only family I have and I want to keep it that way. I just don't want to know my relations, living or dead, and that goes for my father. Sorry about this if it sounds rude.

Yours,
Giles Hills

◆

Via Orti Orcellari 90
Firenze

March 20

Dear Faith,

As you see from above, I have moved. I went round to the old place and they had kept your letter for me. If you do come to Florence this spring, remember we have a date and I am going to cook for you. I am feeling pleased with myself because my first book has just been published. It would be nothing to Francis, who is quite a blasé author by now with half a dozen under his belt. Mine, too, is about putting things under one's belt, in other words, is a cookbook, *Cucina Ben Riuscita* (Mondadori, 20,000 lire).

No, I have never heard of any family secret. Remember, I was six when it happened. Pearmain wasn't likely to give me any revelations, he hardly ever spoke to me. Now I am wondering if I want to know what it is or if I don't. On the whole I think not. I should like to say it can't be worse than what I do know but that is a very challenging statement, asking for trouble. I suppose it is something involving my mother when she was young and I am inclined to say: Don't tell Stewart. I know what journalists are and he will only make it out worse than it was.

You can tell all (the secret too if you must) when you come here. Till then.

All the best,
Jamie

16 Queens Gate Mews
London S.W.7

March 31

Dear Mrs. Severn,

I am afraid I have been thick-skinned. It has taken me a
long time to realize how repugnant to you is the idea of telling
me the story of your aunt and Kathleen March. But you will
see by my use of the name that I have pinpointed it and have in
fact done much more than that.

The files of the newspaper chain for which Chad Hamner
once worked provided me with most of the facts. I wasn't specifically looking for the "secret," just for anything which might
have happened in Myland and later Great Sindon during the
time your grandparents and their young family lived in those
places. Also Mrs. Adele Bacon is still alive, though nearly
ninety. Three of Kathleen's siblings, all younger than she,
survive. I have talked to all these people and seen the records
in the possession of the Essex police, both for 1921 when the
incident occurred and 1979 when the child's skeleton was
found.

Enclosed is my account of what happened. Albert March
has looked at it and says it is accurate as far as he knows. May I
trouble you to read it? You may at any rate have the satisfaction
of knowing that the information did not reach me through you
and yet be able to correct my errors or misapprehensions. The
account will form part of chapter three of my book, a section in
which I shall attempt some kind of character analysis of Vera
Hillyard.

This is a copy so there is no need to return it to me unless
you want to make any actual changes or additions to the text.

I am very grateful.

Yours sincerely,
Daniel Stewart

In the spring of 1916, a young soldier called Albert March became
engaged to be married to a girl who had been his sweetheart since
childhood. Her name was Adele Jephson and she and he were eighteen. A week after the engagement was formed, Albert went out to
the trenches and in July 1917, during the Allied advance on Ypres,
was very severely wounded.

Albert was told that it was unlikely he would ever be able to lead a
normal life. It would, for instance, be unwise for him to marry. In

civilian life he had been a signalman with the London and North Eastern Railway at Colchester and in the opinion of doctors at the hospital where he had received treatment for his wounds to head and chest, there was no chance of his returning to this occupation. Albert, however, was strong-minded and determined. He would always suffer from breathlessness and headaches that prostrated him, but he was determined notwithstanding these drawbacks to marry Adele and continue with his career. He and Adele were married in August 1918 at Great Sindon parish church, the Jephson family being parishioners.

At that time a branch line of the LNER ran northwestwards from the main London–Marks Tey–Sudbury line, branching off at a station called Sindon Road, a mile from the village of Great Sindon. Albert managed to get himself put in charge of the signal box there and he and Adele moved into a cottage in Bell Lane just off the Great Sindon main street. The row in which their house formed the last unit was called Inkerman Terrace, named for an earlier battle in an earlier war. Today the four cottages in the terrace have been converted into the Ringdove Gallery, an arts-and-crafts shop, and is also the home of its owners, Philip and Joy Lees.

Mrs. Adele Bacon, formerly March, says:

"People expect something more when they are starting out in life these days. We had two rooms up and two down; we lit the cottage with oil lamps and drew our water from the pump on the village green along with the people in the other cottages in the row. It was all we needed and we thought ourselves lucky to get it. Of course, at Laurel Cottage next door, they had water laid on and electric light, but that wasn't really a cottage, it was quite a big house by my standards. There was a Mr. and Mrs. Price living at Laurel Cottage when my husband and I moved in next door. Mr. Price died and she sold the house to the Longleys.

"Mr. Longley was quite elderly. I was very young at the time and to me he was an old man. His wife was younger and they had twins who were about twelve, John and Vera. Vera was a pretty girl, very fair and with blue eyes. Later on, she got something the matter with her which made her get very thin but when the Longleys first came she was lovely. She gave me a photo of herself as a bridesmaid at her half-sister's wedding.

"My first child was born soon after they moved in. It was a girl and we called her Kathleen Mary. 'Mary' was after Albert's mother but 'Kathleen' was just because we liked the name. Vera Longley was crazy about the baby. I hardly knew her mother, she was a bit standoffish, thought herself a few cuts above us, I daresay, but Vera was always in and out of my house, wanting to hold the baby and bath her, that sort of thing. And the truth was, I was a bit flattered. Times have changed so much, it's like a different world but in those days a man who'd worked in insurance and who lived in a detached house with electricity laid on was miles above us, there was no comparison. My father was a farm laborer—well, agricultural worker you'd call him now—and my husband was a signalman on the railway. I really thought Vera was condescending coming into my house and I used to bend over backwards to make her welcome and have things nice for her."

In the meantime, less than a year after the birth of Kathleen, Mrs. March was delivered of a second child, a son this time, called Albert after his father but always known as Bertie. The birth was a difficult one and Adele was ill for several months following it. Vera's help was therefore even more welcome and a pattern became established. She got into the habit of wheeling Kathleen out every afternoon during the long summer holidays in the old-fashioned perambulator that had been Adele's own when she was a baby.

Mr. Albert "Bertie" March, who now lives in Clacton and has recently retired from his job with the Anglian Water Authority, told the present writer:

"I was too young to remember anything about that afternoon. Kathleen was a bit over two and I was fifteen months old. My mother never spoke about it. She never said a word at any time, it was just as if I had never had an older sister and of course I can't remember Kathleen. It's only since my stepfather died and Mother came to live with my wife and me that she's opened up at all and once or twice has said things about Kathleen. Like how she was just starting to talk and how she had very curly hair, that kind of thing.

"It was my father who told me about it. I was fourteen and out to work. It was a couple of years before he died. He was only thirty-five but he'd been knocked about in the Great War and that messed him up. He used to have these blinding headaches that came from a head wound he'd got at Ypres. The afternoon we lost Kathleen, he'd had to come home early. He was blind with pain. They didn't like men knocking off with headaches back in 1921, I can tell you, it was a different thing from today. You'd lose your pay for one thing and there wouldn't be any car to send you home in and don't-come-in-again-till-you're-better-Albert sort of thing. Not likely. But my dad had to knock off, he was a danger to the company in that state, a responsible job like he'd got, responsible for hundreds of lives. And of course he had to walk home, though it wasn't much above a mile and that was nothing in those days.

"His way home he took by the back lanes, not the main road. You had to cross the river at a sort of ford we called 'the wash' but there was a wooden bridge for people going on foot. As my father was crossing the bridge, he saw Vera Longley and another girl sitting on the riverbank, and a few yards away from them, under some trees, a pram. The girls had their backs to the pram, which was on high, flat ground, while they had evidently scrambled down the bank. The thing was that my father didn't connect the pram with his own child, it didn't occur to him that his own child might be in it. Probably he wasn't able to think about anything much but the pain in his head.

"He had been home about an hour, he was lying in a chair with a wet rag on his head, my mother was attending to me, when Mrs. Longley came to the door. She was expecting a child herself by then, the one they called Eden. She told my mother Kathleen was gone, she had disappeared from her pram. What always angered my mother was how Vera didn't come herself, she had to send her mother. . . ."

Kathleen March was never seen again. The police were sent for and the village people mounted a hunt. A local farmer had a famous tracker dog which was called in to help in the search. Arthur Longley and his son John were in the search party. It was a bright, moonlit night and the fifty or so men kept up the search until dawn.

What did Vera Longley tell the police? No record of any interrogation of or interview with Vera—if any was undertaken—survives. Here again we have to rely on the March family, or rather on Mrs. Bacon, remembering that Albert March was less than two years old at the time.

"Vera didn't want to see me and her mother didn't want her to. She said it would do no good. But I insisted. It was my child that was lost, wasn't it, my daughter? If she wouldn't come to me, I would go to her, I said, and I did. I went to Laurel Cottage and I saw Vera. Mrs. Longley said she was in a terrible state, sobbing and crying, but she wasn't crying when I saw her. She was just very white and sort of haunted-looking.

"My husband had told me what he'd seen, Vera and her friend sitting talking on the riverbank. Vera said yes, that was right, she had met her school friend, Mavis Vaughan, and they had gone to 'the wash' together. Kathleen had fallen asleep. They left the pram up on a bit of high ground and climbed down the bank themselves to the water's edge. She never took her eyes off the pram for more than five minutes, Vera told me, but I knew that couldn't have been true. She said Mavis sat with her for half an hour and then went off home along the river, leaving Vera alone. She said she kept watching the pram, watching for a movement, you know. If she saw it rock, she'd know Kathleen had woken up. Of course it never did move because there was no one in it by then. Or so she said. When she went up to it, she said, it was empty. Someone had come up behind her and taken Kathleen away. That was what she said. I never knew whether to believe her, but what could I do?"

Mavis Vaughan, later to become Mrs. Broughton, died in 1978, aged seventy-one, but her story of what happened that day is well-known to her daughter, Mrs. Judith Jones, who today lives in nearby Sissington.

"Everything that happened in connection with the missing March child made a deep impression on my mother. Even in the light of what happened later—the murder, I mean—she was convinced Vera Hillyard had nothing to do with it. Vera loved children. Well, I would have thought the circumstances of the murder showed that really. She loved Kathleen March as much as she was later to love her own baby sister. My mother said that Edith Longley being born when she was saved Vera's sanity, she really believed that. As it was, Vera was ill for months after the new baby came.

"A lot of things were said about what Vera and my mother were doing when Kathleen was taken. People suggested they had gone there to meet a couple of boys—you can imagine the kind of insinuations. It was all nonsense. They sat and talked, that was all, and they were never out of earshot of the pram, they were no more than a dozen yards away from it. Mother had been on her way to the shop at Great Sindon for *her* mother—they lived right out in the middle of nowhere at Cole Fen—when she met Vera, and she had to get on and do her shopping. She said she'd wished a thousand times she'd gone past the pram up to the lane so she'd have known once and for all if Kathleen was in there then or not. But she didn't. She climbed up the bank and got onto the footbridge. And it was deliberate, too. It was done so as not to disturb Kathleen. Ironic, wasn't it?

"Later on, of course, after the murder, people who could remember the Kathleen March case said Vera had killed her. They said Kathleen had cried and Vera had lost her temper with her. Vera did have a very bad temper, it was well-known, even my mother said that. But she never would believe that of Vera, not even after she was hanged. . . ."

In the autumn of 1979, Mr. George Treves, who farms six hundred acres of land between Assington and Cole Fen, hired a contractor called Peter Somers to uproot a hedge. His project was that of turning four small fields into one large one in which he intended to raise a barley crop. After three days of working at the destruction of the hedge with a mechanical digger, Mr. Somers discovered, buried at a depth of six or eight feet, an oil drum measuring eighteen inches in height and nine inches in diameter, its open end being roughly sealed with a plug of the yellow clay that runs in strata through the otherwise light, gravelly soil of these parts.

At first Mr. Somers and Mr. Treves thought it possible the drum might contain valuable artifacts such as archaeologists had recently shown an interest in or even the jewelry stolen from Cole Hall ten years before in a burglary which has become something of a local legend. This included a ten-thousand-pound string of pearls among a collection of loot that has never yet come to light. However, what they found inside the drum was a jumble of brownish bones and shreds of cloth. They took their find to the police.

The bones were human. At the inquest conducted on these remains, it was concluded that they belonged to a female child of about two who had been dead at least fifty years. To have discovered this much is nothing short of a miracle of forensic science, and no more was forthcoming. The origins of the oil drum could not be traced. If there were marks of violence on the child's body, time and the decay of more than half a century had obliterated them. The shreds of material mingling with the bones were found to be woolen fibers and Kathleen March when she vanished was dressed in a woolen vest under her cotton dress and a woolen jacket over it.

Was this Kathleen? Certainly the hedge at Cole Fen was no more than half a mile from "the wash" where Kathleen was last seen in her pram. We remember that this is where Mavis Broughton, née Vaughan, lived, at a distance not too far from Great Sindon for her mother to send her to the larger village on an errand. On the other hand, police records show that during a twenty-year period from 1920 to 1940, no fewer than five female children under the age of three went missing in the Great Sindon–Cole Fen–Sissington area of Essex. And of these baby girls, the body of only the eldest, a three-year-old from Sissington, was ever discovered.

It is unlikely that we shall ever know. But if Vera Longley committed this crime, there seems no possible reason or motive for it. Jealousy of attention given to the child can hardly have entered into it since Vera had only to make an excuse to Adele March in order never to see Kathleen again. Reason and motive played so large a part in the later crime that our aim to understand Vera Hillyard's character is not served by attempts to show her as an unreasoning psychopath, for which definition there is no evidence whatsoever.

The March family moved from Great Sindon in the following year, the year of Edith Longley's birth, into the signalman's house which had just become vacant at Sindon Road.

7

I HAVE WRITTEN BACK to Jamie to say I shall be in Florence in May. His mention of his book has struck a chord of memory. When I was about twelve, my mother's aunt died and left me a cookery book. Of course she was no relation to Jamie, being on the other side of my family, the sister of my mother's English mother. She had been a cook years before in a great house called Lytton Lodge at Woodford Green—that is, she had been *the* cook, a personage of some importance with kitchen maids under her, an artist creating banquets. I remember her as a handsome old lady, very religious, almost totally deaf, the peak experience of whose life had been when the Prince of Wales, he who became Edward the Eighth and then Duke of Windsor, came to dine.

She died in the little room she rented in Seven Kings, and all the stuff in the room, which was everything she possessed, came to my mother, her only surviving relative. There was a New Testament with passages marked in red, a pair of folding scissors that had hung from her belt with her keys, a lot of framed photographs of people my mother couldn't identify, some ugly jewelry in old-fashioned settings, bombazine dresses and white lawn aprons that would fetch a small fortune today if we had kept them, and the cookery book. So I suppose that strictly it wasn't left to me but given to me by my mother.

It was called *Mrs. A. B. Marshall's Cookery Book* and it had been published in 1884. Unlike *Cucina Ben Riuscita,* which I suppose Jamie has written for ambitious housewives, Mrs. Marshall, who had run a cookery school, had devised this book for cooks with dinners of a dozen courses to prepare for two dozen guests. I used to read it during the war when the worst food shortages were on. I used to read it while eating sandwiches of gray bread, margarine, and reconstituted egg. At Sindon I sometimes sat reading it on the riverbank down by "the wash," though I did not yet know at that time that this was where Vera had been sitting when Kathleen March was lost.

Mrs. Marshall gave a menu for a ball supper for "400 to 500 persons" which consisted of three hot dishes, a consommé, lamb cutlets and quails, and no less than thirty cold dishes that included more quails and something called Siamese Twins that were double choux puffs iced with green icing and filled with cream that had been colored with carmine and flavored with rum. There was also a menu for a *"déjeuner maigre"* that presumably means a light luncheon but which I translated as a thin dinner, and then there was what Mrs. Marshall and my late great-aunt no doubt thought of as a normal dinner, six courses not counting the vanilla soufflé with pineapple, the gâteau Metternich, and the Parmesan fondue.

Vera took umbrage. She saw my reading *Mrs. Marshall* as a reflection on her own culinary efforts, as indeed it was, though through no fault of hers, as I eagerly pointed out. Reading it in these circumstances was, of course, an odd thing to do, I knew that, and Vera did not like people, notably her own family, doing odd things. One was expected to conform, yet within that conforming to excel or at least do rather better than the standard set. She was a snob, professing to have had no idea that "ancestors" of my mother's had been in service.

"I hope you won't say anything about where that book came from, Faith," she said to me when its provenance had first been explained to her. "I mean in front of people who come here. The Morrells, for instance."

I already knew why not. Richard Morrell's cousin was the Master of Balliol. And somewhere in his background, related to him by a tortuous route among the bypaths of second cousinry, removes and marriages, was an earl's daughter.

"What shall I say if they ask, then?"

"You can say you don't know, can't you? You can say you found it on the bookshelves at home."

Francis said, "You mean she's to lie about it?"

"No, of course not. You always twist my words. It's true anyway. It would have been on a bookshelf in her home before she brought it here."

"They were very good psychologists, those old lawyers," said Francis. "They had people like you in mind when they formulated the oath. I swear to tell the truth, the *whole* truth, and nothing but the truth. They knew all about leaving bits out and putting bits in."

I wonder if Vera remembered that conversation when she stood in the dock at the Central Criminal Court and took that oath. Probably not; she had other things to think about. I never did lie about the cookery book, for if anyone came while I was reading it, I quickly took it away to my room. This room was mine exclusively now Eden was gone—to Portsmouth, we all guessed, though we were not supposed officially to know.

I was at Sindon for the long summer holidays only, for blasé now about raids, my parents had had me back home for Easter and there I had stayed, reverting to old school and old friends. I was never again to "live" at Laurel Cottage, only to go back for holidays, drawn by the prospect of time spent with Anne. Vera, too, had written to ask me. I was surprised by this and immensely gratified. Why is it that when people are never specially nice to us or warm, we long all the more for their affection so that the least little crumb they let fall is bounty? I didn't like Vera, I didn't admire her, and I'm sure she never liked me, and yet I was inordinately pleased at her inviting me. Why, soon she would be letting me stay up till ten and confiding in me the truth behind all those secrets!

"Now Eden has gone," said my mother, "Vera will want a young girl in the house to mold into a true Longley woman. Not so much *Kinder, Küche, Kirche* as *Kauf, Klatsch, Kettelnadel.*"

We were all in the habit in those days of quoting Hitler's more hackneyed sayings. But only my mother, being half Swiss and a German speaker—something she concealed outside her own home in those war years—could be witty about them. She laughed and my father looked cross. I looked up the words in the German dictionary and found they meant "shopping, gossip, embroidery needle."

Was that what Vera wanted me for? Certainly the crochet squares, uneven pieces of work and no longer very clean, were awaiting me. So was Eden's room, virginal as ever, Peter Pan in Kensington Gardens up on the wall, poised on that curious anthill he stands on, still communing with the wild creatures. The white lace mats lay on the dressing table but the hairbrush was gone and so were the cleanser, the toner, and the skinfood. Eden's bed was not made up, not even apparently made up, which is what one would have expected at Laurel Cottage, but counterpane and blankets and pillows in plain white slips laid on the mattress in a neat pile, to keep me out presumably in case I had had any ideas of getting in there instead of into my own. That evening, while Francis was off doing his disappearing trick, and Vera, incapable of learning from experience, was running round the garden calling his name, I succumbed to temptation and explored all the drawers in Eden's dressing table. Of course it was wrong of me, it was spying and a betrayal of hospitality, and I was quite old enough to know better. The truth was that I was bored stiff with crochet, not a bit tired at eight, and outside it was still broad daylight.

The drawers were full of aids to beauty. The objects in them represented not only a great deal of money but also the time Eden must have spent queueing for these things and the effort put into wheedling, cajoling, and bribing shopkeepers to keep them "under the counter" for her. Very little was what a young girl would have today. Nothing for the hair or the eyes and very little for the body. The scent that emanated from those drawers as I opened them and peered in and sniffed was a mingling of talc, rosewater, lemons, and acetone. There were dozens of lipsticks, literally dozens, for I counted one evening and made it a hundred and twenty-one. They were of all possible reds and there was one that was orange and only went red when you put it on your mouth. I knew that because I tried it out. I tried out most of the things in those drawers during the following weeks—the toners, the skinfood, the gloriously scented stuff mysteriously called "mercolized wax," the Creme Simon, the Evening in Paris rouge. The notion in the forties of woman's role, the ideas of what constituted women's lives, were reflected in the quantity of preparations for the hands and nails. Such a collection today would consist mainly of shampoos and conditioners, body lotions and deodorants. Daringly in advance of her time, Eden had one deodorant, a red liquid in a small bottle that you put on and allowed ten minutes for drying while you held your arms up above your head.

It did not occur to me then—nor perhaps would it have done to an adult—what all this would signify to the psychology-indoctrinated observer of today, that Eden was both terribly vain and terribly insecure. I thought only, if she had left all this behind, what had she taken with her? More, surely. The *crème de la crème* in every sense.

Thinking of what was at Laurel Cottage as her rejects or at any rate
as her spare set somewhat comforted me when guilt about my use of
her Tangee lipstick and Arden's Orange Skinfood got too strong

Eden had gone but before she went she had brought home a boyfriend. Not that Vera would have used this word (it wasn't in anything like the general use for "lover" it is today, signifying a
sixty-year-old live-in common-law husband, for instance), or even
have implied there might be anything remotely sexual in Chad
Hamner's interest in Eden or hers in him. Vera would probably have
referred to Chad as Eden's "friend" if she had mentioned him at all
or introduced him. These, though, weren't her ways. I came home
dutifully at seven-thirty from an afternoon and evening at the Cambuses' to find a strange man sitting in the living room with Vera
and—wonder of wonders at this hour!—Francis. They were all
drinking sherry, something one never saw anymore and had never
seen at Laurel Cottage.

I was astonished. I stopped in the doorway in the attitude in which
certain novelists of the thirties described as that of a startled fawn. I
knew this because Francis said so.

"The startled fawn," he said.

He was drinking sherry like the others and there was a high color
up on his cheekbones. I colored too; I could feel it burning my face.
Vera always filled stark or awkward moments with bustle, for which
one could sometimes be thankful.

"Well, I'm sure I hope you've had your tea. You never said if
you'd be eating with those people. I haven't got anything here for
you unless you feel like a sausage sandwich, that's all there is."

"Give her a drink."

This was the strange man. Vera rounded on him, but not at all in
the way she would have done on Francis or me. There was something
coy and sprightly in her manner when she scolded Chad.

"Don't you dare! I can't think what my brother would say. She's
only thirteen, she's not so old as Francis, and goodness knows, she
doesn't even look that!"

"I don't want any," I said, a remark that inevitably sounds sour
and indignant.

Chad got up, held out his hand to me, and said, "How do you do?
My name is Chad Hamner and I'm a friend of Eden's."

"Well, of us all, I hope, Chad," said Vera.

"Of you all, of course."

I shook hands with him. I remember what I was wearing at that first meeting, the voile dress of the group photograph, a dress that had been handed down to me by a neighbor's daughter who had grown out of it, the material a little tired and with pulled threads on the faded orange nasturtiums. My hair was in two thick, untidy, long pigtails. Vera had tried to make me wear ankle socks until ankle socks became impossible to buy and I won the right to go about barefoot in old Start-Rite sandals. He treated me from the first as if I were grown-up. There was no cult of youth then, no frightened deference to teenagers. You wanted desperately to be older than you were or at least taken for older. Chad spoke to me always as if I were the same age as he, that is, the late twenties. Nor did he seem to distinguish me as female, any more than he did Vera, something that later was a source of bitterness. But at any rate to him I was a person worthy of respect, and this I loved.

Though Vera uttered a shriek, disclaiming all responsibility for results and my possible fate, he insisted on giving me sherry in a small tulip glass. The bottle of sherry had been given him by a man he had interviewed and done an article about in his newspaper, the new president of the Rotary Club or the Horticultural Society or something of that sort. Chad was a reporter with a chain of local papers called North Essex and Stour Valley Publications Limited. He was nothing much to look at, neither tall nor short, thick-set nor thin, fair nor dark. In the street no woman would have given him a second glance. Like many such nondescript people, he was transformed by his smile, not a radiant, broad smile but one of mysterious irony that enlarged to total open charm. And he had a beautiful voice that I, in my later dreams about him, likened to that of Alvar Liddell, the radio announcer.

No jeans in those days. No zipper jackets. No plastic synthetics. Young men and old men dressed the same. Young men and boys dressed the same. That evening I was in my aging orange voile, Vera in a dress made out of two dresses, brown sleeves set into brown-and-orange-spotted bodice, surely in 1941 the prototype of such a fashion, Francis in gray flannels, gray pullover, gray school shirt, Chad in gray flannels, cream Aertex shirt, grayish-blue-mixture tweed jacket. He asked if I had intentionally been given the same name as Vera.

"We haven't got the same name," Vera said. "She's called Faith."

This, of course, he might not have known, since no one, not even I myself, had mentioned it. She seemed to remember. "Didn't I say? Didn't I tell you she was my niece Faith?"

Extraordinary the thrill, the warming sensation, of hearing those words "my niece" uttered calmly, indifferently, *acceptingly*, by Vera. Why did I care?

"That's what I said. You have the same name. 'Vera' means 'faith.'"

"'Vera' means 'true,'" said Vera. She seemed a little displeased.

"'Vera' means 'faith,'" said Chad. "Russian for 'faith.' *Vjera.*"

Vera looked as if she were going to argue. She wore her mulish expression. With the awful scathing savagery he reserved for his mother—he was unpleasant to everyone except Eden and Helen, but he was savage to Vera—Francis said:

"He knows, doesn't he? It's not probable you'd know better than him, is it? Well, is it? You're not going to set yourself up against him *philologically*, are you? He's been to Oxford, he's got a degree. Well, then. It's rather laughable when someone like you sets up against him."

Although I didn't know it at the time, Vera *was* right and *"vera"* is the feminine form of the Latin "true." Perhaps it is Russian too and they were both correct, or else Chad, in this as in other matters, was not the infallible authority Francis at that time claimed him to be.

Vera looked at Francis. "My own son," she said. She sounded almost proud. It was as if she were fascinated by the possibilities of how far Francis might go. "If I had spoken to my mother like that, my father would have killed me."

"Fortunately my father is in North Africa."

"You're not supposed to know that! You're not supposed to say!"

"Careless talk costs lives," said Francis. "Of course this room is full of people who can't wait to get out of here and tell the Germans Major Gerald Hillyard, the mainstay of British Intelligence, is currently at the gates of Tobruk, making history." He turned to Chad. "My parents have a code that's defied even the censors. Exclamation mark for Egypt, inverted commas for Tripoli, colon for Far East, et cetera."

"Francis," said Vera, her voice shaking.

"The last communication was laden with dialogue. *Quod erat demonstrandum*. Heaven knows what they will do if our armed forces ever reach the point of actually *invading* Europe. They haven't arranged for that. It doesn't show—"

Vera jumped up, covered her face with her hands, and ran out of the room.

"—much optimism, does it? Not what you'd call much faith or *vjera.*"

Most grown-ups I knew would have reprimanded Francis for his behavior to his mother. Chad did not. He merely shrugged. It was his way to give enormous shrugs, rather Gallic, though he was as English as they possibly come, as English as his name.

"I was conceived in Chadwell Heath," was how he explained it— explained it in fact to me that evening under pressure from Francis. The truth was that it was a name which had been in his family since it was given to his grandfather at the time the Victorians revived medieval Christian names. Vera, I was later to learn, had considerable respect for Chad's family, who were minor local gentry, Masters of Foxhounds and with plaques on the church walls at Sissington, commemorating sons fallen in the Great War. How he came to have his tin-pot job on the *Sissington and Upper Stour Speaker* is another story. For war service he was apparently unfit, having had rheumatic fever as a child. Eden he had first seen in the magistrates' court in Colchester, where she had come with notes for her boss, and he had been in the press box. Of course (this was all Vera's story), they had later been properly introduced by some suitable person, a Chatteriss probably.

Vera came back into the room pink-eyed and tight-lipped to find Chad having a look at *Mrs. Marshall,* which I had forgotten to put away, and saying that what he particularly fancied at that moment was Little Salpicons of Salmon à la Chevalier. Francis timed his remark to his mother's arrival and said that I had got it from my grandmother, who was a cook.

"Her great-aunt, not her grandmother," said Vera, as if the collateral relationship improved things.

Chad sounded interested only, not in the least repelled. "You never told me you had an aunt in service round here. Who was she with?"

Vera nearly screamed, she was in such a state. "She wasn't *my* aunt! She wasn't anything to do with us! She was Faith's mother's aunt or something like that, something on Faith's side."

The devil entered into me and I told him how she had cooked dinner for Edward the Eighth.

"And Mrs. Simpson?"

I said I didn't know.

"Why do we have to talk about cooks? It's ridiculous anyway, reading a cookery book these days, it's enough to make you ill. Personally, I should think it's time that wretched book went the way of your great-aunt or whatever she was, Faith."

Francis, who had been reading Saki, said, "She was a good cook as good cooks go, and as good cooks go she went."

He was rewarded by congratulatory laughter from Chad and a glare from his mother. For a moment or two he sat in one of his mystifying silences, not exactly smiling but looking immensely pleased with himself without smiling, and then he got up and said he was going to bed. Vera was thus foiled and had to take her frustration out on me, asking me as a preliminary if I knew what time it was, and then proceeding as if twenty-five minutes to nine was the small hours. I went upstairs and consoled myself by daubing my face with Miner's Liquid Makeup and Tangee lipstick. Chad soon went home. I heard Vera go out into the kitchen to wash the glasses before settling down with the *Daily Telegraph* crossword.

Family connections Vera was proud of were the Chatterisses, who had everything to recommend them as relatives. She always spoke of Helen as "my sister," never "my half-sister," and Helen's husband as "my brother-in-law, the general." They lived at Walbrooks, where Helen had been brought up and which she inherited when her grandparents died. It was there, of course, in the days when the old Richardsons were still alive, that Vera had performed her spectacular rescue of Eden from under the tree in the storm.

I was told by Vera that I must call them Uncle Victor and Auntie Helen just as I called her Auntie Vera, though Eden was always just Eden. Vera was very anxious, before that first visit, that I should behave well. The following year I was adjured, on pain of "never being taken anywhere again," not to breathe a word to Helen about the cookery book. That first time I minded my manners and did what Vera said, only to have Helen repudiate "auntie." She said it was vulgar, which made Vera sit up a bit.

"Not 'auntie,' darling, I beg." Helen talked, and still talks, with all the panoply of twenties slang and terminology and Mitford-girls expressions. "It makes me feel like someone's old charwoman with *corns* and *false teeth* and *whalebone corsets*."

This was so much an antithesis of what she was that I stared.

"You call me Helen and him Victor and if you can't bring yourself to do that, call him 'General.' I always do, it sounds so grand and Victorian."

She did, too. "General, darling," as often as not. Like some lace-winged creature caught in amber, she remained forever trapped in the twenties—more than that, in a hill station in the twenties, her frocks waistless and diaphanous, a pith helmet planted on her crimped golden hair whenever the sun shone. She smoked black Russian cigarettes—heaven knows where she got them in 1941—in a carved ivory cigarette holder. Her daughter was in the WAAF, her son a fighter pilot, and she and the General were alone in that big house where the Richardsons had created a library, a music room, and outside a ha-ha, a gazebo, and a shrubbery of exotics that battled on through the East Anglian winters. Two old women, one from Stoke Tye and one from Thorington Street, daily cycled over to wait on them. I believe the General did the cooking while Helen, in mem-sahib gear, swanned about the garden picking flowers and making magnificent arrangements all over the house of dahlias and astilbe and silver-mauve hosta.

I liked her very much. It is a long time now since that liking became love. She was very unlike Vera, being easygoing, lighthearted, easily amused, generous. All those things she still is. For a long while, until his *détente* with Jamie, she was the only member of our family with whom Francis continued to keep in touch. With her he seems to have had a special affinity, and it wasn't hard to see why. Of course Helen was nice and there was no humbug about her, but he and she had something else in common that specially endeared her to him. They had both been abandoned—"discarded" was the word Francis used—by a parent when they were children, Francis's mother having sent him off to boarding school in order to devote her time to her sister, Helen's father sending her off to her grandparents and not having her back again even when he had a new wife and home. . . . I am not sure what Daniel Stewart means when he says "the separation still rankles" with Helen. The story of how Arthur Longley had brought his bride Ivy to the school gates to be shown to Helen was well-known in our family and Helen used to tell it with no apparent resentment.

"Grandpapa and Grandmamma were such perfect angels," she said, "that going to live with them was utter bliss. What sometimes terrified me was that my father would take me back, and that I couldn't have borne. Do you know the first thing Grandmamma did when I first came to them, the very first evening? She brought me these two Siamese kittens in a basket and said their mamma had died too and they would be so unhappy if they couldn't sleep on my bed."

The next time I called Vera "auntie," she said in an embarrassed way that "aunt" might sound better. Would I try to get into the way of calling her "Aunt Vera," as "auntie" was rather vulgar? My first successful effort was overheard by Francis and it filled him with glee. He proceeded to drop the "-ie" or similar-sounding suffix off every word that ended like that, ultimately driving Vera into hysterics.

At breakfast: "Thank you ver much. I don't want an more coff. No postal deliv toda? How absolute craze," and so on.

She was rubbing her hands together. "Why are you doing this? Why do you torment me?"

"Avoid vulgarit at an price."

The result was that I stopped calling Vera anything at all.

On a visit to Stoke I overheard her telling Helen she would have liked another child. When I say "overheard," I don't mean I was listening outside a door or behind a curtain—though I daresay I was capable of this—but that although they knew I was present, Vera probably thought me too stupid to understand and Helen didn't care. Or they believed me just out of earshot if they kept their voices low. It was rather what I suppose the attitude of a Victorian pair of lovers must have been to the duenna planted in the same large room with them.

This was before my mother had told me the story of the lost child, Kathleen March, and before I had heard of the adolescent Vera's devotion to her baby sister. It surprised me to hear that Vera was fond of children and liked babies. Was this why she had invited me, who was still a child? Did she love me really and was somehow incapable of showing it?

"You know how I love children," she said to Helen.

If Helen was skeptical she was too kind to show it.

"Why don't you have another one, darling? You're young still, you're only a baby yourself. Why, you're *aeons* younger than poor old me, you might be my daughter."

To me it seemed incredible. Vera was thirty-four, with faded hair and a stringy neck. She was middle-aged.

"There is the little matter of Gerry being goodness knows where."

"The war won't go on forever, darling."

"Won't it?" Vera said bitterly.

"You're missing Eden, too, aren't you?"

Vera was silent for a moment. She had developed a strange nervous habit that I think was unconscious. I have never seen anyone else do it. Standing or sitting, she would clasp her hands tightly and lean forward bearing on those clasped hands as if in acute pain or as if trying to exert great pressure on something. The nearest I can get to it is to say it was like someone stuffing a swollen cork into a bottle with a narrow neck. It lasted a second or two and then she relaxed. She did this now while Helen watched her with sympathetic curiosity. Then she said:

"Eden will never come back."

"Darling, of course she will! What can you mean?"

"Not *that*. Her life's hardly in danger being a wireless telegraphist in Portsmouth. I mean she'll never come home again to live with me. This is the breakaway, isn't it? When the war's over she won't want to come back to Sindon, she'll want to live on her own."

"By the time the war's over," said Helen, "Eden will be married."

"There you are then. It amounts to the same thing."

But she was wrong, for Eden did come back and so did Uncle Gerald, and before the end of the seemingly endless war.

In the meantime, though, life went on much the same at Laurel Cottage. Francis and I were reprimanded for eating with our right hands, hunted down at bedtime—I successfully as often as not, he nearly always escaping—admonished for falling below the standard of gentlefolk; daily the crossword was done, weekly a letter was written to Uncle Gerald and rather more often than that to Eden. Was Vera worried because weeks, months, had passed since she had last heard from her husband? Women knew they must expect these silences. A week before I was due to leave for home and go back to school, a letter came.

Her relief at its arrival was plain to see. But she did not seem to want to read it. After breakfast, she took the letter upstairs and shut herself up in her bedroom with it. Francis liked shocking me and in those days he always succeeded. He said:

"I read in a book that couples fuck more in the first two years of marriage than in all the rest of their lives. What do you think?"

"I don't know," I said, going red.

"You're blushing again. I wish I could do that. So innocent and charming. You will have to teach me sometime."

For the last few days of my stay, Francis went off to visit friends. He had everything his own way, he did just as he liked, and when Vera asked him who these people were and where they lived, he refused to tell her. She threatened to withhold his train fare but Francis didn't care about that. He always had money. I don't know where it came from. Teenagers in those days didn't take on menial tasks to earn money, at least middle-class teenagers didn't, and Francis doing a paper round was in any case unimaginable. But he said he earned it, smiling enigmatically, and when asked by doing what, replied, "Oh, this and that." The day before he went, he carried out the most ambitious Vera-tease he had ever attempted.

In one of her letters, Eden had mentioned a naval officer, a Commander Michael Franklin. He was her boss or commanding officer or someone in authority over her, and had praised her. This, apparently, was in fact all it amounted to. But Eden, being Eden and a Longley, had also mentioned that Franklin was an Honorable, the son of Lord Somebody-or-other. Anyway, Vera had been very impressed, and had talked about Franklin to the Morrells and the Chatterisses and anyone else who would listen, managing to give the impression that Eden's connection with him was something more than that of clerk and boss, in fact was romantic. I think she persuaded herself it was. Chad Hamner wasn't spared this either, even though he seemed to be regarded—particularly by Francis—as Eden's accredited boyfriend.

One evening the phone rang. This was itself unusual. It was bound to be Helen, Vera said to me, going to answer it. We were alone, making a joint onslaught on the crossword, perhaps the only common ground we had, while the clock approached the witching hour of eight. I couldn't hear what Vera was saying. Triumphant at finding the answer to a clue before she had, I was writing in "Manning" for "Cardinal deployment of work force" when she came rushing back, all excitement.

"Who do you think that was?"

Vera was always asking this and being scathing if one guessed wrong.

Of course I said I didn't know.

"Commander the Honorable Michael Franklin, R.N."

"Really?" I said. "That man Eden works for?"

This wasn't the way Vera would have chosen to put it.

"I don't think it's necessary to use those terms, is it? 'Works for'? 'Works with' might be more appropriate, or even 'friend.'" She became heavily sarcastic. "Yes, I don't think we should be going too far if we said 'friend,' Faith. On our side of the family we may not quite aspire to relatives who *cooked* for the Duke of Windsor but we do know some nice people we can call our *friends,* some well-bred people with nice backgrounds. I think we can say we do."

She was extremely excited, something which always let loose her aggression. She gripped her left hand in her right hand and bore down, contorting her face. I asked her what he wanted.

"To come here and see us. Well, to see me, if the truth is told. I don't suppose he aspires to see you or my son. It's me he wants to see as Eden's sister. Those were his words. He has to go to Ipswich on something very confidential and hush-hush and might he call and see Eden's sister?"

It would be at lunchtime on the following Wednesday. He didn't want lunch, didn't expect it in these hard times, rather not, he would have a sandwich somewhere, but nevertheless it would be at lunchtime he would call. Oh, Francis was very clever, very subtle—he knew his mother. She invited the Chatterisses, the Morrells, and, oddly, Chad Hamner. Chad was Eden's boyfriend but just the same she invited him to meet the man she hoped would be his supplanter, and hoped it on no grounds but that Franklin was the son and heir to a viscount. (Vera had found this out at the public library.) And Chad a scion of a no longer very gentle or landed house. She was not a very nice woman and some might say she deserved all she got but she was pathetic—oh, she was pathetic in her aspirations and her downfall!

They all accepted. There was no meat around to speak of and all our combined rations would be too meager to feed nine people. Vera got hold of two rabbits, not wild ones but the kind you keep in hutches. These were Old English, the white sort with brown blotches, and Anne and I had gathered sow thistles and chickweed to feed them. When I protested, Vera told me not to be a sentimental fool. She roasted the rabbits and did roast potatoes to go with them and carrots cooked in cider, and runner beans, with blackberry pie and summer pudding to follow. I picked the blackberries. The vegetables she had grown herself in the beds which had once been Grandmother Longley's rose garden.

Of course Franklin didn't come. By that time, as we later discovered, he was on the high seas protecting a north Russian convoy, his vessel destined to be among the thousands of tons of British shipping lost in the following year and he with it. General Chatteriss, drinking the sherry which Chad had again produced from somewhere, kept looking at his watch and remarking from one till ten past:

"Feller's late."

And from ten past till the half-hour:

"Feller's not comin'."

Chad knew it was Francis's doing. Not all the time, I think, but only from midway through this miserable drinking session in which the Dry Fly was soon exhausted and Vera was in a pitiable state wondering what to give Franklin when he did come.

Or perhaps he had known all along. It must have been someone's home, not a phone box, from which Francis made that call, disguising his voice or maybe not disguising it. Her son speaking warmly or pleasantly would have been disguise enough to deceive Vera. But I don't think Chad connived at it; I didn't then and I don't now. Basically he was kind. And if he was desperately in love, ill with love, so that all stratagems which seemed to further his love were permitted, he nevertheless stopped short at cruelty. For in his way I think he loved Vera too. Everyone associated with the object of his love came into its orbit and was lit by it.

Eventually we ate the roast rabbit. It was dried up and flaky by then and the carrots tasted as if arrested in a phase of wine-making. Many an agonized bearing down on clasped hands, many a twisting of facial muscles took place before that wretched meal came to an end. And afterwards everyone left rather quickly.

Francis made the truth known to Vera in the classic fashion of all such revelations, by uttering a sentence in the voice of the man he had impersonated:

"I wouldn't expect luncheon in these hard times, Mrs. Hillyard, rather not. . . ."

8

MADAGASCAR IS A name that affords children much amusement. It is splendid for charades, for instance, if you don't mind making the game into a five-act play. I don't suppose Vera and Gerald had allowed for it in their code of possible war zones, though, so there must have been months during 1942 when Vera had no idea where he was.

British forces went in there in May in an endeavor to wrest it from the Vichy French. There was the idea around that the Japanese might do so if they didn't, and the Japanese would have had Vichy collaboration. We heard all about it when my Uncle Gerald eventually came home on leave the following spring, but at the time we thought he was still in North Africa. Eden had leave that summer and came to stay a night with us, only one night, she explained, or Vera's feelings would be hurt.

She looked wonderful in uniform. Wrens wore hats, not caps, and Eden's hat particularly suited that thirties-film-star face. She had lost weight, or "fined down" as my mother put it. Her face would be too beautiful for today's taste, too flawless, with those perfectly regular features, large soulful eyes and dreamy look. It was the first time I had ever seen her out of her natural environment of Laurel Cottage and at first she was a little stiff with us, a little reserved and wary, sitting on our sofa with her knees and ankles pressed closely together. It had been a problem deciding where to put her for the night.

Should she have one of our unused bedrooms or share the shelter in the hall with me? Our proximity in the latter case would have been almost embarrassing, a far cry from the bedroom at Laurel Cottage, for the shelter, an affair of sandbags and corrugated iron, measured only seven feet by four. Eden was a member of the armed forces and if not exactly on active service, my mother pointed out, at least accustomed to bombings and gunfire. Of course, my father could only see her as his little sister still. At last it was decided Eden should sleep upstairs but under strict instructions to get up and come down to the shelter if the sirens went.

My mother and I took her up to her room as soon as she arrived. It was not in my mother's nature to make rooms "nice" for guests, she would not have known how to do this or understood the need for it. The sheets were clean, the carpet brushed, and the surfaces dusted. What more was necessary? It was I who had put flowers in a vase, *Woman* magazine and *Rebecca* on the bedside table, and checked the bulb in the bedlamp. Eden said:

"Oh dear, fancy you putting me up here while you're all snug and safe downstairs. Look at that great big window. I can just imagine the flying glass."

"It's weeks since we had a raid," my mother said.

"Don't tempt Providence."

Eden repeated her remark about my parents being safe downstairs while she and my father were settling down to the crossword. He said at once that in that case he and my mother would also sleep upstairs to give her confidence. The bed in their old room would be made up and aired and they would sleep in it.

"You'll make it up and air it then," my mother said.

In fact she did do this herself, though with a bad grace. I think she genuinely wanted to make Eden's short stay pleasant but the adulation Eden got from my father and the deference she received annoyed her. Besides, she read into Eden's attitude to her over every small thing a subtle unspoken criticism, and sometimes her resentment was justified. The sausage left on Eden's plate, the strawberries she had queued for picked over and the slightest unripe bit cut out, the bread crumbled and left. If we wasted food, we would get from my father an admonition to think of the starving Rumanians (or Greeks or Yugoslavians), but Eden was exempted from reproof.

Though Eden did not mention poor Michael Franklin, who was very likely dead by then anyway, she talked a lot about the people she had met in Portsmouth. Naval officers, of course, abounded and it was possible for any girl "who didn't look positively like the back of a bus" to have a wonderful time. The Americans had entered the war by then—the attack on Pearl Harbor having been made the previous December—and Eden had been surprised to find the members of the U.S. forces she had met so nice, so *civilized*.

"Officers, of course," she said. "I can't speak for the other ranks and ratings. I know two girls who are engaged to American officers and really you can't blame them, considering the sort of future that's offered them."

It was a new idea to me—outside the pages of Victorian fiction, that is—that women would get married for money, security, and position; I had thought it was always for love. Eden talked a lot about money and security and what some friend of hers, engaged to a Major Wayne D. Lansky, had told her was in store for her in Norfolk, Virginia, when the war was over: a car of her own, hired help, an oceanfront home. My mother had not been in the room while this was discussed, so it was not bitchiness but genuine interest which made her inquire after Chad Hamner and ask when Eden would be seeing him. I, of course, had told my parents about Chad, not supposing there was any need for secrecy even in Longley terms. In 1942, the result of being in love was that you got married. A boyfriend invited home meant marriage was in the air. Marriages might be made on other foundations (such as cars and hired help and oceanfront houses) but it was still on the whole unthinkable that love could be consummated in any other way.

Eden looked very put out. She passed it off with a quick "Oh yes, I'm sure to see him. He will be bound to look in when he knows I'm home." Later on she had it out with me. Incongruously, this scolding took place in our air-raid shelter, for the inconsistencies of life being what they are, the Germans chose to bomb London that night—or at least deceived us into thinking they would do so. I can't recall hearing gunfire or the distant thunder of bombs, but the alert sounded at one in the morning, and everyone came down and woke me up.

Very soon my father went back to bed. My mother was in the kitchen making us all a cup of tea. Eden and I sat facing each other, I on my bunk, she on an upturned orange box with a cushion on top. Her beautiful face, an amalgam of those now forgotten film-star faces, Veronica Lake, Annabella, Alice Faye, glistened with a skin-food not consigned to the obscurity of a drawer in Laurel Cottage. A

pale blue chiffon scarf turbaned her head and she wore a dressing
gown of blue flowered cotton. Her manner of telling me off took a
curious form.

"I was very disappointed, Faith, to hear you'd been telling tales to
your father."

At that point I really didn't know what she meant and I said so.

"Now don't pretend. You've been gossiping a little, I think, and
now you want to wriggle out of it. What can have made you think
Chad Hamner was my fiancé?"

"I didn't say that."

"Chad of all people! Poor me, I should like to think I could do a
wee bit better for myself than that. I'm quite sure Vera didn't tell you
I was engaged to him. I don't wear an engagement ring, do I? Well,
then. Chad is just a friend, a friend of the family, not me in particular. Have you got that straight?"

"I'm sorry," I said. "He told me he was *your* friend."

"Oh, Faith, dear, one day you'll learn that what a man says in
those circumstances and what is actually the case are two very different things. I expect Chad would like to be engaged to me. Don't you
think he would?"

Humbly I agreed. I would have thought anyone from Gary
Cooper to Lord Louis Mountbatten to General Montgomery would
have liked to be engaged to her. She became confidential and sweet
once more.

"Frankly, I always knew I should have trouble in that quarter from
Chad. We met at the Tregears, you know"—George Tregear was the
solicitor she had worked for—"at a cocktail party and he was making
sheep's eyes across the room at me from the first. He *pursued* me with
phone calls—Vera and I were in fits—and really I think I only went
out with him to put a stop to that everlasting ringing."

There was a good deal more of this in the same vein until my
mother came in with the tea, crawling in, rather, through a gap in
the sandbags. It had struck me from the beginning that Vera's story
and Eden's of how she and Chad had first met did not match. Vera
had said in court, but according to Eden it was at a party. Probably it
wasn't important. I was upset that Eden had reproved me, gratified
that I had been received back into favor.

Next morning, Eden left, but not to go straight back to Great Sindon; that would have to wait till late afternoon. First she would be
having lunch in the West End with some American army officer. The

way she talked about it at breakfast made it sound as if this were a business meeting, an important "liaising" between representatives of the British and the U.S. forces, and my father, forgetting Eden was a wireless telegraphist, seemed to swallow this. But Eden, to my surprise, while maintaining a serious expression, slightly touched my foot with her toe under the table as she mentioned the American's name for the second time.

After she had gone, my mother went into Eden's bedroom to take off the sheets. Being my mother and the way she was, she was very likely speculating as to whether, rather than go into the wash, they could be used on the bed shared by herself and my father. She saw things in that bedroom that made her very angry. It had been cleaned. You might think that a woman who does not keep her house spotless neglects to do so because she is oblivious of dirt, but this isn't always so. Sometimes she simply can't be bothered. Moderate cleanliness is enough. Every spot of dust need not be scoured away even if it is more than visible to the naked eye. There had been a little fluffy dust round the legs of Eden's bed where they touched the floor. This had been cleaned off, apparently with a damp cloth. The lampshade on the central hanging lamp, a parchment affair, which my mother said she had been meaning to "give a wipe to" for weeks, had been carefully washed with soap and water. And in the bathroom things were even worse. Unlike most guests, who leave a ring on the bath, Eden had not only cleaned off her own ring and dried basin and bath, but had removed from the half-hidden tangle of pipes behind basin and lavatory the accumulated cobwebby gray fur of years and left it in a neat little heap on one of my father's squares of shaving-soap newspaper.

It was this, not something Vera did—I remember now—which sparked off in my mother the telling of the Kathleen March story. Of course Eden was in no way involved, she wasn't even born, but I think my mother wanted only to make an attack on the Longley women generally, to illustrate their imperfections, their clay feet, if you like.

"No one is saying she did anything to that child," I remember she said, "but she must have just abandoned it. She can't have been looking after it, she was indifferent. They're like that, self, self, self, and making an impression. It's all outward show and surface. I suppose she was there by that river or wherever it was and this friend came along and started flattering her, telling her how wonderful she was or something, buttering her up, and she forgot the little baby in her care. She was too wrapped up in herself to see some madman come along and snatch it away."

I was learning tact. I was beginning to understand the small satisfactions and the influx of trouble attendant upon "stirring it." So I said nothing about Vera's remarks to Helen on the subject of babies. But my mother, by some exercise of a sixth sense or by the telepathy which often operated between us, said she wouldn't be surprised if Vera had more children after the war was over.

"She'll want to add to her family, you'll see. Now Eden's gone, she'll want at least another one. A girl preferably. Too bad we can't choose these things."

"Won't she be too old?" I said.

My mother was indignant. "She's younger than me!"

The sheets were taken off and thrown into the wash, my mother's reason being that "some of that muck she plasters her face with" had got onto the pillowcase. She and my father had a nice little thank-you note from Eden by the morning's post—she must have written it in the train. The next time I saw her was in Helen's garden, where she told me how Vera had saved her life.

Yesterday Helen came to tea with me. A cup of tea and a biscuit each it was really, ten minutes' pause, and then on to the drinks. That is what Helen likes. She calls it "staying for cocktails" and drinks sherry or likes me to make her just two dry martinis, stirred not shaken, with green olives not lemon, and the mild joke must always be repeated that the nearest the vermouth gets is to show the bottle to the gin. Jamie had a job in a bar in Half Moon Street between leaving school and going to Bologna—in the circumstances, Oxford wouldn't quite have done, they said—and the day after he started, an American came in and asked for a dry martini. Jamie hadn't the faintest idea how to make it but he knew Martini was vermouth so he did his best. In a little while, the American brought it back to him and asked if he had put any gin in it.

"Certainly not!" Jamie said, quite indignant.

The American laughed and showed him how to make a dry martini and when he left he gave Jamie ten shillings, which was an enormous tip in 1962.

When the General died, Helen gave up Walbrooks to her son, who had married for the second time by then and had a little girl. It is a beautiful house and the grounds are lovely, and it amuses me to think how nearly it was mine. But about that I have no regrets. She came to London, to a flat in Bina Gardens, just off the Old Brompton Road. I think she expected London to be much the same as when she had last spent much time there. That had been in 1918 when she had a single London season under the wing of a cousin of old Mrs. Richardson's. Helen found it different but behaved as if it were the same, dressing much as she had done in those days, going everywhere in taxis, furnishing her flat in a mixture of art deco and Anglo-Indian, lumpy white furniture and Benares brass, with a touch of the Syrie Maughams. Every day she has tea at five and makes herself a cocktail at six; every other evening she phones her daughter, and the alternate ones she phones her son. They often come to Bina Gardens to see her, and her grandchildren come. She takes them to Claridge's Brasserie for the cut-rate smorgasbord lunch. And she has me, living a stone's throw away in Vicarage Road.

Helen is my aunt, of course, my half-aunt. But that half-blood, which Vera was all too happy to forget and call Helen her sister, somehow in my eyes deprives Helen entirely of aunthood. I have never called her aunt (by her own wish), and when I introduce her to people I say only her name, occasionally, though rarely, prefixing this with "my friend." I have never thought of her as my aunt, still less by that other title I once had the right to use.

She is eighty-nine, thin still, willowy even, but the willow tree is rheumaticky with creaking joints. Chiffon and other clinging diaphanous materials are still favorites of hers and she still invariably wears a hat. But she has given up those twenties styles at last and now dresses very much like the Queen Mother, in pale blue and with big hats. The gilt hair is snow-white but still done like Gertrude Lawrence did hers for the first production of *Private Lives*.

I had considered also asking Daniel Stewart. Helen put a stop to this with a very adamant negative when I asked her what she thought. She calls him the "bookmaker" though she knows very well what a bookmaker is and what it is not.

"I don't mind talking to the bookmaker tête-à-tête," she said, sitting down but keeping her hat on as she always does. "Well, I do mind, of course I'd prefer not to, it's no joke having to talk in that way about poor Vera, but what I mean is I can stand it when it's just the bookmaker and me, but a third person present, even, darling, you, would make it so dreadfully *public*."

Perhaps later on, I suggested. She could prepare herself for such a confrontation, come along armed with Valium, for instance. And when Stewart's book came out she needn't read it. She gave me that wry look of hers she offers her companions when they speak of the future, of next year even. It means that the chances are there will be no next year for her.

I made tea and we each had what was described on the packet as a muesli biscuit. Helen nibbled hers under the shadow of a blue silk brim laden with nylon delphiniums. It is rare for us to talk about family at these meetings of ours, either on the occasions when she comes for tea and a drink or when we go together to visit Gerald. One way and another, family is a sore point with both of us and we feel we are friends in spite of our family, not because of it. But there seemed nothing else to talk about. Besides, it was Vera's birthday. Had she lived, she would have been seventy-eight.

As people grow old they lose their good looks. This is a commonplace, a cliché. Losing beauty though is only the beginning of a chain. The next link in the chain is the loss of sex. At a certain age, perhaps the late seventies, old women can only be distinguished from old men by their clothes, by skirts and style of hair. And then there comes a point, from which good Lord deliver us, when humanity itself is gone and old apes sit in human clothes. . . .

It is true that Helen, with her flat chest and her gnarled hands, might have been an old man, but there is plenty of humanity left there. The cracked voice is full of life. The blue eyes sparkle, unwearied. And she smells wonderful, of something called Magie Noire, the way no old man ever smells. I wanted to move on with Stewart to 1943, so I asked her about Gerald's return.

"He came on leave that spring, darling, but then he was at the War House for a bit."

I wanted to know how he had got home and why. When I was fourteen or fifteen, no one had told me these things. All I knew was that he had been in North Africa, then in Madagascar (thus missing the Battle of El Alamein), and early in 1943 he had come home. To fill in the gap I had looked up the Madagascar incident and found that the British had gone in there in May 1942 and captured a naval base called Diego Suarez. The hope was that the Vichy French governor would agree to a rapprochement and give up the remainder of the island but in fact he was only waiting until the rains would come in October. So the British attacked Antananarivo, the capital, and the pro-Vichy forces withdrew southwards. There was a further advance and further victories; in November hostilities ceased and the governor was interned.

"I think we must have got out of there altogether in the January or February," Helen said. "We put a Frenchman in as governor, one of de Gaulle's people. Bill Platt was in command of our troops—such a nice man, he used to dine." This, of course, is Helen's way of saying that General Sir William Platt used to come to dinner with her and her husband. "He sent Gerry home, you see, in a bomber. He was to report on the military situation there to someone very high up. It may have been Churchill for all I know. Or whoever the Minister of War was. If only the darling General were alive he could tell you so much better than I can. That business with poor Vera was the death of him, you know. I mean it literally killed him."

Perhaps this is true. Helen and the General stuck it out in Stoke after Vera's death but it was hard for them. They were ostracized. The half-blood was of no account then. Generous Helen had called Vera her sister to the world and now Vera had committed the worst of crimes and met with the worst of ends, she was not going to deny the relationship. It would have been little use to try anyway. Everyone knew. Everyone always does know in villages. The ostracism was not entirely due to a drawing aside of skirts, a not wanting to be associated with such people. A lot of it stemmed from diffidence and embarrassment, from simply not knowing what to say to Helen or Victor if you met them. I saw a lot of them in the years that followed, naturally I did, and I was actually in the house when the General had his first stroke. After that he was never really well again. Five years after Vera's death, he too died. In Helen's arms, as she liked to say, though I doubt if anyone ever actually does die in another person's arms.

"Gerry was quite bright," Helen said. "The General always said he was. He was such a stick, you know, with not a word to say for himself. Imagine being married to a man who never made you laugh." I wouldn't have thought Victor Chatteriss any sparkling comedian but of course I didn't give a sign of what I felt. "A crashing bore, frankly, but the General always said there was more to Gerry than met the eye. I mean, there had to be, darling, when you think of what does meet the eye, that dreadful blank look and those sticky-out eyeballs like, what's it called, Bright's disease. He was like one of those things they have in the West Indies. Well, they have in films. A bongo or a zobo or something."

"A zombie," I said.

"That's it, a zombie. A zobo is a cross between a yak and a cow, we used to see them in India, but Gerry wasn't in the least like one of those. Anyway, as I said, he was quite bright in his way and that must have been why Bill picked him to carry back this important info. That must have been in January 1943 because Vera and Eden and Francis had all been with us for Christmas and Vera hadn't a clue he was coming then. Eden only spent one wartime Christmas with us and it couldn't have been the next one, could it? And '42 we weren't at home, we went to the General's sister in beastly Gleneagles.

"Isn't it funny," Helen said, "how I can remember so perfectly what happened forty years ago but if you asked me what I did yesterday I couldn't begin to tell you? They say it's because of all those millions of brain cells being destroyed or falling out or whatever they do—like one's poor hair, you know—and uncovering the memory cells that have been obscured for years. It doesn't really matter, does it? One might just as well have old memories as new ones, better really. I'm sure I was having a nicer time then than yesterday. Well," she said, remembering, "up till you-know-what anyway."

Helen always calls Vera's execution "you-know-what." The pain of it is not to be expressed without euphemism. She told me once that not a day had passed without her thinking of it and wondering what being hanged was like, what happened to the mind and the body just before.

"They came to see us in London," I said. "Not to stay, though. They stayed in one of those hotels that used to make people laugh and look knowing—the Strand Palace or the Regent Palace. Gerry told my mother they were having a second honeymoon."

"They were *mating*, my dear. That's what they were doing, or poor Vera was doing. She was using the poor chap to get another child, I fear."

I got up and started mixing our dry martinis. Helen eyed the Cinzano Secco warily.

"Just show the bottle to the gin, I beg. That summer he went off to Sicily with the Eighth Army. Well, he'd been with the Eighth Army before Madagascar. The Americans were in on that too, their Sev-

enth and our Eighth. I'm afraid I can't come up with the date, darling. I know it was before old Musso stepped down."

"It was July the ninth," I said. "July the ninth, 1943. I looked it
up. He didn't come home again till the war was over."

My husband came in. He went up to Helen and kissed her and
asked if there was enough dry martini for him to have a small one. I
rejoice that he and she get on, that they are friends when, the situation being what it is, they might so easily not be.

"We were talking about Gerald," I said.

"This isn't your day for visiting him, is it?"

I shook my head. Gerald lives, and has lived for years, in a home
for retired officers at Baron's Court and Helen and I sometimes go to
see him. He is stone deaf and though younger than Helen, seems
older.

"We were talking about what he would have called 'his' war," I
said.

"The General," said Helen, "used to say Gerry had had a good
war, all things considered, and I said jolly good show because he
never had a very good peace. And, my dear, I nearly forgot to tell
you—who do you think I met at Lucy's the other day?"

Lucy is her granddaughter. She is married to a diplomat and gives
large parties in one of those flats in Hyde Park Gardens that have roof
terraces. I said I couldn't guess. My husband gave Helen the second
of the two martinis to which she rationed herself.

"Lady Glennon! What do you think of that?"

Nothing. It meant nothing. "We don't move in these exalted cir-
cles, Helen," my husband said.

"Well, you remember Michael Franklin, I suppose? She's his
sister-in-law. His brother inherited after he went down with his ship.
You must remember that dreadful day and poor Vera's roast rabbits
and our dawning conviction that absolutely no Honorable Michael
was going to breeze in. He would have been Viscount Glennon but
for a German torpedo, and things would all have been different and
maybe it would have been darling Eden I met as Lady Glennon at
Lucy's."

"She never knew him," I said, "except to say 'I've got the message
in triplicate for you, sir.' "

"I do wonder if you're right. Vera seemed so sure. Sometimes I
think I mix him up with that other naval officer of Eden's, the one

that went down with his ship. You're not going to say he wasn't real, are you, darling?"

I said I didn't know. How would I know?

"That would have been in September 1943, somewhere off Ireland."

"What a memory you have, Helen," said my husband. "You're an example to us all."

"Ah, but you could tell me what you had for breakfast this morning, darling, which is more than I could. *Apropos* of which, Mrs. Anstruther in the flat below went on the wireless, on *Woman's Hour*, talking about some diary of her grandmother's that's been published. She's as old as me actually, Mrs. Anstruther I mean, not the grandmother, who would naturally be *aeons* older if she were alive, which she's not. Before they started whatever they call it, recording, they said they'd test for sound and to say something into the microphone. Well, naturally, Mrs. Anstruther didn't know what to say—you don't, do you, in a case like that?—so the interviewer said, 'Just say what you had for breakfast this morning.' But Mrs. Anstruther couldn't. She couldn't remember. She said, 'I can't remember what I had for breakfast' into the microphone, 'I'm too old,' and they all laughed, though of course she hadn't meant it to be funny.

"Eden was in Londonderry then," Helen went on. "They'd transferred her to Londonderry in the spring. The ship came in for a refit or some such thing, and then off she went to Goose or Gander or one of those bird places, but she never got there. Londonderry was full of Americans that summer. I've still got a letter from Eden somewhere telling me all about the lovely Americans, so rich, you know, and dripping with presents. The General used to say 'Beware of the Americans bearing gifts.' He said it to Patricia when she brought a girlfriend of hers to Walbrooks on leave. It came from Virgil, he said, which he'd done at Eton, but I always had my doubts on account of America not being invented in those Roman times, don't you feel?"

My husband put her into a taxi to drive her round the corner. Daniel Stewart would want that letter, I thought. I sat drinking my very dry martini, the last of it, and thinking about that summer, the only one in ten summers I did not go to Sindon for my holidays. I was due to go, I was packed ready to go, but my mother had an emergency hysterectomy, a very major operation in those days, and for weeks afterward she was frail and unable to do much. I stayed at home to look after her. Vera and Francis must have been alone at

Laurel Cottage for all that long holiday between the summer and the autumn school terms. Still, it was the last long holiday they were ever destined to spend together without additional company.

The letter Vera wrote to my father in the autumn of 1943 is lost. Perhaps it came too early in the year for us to have had a fire. That it once existed I know very well. I remember it or bits of it being read at breakfast. The date must have been some time in October. When I saw Vera's writing on the envelope I resigned myself to the reproaches directed at me I was sure it would contain. That August I hadn't been to Sindon and though my mother's illness was excuse enough and Vera knew it, I thought it likely she would mention my defection, asking, for example, why I couldn't have come during my mother's stay in hospital if not during her convalescence. "Faith couldn't put herself out to come down here," and "I don't suppose Faith could be bothered now Eden is away" were the sort of thing I feared and which my father would deal with by asking me to write Vera "a nice letter." But in fact there were no reproaches and I was mentioned only along with my mother as a recipient of her love. My father said:

"Vera is expecting a baby."

This announcement had the effect of making me blush. I suppose it embarrassed me. Luckily, there was no Francis present to point it out.

"Well, goodness," said my mother, "she's left it a long time. Francis must be . . . what?"

"Francis was sixteen last January," I said.

"Oh yes, she says so here. 'Francis will be seventeen in January so I am afraid there will be a big gap when the new baby comes along in April. I should dearly love a little girl this time but shall be happy with whatever comes. . . .'"

My father began worrying about Vera. Her husband was away— in Italy, their code told her—and he was on active service in considerable danger. Her son was at school and I think my father knew as well as I did that he could in any case have been of no help or comfort to her. Eden was now in Londonderry, from which port the North Atlantic convoy escorts set out. Vera was alone, pregnant, and likely to be alone unless the war miraculously ended—until the baby was born and beyond that. So he worried about her and fretted and finally made up his mind to go and see her. He would go and see her and invite her to come and make her home with us. A while back that would have been unthinkable but 1943 had been the quietest year of the war. Once more we were all sleeping upstairs. And it was suggested that those people who still spent the nights in the London Tubes did so more for the company, "the light and gaiety," than in the interests of safety. There were still a couple of months to go before the "Little Blitz" of the spring of 1944. In our suburb, Vera, it seemed, would be in scarcely more danger than in Great Sindon and she would be a lot less lonely.

Of course the idea did not appeal to my mother. Presumably this baby was not an accident, she said, presumably it was planned. Vera knew what she was letting herself in for. What my father said to her in private I don't know. He said very little in front of me. He was not the sort of man to discuss the possibility of pregnancies being accidents or otherwise in front of his fifteen-year-old daughter. My mother eventually agreed, with a bad grace, that Vera should be asked. She wasn't going to Sindon with him, though, not she. He and I talked a little in the train.

"From the tone of her letter," he said, "I wouldn't say she was—well, how shall it put it?—blissfully happy."

"I once heard her telling Helen she longed for another baby."

"Did you now?" He seemed to cheer up at this. "That's a comfort then. When you were going to be born, we were so thrilled, we were so excited." He shook his head. "We were very young, of course. So you think Vera's happy?"

What a question! Had I ever known her happy? What form would Vera-happiness take? I had seen her busy, bustling, hysterical, panic-stricken, jubilant, triumphant, frustrated, petulant, angry, but I had never seen her happy.

I said firmly: "She loves children. She was longing for a baby. Of course she's happy. You can't tell from letters."

That calmed him. He sighed. The train was late, the bus had gone, and we waited hours, it seemed, for the next. Vera was there, hanging over the gate, scanning the street, this way and that, the way she used to look for Francis when he wouldn't come in at bedtime.

"I'd given you up, I thought you were never coming. What held you up? I've got two pheasants, Richard Morrell shot them, but I expect they're spoilt by now, they'll be done to a crisp."

Pregnancy had not changed her—that is, her character was unaltered. Physically, she looked ill. There was a greenish look about her and her hair was exactly the color of barley in the fields a month before they harvest it. She was yellowish-pale. The pregnancy, which even then I had observed does not show itself in most women before five months, had already swollen out her waist. With clothes rationing in full swing, a topcoat costing eighteen points and a dress eleven out of a possible sixty-six for fifteen months, no one was going to squander coupons on maternity clothes. Still, Vera, once so clothes-conscious, could surely, I thought, have done better than she had. She wore an old georgette dress with a small red-and-white pattern on it, the belt necessarily removed but the tabs through which the belt had passed still there, the hem uneven, a green cardigan over it, bedroom slippers, and no stockings though it was November and cold.

We were rushed to the table. The pheasants—the first I had ever eaten—were wonderful, not overdone at all. Vera remained an excellent cook, quite in Mrs. Marshall's class. All through the meal she talked about Eden, her promotion—she had become a Leading Wren—her friends, all high-ranking officers, British and American, the beautiful photograph she had sent her. Hadn't we had one? Eden had promised to send one to my father. Still, she, Vera, had two. And that is how I happen to have had in "the box" the portrait of Eden with the Veronica Lake hair that the Londonderry photographer took.

"We want you to think about coming to stay with us, at least until the child is born," my father said.

"I don't need to think about it. It's out of the question. I couldn't possibly. I wouldn't dream of it." Vera's yellowed face was flushed with color so adamant was she. She remembered her manners. She said, "It's very sweet of you, John, I do appreciate it," and added, "I can't imagine Vranni would be too keen on *that* idea."

"Oh yes, she would. Vranni feels just as I do. You shouldn't be alone here. Not in your condition."

"I've got my friends. Eden will have some leave. Helen isn't far away."

We tried to persuade her, or my father did. I backed him up rather halfheartedly. Now it had come to the crunch, as they didn't say in those days, I wasn't all that keen on having Vera a permanent guest. After lunch she settled down to an inevitable task—making baby clothes. To this end she was painstakingly unpicking an old white jumper of Eden's, carding the wool preparatory to washing it to get the kinks out. Yesterday's washed wool had to be wound into a ball. I held the skein for her while she wound away. Francis was coming home on half-term tomorrow. Why didn't I stay on to see him?

This invitation I managed to decline politely. I walked up the village street to see the Cambuses. Anne and I had one of those friendships that I believe are common among adolescents. My friends at home were my permanent companions, she was my occasional friend, but nonetheless needed for that, having a peculiar and special place in my affections as she was always to have and still has after forty years. Such friendships were even more usual then, in those days of the constant movement of children from refuge to refuge and back again, than they are today. We seemed always to pick up the reins where, six months or a year before, we had let them fall. Our absences gave us much to talk about. Anne told me a curious thing.

One morning in September she had been on her way to school, which necessitated passing Laurel Cottage, when she had seen Vera come rushing out, her face contorted, the tears streaming down her cheeks, and run across the road towards the rectory. Anne knew the Morrells were not there. Richard Morrell's mother had died and they were both in Norwich for the funeral. Sure enough, Vera came stumbling back—Anne was waiting at the bus stop by now—and returned to the house, still crying, her hands up to her face.

"Francis," I said. "It would be something Francis had done."

"I suppose so. He wasn't home much in the summer holidays. He was away nearly all the time."

In Eden's bedroom that night I noticed signs of her recent occupancy. She had been home on leave. The contents of the dressing-table drawers had changed. One had been cleared of cosmetics and filled instead with fine silk underwear, slips and French knickers, mostly in apricot, oyster, powder blue, silk stockings in envelopes of thin paper. In another, along with the Tokalon Biocel Skinfood and the Mercolized Wax, was a bottle of Chanel No. 5 perfume. I had seen pictures of this perfume before but never the thing itself. I gazed at it, tried it out on my wrist, sniffed it—rather like some poor primitive, I suppose, in possession for the first time of an ichor of civilization.

That was the last time I ever looked into any private caches of Eden's. I was fifteen, after all, and my conscience now troubled me too insistently to be ignored. I closed the drawers and, lying in bed in the icy room—no one heated bedrooms in 1943—contemplated the

Madonna-like photograph of Eden that Vera had given us, wondering if I would ever attain to such beauty and hoping desperately it might be so.

We were to return home after lunch next day. Where was Francis? Vera said she didn't expect him till teatime. I thought it rather odd to come home for your half-term on a Sunday afternoon. Why not the Friday? Francis's disappearances were always mystifying.

My father seemed pleased when Chad Hamner turned up on Sunday morning. He was young still, my father, not yet thirty-eight, very young to be my father, but he was as old-fashioned in his ideas and ideals as a sixty-year-old. His life had been sheltered and narrow, he had been strictly and carefully brought up, and he had married at twenty-one. Nothing Eden had said on that visit to us had affected his belief—planted there originally by me—that Chad was Eden's accredited suitor. In his personal Utopia, women, especially his sisters and his daughter, would each have one lover all their lives, an adorer to whom they became at last engaged, then married, then lived with ever after, happily or not as the case might be, but he would take happiness in those prescribed circumstances for granted. Chad, in my father's eyes, was that suitor and Eden's haughty denial of that fact he took for modesty, a coyness he honored. So when Chad arrived, he was gratified to meet him, seeming to find nothing odd in the man he regarded as Eden's lover dropping in while Eden herself was hundreds of miles away in Northern Ireland.

To this he alluded at once. After, that is, Vera had told Chad how pleased he ought to be to meet her brother at last.

"We're poor substitutes for my sister Eden, I'm afraid."

"Oh, Chad saw Eden when she was home a fortnight ago," Vera said. "I expect he had more than enough of her." It was the first time I had ever heard her refer with even the mildest disparagement to Eden and I was astonished. If the world didn't exactly turn over, it tilted for a moment to one side. "Of course I don't mean that. It was lovely having her, only we have to carry on with our humdrum lives regardless of all this excitement from the outside world."

It was a remark worthy of Vera at her most obscure. I recalled uneasily what Mrs. Cambus had said to me the day before, what Mrs. Cambus ought perhaps not to have said to a girl of fifteen. But she was a gossip and known for it in the village.

"Never tell my mother anything," Anne used to say. "Absolutely *not anything.*"

What Mrs. Cambus had said to me was: "That young newspaper reporter is always round at Laurel Cottage. People do remark on it. Of course, it's hardly for you to say anything to your aunt, but your father might drop a hint."

I repeated this to no one. It was extremely distasteful to me, giving me a crawly sensation on my skin whenever I thought of it. My skin crawled then as I looked at Chad, sitting so easily, so very much at home here, taking it for granted he would be asked to stay for lunch—cold pheasant eked out with canned Prem come over on Lease-Lend—knowing where the cutlery was kept, laying the table, pouring us glasses of Vera's homemade elderflower wine. And Vera's eyes were on him a great deal, watching his movements as if he fascinated her. I expected him to go when we did, his accompanying us to the bus stop signifying to me that he also intended to catch the bus, but when it appeared on the horizon, visible from at least a mile away on the Sissington road, he shook hands with both of us, saying:

"Back to a quiet afternoon of Make Do and Mend."

My father looked a little puzzled. I knew Chad meant he would be tête-à-tête with Vera, holding her skein of wool, reading the *Sunday Express* to her while she converted bits of three old dresses into a maternity smock, making a log fire and talking secrets with the door closed. Until Francis arrived and disrupted everything. Or would the two of them have been doing something quite other?

My parents had had the telephone since 1937 but they had never become used to it. It was a sacred instrument into whose mouthpiece you protruded your lips till your breath condensed on the Bakelite and enunciated each syllable carefully and at a louder pitch than in normal conversation. It was for making local calls or use in an emergency, not to be handled lightly or wantonly, and long-distance calls, even over the comparatively short distance of sixty-five miles which separated us from Great Sindon, unthinkable. My father and Vera communicated by letter as they always had. Eden hardly ever wrote except at Christmas and birthdays, yet, strangely enough, it was Eden who took over the communication of news to us about Vera's baby when Vera herself fell silent.

At first, Vera's idea had been to have the child at home, something that would have been by no means unusual at that time. It was mildly frowned on to have a first baby at home but in no way vehemently denounced and more or less prohibited as it is today. Besides, this would not be a first baby. Later on, however, she changed her mind and booked into a nursing home in Colchester. We knew all this through Eden, who occasionally phoned from Northern Ireland—to my father an awesome act and none the less astounding because paid for by the government. Vera's letters, none of which survive, were infrequent, pedestrian accounts of the weather, the winter illnesses of her neighbors, and of her own apparently steady good health. Uncle Gerald was sometimes mentioned, but not where he was or where she thought he was, only as a subject for speculation of an an I-wonder-what-Gerry-would-think-of or Gerry-wouldn't-believe-it-possible kind. Gradually, the secrecy, so dear to Vera's heart, so much a part of her character, closed in. The letters stopped and it was left to Eden.

My father began to worry. As April lengthened and ended and May began, he would say most evenings:

"I think I ought to phone Sindon," as a person today—though only a person of straitened means and lack of sophistication—might say, I think I ought to phone Australia.

My mother, of course, never supported any plan of his that seemed to indulge his sisters. She would remark on the cost of phone calls or say something quite unjustified but irrefutable, such as:

"Suit yourself, you'll get no thanks for it."

Eden, we knew, was due for leave and my father was comforted by hearing her voice when at last he did phone, first making great mental preparations and ensuring total silence in the house, wireless off, windows closed, before asking the operator to get him the Laurel Cottage number. Vera was well, very well, but no, there was no sign yet of the baby. Yes, it was overdue, but babies were often later than one expected, weren't they?

"And how's that young man of yours?"

Eden must have said a perhaps irritable "I don't know what you're talking about, John," for my father laughed and said he had no doubt there would soon be wedding bells. Then he sobered, recollected things. Of course, they were waiting for the war to end, was that it?

He ended rather pathetically. She would keep in touch, wouldn't she? She would send him a "wire" when the baby came?

My parents' marriage was not a particularly happy one. They had married very young, they came from very dissimilar backgrounds. The young people today, my own children, say triumphantly to me:

"It lasted, didn't it? They stayed together. Isn't that the test?"

But the answer is no, it isn't. People did stay together in those days, ordinary middle-class, not-very-well-off people. Other possibilities were not really open to them. They had not committed adultery or been cruel or deserted each other. They had their home they had made together, their child, they were used to each other. And if they were not compatible, not united in soul and body, not blissful together and wretched apart, was this ground for dissolving a marriage at great cost in scandal, astonishment, deceit, and money? I doubt if they ever considered it. My father continued to rile my mother with his silly, starry-eyed worship of his sisters, his old-fashioned, courteous, empty, and meaningless idealization of women; and my mother, in her carping jealousy, never missed a chance of belittling his family and sneering at its members, winding up with a general denunciation of the English bourgeoisie.

I overheard her say to him:

"Gerald was in those Sicily landings. That was on the ninth of July last year. The ninth of July. You can't deny it, it's history."

He came out of the room, his face white and set. I, too, had been doing my sums. Who could resist it? This must have been, I thought, the longest pregnancy on record. Eden's telegram came on May 10. *Vera has son. Both doing well. Love, Eden.*

9

IT HAS BEEN said that we can remember only from the time when we first learned to speak. We think in words, so memory also operates in words, and we can remember nothing of those first two or three years before we could speak. On the other hand, there is the school of thought which would have it that recall is possible from our time in the womb. Jamie has told me he can remember nothing of what happened to him before he was six (except for something which never happened), the reason, he alleges, being that he was too unhappy. His psyche, defending itself from further pain, blocked off the memories. I remember his early years, or episodes in them, very well. He could not have been unhappy. What more could a baby, a small child, need than such unwavering devoted love from a mother as Jamie had from Vera?

Is it perhaps that knowing what happened and how he was used as a pawn in a game, he believes his early childhood must have been wretched? I think this is the truth of it for I know I have not falsified the past, so deeply did the change in Vera impress itself on me that summer. No trauma has distorted my memory, no bias or fear altered what I saw and heard. For me, of course, there was no involvement of the emotions, unless to contemplate maternity and wonder how one will oneself approach it when the time comes is involvement.

Jamie was christened in August. I was going to stay with Vera for two weeks, my father joining me for a day and a night to attend the

christening. It was as well we were there, for no other members of the
family were, not Eden, not Francis, not Helen. Already formed in
my mind was an image of how Vera would be with a baby. Routine-
driven, I thought, everything done by the clock, a fanatical emphasis
on hygiene, cot sheets ironed as well as laundered, and napkins too, I
wouldn't have been surprised. He could not disappear at bedtime
and be hunted through the house and streets, but it could be impressed upon his infant ears that six o'clock was the crucial hour, the
point in time after which no well-conditioned baby should be out of
his cot.

It was not like that. He was a beautiful child, a blond angel. Vera
had written that his eyes were a deep, intense blue, and only in this
respect did he fail to accord with her adoring description. His eyes,
clear, large, and full of intelligent regard, were a curious, changing
agate as if the blue they had at first been were being washed out by
amber-colored water. His face, his cheeks, his limbs, his wrists and
ankles, were rounded and satiny. He was three months old and he
had begun to smile, all his smiles being directed at Vera.

For once she was not at the gate, not scanning the street, preparing
to tell us how late we were, how she had given us up, how she thought
we were never coming. She came to the door carrying Jamie in her
arms and when we followed her into the living room she laid him
down on the floor on a blanket and let him roll and flex his limbs and
kick. I won't say I would not have known Vera if I had met her in the
street. Of course the contours of the face were familiar, the quick
bodily movements, but this was rather the Vera of the early photographs, the pretty, thin, fair-haired girl, than the sharp shrew with
tight mouth and wrinkled eyelids. She was transformed by a serenity
that clung to her like the most becoming of dresses, its rosy color
reflected in her cheeks, her knowledge of its flattery shining in her
eyes.

"You're looking very well," my father said, unable to stop looking
at her, looking at her in a way so filled with admiration that I could
not help thinking with resentment that he never looked at my mother
like that and how gratified she would have been for a fraction of that
admiring regard.

"I haven't felt so well for years," Vera said. "But never mind me.
What do you think of Jamie? Isn't he beautiful? Isn't he adorable?
When you think how I wanted a girl! I wouldn't change him for the
loveliest, best-behaved girl. Not that he's not well-behaved—he's

perfect, he never gives a scrap of trouble, do you, my angel, my lamb?"

I could not agree that he was no trouble. To me he seemed a terrible handful, a source of endless labor, much of it exacerbated by Vera herself and her insistence on holding him constantly, spending an hour more over his feeds, rocking him to sleep in her arms or against her shoulder. Gone was the sewing, the fine embroidery, the unpicked garments and cards of wool, gone the repeated references to Eden, the proud boasting about Eden's achievements, and gone, too, apparently, the vindictive gibes at absent Francis. In fact we had to ask in order to know.

"Oh, Francis won't be home. He's so jealous of Jamie, though he won't admit it. And as for coming to the christening, he says he hasn't believed in God since he was seven. 'What do you believe in, then?' I said, and he just said, 'Me,' meaning himself. Charming, isn't it?

"It's a pity Eden can't be here," said my father.

"You wouldn't expect her to come all the way from Gourock for a christening, would you?"

"Gourock?" said my father. "I thought she was in Northern Ireland."

Another secret, evidently, another mystery. . . . Vera slightly averted her eyes and a flush appeared on her cheeks. She wasn't upset, she wasn't displeased, though she had been caught out in a lie or at any rate a prevarication. "Oh, what does it matter where she is? 'Somewhere in England,' as they say. We're not supposed to know anyway, are we?" And she used the catch phrase everyone employed, from shopkeepers who had received requests for unobtainable goods to mothers criticized for unappetizing meals: "Don't you know there's a war on?"

Jamie never cried. He wasn't allowed to. Babies who are carried, cuddled, their every want attended to, don't cry. Vera dressed him in the robe of white nun's veiling, trimmed with lace made by Great-aunt Priscilla Naughton, which she and Eden and my father and, no doubt, Francis too, had worn to be christened in. It was a warm sultry day, no wind, the sky overcast. For the first time since I had visited there, the garden had been neglected and weeds grew in the flowerbeds, willow herb and giant hogweed and the six-foot-tall great mullein, its gray leaves and yellow flower buds eaten into holes by caterpillars. We walked to the church, Jamie in Vera's arms rather than the high and shiny black pram which had once been Francis's. We walked in a little procession, for Chad had arrived and joined us, along the main street and down the lane to St. Mary's. The cattle and sheep which had been in the meadows when first I came to Sindon had largely disappeared and the fields been plowed up for the war effort, for the growing of grain and sugar beets. Jamie's magnificent robe flowed over and half-covered the tired, shabby dress of Maccles-field silk Vera wore. She waved to people in their gardens as she passed, something I could never have imagined her doing.

My father was Jamie's godfather. There were no other sponsors. I should have loved to be his godmother but it had never been sug-gested and I was too diffident to ask. Anyway, this is the great nonre-lationship, the meaningless function, godparents mostly being selected for their ability to give generous birthday and Christmas presents. Being his godfather gave my father no guardianship rights over Jamie when the time came, made him no surrogate parent. Nor, I suppose, did he, when Jamie was fourteen and at boarding school and holidaying with the Contessa, remember it was his duty to bring him before the bishop for confirmation. He whimpered a little when my father held him and again when he felt Mr. Morrell's wet fingers on his forehead.

When we left the church I thought Chad would go home but he didn't. He returned with us to Laurel Cottage and he was nervous and preoccupied as if he were waiting for something to happen or someone to come. My father talked to him about Eden, not going quite so far as to ask when they intended to become officially engaged but implying the question in almost everything he said. Not in the role of the heavy brother inquiring into a suitor's intentions, I don't mean that, but warmly and enthusiastically as if there could be noth-ing in his opinion Chad would want to talk of more. I could see that he had weighed Chad in the balance as a future brother-in-law and found him substantial enough. At last Chad said:

"John, I think I should tell you there's no prospect at all of Eden and me getting married. I don't want you to be under a misappre-hension. I feel you are and it may be my fault. I'm flattered, of course, very much so, but it won't ever be."

Vera, who had laid the sleeping Jamie into a nest of blankets and *broderie anglaise* pillows on the sofa, averted her eyes. She clasped her hands together and pressed down, exerting her strength. It was the first time I had seen her do this since we arrived. My father looked embarrassed and upset. He had become rather pale. But he tried pathetically to pass it off with humor.

"Turned you down, has she?"

"You can put it that way it you like."

"Faint heart never won fair lady, you know."

"Brave hearts don't always triumph either." Chad said this, it seemed to me, with infinite sadness. "There's a sort of prevailing belief," he said, "that if you want something enough, you can have it. Only try hard enough and you can have it. It just isn't true." He was one of those few, rare people I have known, the first of those few I have known, who could talk freely and without embarrassment about the emotions.

My family, on an imaginary scale of openness, could have been placed on the other extreme end of it. My father could almost be seen to be curling himself back into his shell when Chad said this, and Vera had begun to look angry, fierce in the old way I was used to. And then Chad smiled the smile that transformed him, making him look young and handsome.

"Well, I have a train to catch," said my father.

Chad stayed and we had one of Vera's magnificent teas, changed but not spoiled by austerity, the cakes made with mashed potato and dried egg tasting no less good. He produced one of those bottles of sherry and we wetted Jamie's head with it, there no longer being any talk of sending me to bed. But I couldn't forget what Mrs. Cambus had hinted at and I found myself watching Vera and Chad for signs of the relationship she had seemed to suggest. Exactly what this relationship would be, I was not clear about. All I knew of love affairs, clandestine and otherwise, was drawn from films. I was an ardent cinema- and theatergoer. Adultery was a popular and compelling theme in the 1940's. It was *the* theme, whether the drama was historical or a light comedy or a war tragedy. If there were truly "anything between" (Vera's own phrase) Vera and Chad, I thought I would detect it. I thought, for instance, I might come into the room where they were and find them locked in each other's arms, only to spring guiltily apart at the sight of me. One thing I was certain of. I was too sophisticated, I thought, to be deceived as my father was into thinking it was Eden Chad was attached to. This was a mere blind, a cloak for his constant visits.

Mrs. Cambus's remark had given me a very unpleasant feeling. This had been blunted a bit but I still felt guilty and ashamed over my suspicions, though not enough to stop me watching and speculating. Vera, who had seemed to me ugly, old, and worn-out when first I considered and dismissed this possibility, looked quite different now, years younger. To me, whose standards were high, formed by film stars and Eden, she even seemed passably attractive, attractive at any rate *enough*. But if there were embraces, kisses, whispering together, I saw none of it. Nor was there any attempt to get rid of me and be alone.

Helen came next day. She and the General came to lunch. She was elated, all laughter, hysterical with relief and happiness. Their son, Andrew, missing for weeks, his aircraft shot down somewhere over the Rhineland, was a prisoner in German hands. They had heard only that morning. There had been no more sinister explanation than this for the failure of the Chatterisses to attend the christening. Helen held Vera in her arms.

"You were a brick, darling, not to mind. It is so splendid when the people one is close to *understand*. I just felt I couldn't go to the christening of someone else's boy when my own boy . . ." She burst into wild sobs. Vera gave her some of Chad's sherry. The General patted her thin, shivering shoulders. "Oh, the relief! To know he's safe!" Helen, too, can speak freely of the emotions, but only of a certain kind in a certain way, and that way widely acceptable.

"Your Hun," said the general, "is widely reputed to be a gentleman." He lowered his voice when he said this. Perhaps he thought it came in the "Careless Talk Costs Lives" category. We were all mere women, though; we were safe.

Helen, for some reason, had brought with her albums of photographs of her children, albums and loose snapshots, as if she had grabbed up anything she could find in the five minutes before leaving the house. Patricia, always said to be the favorite Chatteriss child, was ignored now. Andrew was all, Andrew in his pram, on his mother's lap, on a beach, in school uniform, in the uniform of a pilot officer, smiling, young, appearing too young to have been one of the Few. I would like to be able to say that I felt in looking at these pictures some stirring of expectation, some excitement, even some prevision of what was to come, but it would not be true. If I had thoughts of that kind, they were for Chad. As the object of my infatuation, he was beginning to replace Eden, who was growing shadowy, a voiceless, motionless monochrome photograph with a long, pale fall of hair.

But they talked of her, Vera and Helen, that afternoon, while the General fell asleep in an armchair and Jamie lay on a rug on the floor, waving his arms and kicking his legs. Vera's notions of what Eden's future life would be had changed since I last heard her speak in this way of her. Then she had said sadly she was sure Eden would never come back to live permanently in Sindon.

Now it was different. She could have her old job back if she wanted it, she had written to Vera. And if that happened, where better to live than at Laurel Cottage? Eden was somewhere in Scotland at present. She, Vera, knew this because of the code they used, similar to the one she and Gerry had formulated. While she was speaking, Francis walked in. He arrived without warning, almost without sound, to my surprise going straight up to Helen and kissing her. I had never before seen him kiss anyone. She reached out to him one long, red-nailed, heavily ringed, delicate hand and would, I think, have told him at once about Andrew had Vera not still been speaking, continuing as if Francis had not come in, her tale of Eden's present whereabouts and occupation. It was the point about the code he seized on, though not to mock in the same way as he had done once before.

"Let me tell you what happened to someone I know at school. His brother is a prisoner with the Japanese. This man, the prisoner, wrote to save the stamps off his letters for him when he got home, to steam them off. Well, they steamed this one off and underneath the man had written: 'The Japs have cut out my tongue.'"

Helen gave a cry of horror and flung her hands up to her throat. I, too, thought the story horrible. As you see, I have never forgotten it. I swear Vera gathered spittle in her mouth before she spoke to Francis.

"It may interest you to know that your cousin Andrew is now a prisoner of war. Perhaps it will teach you to think of others before you speak. Now apologize at once to Aunt Helen."

Ironically, this was the only time I ever saw Francis obey his mother. Helen cried out:

"Darling, he didn't mean it, he couldn't know!"

"Helen, I am truly sorry," Francis said. He no more called her aunt than I did. Making it worse, "I could cut out my tongue. Oh, Christ," he said, "forgive me."

"He's in a German prison camp," Helen said.

We did not know about the camps yet, nor about the implications of our own bombing of Dresden. Hiroshima was yet to come. We were innocent. Francis, who identified with Helen, who saw his own plight as an image of hers, as an identical link in the Longley chain of indifference or unkindness to children, had grown pale with wretchedness. His coloring was extraordinary, more spectacular than Eden's, the skin a fine, milky white, the hair so yellow, the eyes a hard violet blue. There was sweat in pinprick beads on his short, curled upper lip. His were the features of Michelangelo's *David* in strange colors.

He looked at the baby on the rug as if he would have liked to kick it. I felt a momentary real fear. Francis was so strange, so unlike other people. I could conceive of a situation in which he killed Jamie and then coolly informed Vera of what he had done. The General slept on, having in his sleep managed to smother his face with the *Sunday Express*. Jamie began to whimper and Vera immediately picked him up, holding him against her shoulder, his round cheek against her thin one. Helen said, the subject utterly changed, though not much for the better:

"You know, darling, I do believe his eyes are going to be brown. If they are, he'll be the first Longley to have brown eyes."

Francis, very still, watched her.

"I can't remember if Gerry has brown eyes," Helen said. "Isn't that too awful of me? Not to know the color of one's brother-in-law's eyes? That's what war does for you. I do believe they are hazel. Is that right?"

"My father's eyes are blue," said Francis in a dead voice. The sentence sounded curiously like the opening line of a play, a lost, never-acted Chekhov perhaps.

Jamie, however, had closed his eyes and fallen asleep in Vera's arms.

She breast-fed him. What will Daniel Stewart make of *that*? Jamie himself has made too much of it, to some extent a secure world. It has allowed him to shirk (what he calls "to face") the truth about his mother. Francis, of course, denied that it ever happened. He remembered the feeding bottles boiled up on the kitchen stove in the big double-handled pans Vera used for jam-making. So do I remember. It has never been suggested that she had enough milk to feed Jamie without supplements. He got the "government" powdered milk in bottles as well. Eden was incredulous.

"Vera feed Jamie?" I remember her saying. "Like that, do you mean?" And with the true vulgarity of the mealymouthed, she held up her hands, palms inwards, an inch from her own breasts. "Oh, never, impossible! Why, she didn't even do that for Francis!"

I had never before seen a woman suckle a child. For one thing, she would have had to be something of a bohemian to have done so in the presence of anyone save her husband or her mother. There was no scooping up of T-shirts in tube trains in the 1940's. It was a subject I had never really thought about, though breast-feeding was coming back into fashion. When I opened Vera's bedroom door in response to her "Come in!"—I wanted to tell her I was going swimming with Anne—I was embarrassed by what I saw. It seemed to have a raw earthiness about it not associated with Longleys. I had noticed on my arrival a new plumpness about Vera's bosom. She had always been rather flat chested. The round white breast Jamie sucked at would fill out the bodice of a dress becomingly alongside its fellow, this other not covered as one might have expected, knowing Vera's modest ways, but also bared and with a single drop of milk pendent from the nipple.

Vera sat in a chair I had never seen before, a wooden one with a high back, squat legs, and a round seat, a traditional old nursing chair that had in fact been used by my grandmother and her mother to suckle their babies. She sat upright, her legs spread apart, her head bent as she contemplated the steadily sucking child. He lay in the crook of her arm. Her other hand was lightly closed round the back of his fair, downy head. The look on her face I had never seen before, it was so young, so tender, so infinitely sweet and adoring.

I wish now that we had spoken of what she was doing. It might have made things clearer, it might have helped. As it was, she said not a word, only seeming in a curious way to offer to my eyes the spectacle of this deeply physical, profoundly emotional act. I was shy, I looked away.

"Is it all right if I go swimming?" I said. "Down to the weir?"

She looked up and smiled. She nodded. I got my swimming things and ran down the stairs. I think I ran most of the way to Anne's. It was not that I was so deeply embarrassed, certainly I was not afraid or shocked. My body seemed full of excited energy that had to be dispelled. It was the first time I had been to the river since my mother told me the story of Kathleen March. Because I couldn't imagine Vera with a baby, it had never seemed real to me. Now it did. My mother had not gone so far as to suggest that Vera herself had harmed the child, only that she had neglected to look after it. I asked

Anne if she had ever heard the story, but in asking I left out mention of Vera, telling her only that a baby left in its pram on the bank here had been taken out of it and never seen again.

Anne said she had heard about a lost baby, but no details. We walked along the riverbank to the part where, for some reason to do with a pumping station, the banks had been shored up and lined with concrete, creating a deep pool. There was so much more wildlife then than there is now, such a proliferation of wildflowers and butter-flies and dragonflies. The cleaning up of the English countryside, the sterilization, had not yet begun. The hedges were still there and the deep, moist, unplowed water meadows. We watched a kingfisher swoop and flaunt its colors over the pool.

"Vera is feeding Jamie herself," I said suddenly, I didn't know why. "With her own milk." I would have been shy to say "breast" in front of Anne.

"Yes, I know," Anne said. "She told Mummy. She tells everyone." I was surprised. I knew Vera disliked Mrs. Cambus.

We took off our clothes. We had our swimming costumes on under them. Anne could dive, though she had been told not to dive into the pool. She surfaced and said:

"It's all babies, isn't it? There was Elsie's baby that never was and now there's your aunt's and there was the baby that disappeared. Have you done *Macbeth* at school?"

It had been a set book for school certificate—for her, apparently, as well as for me.

"*Macbeth* is full of babies and milk," said Anne. "You have a look. It's really strange that a play like that which is full of horrors should have all that babies-and-milk stuff, isn't it?"

I asked her if she had thought that up for herself or had her En-glish mistress told her? The English mistress, she admitted. I prom-ised to look just the same, for Vera's story was full of babies and milk too.

The day after I went home I went to the theater. That was my year for going to the theater on most Saturdays. It sounds grand but in fact, what I was doing was going in the gallery, queuing up for a stool first thing in the morning, securing my seat on what seems a pittance now, half a crown or three shillings, and often attending a matinee as well as an evening performance. Two or three of us, all school friends, would go.

I wish I could positively remember what I saw that Saturday

night. I think it was at the Cambridge and I think it was a musical called *Song of Norway*. Daniel Stewart can check up on that if he thinks what I have to tell him about that night is relevant. I saw so many plays that year and the year before and the year or two afterwards: Richardson and Olivier at the New in the Shakespeare Historicals and *Oedipus Rex* and *The Critic, Blithe Spirit* at the Piccadilly, and *Private Lives* at the Fortune. But I know it was a musical I saw that night and in a big theater where the gallery was up in the sky and to look down over the rail gave you vertigo even if you had a head for heights. We were lucky. We were in the middle of the front row.

Someone said, quoting *Lear*, which we had recently seen:

"How fearful And dizzy 'tis to cast one's eyes so low. . . ?"

We were all, of course, casting our eyes down over the rail on to the tops of heads in the stalls far below us. The temptation was to drop things onto those heads, orange pips being traditional. None of us had seen an orange for years. I looked down on a golden head and as I did so, it turned to look upwards, though attempting nothing higher than the dress circle. The head was Eden's.

My reaction was rather strange. I immediately—with a jerk, I think—looked away and sat back in my seat. There was nothing to look at up there but the ceiling, the usual ornate baroque mingling of cherubs and flowers. I made myself look down again and the head was still there, still turned, with the chin lifted. There was no doubt it was Eden. The chignon had just come into fashion and her hair was done up in one, the crown of it a study in complexities, curls and swirls nestling in a deep wave, almost as if designed for an aerial viewing. Veronica Lake had given place to Alexis Smith. I could not see what she was wearing, only that it was white and of some soft, thin material. What it definitely was not was a WRNS uniform. The man sitting next to her was her escort. I knew that because I saw him touch her. Her head was turned towards him. She must have got something in her eye. Their faces came very close as his hand, holding a radiantly white handkerchief, a handkerchief that positively gleamed down there among the blacks and golds and dark colors, approached her eye and, no doubt dexterously, made to remove the lash or grain of dust. I was at once convinced, for no more reason than this, that he must be a doctor. He wore a dark suit. The top of his head had a small bald spot in the middle of brown curls.

The lights dimmed and went out and the curtain came up. I couldn't quite put them from my mind. The play couldn't dispel them. The extraordinary thing was that I was very certain I did not want Eden to see me. I sensed, you see, that she didn't want it known she was in London and would hate to have me see her. She was in Londonderry or else she was in Scotland. Had Vera not told me, less than two weeks ago, that she was in Scotland and having recently had leave could expect no more yet?

There were two intervals. I was relatively safe from being seen because of the segregation of the audience in the stalls, dress circle, and upper circle from us poor galleryites, who even had to use a different entrance door. Nevertheless, I dreaded running into Eden and her doctor friend. Somehow I knew that if this happened, Eden would take me aside and tell me lies. How I knew this I don't know, but I did. She would ask me not to tell Vera or my father that I had seen her and then give me a totally fabricated reason why I was to say nothing, such as that she was in London on some secret matter to do with the war. This I was afraid of, perhaps because I still kept the remnants of my "crush" and total disillusionment is something one never courts even if one desires it. In the second interval I stayed behind in the auditorium while the others went out.

Why had I forgotten that the greatest risk would be afterwards, outside in the street? I had. I felt that the danger was over when the curtain fell and we stood for the National Anthem that in those days was always played.

It may have been the Strand outside or Shaftesbury Avenue or the Haymarket. But I think it was the Charing Cross Road where Shaftesbury Avenue comes into it at Cambridge Circus. The long tyranny of the blackout had almost come to an end by then and a dim-out was to be allowed in its place. At the end of August, though—and for weeks to come due to a shortage of manpower and light bulbs—the West End continued in darkness. There was a full moon that night, and the moon was not obscured then by smog and pollution. We walked along the pavement with the crowd. It seemed to part as if by some stage instruction or command from a director, and there on the edge of the pavement in front of me stood the two of them, waiting to cross, her arm in his. In these days they would have been waiting for a taxi; then, they were making for a tube station, probably Leicester Square.

No more than three yards separated us. My weak smile was al-

ready forming, the "Hallo, Eden" shaping itself on my tongue as her
eyes met mine, lingered there, staring and wide—and looked away.
In that moment I lost whatever feeling I had ever had for her. I was
astounded, for in my eyes she was a grown-up and I still half a child,
and I was also ashamed for her and dismayed. There was no doubt
she had seen me. I knew she had seen and recognized me. Nothing
kills like contempt, and contempt for her came upon me in a hot flood
of blushes so that I put my hands to my face, cooling it with my
fingers. Eden and her man crossed the road and lost themselves in
the crowd, but when I closed my eyes, there she was, I could still see
her, on the black retina, her beautifully made, fine-boned face like
Francis's, the lipstick red as a clown's, pillar-box paint against that
white skin, the eyes as blue as marbles and the hair as gilded as a
cherub's on a ceiling. Her dress had been white, a cross-over and
draped, her legs bare and her feet in white Betty Grable shoes with
heels made for a high-stepping trot like a horse's.

If I had mentioned it to my father, he would have said I was mistaken. I thought about it a lot. I thought of how I should have had to
describe her, had he asked, and how, when he heard of the Grecian
dress and the golden topknot, he would have said:
    "That doesn't sound like my little sister. You mistook someone else
for her."
    Of course I had not. It had been Eden and she was in London
when everyone believed her in Scotland. The mysteries and secrecies
beloved of the Longleys had a new mystery and a new secret. I wondered if Eden was still a Wren even and if she were living in London
or only staying there. I even wondered, so paranoid an effect can this
kind of thing have on one, if it was only I that was excluded from this
secret, if all along, my father and my mother, too, had known Eden's
precise whereabouts and had kept the truth from me for reasons un-
fathomable; if Vera had known when she told my father one day that
Eden was in Londonderry and the next in Gourock. And what of
poor Chad, who had spoken, so it seemed to me, so sorrowfully of his
failure to achieve Eden's love, though not for the want of trying?
    I find myself creating mysteries, too. It is not for nothing that I am
a Longley. Of course, I am trying to arrange these recollections of
mine in sequence, not remembering events and revelations, so to
speak, out of order. It was a good while later, though, years, before I
did discover the truth of this. This was at the time of the uncovering

of many truths. Eden *had* left the WRNS. That August, it was three-quarters of a year since she had been Leading Wren Longley, stationed at Londonderry, and in Scotland she had never been. In London she had a job as secretary-companion to an old woman in Belgrave Square called Lady Rogerson. The odd thing was that she got this job through one of those gentlefolk relatives of Chad's that she had met through him, though Chad was ignorant of it all. Eden simply used him in her progress towards the main chance as she used everyone useful. She lived in Belgrave Square and after a while (she once told us), Lady Rogerson looked on her almost as a daughter—well, a niece. The man with the brown curly hair was a sort of cousin of Lady Rogerson's and he too had a title, though I can't remember what. It was not he, anyway, whom Eden finally caught as a result of living in Belgravia.

All this was well known to Vera all the time.

10

I WAS SO USED to thinking of Laurel Cottage as Vera's house that it came as a shock to hear my father tell my mother that he supposed it would be sold now and the proceeds divided between Vera, Eden, and himself. That, of course, was the way my grandmother had left it. My father had waived his right because Vera needed somewhere in which to make a home for Eden, and then the war had come, disrupting everything. The sale of Laurel Cottage might with luck realize fifteen hundred pounds and my father talked a lot about how he would use his five-hundred share—build on to the house perhaps, move house, buy a car, refurnish the living room, go to Switzerland and see my mother's relations—spending it in imagination several times over. For a bank manager, which he had just become, he was naive about money.

Harder-headed and altogether more realistic, my mother never believed in that money from the start. She was a woman who had no compunction about saying "I told you so." "See if I'm not right" was another phrase of hers, and she usually was.

"When your mother died, I told you to sell the house. Gerald would have got a house for Vera, and Eden could have lived with us. Things would have been very different if that had happened."

They would, indeed.

"Eden wouldn't have been made too big for her boots for one

thing," said my mother. "It doesn't do people any good to be idol-
ized."

My father said in an unpleasant tone that there was not much risk
of that round here. It was interesting to speculate what it would have
been like having Eden as a sort of big sister. I had no idea this had
ever been proposed. Would it have interfered with what George Eliot
calls "the stealthy convergence of human lots," altering the course of
things, so that Vera on her seventy-eighth birthday might have come
along to tea with me and Helen last week? And might Eden have
been there too, a sprightly, blonded sixty-three? Might Francis have
strolled in among us to throw a word of disaster in that way he always
had, as Ate flung the golden apple among the party guests? And
Jamie, his name unchanged and his own, not a self-appointed exile?
Who knows? I think somehow that things would have been much the
same, given the war and the personalities of the players in the drama.

Eden never wrote. Vera often did and continued to mention Eden
as being in Scotland and still in the WRNS. My father never wav-
ered in his custom of reading her letters aloud at the breakfast table,
and as I heard details of Eden's life relayed, though I didn't doubt my
own eyes, I began to think she had been guilty of no greater subter-
fuge than that of coming to London on leave without visiting us or
seeing Vera. We were enduring V1 attacks which only came to an
end when the Allies overran the V1 launching sites in the Pas de
Calais. But Duncan Sandys was a bit premature when in September
he said that "the Battle of London is over except for a few shots."

That same month, the V2's started, those first rockets, which trav-
eled so fast that one could not hear them before they exploded. By
that time one was either dead or not, as the case may be. We called
them "flying gas mains," just as we called the V1's that droned more
loudly before they cut out and exploded "doodlebugs" or "buzz
bombs." One of the last of these V2's to reach England fell on Colchester, making a direct hit on the nursing home where Vera had had
Jamie and causing hundreds of casualties, more than fifty of them
fatal. My father flew into a panic about Vera and Jamie. Suppose this
were a new phase of the war, a kind of swan song of aggression to be
unleashed on East Anglia?

Five months later it was all over. If Eden were still in the WRNS at
the time the war ended, she must have been one of the first of the five
million servicemen and women to be demobilized. Ernest Bevin announced that releases would begin on June 18, and a week later Vera

wrote to say Eden has been "demobbed." Even my father thought that strange. Gerald had to wait a good deal longer and was not to reach home till the autumn of 1945, by which time Francis had gone up to Oxford and Vera, for a change, been to us on holiday.

My mother consented to this, I think, because she enjoyed the company of small children, a rarer quality in women than one might think. Most people, whatever they may say, find the company of little children boring. My mother, though intelligent and quite quick and brusque with adults, had infinite patience with children. She used to say she liked the way they had not yet learnt the shifts and slyness and affectations of grown-ups.

Jamie was about fifteen months old by this time. He had curious coloring, very attractive but unusual, his skin being a light, clear olive while his hair was brightly fair. His eyes were brown; not light brown or hazel or speckly blue-gold, but an uncompromising rich dark brown, as deep a shade as a Spaniard's or even an Indian's might be. And he didn't look like anyone in the family. You know the way babies have a definite "look" of some uncle or aunt or forebear, so that the overall impression is of a copy of that person, but when you examine the face feature by feature the similarity breaks down. I used to pore over albums of old Longley and Naughton photographs and saw this again and again, how the infant Vera, for instance, seemed a reincarnation of Great-aunt Priscilla, how my father immediately brought to mind old William, the shoemaker. Eden and Francis, as I have said, might have been taken for twins. Jamie, though, was himself and only himself. He looked no more like the Longleys (except for his hair) than he did like Gerald, who has a very long face and almost pointed head that Helen says he used to attribute, I don't know how accurately, to his mother's narrow pelvis and the fact that he took an unconscionably long time being born. I decided Jamie must look like some Hillyard forebear, but no Hillyard family albums were available to me.

He was devoted to his mother. This was only to be expected since he had lived since his birth almost exclusively in Vera's sole company. I know my mother would have liked to play with him and talk to him and hold him on her lap, but of this she had very little chance. Jamie didn't cry much. He simply didn't respond to others. He would sit silent or stand with his thumb in his mouth, neither accepting nor rejecting overtures, and if you took him on your knees, he suffered your caressing hand, your smiles, and your encouragement in wary tenseness, his body growing stiff, at last slipping down and going to Vera with his arms held out. To do her justice, she did not particularly encourage this. I thought her nicer than she used to be. She was much pleasanter to my mother, for one thing, adjuring Jamie to "go to Aunt Vranni." (Since Helen's comments, Vera had never again advocated the use of "auntie.") She even agreed to going out with my parents one evening and leaving me to baby-sit. Jamie, she said proudly, had been brought up to know six was his bedtime and because of this he never gave her bad nights.

People loved going out and about London that summer. Austerity was with us and there was nothing nice to eat and nothing nice to wear, no luxury or even comfort, not much petrol, but the theater had never been better, or the cinema. And there was a delicious intoxication about wandering lighted streets in freedom and safety, knowing there would be no darkness to fall from the air. Vera said, without self-pity or touting for sympathy, quite cheerfully even:

"This will be the first time I've been out in the evening for over three years."

Jamie woke up ten minutes after they had gone out. I believe now that somehow all the events of that evening—not the waking of Jamie, of course—were engineered by Vera and Eden for the furtherance of their purposes, but things had gone wrong. They had got the wrong evening. Or one or other of them had. Eden, probably. These things are not easy if you communicate mostly by letter. Vera had been very keen to go out on the Friday night, not the Saturday, so I assume all this had been prearranged by them for the Saturday, but Eden had made a mistake. I believe now that they wanted to give, in the presence of my father and mother, and secondarily in that of Tony Pearmain, a *demonstration*. They wanted to show those three people, those most important three people—I don't think I counted much, I was only seventeen—how they had made their lives and how they were to be accepted before proceeding to the next phase.

Jamie's waking like that put me into a minor panic. I knew very little about babies and had no idea how to handle them when they cried. My instinct was to shut the door on Jamie, go out of earshot of his cries, or stuff cotton wool into my ears.

Of course I didn't do this. I opened the door stealthily and looked in. At sight of me, his crying changed to screams. He was in a cot that had once been mine, encaged, standing up, shaking the bars, and I remember thinking how odd it was that we put our small children in cages, that we didn't construct a cot that had some other confining arrangement instead of bars. That was the last coherent rational thought I had for a long time.

Jamie had worked himself into a panic and at first he wouldn't let me touch him. He flung his body backwards and forwards, pushing and punching me when I tried to get hold of him. I suppose I have since then heard children make worse noises, my own children for instance, but the noise Jamie made that evening has stuck in my mind as being uniquely horrible, perhaps because it was an absolutely uninhibited expression of real distress, real pain and loss. I am sure Vera genuinely believed he wouldn't wake up because he hadn't done so for months and months, I am sure she wouldn't have gone out if she had thought he would wake. Never before had he wakened to find her not there—worse, to find her not there and someone else there instead. His misery and terror seemed boundless. At last I succeeded in picking him up and getting him downstairs. He was sodden all over, from tears, dribble, urine, and sweat.

There was nothing I could do to stop him crying. Vera no longer breast-fed him but she had weaned him onto a cup, not a bottle. No Longley child had ever been allowed a dummy. I tried to stick his thumb in his mouth but he screamed all the more and I later learned that Vera had spent months getting him out of that one by putting aloes on his thumb. I couldn't stop him yelling so I let him yell while I very inexpertly changed his napkin and his pajama trousers and dried his face. By then I was in almost as much of a panic as he was. He had been screaming for half an hour and his face was purple, the veins standing out on the forehead. I had heard of babies having convulsions and I was afraid he might have one, might in fact have been having one at that moment, for I doubted my ability to recognize a convulsion if I saw it.

I shouted at him, "I will never baby-sit for anyone else as long as I live," a resolution I have very nearly kept to, and at that moment the doorbell rang.

We had lived through violent times, we had lived through a war, but somehow one had a far greater sense of safety in those days. Alone in the evening with a baby in a London suburban house now, I would hesitate before opening the front door, I would certainly call out to know who it was. Then, it wouldn't have crossed my mind. Holding the screaming Jamie under my arm in the way I had seen

market-going farmers in picture books carry squealing pigs, bellow-
ing at him to shut up, I opened the door. Outside on the step stood
Eden and a man.

"Goodness, darling, I never heard such a fearful noise in all my
life! You can hear it all the way down the street."

"Were you trying to kill it and we interrupted you?" the man said.

The way I was carrying poor Jamie must have inspired this. I
hoisted him onto my shoulder, where he hung, sobbing.

"Aren't you going to ask us in?" said Eden. Typical Longley. The
quintessence of Longleyism was to ask petty, pointless, rhetorical
questions when one was up to one's neck in trouble. I opened the
door wider and stood back.

Bludgeoned as I was by Jamie's roaring, there was enough aware-
ness left in me to notice their appearance and be astonished by it.
Parked at the curb was a red sports car. (Had Eden really heard
Jamie down the street inside *that*?) The two of them looked as if they
had been dressed up to advertise it in some glossy magazine published perhaps in South Africa or New Zealand, since we had nothing glossy here, neither magazines nor clothes nor people to wear
them. But these two glowed like no one but film stars. They even
looked cleaner than the rest of us, and what with fuel scarcities and
soap scarcities, no doubt they were. Eden had on a blue linen suit
covered with a pattern of white flowers, her companion a blazer with
some sort of badge that indicated he had rowed for something or
played cricket for something and a shirt that glowed with whiteness,
crisp and frosty as Wall's ice cream. He looked young even to me,
in his middle twenties, a fresh-faced, brown-haired man, a lot like
Richard Burton whom no one had heard of then.

Eden, of course, wasn't going to introduce him. Oblivious apparently of the din, she stood looking round her at our shabby hallway
from which the air-raid shelter had been removed, leaving scars on
the oak parquet floor, and where the blackout curtains still hung di-
spiritedly at the window by the front door.

"I'm Tony Pearmain," he said. "How do you do?"

I said who I was but Eden had already told him, giving him a run-
down in the car, I expect, on what he would find when he got here.

"They're all out," I said, shouting above Jamie.

"All?"

How was it that I seemed to know, even then, that she was acting?
Perhaps because she was no actress.

"Didn't you know Vera was here?"

"Vera? Here?"

It was surprising, of course. Or it would have been a surprise if she hadn't already known.

"Well, of course. This is Jamie. Don't you recognize him?"

"They change so quickly at that age. Can't you stop him making that ghastly noise?"

Tony Pearmain put out his arms and took Jamie from me. The result was magical. Did he smell wonderful, radiate self-confidence, communicate in some mysterious fashion beyond the five senses, through his pores or his nerve ends, that here was security, here was infinite warmth and kindness, here were the everlasting arms? Whatever it was, Jamie recognized it and shut up. He laid his once more wet, sticky, sweaty face against the sleek pile of Tony Pearmain's blazer and grew silent, only gulping occasionally as he got his breath back. Poor Tony had this gift with children. Because he loved them, they loved him, and all gravitated towards him, pins to a lodestone, and his presence made them quiet and good. The abiding tragedy of his life has been that he has never had children of his own and that the one child he might have loved and been loved by, circumstances made repugnant to him.

That evening was the occasion of Jamie's first meeting with Tony. I have told him how Tony held him and quieted him but he shied away from this, he hated being told, and insisted I must be mistaken. This must have been some other boyfriend of Eden's, not "Pearmain," who was so cold and distant with him, who sent him away as soon as he could—thus, of course, carrying on the Longley family tradition which had begun with Helen and continued with Francis. But Tony it was, Tony who performed this miracle. I stood in the hall, engulfed in relief, savoring the glorious peace, hardly aware for a while that Eden was there behind me.

"Where have they gone?"

"Out somewhere. To the West End. Perhaps the pictures."

"How awfully annoying!"

I took them into our living room. Their sleek young presences, their smart new clothes, showed up the deficiencies of a house that hadn't seen a coat of paint, a change of furnishings, during six years of war. The springs of the chair Tony sat in, his arms full of Jamie, were broken and the seat descended to the floor. There was no alcohol of any kind in the house, no coffee, and not very much tea. I sensed that at any minute Eden would ask me if I was going to offer them anything to drink. All I could produce was orange squash of a very ersatz kind. I was tempted to offer Jamie's "government" orange juice but feared Vera's wrath if I did. We had no refrigerator, of course, and the orange juice was lukewarm.

It was only about eight o'clock and unlikely that my parents and Vera would be back before ten-thirty. Jamie fell asleep and Tony carried him upstairs. Instead of coming down at once, he sat up there by the cot, waiting to make sure he was going to go on sleeping. Eden was wearing a very beautiful pair of white leather shoes with low-cut perforated tops and high heels. The rest of us were reduced to wooden-soled clogs. I still don't know where and how she got those shoes. Two, three, and four years later we were still standing in long lines on the chance of obtaining a pair of "Joyce" sandals. But Eden always knew people who could get her things, who had fingers and feet in the black market, who brought things into the country in diplomatic bags and bookbags, who sold clothes coupons and bypassed queues and kept things "under the counter" specially for her. She sat in another, slightly less dilapidated chair, contemplating those shoes, lightly stroking the right leg that was crossed over the left, looking at the right shoe with her head a little on one side, a long lock of golden hair falling forward. Without looking up, she said to me:

"He is one of *the* Pearmains, you know."

I didn't know. She made me very aware of my old white blouse and dirndl skirt.

"I suppose you go shopping sometimes, don't you?"

"Oh, *that* Pearmain," I said. "You mean Brewster and Pearmain?" Swan and Edgar, Debenham and Freebody, Marshall and Snelgrove, Brewster and Pearmain. I felt quite overcome. I felt shy of Tony, whereas I hadn't before. I had been going to ask her about that evening at the theater, why she had looked through me, but somehow this revelation about Tony Pearmain made it impossible. And Eden, capitalizing on it, so to speak, as if she sensed the awe she had inspired in me, added:

"I met him at a party at Lady Rogerson's."

Should I have known about Lady Rogerson? Had Vera perhaps told me when she spoke of Eden's being "demobbed"? All this brought home to me how little I belonged even by then.

"Lady Rogerson looks on me more or less as a daughter. Naturally

I went with her when she stayed at Fontlands. We'll be going again for the twelfth."

This was incomprehensible. I think it was a couple of years before I understood that Fontlands was the Pearmains' country house (with grouse moor) in Yorkshire, Lady Rogerson the old woman she was being a companion to, and the twelfth the twelfth of August, when grouse shooting begins. Eden asked me what time the others would be back, and when she heard it would be a couple of hours said she didn't think they would stay. Tony came back and said the "poor little chap" was fast asleep and had I listened to the wireless that day? I shook my head. What was there to listen to anymore?

"We've dropped a new sort of bomb on the Japs," Tony said.

"What sort of bomb?" I said, not very interested. "A kind of V2?"

"Bigger than that, it seems," he said. "Place called Hiroshima, or however you pronounce it." He pronounced it Hero-sheema. "The war in the Far East will be over now, you'll see. I left the little chap's door open so you'll hear him if he cries again."

Off they went in the red sports car. That remark of Tony's about was I trying to kill Jamie was the only even faintly witty thing I ever heard him say. His family owned a huge department store, his brother had married into the Italian nobility. He was, is, as dull as ditchwater and as rich as a gold mine. He was also good-looking, a far cry from Chad, who was poor and nothing much to look at and never opened his mouth without saying something interesting or amusing or provocative. Eden seemed pleased with herself when she left, the bad temper she had shown when she found Vera and my parents were out quite gone. But, of course, even in their absence she must have accomplished most of what she set out to do by that visit, and if nothing at all had been done for Vera, if matters had been made a little worse—well, *tant pis*.

My father considered himself middle-class. He was constantly saying so with a kind of shameful pride. What he never said was that the middle class don't commit adultery whatever the upper and lower may do, but it was a deeply felt aspect of his creed. It would not have crossed his mind that a sister of his could be unfaithful to her husband. He and my mother did not get on well, nor can I say that at the bottom they loved each other, for I am sure they did not, but while she lived my father would never have had to do with another woman. It would have been the same for him as stealing or engaging in some fraud at the bank. Therefore, when Gerald came home and he and Vera almost immediately parted, my father's course was not to wonder why and come to the conclusion most people did, that Vera had been having a love affair with Chad Hamner, but to put the blame on Gerald. At first, though, he would not admit that a separation had taken place.

Vera didn't tell him about it. That wasn't her way. There was no question, of course, of Gerald being demobilized. He was a regular soldier. We had all supposed he would come home on leave and then, wherever he might be sent, possibly to Germany with the army of occupation, she would go with him. Laurel Cottage could then be sold and the proceeds divided three ways. However, Vera's letters made no mention of her accompanying Gerald when in the autumn he went with his regiment to somewhere near Lübeck, nor did she give any explanation or reason for her staying behind.

Eden quite often came to see us that winter, usually alone but once bringing Tony Pearmain to meet my parents. She was silent in a mysterious way on the subject of Vera and Gerald. That is, she gave the impression of knowing everything but of being unwilling to betray. It was Helen who told us.

She and my father had never really got on. He had always disliked her. He came near to admitting that he resented her being better off and having a higher social position than the children of my grandfather's second family. And his feelings were unaltered by the fact that Helen only had these things because her own father had rejected her. She was impossibly affected, he used to say. But they had never been not on speaking terms; there had never been an open quarrel. Helen wrote to him to ask if he would have any objection to her giving Eden's wedding reception at her house, and in this letter she mentioned the Vera-Gerald split.

At least my father already knew Eden was going to marry Tony Pearmain. Only just, but he had been told. Eden rang him up with the news the night before it was in *The Times*. Of course she shied away from telling him, because although Tony was more than suitable, was a great catch in fact and all that he should be in the eyes of an older brother, he was not Chad Hamner. My father really did go on about this sort of thing, behaving as if human beings were biologically monogamous, imprinted with the image of a single partner as the gray goose is or the gibbon. In his view, changing the mate you had first selected was tantamount to a defiance of nature. He looked gloomy when he put the phone down and came across the room to us shaking his head. I could find it in my heart to feel sorry for Eden, who had been bubbling over with excitement and had surely not expected her brother to be quite so aghast.

Apparently he had believed Tony was some sort of relative of her employer (we all knew about the Lady Rogerson setup by then) and that Eden occasionally acted as his secretary. My father was able to convince himself of anything he really wanted to be the case, however improbable, if only he tried hard enough.

"I had no idea," he said, passing his hand across his forehead in a bewildered way. "I thought she was all fixed up with that nice chap we met at the christening. I don't understand all this chopping and changing. What didn't she like about that journalist chap, I wonder?"

"Hadn't got enough money," said my mother.

"People don't always have to stick to the same person all their lives," I said, forseeing difficulties of my own in this area and not wanting, when the time came, to face too many inquests with my father. "Not when they meet them when they're eighteen, not for sixty years, surely?" It seemed appalling. "I don't think Eden was ever in love with Chad anyway or he with her. I don't think it was that kind of thing."

"What was it, then?" said my father. "He didn't come to the house to see my sister Vera, did he?"

This was said in the scathing tone of someone presenting a totally absurd proposition unworthy of serious consideration. It is rather disquieting to hear, as in this case, sarcasm and innocence combined. He was innocent. In the same tone he would have suggested Chad might have been coming to the house in order to make an offer for it or because Vera's wireless had better reception than his own. I said nothing, watching knowledge dawn in my mother's eyes and a smile twitch the corners of her mouth.

Next day we read the announcement in *The Times*: "The engagement is announced and the marriage will shortly take place between Anthony Fairfax Pearmain, only son of Mr. and Mrs. Oliver Pearmain, of Fontlands, Ripon, Yorkshire, and Edith Mary, youngest daughter of the late Mr. and Mrs. Arthur Longley, of Great Sindon, Essex."

Helen's letter came a few days later. This was not one of those my father read aloud at the breakfast table. He read it and walked out of the room, taking the letter with him. Presently he came back, looking very flustered and upset, and gave the letter to my mother, the first page first, then, reluctantly, the second.

"A very nice place to have a wedding," he said, making an effort. "That's a lovely house they've got there." He seemed to remember, which restored his gloom, his resentment of Helen's possession of Walbrooks, though he could surely never have convinced himself any other member of the family had a right to it. He turned pettishly to my mother. "You see what that silly, affected woman says."

"About the wedding, do you mean?"

She knew very well he didn't mean about the wedding but she said that to provoke him.

"Of course not about the wedding. About my sister Vera. Pernicious troublemaker, that woman is. Naturally my sister doesn't want to go off living in married quarters in Germany of all places."

But the damage was done. Or the truth was told. My mother just looked at him in that way she had developed lately when he made out, as she put it, that his sisters were "a double reincarnation of the Virgin Mary." She put her head on one side, opened her eyes wide, and raised her eyebrows as high as they would go.

What exactly had Helen suggested? I never saw that letter and it was lost long ago. Probably my father destroyed it that same day. I doubt though if Helen went so far as to put forward what was in my mother's mind, what she actually retorted to my father some months later when she was suffering during one of their quarrels from being unfavorably compared with his sister.

"Gerald knows very well Jamie isn't his child. He knows he can't be his child. He may be a fool but he's not such a fool he doesn't know a woman isn't pregnant ten months!"

I was embarrassed that I had overheard. I wanted no more of it and began to long for the autumn when I should go away to Girton and no longer hear them getting into each other's skin, under the scabs where the sores never quite healed. For a long time now I had come to my mother's conclusion, had done the requisite arithmetic and noted Vera's impossible gestation of something around 312 days. I had got used to the idea of Vera and Chad, too, and had almost persuaded myself that I had actually witnessed their embraces, their kisses. While I had been sleeping in Eden's room, I told myself,

Chad had come quietly to Vera, creeping up the stairs. It did not seem like him to do this. The whole affair seemed incongruous, Vera his senior and looking so much older, their sense of humor not at all the same, their tastes so divergent. But I had already learnt by then what a mysterious area sex is and how the reason for sexual relationships defies analysis. Jamie, of course, was Chad's child and that was why he had come to the christening—why also so many other people had not. Jamie had Chad's dark brown eyes and pale olive skin. I supposed there would be a divorce and Chad would marry Vera and this vaguely disappointed and irritated me. At the back of my mind was always the feeling that if only he would have waited, he could have had me.

It soon became very clear that Vera was going to live indefinitely at Laurel Cottage. I think there was some correspondence and a few phone calls as well as one interview between my father and Eden on this matter. There was no hardship for Eden. She was marrying a man whose family owned, Helen told me, no less than five country houses. Tony and Eden would be able to take their pick of which one they wanted to live in.

"Good-bye, new house, new car, holiday in Switzerland," said my mother.

"We couldn't have had all those, anyway," my father said.

"Just one of them would have been nice."

I should have liked to say to them that quite soon, no doubt, Chad would provide a home for his child and the mother of his child, but of course I didn't. To my father, Chad was the rather nice chap who still carried a torch for Eden. And my mother, who took an almost gleeful pleasure in the fact that Jamie could not be Gerald's child, never went so far as to provide an alternative father for him, speaking as though Vera had produced him by parthenogenesis and as if this in itself were a solecism that put her beyond the pale.

Eden was married to Tony Pearmain at St. Mary's, Great Sindon, on a fine, sunny Saturday in the summer of 1946.

11

WILL YOU BELIEVE that I was one of Eden's bridesmaids? My dress cost me not a single clothing coupon, for all the silk came to Eden from Hong Kong, brought in by someone she knew in BOAC. Part of the time I stayed at Helen's, part with Vera. It was during the week before the wedding, while I was at Laurel Cottage, that Vera and I and Jamie took that walk which led us past the cottage where Vera as a child had found old Mrs. Hislop's body. She was more expansive that day than I had ever known her but not so open that she could speak of the disappearance of Kathleen March.

The strange thing is that I have reached this point in my private reminiscing, my chronological going over in my thoughts of all my memories of Vera and Eden, of Chad and Francis and Jamie, when Daniel Stewart writes to me with his remarkable discovery. I even dreamed of Kathleen March the night before his letter came, having cast myself in the role of invisible onlooker watching Vera and Mavis sitting on the riverbank and the unguarded pram with the child in it standing among the willow herb and the meadowsweet. Kathleen's father passed me on the bridge, blinded by headache. What woke me was the horror that came out of the bright meadows, the blue sky, a black and scaly monster one can hardly believe a woman of my age would fantasize, a thing that stepped straight from the illustration to an Andrew Lang fairy story. It snatched the child and I woke up with one of those thin cries that are the dreamer's attempt at a scream.

The evening before I had been reading M. R. James's story *The Mezzotint* in which a similar incident to this takes place.

The morning post brings from Daniel Stewart a new chapter. He has stumbled on these facts by chance. He was sure no one else had spotted the connection. What did I think?

In the annals of unsolved murders, I read, the Kirby Theiston case must be one of the most bizarre and also the most neglected by criminologists. Is this because it has so many features in common with the Constance Kent mystery? Or because, until very recently, the apparently most important characters in the drama were still alive?

Constance Kent, a young girl still in her teens, living in the village of Rode in Somerset, was tried for the murder of her infant half-brother and acquitted. May Durham, a girl of seventeen, living in the village of Kirby Theiston in Norfolk, was arrested for the murder of her two-year-old half-sister but released without being brought to trial. Constance, always suspected, always looked on askance, ended her life in a convent. More than half a century later, May Durham, equally ostracized, was exiled by her own family to Australia in the company of an aunt, where five years later she died of tuberculosis. In neither case was the true perpetrator ever found.

Kirby Theiston is a village with a population of around five hundred lying to the west of Norwich. In 1922 the population was rather greater than this and the dual-carriageway road which now bisects the village had not yet been built. The church is Saint Michael and All Angels and the principal house, Theiston Hall, once the seat of a branch of the Digby family of Holkham, was occupied as it had been for the previous twenty years by Charles Ethelred Durham and his family. A fine English country house is Theiston Hall, parts of it dating from the fifteenth century, but largely rebuilt at the end of the seventeenth by Henry Dill, a pupil of Archer, in the baroque style with a bowed south front, octagonal drawing room and hall with ceiling paintings by Thornhill. Durham was the grandson of a wealthy Victorian manufacturer of cotton goods from Rochdale, but neither he nor his father had ever had any occupation beyond that of country gentlemen. No less a landscapist than Loudon had designed the gardens in the late nineteenth century, but Durham, a dilettante with artistic aspirations, uprooted the herbaceous borders, the parterres, and the rosebeds soon after he came to Theiston and set about creating gardens on the model of those he had seen while traveling in

Italy, at Bagnaia, at Settignano and the gardens of the Villa d'Este at Tivoli. Large quantities of statuary were imported and as late as 1922 men were still at work on the steps, ornamental ponds, follies, and temples necessary to the "Italianization" of the garden.

Durham was forty-six years old and had been twice married. His first wife, Honoria Filby, died when she was only twenty-seven, leaving him with a son, Charles, always called Charlie, and a daughter, Honoria Mary, known as May. Durham married again seven years later in 1917 the daughter of a doctor with a prosperous practice in Norwich. Her name was Irene McAllister and by 1920 she had borne him three children, Edward, Julius, and Sonia. This last was something of a vogue name in the late teens and early twenties of the century, due not to Russian influence, the Russian Revolution having taken place in 1917, but to a novel by Stephen McKenna with a heroine and title of that name, published the same year. The little girl, however, was always called Sunny, partly due to her particularly sweet nature and partly to her brother Edward's having made this diminutive of "Sonia."

The household, therefore, at the time of the murder was a large one, consisting of Mr. and Mrs. Durham, Charlie, May, Edward, Julius, and Sunny, with their servants, a butler called Thomas Chapman, Mrs. Deedes, the housekeeper, Mrs. Brown, the cook, two housemaids, a parlormaid, a kitchen maid, Sarah Keringle, the children's nurse, and the undernurse, Bessie Stonebridge. Three gardeners were also employed, John Williams, the head gardener, Thomas Pritchard, and Arthur Bailey. The land adjoining Theiston Hall was extensive and included thirty acres of woodland. Pheasants and partridges were preserved and Durham employed a gamekeeper, Robert Jephson, who occupied a cottage on the property next door to that in which John Williams, the head gardener, lived. In the month of May of 1922, the only member of this household not at home was Charlie, he being up at Oxford in his second year at Worcester College. Everyone else was present and the usual number was, in fact, augmented by the presence of guests in Jephson's cottage, for his sister, her husband, and their two children were staying with him and his wife as they usually did at this time of the year. This visit served the double purpose of providing them with a holiday and securing help to Jephson in the rather finicking and time-consuming task of collecting the fallen eggs of game birds and setting them under hens or already sitting pheasants. The pheasant was a sacrosanct bird in those parts, precious at every phase of its life cycle, and there had been an unpleasant incident some years before when Jephson's predecessor, an elderly man called Brimley, had shot May Durham's pet cat when he caught it taking and decapitating pheasant chicks. Charles Durham had not exactly dismissed the man but had retired him on a small pension, depriving him of the cottage he had lived in for forty years.

May Durham was an extremely good-looking girl of seventeen years and nine months, with fine dark eyes and black hair so long she could sit on it but which she was considering having bobbed in the current fashion. She had been educated at home, her governess having left the previous Christmas, and Charles Durham had intended sending her to finishing school in France but that spring May had met the young Norwich architect Thierry Watkin. He had asked her to marry him but Durham refused to sanction an official engagement until they had known each other longer. May, therefore, was living at home with little to do but go calling with her stepmother, arrange flowers, play tennis. She seems to have had no hobbies or intellectual interests of any kind and although considered an accomplished pianist never lifted the lid of the piano after her governess left. Her relationship with her stepmother was an uneasy one, though she seemed to have got over the intense, fierce resentment she had shown when her father first remarried. Of her small half-brothers she was fond, playing with them, taking them out, and lavishing a good deal of attention on them, so that family friends smiled their approval at the projected marriage with Watkin, seeing May as the maternal type.

Sunny, however, she is said to have disliked. It is hard to imagine a beautiful, healthy, comfortably situated girl of seventeen disliking her two-year-old half-sister, especially as the child was known for her easy disposition and "sunny" temperament. On the other hand, two things about Sunny might, if we are to see May as paranoid, or a near-psychopath, have inspired a pathological dislike in her. She bore an extraordinarily close resemblance to her mother, Mrs. Irene Durham, and she was adored by her father to the extent perhaps of displacing May in his affections. Georgina Hallam-Saul, the only writer to have dealt at any length with the Kirby Theiston case, put forward a curious postulation. This is that in the first half of the twentieth century, more specifically from 1910 till about 1940, there was a definite cult of aligning blondness with beauty, so that a dark-haired woman was considered less well-favored than a fair one, often irre-spective of other claims to beauty such as feature, figure, or eye color. Now May Durham, as has been said, was dark-haired and with very dark coloring, olive skin, brown eyes. She favored her mother. Charles Durham inclined to fairness, his second wife was a very fair, pale-skinned blond and their daughter Sunny had golden hair and blue eyes. Miss Hallam-Saul suggests this as a cause of envy and resentment on May's part of her half-sister but Miss Hallam-Saul, of course, is committed to her theory of May as perpetrator.

It seems clear that May seldom chose to be accompained by the little girl when out in the garden or the grounds, while the little boys were always acceptable company on a walk or a visit to the various pet animals the Durham family kept—a pony, the sheepdog who had his kennel out in the stableyard, the guinea fowls in their run, the Olde English rabbits. However, on this particular Tuesday morning in May 1922, when May Durham set off with Edward and Julius to show them for the first time the kittens to which her cat (successor to the one shot by Brimley) had given birth a week before, she also took Sunny. This was the second brood of kittens the cat had produced and, like the first time, she had chosen to have them, not in the lying-in quarters prepared for her by May Durham in May's own bed-room, but in the hollowed-out trunk of an oak tree.

What happened during that visit no one knows. Now no one will ever know. May's account was simply that she lost Sunny. The cat, though gentle with its owner, scratched Edward when he touched it and for a few minutes all May's attention was given to him, comfort-ing him and wiping away the blood with her handkerchief. The tree where the cat's litter was was on the edge of the woods, not too far from the house but separated from it by the stable block and a pad-dock. According to May, she believed Sunny to be sitting on a log next to Julius, but when she turned round, Julius was still there and Sunny had disappeared.

Julius Durham, now sixty-six years old, remembers nothing of that day. He was only three. His brother, Edward, eighteen months his senior, recalls details of that morning, though he admits that much of what he "remembers" may be derived from what he was later told.

"May's cat scratched me on the hand. I suppose it was the first real pain I had ever felt. I don't remember blood, only May hugging me and telling me to be brave. Of course I was bawling and screaming. May tied her handkerchief round my hand and then I think we all started looking for Sunny, but as you know, we couldn't find her."

May seems not to have been too worried. She thought the child had gone back to the house on her own, rather a curious conclusion for her to have come to, considering Sunny was only just two and seldom walked any distance without being carried. And when May got back to the house with the boys, she made no enquiries about Sunny. The reason she gave the police for not doing so was that, in the distance, in the lane which linked the stableyard with that part of the grounds where the gardener's and gamekeeper's cottages were, she saw Bessie Stonebridge, the undernurse, talking to a woman and with them was a small girl she took for Sunny. In fact, this child was not a girl but a boy, nephew of the gamekeeper, and the woman was his mother. May Durham was shortsighted and it was vanity that stopped her wearing glasses.

It was therefore more than an hour later that Sunny was missed. The Durhams were giving a tennis party that afternoon to which the young people of the neighborhood were invited to play and their parents to watch. Pritchard had freshly marked out the court and May was with him checking the height of the net (one tennis racket's vertical height plus the measurement of the head held horizontally) when the nurse, Sarah Keringle, came to her to say it was time for Miss Sunny's luncheon. May, aghast, admitted she thought the child was with Bessie, but Bessie, for the past half-hour, had been in the nursery with the two little boys.

A search for Sunny was mounted, the searchers initially being Charles Durham, John Williams, and Arthur Bailey. They were later joined by Mrs. Durham and May. The first guest to arrive for the party—no one at Theiston Hall except Edward and Julius had had any lunch—was Thierry Watkin, and he too joined in the search. Sunny, however, could not be found and Charles Durham phoned the local police. To Thierry Watkin fell the unenviable task of turning away the party guests as they came.

The police arrived promptly enough, a village constable and later a sergeant from Norwich. They set about interviewing everyone who might have seen Sunny, beginning with the indoor and outdoor servants at Theiston Hall and proceeding to Theiston Kirby village. No one admitted to having seen her since eleven that morning. The occupants of Theiston Hall were obliged to go to bed that night without news of Sunny's whereabouts.

Next morning the child's body was found by Jephson's dog no more than fifty yards from the log where she had been sitting next to her brother. The body was in a shallow grave made by scooping up the leaf mold, a task that could easily have been done with the bare hands. Her throat had been cut.

There was no doubt it was murder. The mode of death put accident out of the question. Norfolk CID came and questioned May. Sarah Keringle had told them that when Miss May came for the children she had been wearing a blue print cotton frock but later, when checking the height of the tennis net, had changed it for a linen skirt and black-and-white jumper. Why, the police asked, had she changed her dress *before* checking the net, why not after luncheon and before the party? May said there had been blood on the blue dress from Edward's scratched hand. It was then that the police took May to Norwich to the police station.

She spent one night there and was released next day. Chief Inspector John Finch had satisfied himself by then that Edward had been scratched by May's cat and that Sunny's killer would not have got a few spots of blood on his or her clothes but have been liberally splashed with it. He and his men next turned their attention to the village and the various men living there known to be less respectable than their neighbors—one, for instance, who had spent a night in jail on a drunk-and-disorderly charge; another who was a known poacher. Needless to say, there was no one in Kirby Theiston who had ever remotely been suspected of child molestation, let alone the brutal murder of a child.

It was at this late stage that they finally came to question those relatives of Jephson who were guests in his cottage. An extraordinary aspect of the Kirby Theiston murder was that although Finch was told on that day of the discovery of Sunny's body that Jephson had his sister, his brother-in-law, and his two-and-a-half-year-old nephew staying with him, he showed no interest in them and made no attempt to talk to them until *five days after* Sunny disappeared. When he did come to question them, their visit was over and they were about to return to their own home at Sindon Road in Essex.

Robert Jephson's sister was named Adele and her husband was Albert March.

A year before, the Marches had also lost a child, also a girl, also two

years old—their daughter, Kathleen. This fact, it seems, was unknown to Chief Inspector Finch and his questions did not elicit it.
Miss Hallam-Saul, in her examination of the Kirby Theiston case,
does not mention it. Her mention of the March family is confined to
two paragraphs in the chapter on the characters and antecedents of
the outdoor servants at Theiston Hall.

In his collection of murder case histories, *Murder in East Anglia*,
James Moore-Whye gives pride of place to the Kirby Theiston mystery but he does not refer to the Marches beyond this slight reference
in the following paragraph: "Chief Inspector Finch asked permission
of Mrs. Jephson, the gamekeeper's wife, to search the cottage. The
hunt was on for bloodstained clothing and the knife which was the
murder weapon. Mrs. Jephson told Finch he could search all he liked
as she and her husband would not be there for an hour or two. They
were going to Norwich with her brother and sister-in-law, who had
been staying with them, to see them off at the station."

What questions, then, did Finch ask of Albert and Adele March?
Only, apparently, if they had ever seen the child Sunny and if they had
ever seen anyone suspicious hanging about the grounds. To both they
replied in the negative, left the house, and were never questioned again.

Sunny Durham's killer was never found. Irene Durham believed
her stepdaughter responsible, citing May's uncontrollable jealousy as
motive. Herself on the verge of a mental breakdown—she had been
pregnant when Sunny was killed and miscarried a week later—Irene
struck May in the face when the girl tried to offer her sympathy and
told her husband she and May could no longer continue to live under
the same roof. There had been no positive engagement with Thierry
Watkin, though something more than an understanding, but Watkin
did not renew his proposals. He called only once after the day of the
tennis party and shortly afterwards left the neighborhood. Gradually
it became obvious that the village believed May had killed her half-
sister and had never been brought to trial only through lack of proof.
One day she was stoned by a group of boys in the village and had
stitches inserted in her forehead.

Did her father think her guilty? Instead of a finishing school in
France, May was sent to a sanatorium near Brunnen in Switzerland,
her health, it was suggested, having given way under the strain. Prior
to this there had been no hint of May being phthisic, but it was of
tuberculosis she died five years later, having passed the previous four

in Melbourne in the company of her father's sister, Miss Mary Durham. Or did the Durham family somehow manage to hush up the fact that May, in fact, committed suicide?

Charles Durham died in 1939, his second wife, Irene, in 1962, his son, Charlie, five years after his stepmother. The son Irene gave birth to in 1925, christened Colin Jonathan, was killed climbing in the Himalayas in 1964. Only Edward and Julius Durham survive of the Durham family of Theiston Hall. The house is now a conference center. John Williams, the head gardener, died in 1932; Thomas Pritchard in 1942; Arthur Bailey in 1946; and Sarah Keringle in 1952. Bessie Stonebridge married, became the mother of four children of her own, and now, as Mrs. Dryburgh, aged eighty-one, lives with her married daughter in Aberdeen. Of the other indoor servants, only the kitchen maid, Margaret Otter, survives. At eighty, a single woman, she still lives in the neighborhood of Norwich. Robert and Kitty Jephson, a childless couple, died within months of each other in 1970. Adele March died at the age of ninety a month before this was written, having survived her first husband, Albert, by fifty-five years and her second husband, William Bacon, by sixteen.

Kathleen March was two when she disappeared. So was Sonia "Sunny" Durham. Each was in the care of a young girl and each young girl thereafter carried a stigma through life, the stigma of a universal, whispered belief that she was a child-killer. But the common factor in these cases surely is Albert March, known to have crossed the bridge at Sindon Weir round about the time of his child's disappearance, known to have been at Theiston Hall at the time of the disappearance of Sunny Durham. In the ten years between 1920 and 1930—from a year after March's marriage, that is, until the year of his death—no fewer than five female children between eighteen months and five years disappeared in the North Essex–South Suffolk area. March had received a head wound while in France in the war of 1914–18 and this had left him liable to crushing headaches of the migraine type. Had it also caused brain damage of another kind, so that while afflicted with this almost intolerable head pain he was driven to commit acts for which he was in no way personally responsible and which he forgot once the headache was past?

I laid down these sheets of manuscript as shocked and moved as Daniel Stewart would have had me, but not for the reasons he would have expected. It is true that I took in the burden of what he was saying, that all the evidence now pointed to Albert March having been guilty of Kathleen's murder and that therefore Vera must be exonerated, but I took it in with indifference; I had never thought Vera capable of killing a child.

What touched my feelings with a cold finger, what made me lay down the pages and find myself staring unseeing into the past, was the name Jonathan Durham. A Jonathan Durham had been Tony Pearmain's best man and had later married one of my fellow brides-maids the way best men are supposed to but seldom do. Was it the same Jonathan Durham? It must be. I remember he was a climber and that he came from somewhere in Norfolk. And he would have been the right age. Here indeed was the stealthy convergence of human lots. I remember him well as I remember everything about that day, Eden's wedding day.

Sweet-pea colors we bridesmaids wore and I was the one in pale purple. The sugar-pink one was called Evelyn Something and it was she who later married Jonathan. Eden had refused to wear slipper satin which was the fashion and had a billowing dress made (she told Vera and me) out of twenty yards of white tulle. She spent the night before the wedding at Laurel Cottage and Vera was the first to see her dressed in this amazing confection with its tight bodice and sleeves and huge skirt. A girl who worked for a local hairdresser (and who lived with her parents in Inkerman Terrace next door to the house that had been the Marches') came at nine in the morning to do her hair first and then Vera's. My hair, being very long and straight, didn't need doing. The night before, it had been quite like old times, Francis sleeping in the room on the other side of the landing, Eden and I sharing her room, the beds still as far removed from each other as possible. When she opened one of the drawers in the dressing table to hunt about for a pair of eyebrow tweezers, guilt got hold of me and I wondered if she had ever noticed my incursions into her privacy, if I had left a long brown hair behind or the marks of none-too-clean twelve-year-old fingers. But it was soon apparent that she had discarded every cosmetic and perfume that dressing table contained. She had gone up the scale now and nothing but top-rank French toiletries would do for her. But her sophistication did not extend to the appointments of the room. Before she got into bed, she unhooked the Peter Pan photograph from the wall.

"I mustn't forget to take that with me," she said. "That's absolutely my favorite statue, you know, Faith. It was wonderful being in London and seeing it every week."

I couldn't help remembering how she had been in London and had seen me but for reasons of her own chosen to ignore me.

"I suppose this room is going to be Jamie's," I said.

"Really, I haven't thought about it," she said. "You'll have to ask Vera."

Eden did not like children. Or so it seemed to me, seeing her with Jamie. She took very little notice of him except to tell him not to do things, more specifically not to touch things when the things were hers. She sat up in bed and transferred her engagement ring, which she wore night and day, from her left hand to her right. It was a spectacular ring, not so much a cluster as a *dome* of diamonds on a thin platinum band. Eden told me next morning that she hadn't slept a wink all night, and perhaps this was true. Since I *had* slept, I was in no position to judge.

Her face looked a bit drawn and her eyes puffy. I was getting my energy together to get up and go for my bath. We all had to have a bath and since I was the least important I was to have mine first, at seven-thirty, to allow time for the hot-water tank to heat up again.

Eden said, "Wait a minute," and astounded me by making me the recipient of the first confidence I had ever had from her. And what a confidence! I had begun to get over my awkward habit of blushing by then but I felt my cheeks burn and I looked away, not meeting her eyes.

The words burst from her, unchecked. "Is he going to know I'm not a virgin?"

"I don't know," I said. "How should I know?"

The six years between us were nothing, the relationship of aunt and niece was everything. A deep embarrassment conquered almost every other feeling. It wasn't until later that I reflected how incongruous it was that the girl who asked me this question was the same one who had stormed at my father over my failure to write a thank-you letter, the same one that had ignored me in the street.

"Only I'm not," she said. "They say men know."

"Only if they've slept with lots of girls, I should think," I said, common sense asserting itself. "Has he?"

She said she didn't know. She sat up, wrapping her arms round her knees. With her head tied up in a chiffon scarf, she looked like Hope sitting on the world in that picture. Grandmother Longley used to have a print of it in sepia, which disappeared when Vera took over.

"Why ask me?" I said. "Why not ask Vera? She's more likely to know."

"I can't." Crisp and desperate. "It's out of the question."

"I read somewhere," I said—all my experience came from books—"that you get the same results from riding. Horses, I mean. Did you used to ride?"

She shook her head. "That's something else I've got to tell him, that I've never been on a horse. He thinks I have. He's never known anyone who can't ride."

With difficulty I kept a straight face. "Well, don't go and tell him, will you? Not about the riding, the other thing. Remember what happened to Tess of the d'Urbervilles."

But Eden had never heard of Tess. While I was having my bath I wondered which of the men it was Eden had lost her virginity to. Chad? Surely not, if he was Vera's man and Jamie's father. I flinched at the whole idea. The naval officer, the Honorable, who got drowned? The man she had gone to the theater with? Or perhaps they had all been lovers of hers. I was intrigued and a bit shocked. This was 1946. The idea of a woman having lovers outside marriage was no longer horrifying, unspeakable, or the daring prerogative of an upper class, but it was still shocking to older people, and to my generation and Eden's, something to be discreet and reticent about. That, I thought, was why she didn't want to ask Vera's opinion. Vera was nearly forty and things had been different when she was young. I don't know how I managed to hold this view while at the same time believing that Vera had been unfaithful to Gerald and was having a love affair with Chad, but I did.

This must be the only instance I have ever known of a woman being given in marriage by her own nephew. My father had been hurt by Eden's failure to ask him to give her away. She gave him (on the phone) a typical Longley excuse—you couldn't call it a reason— for not asking him. He put the phone down and came back to my mother and me, putting a brave face on things.

"She says it wouldn't do, not when I've got a daughter of my own. She says it would be another thing if you were married and I'd already given you away."

"I'm afraid Faith can't get married just to oblige her," said my mother.

Francis was to do it. He came down to breakfast wearing the pin-striped trousers of his morning suit and the white shirt that went with it, though no tie. Vera fussed about, saying he would get egg on his clothes. Francis, of course, played up to this with a tease I had seen once before. He left the table, sat in an armchair, and balanced on one of its arms a full cup of tea in a saucer. Now, I had scarcely ever seen Francis do a maladroit thing; he was a very graceful, manually dexterous person, who never dropped or spilt things except on pur-pose. And if I knew this, Vera must know it much better. But she never learned. Francis played up to her anxieties, moving his elbow in such a way as to come within a quarter of an inch of the cup, shifting in the chair to make it rock, lifting the cup to his mouth and replacing it off-center in the saucer. If the tea had spilt, it would have gone all over his trousers and shirtsleeves too probably, or else onto Jamie, who had chosen that particular patch of carpet to sit on and play with a stack of old wooden bricks that had once been my father's.

Vera could move Jamie. She did, and he set up a howling until he was allowed back again. With Francis she could do nothing but beg him to move the cup. She even gave him a small side table, first removing all the knickknacks with which it was loaded. Francis re-sponded by placing on it the newspaper, his cigarettes, and an expensive-looking gold cigarette lighter. The tea he had hardly touched.

"It's got cold," he said. "I'd better have a fresh cup," and he tipped the tea away, refilling the cup and putting it back on the arm of the chair.

Why is it that really beautiful women when *en déshabillé* can look so much more awful than ordinary-looking ones? I have noticed this again and again. They think it unnecessary to bother, I suppose. Men have told them they would look beautiful in a sack and possibly they would, indeed they would, a sack might not be an unflattering garment; it is not sacks we are talking about, though, but grubby old blue flannel dressing gowns and tatty stained headscarves, dirty marabou mules and flaking nail varnish. Eden sat at the table exhib-iting all these, eating nothing, her face greasy, a bit of cherry skin from last night's supper trapped between her front teeth. Jamie, who was beginning to lose his total dependence on Vera as the only person in his world, went up to Eden with a toy car in his hand. She turned to him a face of impatient despair and without exactly pushing him away made at him that sort of gesture one makes when someone else's cat or dog is importunate—a brisk dismissive sweep of the arm.

Vera would never reproach Eden. They seemed less close than they had been, but this rule still held. She looked wretched.

"Come to Mummy, my darling," she said and she held out her arms to him.

It was extraordinary what happened then. The tea in the teacup having served its purpose, Francis poured it away, and going to Eden, raised her up into a standing position, took her in his arms, and hugged her closely.

"Bear up, my old love."

She hid her face in his shoulder. They stood there embraced, swaying slightly. I sat there at the table alone while on one side of me Vera hugged Jamie and on the other Francis hugged Eden, and at first I felt bored by them and then—the old feeling back again—left out.

Vera said in a dreary, neutral sort of voice:

"The hairdresser will be here in ten minutes."

Eden gave a little scream and let go of Francis.

"I have to talk to you!"

"Do you, sweetheart?" he said. "I expect that can be managed. My time is all yours. I am giving you my day."

I guessed she was going to ask him what she had asked me. And somehow I knew he would know the answer. He was the kind of person who always knows things like that.

"Go get your bath," he said, "and then we'll let our hair down and take our knickers off or whatever girls do when they talk."

"Francis!" Vera shouted at him. She held Jamie tight against her as if someone were menacing him. I thought she was going to reproach Francis for that remark about knickers. "Smut" she would call it. But she didn't. "What do you mean, 'talk'? What can you have to talk about? Eden's getting married at midday."

It was curious. I had the feeling she was talking to Eden, yet it was Francis she addressed in that hectoring tone she would never have used to Eden. Is it hindsight that makes me say she looked pale and frightened? I expect it is. Stupidly she said:

"I forbid you to upset Eden!"

He burst out laughing. The hairdresser rang the front doorbell and I went to let her in.

For some reason, perhaps because I saw him as Gerald's successor, I expected Chad to come to the house during the morning. But he didn't come and his name wasn't mentioned. My parents were staying at an hotel in Sudbury, the bridegroom and his family at a much grander one in Dedham. There were going to be two hundred people at this wedding. Eden had wanted to spend her last night as Miss Longley at the Chatterisses' house, Helen later told me, had almost taken it for granted she would, having in mind a grand dinner to impress her future in-laws. Helen would have been quite happy to produce the dinner but her heart bled (as she put it) for poor Vera.

"Think how unhappy she would be, darling," she had said to Eden. "Do stay that one night with her, I beg. You have so much and, really, when you come to think of it, she has so little."

And Eden, giving in with a bad grace, had said incomprehensibly, "I should have thought Vera had had quite enough of me."

On my way to dress, I passed Vera's open bedroom door and saw her inside dressing Jamie in blue shorts and white silk shirt. The last time I had seen them in there together, Jamie had been at Vera's breast. Her expression now was no less radiant, committed, adoring. Chad had told me that the way to make a character in fiction lovable is to give him something to love. His old mother will do, his spaniel will do, at a pinch his budgerigar will do. I had always rather disliked Vera but you couldn't dislike a woman who loved a child so dearly as Vera loved Jamie. She was transformed, softened, altogether sweetened by him. The awful word for what he was doing for her is "tenderizing," the process used on steak.

"We thought he could be Aunt Eden's page, didn't we, my lovely?" she said. "But Aunt Eden didn't like the idea. She thought children might be troublesome. Which," she added reasonably, "is quite understandable."

What has become of Eden's wedding photographs? I suppose Tony has them still or, more likely, has long ago thrown them away. He has never remarried and spends most of his time abroad. In the Far. There is one wedding picture of Eden in "the box," posed alone, but perhaps no record now exists of how Eden and Francis looked together, glorious fair-haired twins that they seemed, a Hollywood bridal couple in the days when film stars were beautiful people, films were sleek and polished, and grooming was obligatory before attending any function. They were a little unreal too, waiting there in Vera's living room, standing because sitting more than she had to would have crumpled Eden's tulle. Waxworks they might have been with their smooth faces and gleaming hair, the sheen on their clothes and the stiffness in their fingers, facsimiles of people someone had the forethought to make, knowing that one day Tussaud's might be glad to have them. But it is Vera only who stands in Tussaud's, her effigy plumper and glossier than the real woman ever was, but by some grotesque accident or design, dressed in the suit she wore for Eden's wedding, dark blue with a fall of blue-and-white-spotted foulard at the neck.

When I walked up the aisle behind Eden, one of a bevy of whom Evelyn, who married Jonathan Durham, Patricia Chatteriss, and a Naughton cousin called Audrey were the others, I saw Chad in a front pew on the bride's side but a long way from Vera, who with Jamie was correctly sandwiched between Helen and my mother. On the other side of Helen, between her and the General, sat their son, Andrew, who had been a Hurricane pilot in the Battle of Britain and then a prisoner of war, my cousin but not quite my cousin, for we had one, not two grandparents in common. Darker than any of us Longleys, he had a cadaverous look about him then, his face all hollows, his cheeks wasted. In the camp he had got very thin and had never regained that lost weight. To me there was something intensely romantic about his appearance, something heroic. What must it have been like to have an aircraft disintegrate around you, to embark on that terrible fall amid the fireworks of antiaircraft guns, to drift down through the night sky into the enemy's country where God knew what awaited you? I looked at him and, without smiling, he winked at me. Later on I was pretty sure that wink had been meant for his sister, but at the time I thought it was for me.

Chad was staring in Eden's direction with a peculiar, suffering intensity. It made me wonder if he had turned to Vera when Eden rejected him. I turned my eyes away, fixing them on the back of Eden's veil, not wanting later to be accused by Vera of unbridesmaidenly behavior. What can you say about a wedding? All weddings are the same, all brides are beautiful, all flower arrangements the loveliest one has ever seen, all music the best one has ever heard—till next time. Except in *Jane Eyre,* no one ever does get up and speak of impediments. And for all the curious circumstances surrounding Eden's wedding, the paranoid strangeness of hers and Vera's behavior, no one could justifiably have done so. What had happened did not constitute an impediment in the legal sense, though no doubt it would have done in Tony Pearmain's eyes.

Who had chosen the Wedding March from *The Marriage of Figaro* for the walk back down the aisle? Not Eden, who, I am sure, had scarcely heard of Mozart. Tony, then, or his mother, or his best man. It was a brave attempt at being original which failed because that march was written for an orchestra and defies all arrangements for the organ. The organist—sister of Mrs. Deliss at the priory—did her best, and the instrument jerked and wheezed and pounded and none of us knew how to walk in time to it, finally adopting a kind of goose step. I could see people in the congregation wincing. Chad, who I thought would sympathize with Eden, winced too and then went through the lip-pursing, face-contorting motions of someone who can't repress his laughter. He put his handkerchief up to his face and pretended to blow his nose.

Jamie sat quiet throughout the ceremony and came, quiet and awed, to Helen's house. But there he fell in with the caterers' people, maids who carried him off to the kitchens, swathed him in dinner napkins, and fed him with ice cream. Food was served in the dining room, which had French windows opening onto the lawn, and poor enough food it was in 1946, needy nothing trimmed in jollity, the Richardson silver and the flowers distracting the mind and palate too from chicken and Spam, rabbit vol-au-vent, and mock cream. It was a marvelous, hot day, one of those rare English summer days which are clear as well as sunny and there is no haze to mask the sky. Somehow or other, without help, the Chatterisses had managed to keep the garden going throughout the war. Helen, who looked as if her hands had never done heavier work than fine sewing or the washing of porcelain, had spent part of every day gardening while Andrew was missing, the best method, she used to say, of bringing herself a measure of peace of mind. Knowing nothing about it but modeling her herbaceous borders on those she had seen on a prewar visit to Glyndebourne, she had gone about her neighbors' gardens helping herself to snippets and cuttings of their plants until those borders that in Richardson days had held nothing but roses and lavender bushes now formed long, thick ribbons of color, filled as they were with the crimson and ivory spires of astilbe, with agapanthus, the blue poppy, and echinops, the blue thistle, with nepeta in a blue mist, silvery artemisia and cineraria, with southernwood that is called lad's-love, and alchimela mollis, the maiden's breath. The lawns ran down to the shallow sheet of water, lily-covered, that Helen called a pond and Vera, when speaking of it to acquaintances, "the lake." Standing by the water's edge with a glass of something that was not quite champagne in my hand, feeling with my toes through my thin pumps (satin shoes of my mother's from the twenties dyed purple) the iron-hard, calluslike remains of the great tree stump under the turf, I asked Andrew if they had imported the swans specially for the wedding. They drifted, with a dignity that was indifferent to these human watchers, among the bronze-colored, dish-shaped lily leaves and under the willows that trailed their hoar leaves in the glassy stream.

"They arrived yesterday," he said. "We're very pleased to see them. There've been no swans at Walbrooks since the pair were shot."

"Someone shot swans?" I said.

"Don't you know the story?"

"I never know stories," I said. "I don't know how it is that everyone knows them but me, but that's the way it always is. I didn't know about Vera saving Eden's life under the tree that used to be here until three years ago."

"Oh, *that*." It was Francis. No one could sneer so splendidly as Francis. He had come up behind me with Chad.

"Well, it happened," I said.

"She always had the instincts of a girl guide."

"Tell me about the swans," I said to Andrew.

"My great-grandparents, my mother's grandparents who used to live here, had a little boy. His name was Frederick and if he were alive today he would be seventy-eight. But they lost both their children, their son when he was three and their daughter, my mother's mother, in her twenties. There was a pair of swans nesting on the pond here. Frederick had a nurse who was an ignorant, backward sort of girl, more or less retarded, I suppose. She took him to the pond and showed him the cygnets, and the cob—that's the male swan—attacked him and . . . well, beat him to death with its wings."

"That's horrible!" I said.

"Yes. They dismissed the nurse. My great-grandfather got his shotgun and came down here and shot the cob and the pen and all the cygnets. I suppose he was out of his mind with shock and misery. But now after seventy-five years, the swans have come back."

Francis drawled, "Do you suppose these have a family in the reeds? Perhaps we should get one of the caterers' girls—the one who dropped the sherry bottle—to bring Jamie down here."

There was a shocked silence. Then Chad said:

"Not really amusing, dear lad."

"That depends on your taste," said Francis. "I find I have a particularly sophisticated idea of what constitutes entertainment. For instance, I have often thought how much I should have enjoyed the Roman games. I should have liked to do what Wilde said Domitian did and peered through a clear emerald at the red shambles of the Circus."

Andrew said nothing but his face was very severe and condemnatory. Chad was laughing. He began telling us how his grandfather had refused to let his mother, at the time a woman of twenty-five, keep a copy of *Dorian Gray* in the house. But suddenly he fell silent and quoted, in quite a different sort of voice:

"'There is no name, with whatever emphasis of passionate love repeated, of which the echo is not faint at last.'" He seemed to be addressing the swans. "And thank God for that," he said.

He and Francis went off—to tease someone else, presumably.

"I thought it unfortunate," Andrew said, "their mentioning Oscar Wilde in quite that way and quoting him too in your presence."

I was enchanted by his gentlemanlike, not to say courtly, behavior. I was so overcome I forebore to point out that the quotation was from Landor, not Wilde.

"An extraordinary pair. I find it hard to think of Francis as my cousin."

"Do you find it hard to think of *me* as your cousin?" I said, emboldened by the mock champagne.

"I don't think I do quite. Think of you as my cousin, I mean. Do you want me to?"

"Oh, no."

He looked curiously at me. Patricia and Evelyn and Jonathan Durham were approaching us across the lawn.

"Francis is up at Cambridge, isn't he?"

"Oxford," I said.

"I must say that's rather a relief. I'm going up to Cambridge in October." I did not tell him that I was too. Why tell him something it would be more interesting for him to discover from some other source? "I shall be rather a mature undergraduate," he said, and broke off to introduce Jonathan to me.

I wonder now if Andrew had delayed telling the story of the little Richardson boy and the swans until Jonathan had joined us, would Jonathan have spoken of his own sister, killed at the same age? And if he had, mentioning Jephson in the telling, would I have made the connection forty years before Daniel Stewart? But the swan story was past and Jonathan had not heard it and soon it was time for Eden and Tony to leave for their honeymoon in a borrowed house in Derbyshire. Why is it that the upper classes, or at any rate the rich, from the royal family down, are lent country houses by their relatives for honeymoons while the rest of us go to such more interesting and exciting places as Brighton or Paris or Capri?

Back we went to Laurel Cottage, Vera and I and Jamie. This was pure altruism on my part and I was proud of myself for it. My parents had gone back to London. Helen asked me to stay at Walbrooks "with the rest of the young people" and I would have liked to, I would have liked to very much, and surely it would be more tactful to leave Vera alone with Chad for the evening and perhaps the night?

"Jamie and I will be all on our own, then," she said a little peevishly.

I thought this unlikely. Francis would surely be there. He was in the room with Helen and Vera and me while we discussed this, standing apart and listening in that way he had, like a character in the Jacobean drama, Bosola, for instance, gathering crumbs for future malicious use, I thought. But I said I would go back with Vera. Perhaps I sensed that today she had finally lost Eden forever. I was unprepared for her cheerful manner, a quite unforced contentment, on the way home in Mr. Morrell's car and afterwards as she was getting Jamie ready for bed.

"Things went very well, didn't they?" she said, dipping him into the bath amid his flotilla of toys. "The weather couldn't have been better and it was a lovely service. Didn't you think the music was lovely?"

"Well," I said, "I wasn't too keen on that march they went out to. It sounded as if something had got broken in the organ."

"Blessed is he," said Vera, "who sitteth not in the seat of the scornful."

This was a favorite Bible quote of hers and my father's, Eden's too for all I know. They got it from their own mother. Considering their attitude to life, this is as fine an example of projection as one might come across. I should have known better than to criticize anything connected with Eden. Vera soaped Jamie and gently splashed him and he shrieked with delight and splashed her back. When she said that about the seat of the scornful, her face had creased up and packed itself into a hard, fixed mask. She was already getting that vertical pleating on her upper lip most people don't develop before fifty. But playing with Jamie she was transformed again, young again, with the untried, innocent face of the portrait in "the box."

She surprised me by talking of Eden in a way I had never thought possible. I suppose she was beginning to think of me as grown-up. Up till then she had referred to Eden only to praise something she had made or done or to boast of her friends and her social position.

"If I'm not much mistaken" (another typical Longley phrase, this one), "Eden will have a baby within the year. You can imagine *he*'ll want children—well, he'll want an heir and his father will."

It sounded feudal to me and I didn't feel I had any comment to make on it.

"Yes, they'll want a son. Of course Eden loves children, she worships them."

That was not how it had seemed to me when I saw her push Jamie away that morning or on the innumerable occasions I had seen her ignore him when he spoke to her.

"Eden will want six, you can be sure of that. And since money is no object, I see no reason why they shouldn't have a big family. If I'm not much mistaken, my dear, the next big function we go to will be Eden's son's christening. He'll be a very lucky little boy." This was addressed to the now dry, powdered, pajamaed, sleepy Jamie. "Everything handed to him on a gold platter. But one thing's for sure, isn't it, my sweetheart, he won't have more love than my boy. That's something no amount of money can buy."

Francis had not returned with us and now, two hours later, he had not appeared. Vera, tucking Jamie up in bed, lifted her face from kissing him and said:

"They're so lovely when they're little, and when they grow up they're just people. They're not like you, they haven't got your ways and they're more unpleasant to you than they are to their worst enemy."

I listened, fascinated, amazed at this unexpected sensitivity, hoping for more, destined, of course, to be disappointed.

"He isn't going to be like that, though, are you, my sweetheart? Francis was too much with other people, you know, that was the trouble. His ayah first, then his school. He hardly knew me. Little children are best when they are just with their mothers. You can see that in pictures of primitive people, can't you, savages and aborigines and so on. Those people always have their babies on their backs. I am going to see to it Jamie and I are never apart."

Chad didn't come either. The sun had gone in at about six—if I were an adherent of the Pathetic Fallacy I would say it went in when Eden left—and the long summer evening was dull and gloomy. There is something depressing, anyway, about the evening after a wedding. One feels excluded. The point is that one *is* excluded, everyone is except the two that it was all for, for what they are embarking on no one may share in. It is rather as if one went along to the opera and had tea in the tea tent, walked round the lake, drank the champagne and, just as the curtain went up, was sent home again. I could have said that to Anne Cambus, to Chad, perhaps to Andrew Chatteriss, but not to Vera. So we sat there more or less in silence, she knitting a jumper for Jamie in a complicated Fair Isle pattern, I reading until the light failed. Vera had long given up attempting to teach me to knit or sew or crochet and she seemed resigned to my reading, though I believe she thought it a wicked waste of time. That evening, though, she had the advantage of me for she had reached a plain section of the jumper and could do the stocking stitch without looking at her work. For reasons of economy, presumably, she was always loath to put lights on. She deferred it even longer than usual and when I suggested having the table lamp on just for me, she reacted like the old irritable Vera of my childhood.

"The room will be full of insects. All those moths will get in." It was impossible to convince her that not all moths, indeed not the vast majority, are the kind that eat your clothes. And this was a misapprehension made all the more ironic by the fact that her son was destined to become a distinguished entomologist. "We shall be riddled with moths," she said. "I should have thought it was so peaceful just to sit in the twilight for once."

In the twilight we sat, Vera's fingers moving automatically, and the needles, wooden wartime needles, making a soft click-click-click. What did I think about? Eden's wedding night, I fear. Young people then were more given to prurient curiosity. Experience came later to them and less variously. Principally I wondered how she had overcome, if she had overcome it, Tony's finding out he wasn't the first. Vera's earlier remarks about Eden's fondness for children and the large family she would have interested me hardly at all at the time and

I am surprised now that I remember them. Probably my memory is inaccurate, though I am sure the gist, the essential inner sense of those remarks, remains. I have often thought of them since.

Was she afraid even then? Were her Eumenides gathering, sitting like crows in the trees about the darkening lawn or fluttering against the windowpanes like the moths she so disliked? I think so. I think future events cast their shadows even then, like the real shadows which suddenly flared in long bands across the lawn as the sun appeared briefly again before its setting.

It may be fanciful of me but I expect she thought she had paid. She had rendered up a heavy price: her husband, her freedom, a financially comfortable future, whatever of Francis she might have salvaged, Eden's devotion. She had given this enormous ransom to the Furies and I expect she hoped that they would keep away. One small thing only the gods had to do for her, and why shouldn't they do it? For most women they did it, too frequently sometimes, constituting a curse and not a blessing. So why not here, in this instance? You might also have said of Vera that she wanted only to be left alone. When she said she wanted to sit in peace in the twilight, she meant that in more than a literal sense. I hardly think that the news which came to her almost immediately Eden returned from her honeymoon could have pleased her, though at the time the rest of the family saw it as being particularly to her advantage. Did her heart sink? Did she feel trapped? No doubt she prayed that the next letter would bring her the news she longed for or that one evening the telephone would ring. . . .

The dusk grew depressing. I said that I thought of going down to the Cambuses for a while. Vera uttered her automatic "At this hour?" but put up no more objections. I think this must have been just before she met the new Mrs. Cambus, who was to become her dear friend and support (and principal witness for the defense at her trial), or at any rate before she got to know her well, for in saying good-bye to me she did not mention her but merely told me to be sure and bolt the back door after me when I came in. How far I had progressed in growing up since the eight-o'clock-bedtime days—or how far she had in tolerance! But Josie Cambus was not mentioned as she certainly would have been had this visit been paid two or three months later, when all sorts of messages would have been given to me to deliver, and Vera's love sent.

Anne's mother had died of cancer and within six months her father had married again. My husband says Donald Cambus and Josie had been lovers for a long time and I think Anne suspected this, therefore resenting her new stepmother more than she might otherwise have done. Josie, who had been a widow with two sons, she saw as longing for her lover's wife to die, jubilant at her death, impatient to step into her shoes, though in fact I don't think this was Josie's nature at all. I got to know her well, eventually very well indeed, and I came to understand that her principal trait was *motherliness;* she was one of those people whose mission in life is to look after other people, and in coming to Sindon, giving up her secretarial job, her house in a suburb of London, she was driven as much by a desire to retrieve Donald Cambus's household and care for his children as by the need to be with him always.

But that evening she and Donald were out and Anne and I spent an hour or two alone together, talking about the wedding of course, about Eden's anxious inquiry of the morning (which I am afraid I unhesitatingly repeated), and then Anne grew venomous about poor Josie and what she called her designing ways. For her part, she couldn't wait to get away to teacher-training college, from which, she said, she would never return to her father's house.

I went home to Laurel Cottage the back way, something I had rarely been in the habit of doing at night. The gate in the back fence of the Cambuses' garden led into a narrow lane or path that eventually, after crossing the edge of a field, cutting the corner of a farmyard, and running between high flint walls, passed the back fence of the Laurel Cottage garden. The reason I avoided it was the farmer's dog, a black Labrador with a nasty temper. But this dog I had seen from the Cambuses' living-room window, setting out on a walk, correctly leashed, with its owner, so I took to the path, having switched on my torch. It was a bit after half-past ten.

Very dark. A dense, humid, by now quite cold, moonless night. Nobody knows what darkness is until they have lived in an English country village where the inhabitants stoutly oppose the installation of streetlamps. It was impossible to see anything that night except a sort of lightening of the blackness overhead and a deepening of the blackness where a hedge was or a wall or a tree. It was easy enough to find my way with the torch. I came to the gate in the Laurel Cottage fence and there saw the first lights since I had left the Cambuses'. There was a light on in Vera's bedroom and the faintest gleam or glow of light from the hovel.

It was still standing, still threatening to collapse without going further towards doing so. The falling house that never falls. Eden's Wendy house it had been, where she had played with dolls, washing them and mending their clothes, no doubt, putting them to bed at six. Inside its crumbling wattle and daub Anne and I had acted out, over and over, the tragedy of Mary Stuart, blowing up Darnley and hiding Rizzio in vain behind her skirts. As I came towards it, its broken window flared with light, with guttering bouncing light. How far this little candle throws his beams! So shines a good deed in a naughty world.

They didn't see me. They were otherwise occupied and their eyes were not for seeing passersby. Their light, a candle in a saucer on the gateleg table, was to enable them just to see each other. Out of politeness, I turned off my torch. If this sounds blasé, if it sounds as if I wasn't shocked, horrified, aghast, overturned into a tumult, it is not so, for I was, I was all those things. But discretion did not quite leave me, that and a shrinking from their seeing that I had seen *them*.

I looked once and went on towards the house. Chad and Francis were making love, undoubted, uncompromising sodomy—for I saw all that in their forked-radish nakedness—on the hovel floor.

12

EDEN COULD HAVE had her pick of Pearmain houses. Instead she chose to buy Goodney Hall. My father was delighted and so was Helen. She and Vera would hardly be separated now, they would be able to see each other two or three times a week, for Tony's wedding present to Eden had been a car.

People said it was sweet of Eden, it was considerate of her, to make her home near her sister's. Later on they said it was malicious. I don't believe kindness or malice came into it. Eden had been brought up by Vera to be a snob and she had outdistanced her mentor. All her life, I think, she had longed and longed to be rich and have the power wealth brings, and whereas Vera frankly and honestly basked in the reflected glory of Helen's prestige, enjoying it vicariously, proud just to be able to have Helen for her sister and drop her name in company, Eden had envied her and felt resentment in much the way my father did. Now she could turn the tables on Helen. Walbrooks, after all, was only a farmhouse, if a grand one. Goodney Hall, at Goodney Parva on the Stoke side of the Stour, was what my grandmother Longley called a "gentleman's house," and it was rather better than that, for it had been designed in 1786 by Steuart, who was the architect of Attingham Park in Shropshire and St. Chad's church in Shrewsbury. It had a portico with immensely long columns, a Chinese drawing room and principal bedroom described as Etruscan, and altogether it reminded me of the Pavilion at Brighton. But it was exactly what Eden wanted, it brought her ascendancy over Helen and almost everyone else she knew. When my father next wrote to Vera, he told her how pleased he was, but in her reply Eden and her move were not mentioned. Nor did Eden herself reply to the letter he sent her, asking her, now she was so comfortably settled, to consider he and she making over their shares in Laurel Cottage to Vera. And this may have been just as well, for mention of the project made my mother furious, igniting fearful quarrels between my parents.

"If you do that, I swear I'll leave you," she said to him, "and then you won't be able to give houses away, you'll have to find a home for me."

My father hoped, and constantly expressed this hope, that Gerald and Vera would patch up their differences and live together again. They were not divorced and in those days before divorce became so easy as it did in the early seventies, had no prospect of being so. Adultery was a possible ground, yet I now wondered, in the light of what I knew, if there had indeed been adultery. Ten-month children were not unknown, if rare. Blue-eyed parents may have a brown-eyed child if there are brown eyes among their forebears. Perhaps Gerald had known all this, had known there was no adultery, and the separation had come about simply because he and Vera had ceased to love each other, had grown indifferent or preferred the single life the war had taught them both to live. One thing was certain. Chad Hamner was not her lover and never had been. Jamie was not his son.

So many things became clear as a result of what I saw that night, by candlelight, in the hovel at the end of Vera's garden. So much was changed. I was no go-between, though; I was no traumatized witness of a primal scene. It is true that I slept very little that night; it had been a shock what I saw, but it was rather an *interesting,* a fascinating shock than an unpleasant one. It explained so much, and some of it not unflattering, a relief really, to myself.

As a possible lover of my own, the first perhaps, Chad had been put out of the running by becoming (as I thought) Vera's. After I thought he was Vera's I was not such a fool as to want him or to hope for him anymore. But I had still minded that he could have preferred Vera to me; I was disappointed about that. I believed that he had loved Eden but that this was an early rehearsal for coming to love me; I thought he should have waited for me, and that it was only impatience or weakness of character that made him turn instead to Vera. I

was relieved to understand none of this was so. I looked back, intrigued out of the possibility of sleep or thinking of anything else, by
the revelations, the clarifications of so many words and acts of the
past years.

Those inexplicable visits to the house in Eden's absence, always
the day before Francis was due home or when a phone call from Francis was expected—these were explained. Those declarations of the
hopelessness of his love, his remark to my father that brave hearts and
persistence will not always triumph, his gazing in church, not at
Eden as I had believed, but at Francis, who escorted her—all these I
now understood. And I understood Francis's coquettish behavior, his
posing, his wit, in Chad's presence. Somehow I knew, too, that this
was not a happy love, a relationship of mutual desire and affection,
but one-sided, a case of there being one who kisses and one who lets
himself be kissed. But that not often, perhaps less and less often, and
at a price, Francis occasionally yielding rarefied favors to strengthen
his hold.

And I saw something else, though not that night, not until I was
myself older and better versed in these things. Chad had met Francis
through Eden. How else would they ever have met each other?
Chad—who had moved away, who had succeeded in getting himself
a job on the *Oxford Mail* to be in the city where Francis was—had
worked on the local paper in Colchester then and Eden had been
working for her solicitor. Whether they had met in court or at a cocktail party or in the solicitor's office hardly mattered. They had met
and Eden had introduced him to Francis. That meant she must have
known. That meant that at eighteen, when Francis was only thirteen,
she had known, had connived at and certainly encouraged a love
affair which in the 1940's was regarded by most people as corrupt,
disgusting, monstrous and beyond words, unnatural. In other
words, she had brought home to her sister's house a man who loved
boys and had presented to him her sister's child as his catamite. As
her accredited lover he came, or rather her suitor, so that he might set
about—though not very successfully, not very happily, Francis being
what he was—seducing a prepubertal boy.

I was never outraged, knowing Francis as I did, but I was astounded. I would not have thought Eden had it in her. Why had she
done it? What was in it for her? I have never known and I don't know
now. I can only make guesses. Secrets, having them, creating them,
keeping them and half-keeping them, were the breath of life to her,

and here was a secret she could keep from Vera. Or it may have been more practical and less neurotic than that. It may have been that in those days before she went into the WRNS, when she presented to the world the image of untouched, beautiful, innocent girlhood, a girl within a budding grove, an almost Victorian concept of perfect girlhood, quiet, meek, pure, accomplished, she was in fact engaged in a love affair with someone totally unsuitable. I rather incline to this view, based on guesswork though it is. It is so entirely the kind of thing Eden would have done, secretly met her uncouth or merely married lover, someone anyway Vera and my father and Helen and all would utterly have disapproved of, while Vera believed her in the safe company of Chad. And Chad, for his own purposes, would willingly have connived at this, while Francis watched the game with amusement, occasionally playing a hand or two when the fancy took him. Poor Vera, I had been used to thinking of her as in control, a presiding authority. I began to see her as everyone's dupe. Neither of these descriptions, of course, was entirely true, for she had alternated between the two.

And now Eden was installed, chatelainelike, at Goodney Hall, "a stone's throw" as my father put it, from Great Sindon, though in fact it was ten minutes' drive away, on the Suffolk side of the Stour Valley where the Weeping Hills rise and dip and roll away towards the Vale of Dedham. It was a year before I saw the house, for I had gone up to Cambridge the autumn after the wedding, and the following year when I returned to these places, to this neighborhood, in the long vacation, it was with the Chatterisses I stayed and not with Vera or Eden.

People had started going abroad again for their holidays. Tony had taken Eden to Switzerland, to Lucerne, and Helen had had a postcard with a picture on it of Mount Pilatus, the lake in the summit of which is one of the seven ancient entrances to hell and where Pontius Pilate forever sits washing his hands. Vera's card was of a chair lift and she seemed disproportionately pleased with it, even bringing it with her when she and Jamie came over for lunch next day.

"I expect they are making the most of it," she said. "This will be their last chance to go anywhere like that for a long time."

"Eden will have a nanny for the baby," Helen said. "It won't make that much difference to their lives."

This was the first I had heard of Eden's baby. She was not yet quite two months pregnant. Vera could talk of nothing else. She was over-joyed. Eden had been married more than a year now, she, Vera, had begun to wonder if anything could be wrong, for she knew how pas-sionately Eden longed for children, but now all was well. Vera specu-lated as to the child's sex, what name would be chosen, whom it would look like, precisely when it would be born and what kind of labor Eden would have. This went on all through lunch, kind Helen showing no impatience, listening and responding to Vera, but the General and Andrew and I restless and bored and Patricia, who had come home for a week's stay, frankly asking once or twice (though in vain) if we couldn't change the subject.

"I was the first to be told," Vera said. "Do you know, Eden told me what she suspected even before she told Tony? She said: I think, I hope, I'm almost certain I'm going to have a baby and I want you to be its godmother. I was so happy I burst into tears."

Jamie was three and a bit, articulate in speech now, a "good," quiet boy who still had a sleep in the afternoons and went to bed by six-thirty. He seemed intelligent. He had rather a stilted way of talk-ing which was naturally appealing in such a young child because it was "quaint." He would refer to "adults" instead of "grown-ups," for instance, and get all his past tenses right, never saying "rided" for "rode" or "eated" for "ate." And he was a happy child, he was very happy then, I would vouch for that. I wonder if he remembered that visit, that day at Walbrooks, when he chose to call himself an Italian version of Richardson. After lunch, Helen showed us all the "surprise" the General had given her for her birthday, a likeness by Augustus John of a sweet, plain-faced woman in a dark dress with a lace collar. It was her grandmother, taken in late middle age, and it had been sold when the old Richardsons had died in the twenties by the lawyer who managed the estate for Helen, the heir, and who had not known Helen would have wanted every memento in existence of Mary Richardson. But the portrait had come onto the market again and the perspicacious General had bought it and now it hung in Helen's drawing room.

Helen hardly ever talked about the hard part of her childhood, her father's abandonment of her just when she had lost her mother; she never made a heavy thing of it as Francis did of his deprivations. But she could not speak of her grandmother without passionate feeling, and now as she stood in front of the painting, looking particularly at the folded hands, the third finger on the left hand with its weight of thick gold wedding ring and engagement ring of rubies in a cumbersome Victorian setting, the tears came into her eyes.

"I like that lady," Jamie said. "If I saw her I would sit on her lap."

This was to be favored indeed, for Jamie never sat on anyone's lap but Vera's.

"Would you, darling?" Helen was delighted. "Well, she was a sweet, kind lady and she would have called you her lamb."

"I should like you to call me your lamb," Jamie told Vera, and then, of course, she had to and Jamie took her up on it every time she forgot.

Those holidays, too, we all went to see Eden. It was an extraordinary, dramatic, and upsetting occasion. We went in the General's car, a 1937 Mercedes-Benz that had been holed up in one of the Walbrooks stables while the war was on because the General said the village people might throw bricks at a German make of car. And rightly so, he said. He had had no business to be buying a German car even then, even secondhand, he must have been off his rocker, it was just pouring marks into Hitler's war effort. On the way we called for Vera and Jamie, both of whom were wearing new clothes made by Vera. Vera cut up her old cot blankets to make a jacket for herself and coats and trousers for Jamie. In 1947, if you didn't want to wear Utility clothing you made your own. Vera had made Helen's dress from the skirt of an old crepe-de-chine ball gown. I was wearing the skirt part of an old cotton frock with a cotton jumper my mother had knitted. I mention all this because of what Eden was wearing and what she had brought back from Switzerland.

The house, Goodney Hall? Well, it was—and is, I expect—a fine, elegant, not very large eighteenth-century country house of which I am blasé enough to say there are many in England. The gardens had parterres and herbaceous borders and a pleached walk and rhododendrons that were famous and a greenhouse full of showy flowers. There did not seem much character to the house, no imprinting upon it of the personalities of its new owners. I heard later that Tony had bought it with all its furniture, bought it lock, stock, and barrel, as they say, and perhaps there wasn't much else he could have done. He and Eden knew nothing about antiques and one could hardly have put Utility furniture into Goodney Hall. I remember Eden's house as furnished entirely in pink and green, though of course it can't have been like that. Surely there was yellow in the Chinese drawing room and red in the Etruscan bedroom, but if there was, I don't recall it. What I remember are pea-green carpets and French furniture with pink silk seats and big pink Chinese vases with smudgy patterns, truly boring pictures, mostly mezzotints, of north European towns and ships on stormy seas, and green velvet curtains with heavy tassels of tarnished gilt.

But Eden, you could tell, was immensely proud of it. She was also enormously happy. And she looked quite different. I don't mean she looked well in the sense of being healthy. She didn't. She was thinner and paler and her face was less full. This, I thought, must be because she was pregnant. She looked different in the way rich women do. One might paraphrase that interchange between Hemingway and Scott Fitzgerald and say the rich *look* different, they have more scope. In this particular way, Eden looked different even from Helen Vera and I didn't enter the competition—who, after all, was wearing a homemade dress and had washed her hair herself. Everything about Eden, you see, was of the best, the most expensive top-grade stuff. The best hairdresser in London had cut her hair, she was wearing the most prestigious range of makeup available. She had on her huge diamond engagement ring and an eternity ring Tony had given her two weeks before when she told him she was pregnant. The dress she wore was white *broderie anglaise,* one of half a dozen she had brought back from Switzerland and which she had spread out on the (presumably) Etruscan bed before we arrived. The Swiss were different, too. There was no austerity there and nothing Utility. The shops were full of clothes, Eden told us, dresses and suits and shoes and silk underwear and silk stockings, and she had bought masses, as much as they could—I waited for her to say "afford"—carry home.

Vera was disproportionately grateful for her present. This was a brooch made in the shape of an edelweiss, of bone or horn, I suppose, but it looked like some prototype of plastic. It was a nasty little brooch, not at all well-made. Eden seemed to have bought a great many such things, gentian and edelweiss jewelry, all intended as presents for this friend and that, discriminating not at all between her beloved sister who had been a mother to her and the woman who came up from the village to do the rough work. Then there descended onto the bed from a fine carved wood chest quite a dozen carved wooden animals, exquisitely carved in the way only the Swiss can work so that the reclining St. Bernard looked about to get up and stroll away and you would not have been surprised if the Siamese cat had stretched itself and begun washing its whiskers.

Jamie, of course, became very excited. At first he was simply filled with awe. He had never seen anything like this before. I wasn't very fond of children then, I was never one of those girls who adore young children and want to hug them and take them out and look after them, but just the same, the expression on Jamie's face as he looked up at Vera moved me. He was so entranced, so overcome with wonder, with delight, at these things which literally looked like real animals in little, that first he smiled, then burst into joyful laughter.

"The dog!" he said. "The cat! Look, Mummy, that one's a bear. Look, Mummy!"

He was a gentle child and it was a gentle hand he put out to touch the back of the dog that looked for all the world as if covered with fur.

"No, please don't touch!" Eden said rather sharply.

There were no toys in the shops for children. There were children born at the beginning of the war or just before it who had never had a new toy worth calling a toy, who had inherited siblings' hand-downs, some of whom were lucky enough to have relatives who could sew and knit dolls or carve horses and carts. But Jamie wasn't one of these latter. If Francis had ever had toys—of course he must have, though you couldn't imagine it—they had long been lost or given away. Jamie had had to make do with that old set of bricks that had been my father's, Vera's own worn, bald, fluffy teddy, and such things as kitchen utensils. He took no notice of Eden. He picked up the dog and held it in his hands, close up to his face.

"Put it down! It's not a toy." Eden snatched the dog from him. She said to Vera. "Why do you let him do that? I thought he was supposed to be obedient."

I remembered from long ago the letter to my father: "I think you might teach your child better manners. . . ." My heart didn't often go out to Vera but it did then. She made no retort to Eden, no defense of the child to whom these things were a wonder and a delight. Love had tamed and humbled her. She said nothing. She took Jamie into her arms and he cried into her shoulder. The curious thing was that his crying wasn't the normal, unrestrained howling and sobbing of a child deprived of something he very much wants to have. It was quiet, sustained, more like an adult's grief. And yet you had the impression—Andrew told me afterwards that he did too—that Vera was a rock to Jamie, that even in his misery, it was almost a pleasure to him to have *those* arms, *that* shoulder, *those* gentle, whispered words. Vera, too, drew a kind of sustenance from his unhappiness because it was confided in her only, only she could comfort and support, she alone was humankind to him.

We had to make a tour of the house and a tour of the garden. Vera had recovered and praised everything extravagantly, flattering Eden absurdly, complimenting her as if she personally had planted out and pruned the roses, grown the raspberries, embroidered the petit-point chair seats and painted the lotuses and dragons on the porcelain. She was like one of those sycophants who hung about the nobility in the eighteenth century, like Mr. Collins with Lady Catherine de Bourgh. Eden accepted it all with gracious smiles, but she did not look well, she looked tired and there was something languid about the way she moved, though she brightened up and became enthusiastic again, as effervescent as she had been over the Swiss booty, when we came to the room that was to be the new baby's nursery.

It was on the end of the house, a corner room with windows facing west and windows facing south, and it had been a child's room before, though perhaps a long time ago, for the paper on the walls was all faded Arthur Rackham fairies and between a pair of windows stood a dappled gray rocking horse with worn saddle and harness. I have a very clear, sharp recollection of standing in that room, filled with bright, soft August sunshine as it was, the sunshine making spots and squares on the pink carpet that had a pattern all round its edge of white convolvulus intertwined with improbably pale green ivy. The wallpaper reminded me of Eden's picture, her favorite she had said it was, of the Peter Pan statue, and I wondered if she would hang it in this room. The west-facing windows looked out over the Weeping Hills, that gentle range of slopes and dips and wooded rises so unlike a Suffolk landscape, and the south-facing ones over the broad sweep of lawns ringed by stately trees. All along the terrace below stood at intervals stone urns ornamented like Keats's urn with youths and maidens and people going to festivals and mysterious priests and heifers lowing to the skies and bold lovers never kissing, and in the urns grew *Agapanthus africanus,* the blue lily, and white and purple *Allium,* in rare and special varieties, as Vera the sycophant had taken care to tell us. Vera now leaned out of one of these windows, praising the view. Helen looked a little bored, or as bored as kind Helen could ever show herself to be. Jamie, of course, had climbed onto the horse and this time Eden didn't stop him. She was telling us all how the room was going to be decorated and furnished and how the nanny would have the communicating one. Besides, the horse was old and shabby, doubtless to be chucked out along with the little wooden chairs and table and the brass bedstead, so it didn't matter about Jamie playing with it, did it?

Andrew said, "You ought to have peacocks, Eden. You ought to have a pair of peacocks out on your terrace."

"Goodness knows where you'd get peacocks, darling," said Helen. "Old Mrs. Williams couldn't even get a budgie when her Bobby died."

Eden turned round. "I wouldn't dream of having peacocks." She was suddenly petulant. "Hateful things. Have you heard the noise they make? Have you heard them scream?" Her lips trembled. I couldn't imagine what was the matter with her. "I don't want to be wakened up by screaming at four in the morning."

"Good thing you're having a nanny then."

Eden ignored this quip of Andrew's. "Shall we have a drink before lunch?"

Poor Jamie once more had to be parted from an entrancing toy. He didn't cry this time. He put his hand in Vera's and walked along beside her, down the long corridor, down the balustraded staircase. Tony now appeared. He only went to work in London three days a week and this wasn't one of those days but he had been out somewhere seeing a man about coppicing their wood. At once he busied himself with pouring our drinks and being the sort of man he was— kind, well-meaning, sociable, dull, and totally insensitive to mood or the differences between people or their tastes in contrast with his— treating us while he did so to an account of exactly where and how he had obtained this gin, that whiskey, that sherry, and where he expected the next bottles would come from. They had a great many glasses of all shapes and sizes and it was of the first importance to Tony to use the correct glass for each kind of drink. He even insisted on a different shape of glass being suitable for dry sherry from that suitable for medium sherry, something I have never come across since.

"And now how about this young chap?"

Vera said Jamie could have squash or some of the "government" orange juice she had brought with her, but Tony wouldn't have that.

"Oh, come on, we can do better than that. Personally, I believe in getting a boy used to wine from an early age. It was what my father did for me and I've never had cause to regret it."

"Hardly at three, surely?" said Andrew.

"I wouldn't be too sure of that. I wasn't much past that. My governor was set on my knowing wine, you see, and he said it was never too soon to start."

"I suppose he laid down a pipe of Montrachet for you?" Andrew said very seriously.

I didn't hear Tony's reply. I was conscious only of thinking he shouldn't tease Tony, it was as bad as teasing Jamie would be, and then, looking up, reaching out for my sherry, I happened to glance in Eden's direction and saw blood running down her leg.

It had the effect of freezing me. My fingers had just made contact with the glass and there they rested on the cool, hard, slippery, rounded surface, or rather clutched at it, while my gaze fixed on Eden's left leg. She was standing up. The woman who lived in and looked after them, her husband being gardener and handyman, had come into the room with two platefuls of canapés, bits and pieces of egg and cheese and pickles on rounds of toast. Eden had taken these from her and was in the act of offering them to Helen. As she leant forward the full skirt of her white dress had swung up a little so that the backs of her knees were visible. None of us was wearing stockings—you had to give coupons for them and it was hard to get them anyway—but Eden had on very pale, thin stockings, Swiss no doubt, and the blood in a thick, dark trickle was flowing down the inside of her leg, had reached the knee, the calf, was approaching the ankle and the thin ankle strap of her white sandal.

Oddly enough, I didn't think of what this must mean. I only thought of periods and when things like that had happened or nearly happened to me. Most of all I thought of Eden sitting down when the canapés had been distributed and the blood staining her beautiful ice-white, eyelet-embroidered skirt. But still I didn't know how to handle it. Come to that, I am not sure I would know how today. If I had whispered to her, when she and the plate were in front of me, to come outside with me a minute, I had something to tell her, I am quite sure she would have looked up and laughed and demanded of the company what could *I* possibly have to tell her that everyone might not hear, what could I possibly want to keep private from the rest? She was like that. She was Eden. So I shook my head at the canapés and let her go past me and at last had the presence of mind to catch Helen's eye and give her a look of such entreaty that Helen, so clever, so tactful, so insightful, immediately got up and said to Eden that she must use the bathroom before lunch and she expected I would like to also.

Women didn't ta^{ll} about their periods then. Or not much. Perhaps to contemporaries, and usually with euphemisms. As soon as we were outside the door, I told Helen briefly what I had seen. I called it "the curse." At least that was an improvement on Vera's "a visitor in the house."

Helen laid a hand on my arm. "But, darling, it can't be. She's pregnant."

"Oh, God," I said. "I forgot that."

"I mean, dearest heart, if that's what you saw, she *isn't* pregnant anymore."

And she wasn't. But we didn't have to tell her. When we went back into the room, Steuart's Chinese drawing room that I remember as pink and green though it must surely have been yellow, Eden was gone and Andrew was looking mystified and Tony, who ought to have been looking mystified, not to say anxious, was still going on about instructing children in worldly know-how, having proceeded by this time to the smoking of cigars. We sat there. We waited. Jamie said he was hungry. He didn't like scrambled egg and gherkins on cold toast and I can't say I blamed him. Suddenly Vera said:

"Is Eden all right?"

"Oh, absolutely," said Tony. "She's just popped off to powder her nose." Everyone says "absolutely" now but no one did then except Tony, and he said it all the time.

Vera went upstairs. She had to take Jamie with her because he wouldn't be left, he wouldn't be parted from her. Mrs. King, the housekeeper, came in to say lunch was ready and Tony said, all right, we'd be along in a minute. He went off too, but not to find out what was wrong with Eden as I believed, but to open some wine that had to be allowed to "breathe."

I said to Andrew, "Eden's having a miscarriage."

"Christ."

There was a phone in the room. At that moment we heard it make a sort of tinkle, a sign that the extension upstairs was being used. Somehow we all knew this was Vera phoning the doctor.

"Don't you feel," said Helen, "that we should stand not upon the order of our going—or whatever that tiresome woman said—but go at once? I mean, maybe take Jamie and leave Vera here with Eden?"

"*Not* take Jamie," said Andrew. "Please not. Peacocks would be preferable. But by all means go."

"I couldn't eat anyway," I said.

It was amazingly difficult to put all this across to Tony. Of course, it fell to Helen to do it, to explain, but we were there, we heard it, and his obtuseness was unbelievable. He kept insisting it must be a joke, Eden was teasing him, trying to make him anxious—what must their marriage have been like?—and she and Vera were upstairs "talking secrets," all girls together. Then Vera came down. She was white-faced and grim. Jamie was in her arms, half-hanging over her shoulder.

"I've sent for the doctor. Eden's having quite a severe hemorrhage. I imagine she's lost the baby."

The only one of us to have any lunch was Jamie. Vera looked distraught, deeply wretched, and concerned, but Jamie still came first with her. She took him out to the kitchen and got him something to eat, milk and a chicken sandwich. Helen and Andrew and I went back to Walbrooks and eventually, late that afternoon, I suppose, Tony drove Vera and Jamie home. The doctor had Eden taken straight into hospital.

What happened to her there? I have never really known. No doubt Tony knows—that is, if he can remember, and if he can, will he want to talk about it? Would he want to tell Daniel Stewart? I am sure not. Eden had miscarried and she had some sort of operation. I have since thought that perhaps it was an ectopic pregnancy that she had had, one in which the fetus implants itself in a fallopian tube. As the embryo grows, the tube may rupture, in which case the tube itself must be removed by surgery or the woman will die. On the other hand, the fetus may detach itself and be expelled without damage to the tube. I know only that after this miscarriage it was rumored through the family that Eden would not or should not have children. It would be dangerous for her to become pregnant again or—this was the alternative version—impossible for her to become pregnant. My mother said:

"I can't help wondering if it's the result of the life she led in the Wrens."

I didn't know what she meant. My father didn't know what she meant. We both thought this was some half-formed, half-superstitious, minatory legacy of Victorian morality. But what she suggested was quite feasible, quite medically accurate in fact. She was inferring that Eden, sleeping around, had contracted gonorrhea, one of the possible aftereffects of which is to bring about a blockage of the fallopians. This is said to have been responsible in the past for many one-child families. The bride would catch gonorrhea from her husband at the same time as she conceived, so that one child would be safely born. But the disease by then had done its work and the tube or tubes had been blocked so no further conception could take place. If Eden had indeed caught gonorrhea from a lover, the result could have been an ectopic pregnancy.

There was no real reason to believe this. One hears of the fallopians being blocked after abdominal surgery. Eden had had her appendix out as a child. Or surely it could be simple, unaccountable misfortune. All that seemed certain was that Tony Pearmain had no heir and most probably never would have.

13

FIFTEEN YEARS OR so after all this happened, Chad Hamner told me the story of his life over tea in Brown's Hotel. I had met him by chance in Bond Street, having gone there to have my hair cut at Vidal Sassoon's. Tea at Brown's is a very civilized business. You sink into your armchair and they bring you a small homemade toasted teacake which they drop onto your plate with a pair of tongs. The implication is that this is what you *must* eat, this is what all English gentlefolk eat as a matter of course for their tea. The cakes, which arrive on a three-tier silver stand, are optional but in any case for later. There they are, looking inviting, but the teacake must be eaten first—like at nursery tea.

In this milieu, Chad and I were perhaps out of place. We didn't look out of place, of course, we looked like everyone else, just as elegant and urbane, me with my haircut, Chad grown thinner and his hair beginning to go gray. He was the first man I ever came across to abandon the sports jacket for a casual one with a zipper. It was on the pavement outside Asprey's that we met. He put out his arms and I went into them and we stood there embraced, though the strange thing was that we had never hugged each other before, never kissed or even touched hands as far as I can remember. But the bond between us was a strange one. There cannot be many people who are linked together by a hanged woman.

I don't know why we went to Brown's. Certainly not because

Chad was staying there or had become rich or even habitually went there. As a journalist he was free-lancing, he had a flat in Fulham (which in 1963 was not fashionable or interesting or "upwardly mobile"), and I don't think he was doing very well for himself. For Francis he had ruined his life, he had destroyed all prospects of success. He told me this while we ate our teacakes. For a long time he had accounted the world well lost for love, but the trouble with that one is that love doesn't last and then one remembers that the world was once there for the losing.

He wouldn't have started on it if I, with an emotional rush of desire to confide and confess, had not come out with what I had seen that night after Eden's wedding. I had told no one till then—not even Andrew, not even Louis. Chad looked me straight in the eye, a cool, steady gaze, unexpected really after what I had just told him.

"I was sick with love," he said. "That's what the translation of the Song of Solomon ought to say, not sick *of* love. I only wish I could have got to be sick *of* love. I fell in love with Francis when he was thirteen. Rather classical, don't you think? The Emperor Hadrian and Antinous. An ugly old chap and a beautiful youth."

"Hardly old at thirty," I said.

Chad gave one of his enormous Gallic shrugs. "Age is a state of mind. I felt old when I was with Francis and I felt ugly. What I did was something most people would think abominable even today, but I didn't do it much, he wouldn't let me. And I wasn't the first. Does that surprise you? He used to let me make love to him approximately three times a year. Nineteen-forty-five was my bonanza year—he must have been celebrating the war being over—and he let me do it four times. No wonder I couldn't get him out of my system."

"Francis makes nonsense of Freud, doesn't he?" I said. "Poor Vera wasn't exactly a domineering, possessive mother to him."

"Yes, but Francis wasn't really queer. Not like I am, not to the core. I've never had a woman. Francis was simply all things to all men and women as it suited his book. I used to ask myself why he bothered with me and I came up with two answers. I'm still sure they were true. The first is that it's wonderful to be adored—I mean I should think it is, I've never been adored—wonderful to have someone worship you and know that nothing you can do, no amount of indifference and neglect and downright unkindness that you can mete out, is going to make an atom of difference."

"What's the other one?" I said.

"Francis liked doing things he and others believed to be wrong. He liked to do them simply for the sake of wrongdoing. Actually, that's very rare, it's much rarer than you might think. Even the great sinners of this world—Hitler, say, Stalin, certain multimurderers—believed that what they were doing was right or that the end they were attaining to was right. Hardly anyone sets out to do evil like Milton's Lucifer does, and he never convinces us, he always seems rather a pleasant chap. And it's not a case of 'Evil, be thou my Good.' Francis wanted evil to stay evil, to be his evil, and for that reason to be desirable to him. But none of that made any difference to my loving him. I would have followed him to the ends of the earth."

A chord was struck. I thought of what Anne and I had used the hovel for on rainy days and what Chad and Francis had used it for on misty nights.

"Like Mary Stuart," I said, "following Bothwell in her shift."

"Underpants in my case," said Chad, "only he seldom let me get that far. I missed so many opportunities for him, you know. I was stringer for a national paper and they offered me a job on the staff but I turned it down. I only got to see Francis in the school holidays as it was, but if I'd been in Fleet Street I wouldn't have seen him at all. The *Oxford Mail* job seemed heaven-sent. It was possible to *see* him every day if not to speak to him. And then I got fired. About six months after you saw us together that night, I got fired. And that again was through Francis. I don't mean it was Francis's fault, it wasn't, it was mine, but it was through him it happened.

"I had a job one evening for the paper, covering the annual dinner of a tennis club at Headington. You don't go to things like that, you get a handout beforehand of the general program and pick the rest up from the secretary or someone afterwards. I had no intention of going. I was taking Francis out to dinner, it was going to be the first time I'd been alone with him for a month. You know they say everyone has a peak experience in his or her life? A day or a few hours when one knows the most perfect, the highest degree of happiness, of ecstasy if you like, of one's entire existence. Well, that evening was mine. I thought so at the time and I've no reason since to change my opinion. Francis came back to my flat and we made love and he was kind to me and I was gloriously happy and it was my peak experience. It was also the last time I was happy for a very long while—I mean the last time I was even moderately content. I wrote my tennis-club story from the handout without checking up on it, the paper came out, and the next thing was I was up in front of the editor being asked why I hadn't thought to mention that the guest speaker at the dinner, a local bigwig, had dropped dead while making his speech. So I got the sack and came back to darkest north Essex—where at least I was more likely to see Francis than anywhere else—and because someone had left, they gave me my old job back."

He told me a lot more that afternoon, how he had followed Francis to London, and because Fleet Street wouldn't have him then, had gone to work as a reporter on a local paper out in northwest London called *The Willesden Citizen*. And how Francis had got tired of him at last and one day had struck him, knocking him down three flights of the staircase that led up to his bed-sit in Brondesbury Park. There were even more painful things: how Francis turned his fondness, a fondness he even then still retained, for playing practical and more subtle jokes, upon *him;* how his determination to be rid of Chad had led him to humiliate him in public far more cleverly and deviously than in his boyhood he had ever humiliated Vera. So by the time Francis was in his mid-twenties and Chad over forty, it came to an end and Chad was no longer very well, no longer strong enough to do a general reporter's job in a bleak northern suburb.

"I'm like Hadrian in more ways than one," he said, and he pointed out to me the diagonal crease that crossed each of his earlobes. Apparently these occur in people with a predisposition to coronary heart disease; it is medical fact, this, it is proven, not an old wives' tale. We know from busts of Hadrian and Hadrian's head on coins that he had those lines on his earlobes, and it was from coronary heart disease that Hadrian died.

But before he told me about that, he mentioned how he had been back in Essex, back in his old job by the winter of 1948, the winter that Vera was ill. And he was a fairly frequent visitor to Laurel Cottage. That people suggested he was or had been Vera's lover had never occurred to him, women as sexual partners were too alien to him for him to have thought of it, and when I enlightened him, it was a revelation. No, he hadn't known, it hadn't crossed his mind. If he had liked Vera and been friends with her, it was because she was Francis's mother and the place she lived in was imbued with Francis's presence. He visited her to be in Francis's home and talk about Francis if he got the chance, just as Hadrian, for all I know, might have dropped in on Antinous's mother up there in Bithynia. To be a family friend, he felt then, would be a way of ensuring that he had Francis forever. In small measure, perhaps, remotely, vicariously, not seeing him for years on end, yet tenuously possessing him still, a better portion, far better, he thought it was, to be sure of those crumbs of news, those casual mentions of a name, even with the inevitable pain, than the alternative with nothing.

"You wanted to keep a foot in the door," I said.

"That was part of it, yes. Our relationship—what a word! I hate it but what am I to call it?—our whatever-it-was was so thin on the ground, so hazardous, so *brittle* . . . well, brittle to him, fragile to me. But this way I could at any rate still see myself twenty years from then growing old with Vera at Vera's fireside, confided in, told where he was and what he was doing, his promotions and his publications. If I couldn't have more than that, at least I could have that, I thought, and I couldn't see what could take it from me if I was determined enough to arrange it. I only had to keep on going to Vera's house. And then, still, there was a chance of Francis being there. In theory, he still lived at home. The time would soon come, he had told me, when he would leave for good, he would never go home again. I didn't altogether believe him and anyway that time hadn't yet come and I lived in the present. That's supposed to be a good thing, you know, an ideal, according to modern psychology. Odd, because the truth is, one lives in the present when the past is too bad to remember and the future too dreadful to contemplate."

One day that winter, a week after Christmas it was, he went round to Laurel Cottage because he expected Francis to be there. Francis wasn't there. He had gone off to stay with some people he knew in Scotland for the New Year and of course he hadn't bothered to tell Chad. Chad said it was such a horrible disappointment, such a bitter shock, to find him gone, to know that he would return to Oxford without coming home first and that he, Chad, would therefore not see him for four months, all this so knocked him sideways that for a while he didn't notice that Vera was ill. He didn't really notice it till Vera asked him to excuse her for not offering him tea, for she felt too weak to get out of her chair. Then he saw how pale she was, how heavy-eyed, and when he laid his hand on her forehead, a surge of sweat broke through the skin.

This was the beginning of what Chad told me in Brown's Hotel, going on to say that sometimes he had wondered since how instrumental he had been in stimulating later events. Suppose he had done what Vera asked of him—in the circumstances, what a request for the mother of a little son to make to *him!*—would those terrible convergings of human lots never have taken place? Would all have been well? I don't think so. I think Eden would have found a way and Vera would still have lost out. I told him that, I told him not to let it trouble his conscience. For all his knowledge, I knew them better than he did, they were my people. We parted, never to meet again, never to hear of each other again until Daniel Stewart entered our lives.

I asked him one more thing. Perhaps it was wrong of me. What business was it of mine?

"Is the echo faint at last, Chad?"

He pretended not to understand.

And now I have before me, literally lying on the table before me as it has come out of its envelope, Chad's own account of what happened when he called on Vera that New Year's Eve. He has written it for Stewart at Stewart's request because there is no one else alive who knows, who was there, who was a witness. Chad, though in his seventies now, though stigmatized with the earlobes of Hadrian, seems very much alive, very *compos mentis,* but that style of his, once so lucid, so graceful, so pleasing—what became of it? I suppose it was thrown away and sacrificed for love of my cousin Francis. Stewart wants me to look at this account, to confirm it. That I can't do. I wasn't there. I was in London and Cambridge and sometimes in Stoke-by-Nayland, and all I knew of Vera's illness was contained in one letter which came from her to my father. But I shall read what Chad says just the same. I am curious to know the rest of it, the part he didn't tell me in Brown's Hotel.

I shall try to give you a factual account (Chad writes) without allowing hindsight to intrude and affect my statements. I shall try to write what seemed to me to be true at the time. In 1948, on the last day of 1948, I knew nothing of any mystery surrounding James Ricardo, then Hillyard, whom we called Jamie. As far as I knew he was Gerald Hillyard's son and it had never crossed my mind to question this. The separation that had taken place between Mr. and Mrs. Hillyard I supposed due to some quite other cause. I was equally in the dark as to any breach between Vera Hillyard and Eden Pearmain. For as long as I had known them, they had been devoted to each other be-

yond, so to speak, the call of sisterliness. I believed this to be unchanged, and up to a point, even then, it was.

The thirty-first of December 1948 was a Friday. I had an inquest
to cover for my paper in the morning and once I had written it up
would have had a free day ahead of me. Some half-formed plan had
been made of spending New Year's Eve with the Hillyard family. To
confirm this arrangement I drove home from Colchester by way of
Great Sindon and called at Vera Hillyard's house, Laurel Cottage.

She never locked the front door by day. Those were safer times. I
let myself in, calling her name. The little boy, Jamie, came running
out but Vera herself I found sitting in an armchair and she didn't get
up when I came in. However, it was a little while before I realized
there was anything wrong. I put her despondency down to the fact
that her other son, Francis, had changed his mind and wouldn't be
with us for the New Year. Then she told me she thought she might
have flu, her temperature which she had just taken was 102. I asked
her about fetching the doctor and she said he would only tell her to go
to bed, and how could she do that with Jamie to look after?

I was in a dilemma. Vera looked ill to me and she seemed to be
getting worse. I saw the sweat break out on her face and then she was
shivering and asking me to fetch her a blanket. It seemed wrong to
leave her but on the other hand I could do nothing for her and I had
no wish to catch flu myself. There was one thing I could do to help. I
said I would take Jamie out for a couple of hours so that she could
rest. This she agreed to. So I took the child home with me and made
him lunch along with my own and wrote up my story while he played
with an old Mah Jongg set, and at about four I took him home.

Vera was much worse. She was in bed, or rather, she was lying on
the bed still with her clothes on and turning from one side to the
other, holding her chest and having difficulty with her breathing.
This time I didn't hesitate. I phoned her doctor and asked him to
come as soon as he could. In those days you could phone doctors and
get to speak to them, not a receptionist or, worse, an answering service. And they would come to see you without the heavens falling. I
don't know what this doctor's name was, I can't remember, but he
lived in Great Sindon and he came within half an hour.

Vera's temperature might have been 102 when she took it but
when the doctor did it was 104. She had flu and he thought she might
be getting pleurisy. He told her to keep warm, stay in bed, drink

plenty, and take aspirin, and he would come back in the morning. She was lucky to have me there to look after her, he said. I believe he thought I was her husband. I quickly disabused his mind but promised I would stay the night. What else could I have done?

When the doctor had gone I asked Vera if she would like me to phone Eden, but this she wouldn't have. I was on no account to trouble Eden, especially on New Year's Eve. What was bothering me, of course, was Jamie. I could look after Vera for a couple of days but not a child of whatever he was—three going on four?—as well. However, I did manage to put him to bed and when Vera herself was asleep I tried to phone Eden. The housekeeper, a Mrs. King, answered and said they were both out. It was New Year's Eve, she reminded me. That night I slept in the room that was Francis Hillyard's, setting the alarm so that I could get up and look in on Vera at two and again at five.

"Delirium" is a strong word and I won't say Vera was delirious. But her temperature was very high and she was light-headed. The second time I went in she got hold of my hand and held it and began talking to me in a high rapid voice, a meaningless jumble most of it, as I thought then, and some rather more lucid stuff about life being pointless without children, and then suddenly she recited a verse.

I had never thought of Vera as in the least "literary" but I suppose she remembered this from school, where it had made a strong impression on her.

> For there is no friend like a sister
> In calm or stormy weather;
> To cheer one on the tedious way,
> To fetch one if one goes astray,
> To lift one if one totters down,
> To strengthen whilst one stands.

I went back to bed and Jamie awoke me about seven. He wanted to be with his mother but I was afraid to let him in case he caught the flu. The doctor came, said she could be left if we could find someone to come in and see her two or three times a day. But she was on no account to be left with the child. Again I tried to phone Eden and again she was out. The housekeeper said she would take a message for Mrs. Pearmain to call me when she came back at lunchtime. She was bound to be back by twelve as guests were expected for lunch.

Vera was still breathing unevenly and her voice was strained. I sat on her bed and told her what the doctor had said. I told her that I would have to go but that I had spoken to Josie Cambus and she had promised to come in at lunchtime and again in the evening. However, I said, I would stay at least until Eden phoned back because we should have to make arrangements for someone to look after Jamie.

That had an electrifying effect on her, ill as she was. She seized my hand in both hers. She sat up, clutching my hand. I must take Jamie, I must promise her I would take Jamie and look after him. I can remember her exact words.

"You take him, Chad, he knows you. He will be all right with you. I should be easy, I should sleep if I knew he was with you."

She would soon be better, she said, it was unthinkable that she could be ill for more than a day or two. She could not remember a day's illness since that trouble she had in her teens when Eden was a baby, and that had been anemia, she thought, which would have been cured if anyone had had the sense to give her iron. She rambled on like this, tossing from side to side, gripping my hand. I would promise her, wouldn't I, that I would keep Jamie just till Monday. By Monday she would be better, she would be right as rain. Jamie would be no trouble, he would eat just what I ate, he never woke in the night, all his clean clothes were in the chest of drawers in his room. She would pack them herself if I would bring her a suitcase.

It never occurred to me for a moment to say yes. I thought it a ridiculous request to make of me. I was a single man living in a flat that was little more than a bed-sit with a kitchen. What did I know about the needs, the tastes and whims of little children? Next morning, though it would be Sunday, I had an interview booked with our local MP, the only time he could see me. On Monday morning I would be due at work by nine. So I didn't even consider doing what Vera asked. For one thing, I didn't think there was a chance of her being well by Monday. I told her one of the women would have him, Eden would have him.

She reared up in bed as if she had seen a ghost come in the door. She stared at me as if she could see something dreadful behind me, a specter that had entered and was standing there with arms upheld. In a way she had, though at that time it was invisible to the rest of the world. Clutching my hand, she held on to me as if she wanted to keep me a prisoner.

"Please keep Jamie, Chad!"

She was imploring me, begging me, and I thought her high temperature had made her mad. That's all I thought it was.

"I can't," I said. "Be reasonable. You know I can't."

"It's the only thing I've ever asked you. I'll never ask you to do a thing for me again. Please, Chad."

"It isn't possible, Vera," I said.

"Then will you get Josie to have him. He doesn't know Josie like he knows you but she's a kind woman, she'll be kind to him. Promise me you'll get Josie."

I said I would ask her. I would do my best. Downstairs the phone was ringing. I went down to answer it and of course it was Eden. The housekeeper had given her the message that Vera was ill and once she had had lunch she was coming straight over, she wouldn't wait for her guests to leave, Tony would be there, she would come straight over and fetch Vera and Jamie and take them back with her to Goodney Hall.

It was a great relief. I felt a load lifted from my mind and that our troubles were over. Josie arrived just as I put the phone down, with lunch for Vera, which of course she couldn't eat, and being the rare (for those days) possessor of a washing machine, took away a pile of Vera's and Jamie's washing to do. I told Vera Eden was coming and got a very curious reaction.

She looked at me with mad eyes, but she wasn't hysterical, she didn't even sound delirious. She uttered this mad request in a sane, calm, intense voice.

"Jamie has his sleep in the afternoon. Lock him in his room, Chad, and tell Eden Josie's got him."

What could I say? What does one say to apparently insane demands of that kind? I humored her. I said all right. May God forgive me.

That was all I read of Chad's statement for the time being. I was finding it curiously upsetting. Of course I knew it had been bad, all of it, I knew about Vera's despair, but I didn't know it had been as bad as that. As for verifying things for Daniel Stewart, I couldn't do that anyway. What I could do was find the letter Vera wrote to my father about a week after that Saturday. It is dated January 6, 1948, and is one of the rare winter letters he kept. The remarkable thing about this letter is not what it says but what it doesn't say.

Dear John,

I should have written before to thank you for the postal order you and Vranni kindly sent Jamie for Christmas. Unfortunately I have been laid up with flu for the past week. I have had a really bad go of it, with throat and chest complications, but everyone has been wonderfully kind and helpful, Josie and Thora Morrell coming in to see to me each day and Helen has been an absolute brick, spending hours with me, reading to me, and sending food from Walbrooks.

Jamie is with Eden. I was rather worried she might not be strong enough yet to look after him but she assured me she was feeling quite fit again. It is the best place for him really, to be in that lovely house, and I should be able to have him back with me next week. Eden came over to fetch him the minute she knew I was ill. . . .

This was read aloud, of course, at our breakfast table, my mother listening with her customary expression of wry exasperation.

"I'm glad the boy is with his aunt," said my father. "That's a load off my mind. He couldn't be in better hands. Eden will be kindness itself, it'll be the next best thing to his own mother."

"I don't suppose it makes much difference," my mother said in her neutral voice. By this I took her to mean that in her opinion, Vera and Eden would be equally horrid to any child in their care. My father thought the same, for he threw the letter down and asked her what she meant. She answered him obliquely.

"You know how I feel. I told you at the time it was all for the best your sister having that miscarriage. She doesn't like children, she's got no patience, you've only got to look at her to see that."

They argued about this for a while, my father insisting that the maternal instinct had found its fullest expression in both his sisters equally, they got it from his mother. My mother had never forgotten the incident of Eden dusting her bedroom when she stayed with us. She let fly about Eden's selfishness, lack of thought, eye to the main chance, and so on. I was remembering Eden's wedding morning when she had flung out her arm to gesture Jamie away and would have struck him if he hadn't dodged her hand. I remembered how she never spoke to him if she could avoid it and in my mind's eye I saw Jamie holding the carved Swiss dog and Eden turning on him.

"Put it down! It's not a toy!"

My father got up to go off to work. "I really think that's the best place for him," he said, as if none of this argument had taken place. "He'll be best off with his aunt."

"I would gladly have had him here if I'd known," said my mother.

Nobody once suggested the obvious person to look after Jamie and minister to poor Vera. I suppose the fact was that we had all given up Francis as a potentially useful or helpful or ordinary social being years before. We had almost given him up as a member of the family. It seems from what Chad has written that Vera never suggested fetching him home from wherever he was in the Highlands for Hogmanay. My parents had forgotten his existence. And I, who, if we had been talking about any other family group, would naturally have asked why the sick woman's son couldn't be called upon, never considered Francis in this role. I looked through Chad's statement again, looked in vain for a mention of Francis in this connection, noting only how Chad had passed two nights in Francis's room, in Francis's bed no doubt, and wondering how that had been for him, ecstatic or painful or perhaps both.

I did not lock Jamie in his bedroom (Chad continued). I simply put him in there on his bed with his toys and hoped he would fall asleep for a while. Eden arrived at about three. You want the facts, you want everything I can remember, so I may as well tell you that though she wasn't drunk, she had been drinking a lot. She smelt of wine. Mme. de Pompadour said that the only wine a woman can drink and still look beautiful afterwards is champagne, so I suppose it was champagne, among other things, Eden had been drinking. She shouldn't really have been driving a car. She went straight to Jamie's room and packed a suitcase for him and then she went in to see Vera.

I heard nothing of what they said to each other. Eden's going into his room had awakened Jamie and he was whimpering. I gave him some orange squash and a biscuit. By that time I was desperate to get away. I heard Eden calling my name and I went upstairs and found Vera lying on the landing where she had collapsed and fallen over. She wasn't unconscious, only too weak to get up. I thought she had been trying to reach the bathroom, that was what I thought at the time, but later on I came to a different conclusion. Eden was also out on the landing, her gloves on, her handbag under her arm. I think Eden had said good-bye to Vera, come out of the bedroom, and Vera had got up and followed her, tried to run after her perhaps, and there, in her weakness, fallen over. I picked her up in my arms and carried her back to bed. She lay back against the pillows with her eyes closed. Downstairs Jamie had begun to cry.

Vera murmured, "Jamie . . . please, Chad. . . ." Tears began to fall down her cheeks. I thought they were the tears of weakness, of fever.

"It's best to leave her and let her get some sleep," Eden said. Her speech was the slightest bit slurred. You wouldn't have noticed if you didn't know what her normal voice was like.

We went down to Jamie. He was crying because he had spilt his drink over himself. I cleaned him up and gave him some more. Nothing was said by Eden about taking both Vera and Jamie away with her. Nor did I remind her of what she had said earlier. Vera wasn't fit to be moved. The doctor himself had said she should stay in her room in bed. We had seen what happened when she tried to walk. I was wondering whether I dared leave her when Josie Cambus came in, carrying her knitting and a library book, all prepared to stay for the rest of the day and all night if necessary.

And that was it. Eden put Jamie on the back seat of her car and the suitcase in the boot and drove off. I told Josie I would give Vera a ring on Monday to find out how she was and then I, too, left. By Monday, however, I had flu. I was off work ill for the whole of that week and part of the next and when I finally phoned Vera, Josie answered to say she was much better but asleep just now. I did not speak to Vera again for a long time and when I did, things were very much changed. Eden Pearmain I never saw again. My last sight of her was as she got into the driving seat of her car, the last words I ever heard her speak, those in which she told Jamie to mind his fingers in the door.

Vera was ill for a long time. Her appearance shocked me when I saw her that February and I thought Helen was right when she said Vera wasn't yet fit to have Jamie back.

I was staying at Walbrooks for the weekend, having come down with Andrew on the Friday night. If my father had heard from either Vera or Eden during the past weeks, no news had been passed on to me beyond the information that Vera's convalescence was a long one. I arrived at Stoke-by-Nayland, concerning myself about Vera only insofar as my conscience was mildly troubling me. For reasons that must have been obvious to everyone, including herself and Eden, I now stayed with Helen instead of her when I was in this part of the country. No doubt Vera understood, but I had deserted her all the same.

"Oh, darling," Helen said, "she wouldn't have wanted you. I don't mean it like that, of course, but she's not at all well. She's never got over that flu. But we'll go over tomorrow and you shall see for yourself. She wants Jamie back, she wants us all to go to Eden's and fetch him back, but I don't know. You'll see."

She was so thin I had to stop myself staring at her, and she had that faded worn-out look some fair women get as they age, the look of a dead leaf. Her skin had crumpled and there was a lot of gray in her hair, the bones in her wrists and knees were knobs, and when she smiled her face became a skull. In spite of all this, in spite of her evident weakness, she had spent the past week painting Jamie's bedroom. We all had to go up and admire her work, Helen and the General and Andrew and I. This was the room where I had slept, where I had watched Eden cream her face and put her hair in curlers and had myself experimented with her makeup. It was transformed. Vera had painted the walls white and the woodwork pale blue and had made Jamie a rag rug out of blue and white material scraps, cut illustrations out of Beatrix Potter books and framed them in *passe-partout*.

"It looks heavenly," said Helen. "Isn't he going to adore it? But, darling, are you sure you're fit enough to cope?"

Vera gave her skull smile. "Of course I am. Could I have done all this if I wasn't? Anyway, I don't suppose Eden would keep Jamie any longer. It would be a bit much to ask. She leads a very busy social life, you know. I expect she's fed up with having him, she'll be only too glad to see the back of him."

It was said so brightly, so confidently, so . . . desperately?

"I could have him for a while." Helen sounded anything but enthusiastic. Yet I am sure none of us doubted that she meant it. She would have Jamie if Vera wanted her to. "I happily will, darling, if you don't feel up to it and Eden wants a rest."

Vera didn't say anything. It struck me then that she was frightened. Or does hindsight make me say that? Did I notice anything at the time except her thinness, her tiredness, the way she shook her head, at the same time giving Helen a grateful yet dismissive smile? We all got into the car and drove to Goodney Hall. The house was approached by a long avenue of lime trees, and around their roots and in patches on the parkland lay drifts of snow. The sky looked full of snow. It was deep, bleak midwinter, the worst time of the year, much worse than December, and although the evenings were lengthening, it was dark soon after five.

Steuart's beautiful house rested aloof on its raft of terraces and balustrades and steps. There wasn't even a coniferous tree or an evergreen up near it to break the monochrome, the grays of that house and the sky behind. It was three o'clock and not a light on yet. A curious thing happened as we approached the gravel sweep in front of the terrace. Eden came round the side of the house alone, walking slowly, pausing at the corner where a stone urn stood on the angle of the balustrade, and placing her hands on its pedestal, stared first across the park, then in our direction. She was wrapped in a fur coat with a thick, upturned fur collar that framed her face. I am sure she didn't expect to see us, didn't know we were coming, and was unpleasantly surprised by the sight of us.

Nor could she quite disguise this. She had not been born to this style of life or nurtured in a tradition of social grace, the concealment of feeling, the putting on of an artificially welcoming face. She came down the steps looking cross, then resigned. Her hair was entirely covered by a turban of some sort of dark jersey material and this and the red-fox collar discouraged kissing. No one kissed. Eden said:

"Well, my goodness, how nice to see you all. What a surprise!"

"I told you we'd come on Saturday," said Vera.

"Two weeks ago you said something about probably coming this weekend."

They were both giving the impression that if Vera had tried to make a firm date, Eden would have turned her down. We went into the house. Although there was a fuel shortage, just as there were shortages of almost everything, I had expected Goodney Hall to be warm inside. Eden and Tony would have found ways, I thought. It was cold, colder than college or Walbrooks or my parents' house. A small electric fire was switched on in the Etruscan drawing room. We all kept our coats on and perhaps because of this didn't attempt to sit down. Eden said it was Mrs. King's day off but it was a bit early for tea anyway, wasn't it? Tony, too, was out somewhere.

Vera's voice had become strangely timid. "Is Jamie still having his sleep?"

"Jamie?" Eden spoke as if he were someone whose name she had

once heard and now vaguely remembered from the distant past.
"Jamie? Yes, I suppose he is. I really don't know."

No one said anything. Andrew said to me afterwards that for a
moment he had the curious feeling that Eden hadn't been looking
after Jamie, that he wasn't in the house, that it was all some sort of
delusion on Vera's part. She only *thought* Eden had been looking after
him while all the time he had really been with Josie or Mrs. Morrell.
But this, of course, was Andrew's misapprehension, for Eden, taking
off the red-fox coat and dropping it over an armchair, now said, with
equally devastating effect:

"Shall I ask Nanny to bring him down or shall we go up?"

A little color came into Vera's face. She looked as if she had two
insect bites on her wasted face, one on each cheekbone.

"Nanny?"

"Yes, that's what I said." Eden spoke in a pleasant tone.

"You had a nanny to look after Jamie?"

"We thought the most sensible thing would be to engage a profes-
sional who would know what she was doing, yes."

As if Jamie were autistic or retarded or delinquent, Andrew later
said to me.

"Is he up in that beautiful nursery we saw, Eden?" said Helen,
very sweet, very cheerful. "I'd truly love to see it in use."

Eden shrugged. "Come along, then."

The General declined. He belonged in that generation of men,
perhaps the last, for whom men's and women's roles were utterly
differentiated. Men did not set foot in nurseries, converse with nan-
nies. Men, like sultans, had nothing to do with children, even boy
children, until they attained the age of reason. He picked up the *Daily
Telegraph*—in which, I noted, Eden had half-done the crossword—
and sat on the sofa with it. A man's role was to drive the car, and
when the car was ready to be driven, he would do it. Andrew came
with us, though, and as we went up the staircase, I took his hand.

Eden, when the fox was off, was dressed for the part of lady of the
manor. She wore a tweed skirt with box pleats, a pale blue "twin
set," several strings of pearls, and the eternity ring. Her brilliant gold
hair was cut short and permed in symmetrical sausage curls. She led
us down the long corridor to the corner of the house where the nursery was. It was so cold in that passage that my teeth started to chatter.
But inside the nursery it wasn't cold. I hadn't noticed the fireplace

on my previous visit. I noticed it now. A fire burned in it, a fire
generously fed with good Welsh nuts, not logs, and it sent out a fierce
red heat, more than competing with the two-bar electric fire that
stood between the windows. These were misted with condensation,
the air outside being icy. Last time I had seen this room, the sun was
shining and making patterns all over the pink carpet which had a
border of ivy and convolvulus. This carpet had gone and been replaced by a fitted one of light blue and there were new curtains of
blue rep, the wallpaper was boats on a choppy sea, but the table,
chairs, and rocking horse were still there. A girl a bit older than I,
perhaps Eden's age, was laying this table with a teacup and saucer,
plates, a rabbit mug. She wore a gray dress, not exactly a uniform
yet drab enough to be one. Jamie was on the rocking horse and
seemed to have been jerking it vigorously back and forth. When we
came in, the jerking stopped though the horse naturally went on
swinging. He looked in our direction, then turned his face sharply
away.

Eden went up to the nanny and muttered something inaudible to
her. The girl immediately, as if in response to a button pressed or a
lever thrown, said:

"Say hallo to Mother, Jamie."

She had a thick Suffolk accent so that this command (which was
disobeyed) came out something like: "Sah-allo ter Mawther,
Jarmie."

Vera was sensible enough not to show her bitter disappointment. I
hadn't realized until that moment that she and Jamie hadn't seen
each other since January the first, now six weeks past, and six weeks
is a long time in the life of a four-year-old. Jamie got down off the
horse, went over to his nanny, and stood close by her.

"Come on now, don't be a baby," she said.

Jamie's face crumpled and he began to cry. The girl picked him up
and held him. Rather awkwardly, I thought. Eden had detached herself from the little drama that was developing, gone to the fireplace
and, slipping her carefully manicured and beringed right hand into a
coal glove, started prodding at the fire with a small brass poker.

Unable to contain herself any longer, Vera ran to Jamie and put
out her arms. As anyone but she could have foretold, this had the
effect of making Jamie cling all the tighter to the brawny, gray-
cotton-clad shoulders. He buried his face. Vera gave a piteous cry

and the nanny responded by shoving Jamie at her. The ensuing scene was painful to see. Such scenes—and they usually happen when a mother and her child have been separated over a long period—always are painful. Jamie screamed and fought, struggled out of Vera's arms, threw himself at his nanny's lap, bellowed, embraced his nanny's knees. All the while Eden poked and prodded at the fire. Outside it had begun to snow. Fat, fluffy flakes of snow were drifting thickly past those dewed windows. The nanny sat down, cuddling Jamie, and Vera stood trembling with clenched fists. Helen said:

"He's bound to be a bit unsettled at first, darling. Don't be upset. Shouldn't we just wrap him up warm and collect his things and go? Wouldn't that be best?"

Eden came over. "You weren't intending to take him with you?"

"Yes, of course, darling, I thought you knew that."

"I certainly did not. Anyway, it's out of the question. Look at the snow. He's had a bad cold and it would be very unwise indeed to take him out in this weather, wouldn't it, Nanny?"

I think we were all struck by the unsuitability of this girl as an oracle, and it so happened that she made no answer to Eden's appeal. She merely looked bovine, humping Jamie on to her hip and jigging about with him from one foot to the other. We probably all felt, too, that if anyone were consulted on the question of Jamie's health it should be Vera. Jamie struggled down, sat on the hearth rug, and began sucking his thumb. Vera said:

"You never mentioned a cold."

"No, well, I haven't spoken to you for about ten days, have I? He's had it since then."

"I rang and rang. You were never in. That woman, your house-keeper, always answered."

"Vera," said Eden patiently, "I can't stop in all day on the chance you might ring."

"When can I have Jamie, then?" said Vera like a little girl who, having been denied a treat, tries to extract a fresh promise from a parent. "When can I have him?"

Andrew was starting to get angry and the effect of Vera's humble pleading tone was to make him angrier still. He might be an under-graduate like me but he was much older, older than Eden, nearly thirty, had been in the Battle of Britain, had been a prisoner of war, and was long past the category of "children" of the family, in which I still belonged.

"You can have him when you like, Vera. He's your child. We'll wrap him up and he'll be perfectly all right. We came over here to fetch him and that's what we'll do." He addressed the nanny in a tone worthy of a descendant of the Richardsons, wealthy gentlefolk that they were. "Get his things ready, will you?"

I admired his manner. Emancipated as I was, sticking up even then for women's rights, I still expected a man to be able to "take charge." Helen too looked pleased. I had watched dismay come into her face at Eden's high-handedness. Astonishingly it was Vera who demurred. She seemed determined to placate Eden, though Eden was firm rather than angry.

"If you really think it would be bad for him, Eden . . ."

"I do. I've already said so." Eden went to one of the windows and lifted the curtain away from it, though it was perfectly easy to see the blizzard without that. Andrew said what we were surely all thinking:

"If the car is brought up to the front door he'll only be outside for about ten seconds," and scathingly, "It isn't as if he's got to walk two miles to the station."

"Why don't we say next weekend and make a firm date?" said Vera. It seemed, even then, a very curious way of putting it. "Suppose I said next Saturday, Eden?"

"You'd better make sure my father's free next Saturday," Andrew said, not very warmly.

"Josie's got a car. She'll drive me. Shall we say next Saturday, Eden?"

Eden took her time about answering. The fire in front of which Jamie was sitting, still sucking his thumb (the bitter-aloes-aversion therapy all forgotten now), had been unguarded. Eden slipped her hand into the coal glove, put a couple of pieces of coal on the fire, and placed a wire mesh guard in front of it. When she had finished doing this she took the glove off and in an absentminded sort of way put her hand out and lightly ruffled Jamie's hair. He reacted not at all.

"You can come next Saturday if you like," she said.

"I'll come in the morning and fetch him, then, shall I?"

"Yes, come in the morning."

The nanny came back with tea for all of us on a tray. Eden looked annoyed. She shook her head when the nanny started pouring tea into her cup. Vera sat down in one of the wooden nursery chairs. She looked as if she might have fainted if she hadn't done that. Silence prevailed until Helen began talking about the snow, relating snow anecdotes of her childhood at Walbrooks. During this, something odd, and in the light of what was to come, dreadfully painful, happened. Jamie got up off the hearth rug and made his way over to Vera's side. He stood by her chair. Again Vera behaved quite sensibly, not showing the emotion I believe she was feeling. She put out her arms to him, or her hands rather, in that tendering gesture that offers a casual cuddle if the child wants it. Jamie evidently did want it. He climbed onto her lap. For the first time since our arrival, he spoke.

"Eden is going to buy me a dog," he said to Vera.

"Is she, darling? That's kind."

"A big dog. But it will be little first."

"Oh dear," Vera said. "I hadn't really anticipated having a dog, but if you've promised, Eden . . ."

Jamie nodded. "She's promised." He put his arms round Vera's neck and hugged her.

"Don't let your tea get cold," Eden said, and in her accents, precisely imitated, I'm sure, I heard my grandmother Longley whose voice I thought I had forgotten.

The snow forced us to leave. The blizzard let up but it was apparent more snow would fall and some of the lanes would then have become impassable. As Andrew said later, to be forced to spend a night at Goodney Hall would be a fate worse than death.

Vera seemed much happier since Jamie had come to her and shown her affection. I thought, and I believe Helen and Andrew did too, that this was the only trouble. She had been upset by his indifference. You could see, too, that he did have a cold. His nose was running and occasionally he made croupy sounds. The nursery was very hot and no doubt it wouldn't have been wise to take him out into the cold for even ten seconds. I think we all felt much better about the arrangement by the time we went downstairs and collected the General. Jamie had kissed Vera good-bye, had seemed quite cheerful in the nanny's arms, waving to us from the nursery door. And Eden also kissed Vera. Indeed she kissed us all and, shivering at the snow, begged us to phone her the moment we got to Walbrooks just to let her know we had got there.

That was the only weekend I spent away from Cambridge that term. I wasn't sufficiently interested or concerned to inquire what happened on the following Saturday. If I thought about it at all, I assumed Jamie was back with Vera at Laurel Cottage. I remember I did wonder how Vera would get on with a "big dog," no pet animal ever having been kept by any Longley within memory of the oldest of them.

It was April before I learned that Jamie had never been returned to Vera but was still living at Goodney Hall, apparently with her acquiescence.

14

DANIEL STEWART IS a man who looks very young at first. One's first impression is how young he is, a mere boy. This is because he is thin and straight-backed and wears his hair long and hasn't gone bald. Helen has a theory that for the best effect, women—and men too, for all I know—should dress ten years younger than they are, neither more nor less. Stewart dresses twenty years younger than he is, and it is too much, it is verging on the absurd. After a time one becomes insistently conscious of the lines on his face, so painful when he smiles, and the gray in his hair that the color rinse has not dyed so deeply as the rest of it—copper threads, in fact, among the brown.

But all this is by the way. He is pleasant, a little ingratiating, intelligent. He sits in my drawing room with a whole heap of books on fungi spread around him and we wait for Helen to come. He, of course, has met her before. I am listening to him with half an ear and with the other half for the diesel throb of the taxi that will bring her.

"I want to get this straight," he says. "Was the poison Vera Hillyard used the same as that which killed the old woman she found dead in the cottage?"

"Mrs. Hislop," I tell him. "You're asking me? I didn't even know it was poison that killed her. I knew she used to cook fungi for herself—what I'd call toadstools."

"The inquest verdict was 'natural causes.' The death certificate said 'myocardial infarction,' which is a sort of heart attack. In other words, she died of heart failure, which is what we all die of. At the postmortem, considerable kidney deterioration was found but no comment was made on this. Mrs. Hislop was, after all, nearly eighty. In the cottage was a basket of uncooked fungi and in a saucepan a kind of stew of fungi. Both were analyzed and found to be harmless."

I ask him if the postmortem found any poisonous fungi in Mrs. Hislop's body. I thought I wasn't interested in this kind of thing—for instance, I never read detective stories—but as we talk about it, I find I am.

"There was nothing, hence the verdict. But there was a great deal of talk about poisonous fungi at the inquest, largely, I think, because Mrs. Hislop was known for dabbling with it. Vera Hillyard gave evidence at that inquest, of course, but you knew that."

"No, I didn't," I say, and I am very surprised. This is because I remember Vera telling me how she found Mrs. Hislop but not telling me she was at the inquest. Yet this surely must have made a profound and lasting impression on her, sheltered fourteen-year-old that she was. The implications of her failure to tell me are not lost on me. At that inquest she would have heard all the talk about fungi. She would have stored it up to turn over later in her mind.

"In spite of that verdict," he says, "I am sure Mrs. Hislop did die of fungal poisoning and that the poison she used was the same that Vera Hillyard used nearly thirty years later. Nobody really knows what it was and nobody ever will know now. It's possible only to take the symptoms and calculate from that, to use, in fact, what we do know and make an intelligent guess from that."

"Like the Emperor Hadrian's ears," I say.

He doesn't take me up on that one. "I'm wondering if it was a poison called orellanin that's responsible. It's found in the *Cortinarius* species of fungi. For a long time, *Cortinarius* was considered harmless, and it wasn't until 1962 that the properties of *Cortinarius orellanus* were discovered by a Pole called Grzymala. It damages the kidneys. Death has been caused in children after several days, in adults after weeks or months. The kidneys go wrong."

"Mrs. Hislop was in the habit of regularly eating strange fungi," I say. "You say that the postmortem found kidney damage. Vera told me that when she found her, she looked 'all swollen up.' It could have happened months after she's eaten what-do-you-call-it, *orellanus*." I pick up his field guide to mushrooms and other fungi, read the relevant section, and immediately see objections.

"Yes, but look here, it says that *orellanus* is rare or absent in Great Britain. Vera didn't go to Poland collecting fungi. And the other one, *turmalis,* that's rare or absent here, too."

"I know," Stewart says, "I haven't missed that. But what about the purple agaric that isn't even in this book? Here it is." He hands me a thin, flat booklet published by the then Ministry of Agriculture and Fisheries, some ten years before Vera began on her poisoning course. *"Cortinarius purpurascens,"* he says. "Apparently it's fairly common. It says it has been listed as edible but the word is merely used in the sense that it has been eaten without ill effects."

This book, a copy of it I mean, I have seen before. Although I know Vera was a murderess, although I know that before she used the knife she tried poison, nevertheless, I have that curious sensation we call the heart turning over. The book (called Bulletin No. 23, *Edible and Poisonous Fungi*) is flat and dark green with a picture on its cover of a golden chanterelle such as one sees for sale in French markets. The date of publication was 1940, the price half a crown. In the little text beside the watercolor drawing of the purple agaric, a note explains that the species is difficult of determination even by experts and warns that experiments are not advisable. Nothing about orellanin, though, and just as I am beginning to say this to Stewart, I remember what he has told me, that its properties weren't discovered until twenty-two years after Bulletin No. 23 was published.

"It belongs to the *Cortinarius* species," he tells me, "and therefore very probably contains the kidney-damaging orellanin."

I gaze at the picture and remember with perfect clarity seeing purple mushrooms in the woods at Sindon. It was always late summer that I was there, wasn't it? For a long time it was only in the late summer or early autumn. Anne and I would wander through the woods together. It was near "the wash" where the river was forded and a wooden bridge passed over it, there where Vera once sat gossiping with her schoolfriend and Kathleen March was snatched from her pram, there it was that I had seen *Cortinarius,* growing in clusters through the leaf mold, date-brown olivaceous (as the book puts it), glutinous and opaque, expanded and marked with a raised violet fuscous zone, the stem fibrillose, pallid, the gills bluish, then cinnamon, violaceous when bruised, broad and crowded, the flesh azure blue.

At this point, Helen comes in, and how glad of it I am! The nausea of old remembered ugly things is in my throat. She embraces me, shakes hands with Stewart.

"I have brought my Valium with me, Mr. Stewart, so if you want to talk about you-know-what, could you give me warning? And I can take one in good time."

Stewart asks her only to describe Goodney Hall to him. The people now living there won't permit him to see over it. That won't upset her, will it? She shakes her head. The wide-brimmed hat she is wearing is the rich brownish-violet of the purple agaric, in-curved lilac fuscous, and I am glad when she takes it off and bares her small white, fluffy head.

"I won't take my Valium but perhaps we could have our sherry a wee bit early, darling?"

In wilder moments I have sometimes thought I married in order to have Helen for my mother-in-law. Or was that not the cause but merely the one good effect? Surely I married as I did because I was afraid, young, ignorant, and inexperienced as I was, that if I didn't marry within the family, no one outside the family would have me. No one outside would marry a hanged woman's niece.

Helen can remember thirty-five years back better than I can. I remembered Eden's drawing room as pink and green, the whole house pink and green, but Helen remembers crimsons and yellows. She remembers the Arthur Rackham paper on the nursery walls changed for a plain deep blue that made the room look cold even in summer or even when a fire was burning in the grate. And she remembers Jamie's nanny's name: June Poole. I am amazed at myself for forgetting it, for was not Grace Poole the nurse and keeper of Mr. Rochester's wife? The situations were very different, of course. Jamie wasn't deranged or female or a secret, though for a while he was a prisoner, and there was no part in this drama for a Jane Eyre.

June Poole was a girl from the village, from Goodney Parva, and her qualification, not a bad one perhaps, for being Jamie's nanny was that she was the oldest of seven siblings. She had known no other life than that of minding children. Whether she *liked* it was another matter. Did she even like Jamie? Helen, though, doesn't speak of this. I know she finds speaking of Jamie at four and five intensely painful. I have given her her sherry and she is talking of the rhododendron garden at Goodney Hall, famous all over the county and opened by Eden to the public that spring, when my husband comes in.

I love the way they are so pleased to see each other, he and Helen, and kiss and are at ease as if it were the most natural thing in the world. Yet I have never quite got used to it. I don't think he likes Stewart and certainly he dislikes the idea of Stewart's book.

"I hope you're keeping the law of libel in the forefront of your mind, Mr. Stewart," he says, winking at me behind the old-young man's back.

Illness governed events at this time. First Vera was ill, then Jamie, lastly Eden. What Jamie's illness really was I never knew. Croup perhaps, though he was old for that, bronchitis, pleurisy, I don't know. This illness, though, was the reason given for his not going home to Sindon. Vera's letter to my father, dated March 30, 1949, survives.

". . . Eden has kindly invited me to stay with them at Goodney Hall for a couple of weeks. Tony is sending one of the cars for me tomorrow. . . ."

Poor Vera! Even in the extremity of her dread, snobbery—in this case vicarious snobbery—was not forgotten.

"Jamie has been there for nearly three months now, unfit to be moved since the bad cold with complications he had in the middle of February. I miss him dreadfully as you can imagine but have had to accept what I know to be best for him. Certainly there was no question of moving him, taking him out, etc., during the very cold weather. Eden has been kindness itself, though I know you will agree that any other behavior from *her* would have surprised us. She has lavished every care on him and daily kept me up to the minute with regard to his progress. It will be nice to spend time under the same roof with him. We shall really have to get acquainted all over again! By the time the two weeks are at an end, he should be fit enough to accompany me back to Laurel Cottage. . . ."

These lines are a masterpiece of their kind for concealing true facts and real feelings. They are also perhaps a sop to Providence or a placating of the Furies. If I put a brave face on things, if I make believe all is well, all *will* be well. Yet I, Faith, know so little and there is no one alive who knows more. For instance, had Vera and Eden by this time discussed the question of Jamie's future? Of Jamie's past, come to that? Had Eden made to Vera any actual declaration of intent? Or was poor Vera—and this I think to be most likely—left for all those months in suspense, knowing no more of this aspect of things than she had expressed to us that snowy day in February, no more than she told my father in the letter, but terribly afraid of the worst?

I think, in the light of Chad Hamner's statement and my own memories, that she had been aware she had something to fear from Eden's wedding day onwards, perhaps from earlier than that, the announcement of her engagement. Her fears became concrete, real, not chimeras, when Eden miscarried.

Often, since then, I have wondered what the two sisters said to each other when they were alone together during those two weeks of April. Tony went to London, by train from Colchester, at least three times a week. No doubt Eden's friends came sometimes, Mrs. King would have been in and out, and June Poole too. When they walked or were in the garden and at meals, too, Jamie would have been with them. But what of the long hours when they were alone, just the two of them?

Did they thrash things out, trying to find a compromise, trying to create a sharing future, a communal life? Or was Eden adamant and Vera pleading? Was the identity of Jamie's father ever discussed? Knowing them, these two sisters, I tend to believe that they were never open about any of it. They never said what they felt or meant to do but always spoke in half-shades and half-truths, Eden still keeping up the pretense that Jamie was "delicate," "not strong," Vera terrified of antagonizing her.

Did they reminisce about the past? That surely would have been too painful. Not for them, at that time, to look back into the distant past when Vera had saved the infant Eden's life, had rejected her own son to be a mother to her, had wept bitterly when the war took Eden away, those days when they had loved each other dearly—in the far.

That summer, for part of the long vacation, I went with Andrew to Walbrooks. Of course I married him. Not then, not for another year and more and our Finals were done with and he had taken his First and I my disappointing Lower Second. Then, we were not even engaged. For a few months I was in love with him, but being no Desdemona, I could not love him for the dangers he had passed. The dangers he had passed began to bore me to death and I dreaded ever hearing the words "Battle of Britain" again. If Vera had not been hanged for murder I would have dropped Helen's son as gracefully as

I could and hoped we might have become no more than cousins again.

But this is Vera's story, not mine. What was I then, or at any time but a figure in one of Vera's dreams? A potential ally against Eden? What was anyone to her but that?

She had passed the greater part of that summer staying at Goodney Hall, sometimes going home to Laurel Cottage for a week or a few days, but Jamie had never gone with her. Now he was five, he had become five in May, and the question had come up of his going to school. Naturally, it was taken for granted he would go to Sindon village school and probably remain there till he was eleven. Vera would not do with Jamie what had been done with Francis. Her beloved Jamie wouldn't be separated from her and sent away to prep school. Nor, we all thought, would Gerald be likely to intervene. It would be Vera's decision and Vera's only. I don't think any of us any longer believed—though we never spoke of it among ourselves—that Gerald was Jamie's father. Jamie had to have had a father and it wasn't Chad, so Vera had to have had another lover. My own view at the time, which I never expressed even to Andrew, was that some former boyfriend of Vera's, someone she had known before she knew Gerald, had come home on leave and they had met by chance, and frustration and nostalgia and perhaps an under-the-counter bottle of wine had done the rest. It didn't sound like Vera, but people's sex lives seldom do sound like the people who have them.

Vera asked Andrew and me to help her kidnap Jamie.

We had been to Bury St. Edmunds in the old Mercedes, just the two of us, and driving back went over the Stour at Sudbury into Essex and took in Great Sindon on our way home. It may have been that day that going into Sindon Wood down by "the wash" to pick up pine cones for Helen's drawing-room fireplace, I saw the purple agaric growing out of the leaf mold. Certainly, according to Daniel Stewart's book, *Cortinarius purpurascens* abounds in July and August, and this was July. Or it may have been some other day years before when Anne Cambus and I roamed Sindon Wood, or even years after, when I went back alone.

I don't like to think that if we had agreed to Vera's request murder might never have been done. It wouldn't be true anyway. Only if we had agreed and our efforts been successful could that particular disaster have been avoided. And we know from subsequent events that our efforts would not have been successful.

Vera wasn't expecting us. We called on her by chance. I was all for driving on, avoiding the lane where Laurel Cottage was, but Andrew said it wouldn't look well if someone in the village saw us and passed it on to Vera. He was always a great stickler for appearances.

Josie Cambus was with her. That may have been the day I first heard mention of Josie's son by her previous marriage, for when we arrived she had been talking of this son and how he was reading law. Vera was as thin as when we last saw her, and as aged. But she seemed to have regained her wiry strength. All the time we were there she was on the fidget, her hands constantly picking at the piping on the arms of her chair, and once or twice doing that bearing-down business, straining as if pressing on a drill, her face contorted.

About five minutes after we came in, Josie left.

Vera said, "Did you come in a car?" as if it were possible to visit Sindon by any other means in the middle of the afternoon, the lunchtime bus having gone two hours before and the teatime one not due till five.

As if doubting our answer, she went to the window and contemplated the Mercedes, parked up against her fuchsia hedge. She nodded. She was a pathetic sight, was Vera at forty-two—emaciated, gaunt, looking ten years older. Her mouth, though empty, worked like a gum chewer's.

Suddenly she began to speak, apropos of nothing that had gone before, yet as if this were only the continuation of a conversation she had been carrying on for weeks. And in a way it was, for later on I learned she had made a similar appeal to Josie, to the Morrells, and even to Helen, though Helen had said nothing of it to us.

"If we went over there now," Vera said, "Tony wouldn't be at home. I know that for a fact. And it's June's afternoon off. I've stayed there so much I know all the workings of that household. There would only be Mrs. King with Eden, and Mrs. King's not very strong, she must be sixty if she's a day. We could easily do it. *I* could do it if you'd keep Eden talking. It would be easy."

People with an obsession have their minds so filled with it to the exclusion of all else that they assume others must know what they are talking about without introduction. It was like this with Vera. It seems strange to me now that I hadn't the least idea what she meant and that Andrew hadn't.

"Fetch Jamie, of course," Vera said. She was impatient. "Bring him home. Take him away by force. It's the only way."

We both thought, we found out afterwards, that Vera had gone mad. Andrew said:

"Doesn't he want to come home, Vera? Is that it?" He spoke gently and cautiously.

"Of course he wants to come. He's only five, isn't he? What does he know? It's Eden won't let him. Everybody knows that. Eden wants to keep him because she can't have children of her own."

"Now look, Vera. Wait a minute." Andrew sounded as appalled as I felt. "That can't be true. You're a bit overwrought, aren't you? You don't look well. But you mustn't exaggerate. Has Eden been putting pressure on you to let her adopt Jamie? Is that it?"

"Pressure!" said Vera. She gave a dreadful throaty laugh, and sitting down on the extreme edge of her chair, began to wring her hands.

"Because all you have to do is refuse. They can't take him from you. The law won't let them. Surely you know that?"

She made an impatient, rather violent gesture of shaking her head back and forth. "You've got the car and there are two of you and you're young and strong. You could fight Eden. You could shut Mrs. King up in her room and Faith could keep Eden talking while I got Jamie from the nursery, and if Eden saw before we got away, you could keep hold of Eden while Faith and I got away."

"I can't drive," I said.

Andrew glared at me. I suppose it did sound as if I were taking her seriously.

"Look, Vera," he said, "I think you ought to see your doctor. Get something for your nerves." People did talk about nerves then and not neuroses. "Have a quiet lie-down and think about it. Anytime you want to bring Jamie home, we'll fetch him for you. Okay? Anytime—you only have to say the word." I loved him for that. He was being strong, the way I believed he always was. "Only we have to do it aboveboard," he said. "Let Eden know and be firm about it, but we have to be civilized too, don't we?"

She gave him a look of ineffable scorn. "Why will no one help me?"

"You don't *need* help, Vera. Or not in that way. You need a doctor's help, if you ask me."

"I don't ask you. The only thing I ask you, you won't do."

Neither of us felt we should leave her in that state, though I think we were both beginning to feel a tremendous distaste for the whole business. We thought we understood, you see, we thought we understood about the pressures and the resistances. We suggested she come back with us to Walbrooks and Helen and stay for a few days and maybe see Helen's doctor. She would have none of it. If she went anywhere it would be back to Eden's to be with Jamie.

"But does Eden really want to adopt him?" I asked Helen that night.

"It seems like it, darling. She can't have babies, she never will be able to. And apparently she's been persuading Vera very hard for the past three months to let her adopt him legally. She's told me so herself. Of course, as to keeping him from Vera by force, that's all nonsense."

"Is it though? What exactly happens if Vera says she wants him *now* and she's going to take him? She hasn't got a car. I mean, would Eden physically hold on to him? Would she shut him in the nursery? Would Tony and June Poole help her?"

"I can tell Vera's been talking to you."

"No, she hasn't," I protested. "At any rate she didn't tell me all this."

"The fact is, I suppose, darling, Vera doesn't want trouble. She doesn't want an outright breach with Eden. And of course she doesn't—we've been such a united family."

I couldn't see it that way myself and said so. Arthur Longley hadn't been united to Helen when she was little and he married again. Gerald and Vera hadn't remained united and Francis had never been united with anyone. Those two sisters had always disliked my mother and she them, and my father and Helen had not got on. So much for being united. Andrew said—to my surprise:

"Don't get me wrong but mightn't it in the long run be the best thing in the world for Jamie if Eden adopted him? Vera hasn't seemed entirely sane lately. She's alone. She's not well off. You have to ask yourself how ideal she actually is as a parent."

"Why do you have to ask yourself?" I said. I hate phrases like that. "How ideal is any parent? The point is, surely, that she *is* his parent and the only parent he's got as far as one knows." Helen registered shock at that. When I say "registered," I mean showed it in Helen's special way, making an oooh mouth and putting up her eyebrows. "Vera *loves* him, you don't seem to realize that. She really loves him passionately, doesn't she, Helen? I don't believe you've ever seen them together or you wouldn't talk about ideal parents."

"I was thinking of the child," Andrew said. "I was thinking of his chances. This way he'd have two parents, young parents, too. A beautiful home. Money for his education. The right background."

That disgusted me. "Eden hates him," I said. "She hates children."

"No, she doesn't, darling," said Helen. "I've seen them together, I saw them last week, and she's as doting as Vera now."

That night it was when we began to take sides. No one openly expressed this, no one came out with it and said Eden should have him or Vera must keep him, but silently we took sides. Curiously enough, Andrew for all his initial protestations, came into the Vera camp. I think his sole grounds were that he didn't like Eden and wanted her to get her comeuppance. The General was on Vera's side because he had sentimental ideas about maternity. Helen astounded me by taking up the attitude Andrew had held. In adoption by Eden and Tony she saw unparalleled material advantages for Jamie. Besides, this way the family would be less likely to be split, she felt, for Vera would spend half her time at Goodney Hall to be near Jamie, whereas if Vera won, Eden would never speak to her again. I remembered the profound sisterly love there had once been between them and marveled.

"What a pity it was Vera ever had that flu," said Helen, as if this had brought it all about. But that was what we all thought at the time.

I must not give the impression that the Vera-Eden-Jamie business occupied us to the exclusion of all else. We thought about it a lot, we talked about it, but we had other things too. Andrew and I specially had other things. We were moving from a friendship, a cousinship, into a love affair. Patricia, too, was contemplating marriage, and she brought the man she was living with in London down to Walbrooks for a fortnight. Not that any of that older generation knew she was living with him, it was not something one openly admitted to in 1949, and when they came to Helen's they were given separate bedrooms as a matter of course. There was a good deal of secret padding about the passages of the Richardsons' old house those August nights.

About a week after that visit of ours to Laurel Cottage, Eden dropped in one morning. She came alone, having left Jamie at home with June Poole and Mrs. King. She was on her way, she said, to pick up Vera, who was returning to Goodney Hall with her until the end of the month. I think the question of Jamie must have been preying on Helen's mind, otherwise she would hardly have burst out as she did in our presence and that of Patricia's boyfriend, Alan. It was as if she couldn't contain herself.

"Darling, it really isn't fair to poor Vera to go on like this! You simply must make up your mind what you want to do and do it. And the poor little boy—what must he be feeling?"

Eden was very calm and aloof. She was wearing a dress of fine Indian cotton in large shaded checks of navy blue and yellow with a wide collar and deep décolleté, the neckline being filled in with ruffled lace. The skirt was full and longish and such were the formal fashions of the time, even for driving about the countryside in the mornings, that she had on nylon stockings with pointed clocks and dark seams and very high-heeled ankle-strap shoes of navy-blue glacé kid. Her mouth and fingernails were painted crimson. The perfume she was wearing was a very pungent one, Coty's Emeraude.

"My mind *is* made up, Helen," she said. "Tony and I know exactly what we want. We want Jamie. There's no difficulty on our side. It's Vera you should be talking to."

"If Vera isn't in agreement with you, young lady," said the General, "you'll have to give it up. You know that, I suppose?"

I could see Eden hated him calling her "young lady," as I hated it when he did it to me. It was a term he used to Patricia and Eden and myself when he was less than pleased with us.

"I don't want to talk about private things in front of all and sundry," she said.

"Oh, darling, all and sundry! How can you? We're all family here."

Eden didn't think Alan family, though she hadn't quite the nerve to say so. "Anyway, it's private between Vera and me."

"Not if you're upsetting your sister, it isn't," said the General. It wasn't clear if he meant Vera or his own wife by "sister." The devil entered into me, for I knew that of all people's interference, Eden would hate mine the worst. Well, she would have hated my mother's more.

"Why can't you just adopt any baby?" I said. "Why can't you go to an adoption society? I should have thought you'd want a little baby. Jamie's five."

"I'm well aware how old Jamie is, Faith. Thank you very much for putting your oar in. What business it is of yours, I don't quite know."

"Please don't quarrel, darlings," Helen cried. "I can see you'd want your own nephew, Eden. I can see that. He's a sweet little boy anyway, he's a darling and—you could send him to Eton!"

This was so absurd it made us laugh and went some way to clearing the air. Eden said, still smiling:

"I may as well tell you since you've brought the subject up, that it's all settled. I didn't want to announce it till all the odds and ends are tidied up. We *are* going to keep Jamie, he will be our son, it's only a matter of a few formalities. And of course Vera will spend just as much time with us as she wants until she gets used to the new arrangement."

We were all a bit stunned. Whichever camp we were in, I don't think we had envisaged anything like this happening quite so fast. And I remembered Vera begging us to kidnap Jamie. It was only a week ago that she had appealed to Andrew and me to help her.

"But Vera loves him," I said. "He's everything to her."

Eden was hating me. It was that which gave me courage. "All the more reason why she'd want the best for him."

"You know that one doesn't work. No one is that self-denying."

"I'm not going to talk about it with you, Faith. You're not old enough to understand. As far as I'm concerned, you're still more or less at school."

"I know love when I see it," I said. "Vera told Andrew and me last week to get Jamie away from you. She implied you were keeping him by force."

"Oh, Faith," said Helen.

Andrew let me down. He didn't say a word. His father asked him. He said, "Was that true?" and Andrew just shrugged his shoulders. But if he had supported me, if they had all been made to believe, what could we have done? Patricia left the room, taking Alan with her. She said, "Come on, Alan, let's go outside."

"Do you really think," said Eden with infinite scorn, "that Vera would be coming to stay with me, that I'd be fetching her now, if she was opposed to our adopting Jamie? Do you? Do you think she'd allow it if she was? Why wouldn't she just get hold of Jamie and walk out of the house with him? Or does Faith think I'm keeping him a prisoner?"

There were no answers to that. Eden soon went, parting coldly from all of us. The General was cross with me after she had gone, calling me a firebrand. I had a tremendous row with Andrew in which at last I forced him to admit Vera had asked us to kidnap Jamie. I also got him to tell this to his parents, though he toned down and qualified the truth a lot, making it look as if Vera was hysterical and needed mental treatment.

This upset Helen disproportionately. People didn't accept mental illness then like they do today. They always had to defend themselves by saying there had never been anything like that in their family. That was what Helen did say, but at the same time as being horrified at the idea of Vera's mental disturbance, seemed anxious to blame everything onto it. She said she would make a point of finding out for herself, though. She would go over to Goodney Hall in a day or two and speak to Vera alone.

I should have liked to go with her but she wouldn't let me. Although she didn't put it quite like that, she implied I should only antagonize Eden. The Chatterisses didn't have any notions about economizing by not using the phone so I phoned my father and spoke to him about Vera and Jamie. He was never much good with phones, having come to them too late in life, and he always tended to address the mouthpiece rather than simply talk to the person at the other end. He spoke on phones as if everything he said was being recorded for people unused to the sound of English. This, added to the facts that, like Eden, he believed me too young to involve myself in this matter and also too *presumptuous* as a mere niece, made our talk unsatisfactory. He kept saying he couldn't follow any of it, but Vera and Eden must know what they were doing. The most important thing was that I shouldn't get on bad terms with my aunts.

Helen came back, looking quite cheerful. Vera was perfectly normal, she couldn't imagine what Andrew had meant. She and Jamie had been out together, out for a walk to Goodney Parva, when Helen got there. Surely that could put paid to any ideas of Jamie's imprisonment? Vera had brought him back and sent him off upstairs to June Poole and talked to Helen about Jamie starting school. He would be going to Goodney Parva village school, starting that September.

"I asked her if she'd be living there too and she said, no, she'd be back at Laurel Cottage by the end of August. Then I came out with it and asked her if it was true Eden and Tony were going to adopt Jamie legally. She said she didn't know about 'adopt legally' but they were going to keep him, have him living with them. I asked her why. She didn't say anything, just made a face. She was embroidering one of those ridiculous cushion covers, you know the way she and Eden do, darling, like they needed—what-d'you-call-it?—occupational therapy. She just went on sewing away, not looking at me."

"Did you actually get to the crux?" said the General. "Did you ask her if that was what she wanted?"

"Yes, I did, darling. Don't interrogate me. She said quite calmly that it was absolutely what she wanted and not to talk about it anymore. I don't think she's a bit mental, Andrew, really I don't. More *lethargic,* if you know what I mean."

My father wrote me a letter. He said he had the greatest confidence in his sisters doing the right thing and putting their duty before personal considerations. They had been properly brought up and that was something that would stand them in good stead. There was no history of mental illness in our family, none whatsoever, and he wanted me to believe that. The last thing he wanted was for me to worry about that sort of thing. However, he thought it probable that my mother's dislike of his sisters, which he attributed to jealousy, had affected me and prejudiced me against them. It would cause him bitter sorrow to think that anyone could have attempted to destroy the affection and admiration he knew I felt for Vera and Eden. And so on. Wouldn't I go and stay with them for a few days before I came home? After all, there was no need for me to prolong my stay with Helen, who was only a half-aunt.

Nothing would have induced me to stay at Goodney Hall, always supposing I had been asked. Eden, of course, didn't ask me. Eden being Eden would no doubt have expected a written apology before she even asked me to tea. I stayed at Walbrooks for about three weeks and then I went home to my parents, having promised to return in September and go up to Cambridge with Andrew at the start of the Michaelmas term. It was impossible to make my father understand why I hadn't gone to Eden and Vera. I was growing tired of explanations, more particularly because I had come to guess there were things both Vera and Eden knew that none of the rest of us did, and to act without that knowledge was useless. To speculate was useless. A letter came from Vera but it does not survive. Why, I don't know, as we certainly had no coal fires in September. It told my father that she would be returning to Sindon at the end of the week (she had stayed on a fortnight more than arranged already) and that Gerald wanted a divorce. He had met a woman he wished to marry and would provide Vera with grounds. In those days a woman had to prove desertion or cruelty as well as adultery in order to divorce a husband.

"She'll be well rid of him, he's treated her monstrously," my father said.

Eden became ill at an awkward time for the Goodney Hall household. June Poole was on a week's holiday. Tony's father had had a slight heart attack and Tony was staying in Yorkshire. These things could not have been arranged. They were coincidental. What Eden had the matter with her was not specified and therefore gave rise to a mystery. It wasn't a cold or flu. Might it, we speculated, be another miscarriage? By the time I was back at Walbrooks she had been taken into hospital.

Vera was left alone at Goodney Hall with Jamie, and Mrs. King, the housekeeper, and a woman from the village who came in twice a week to clean. What happened she told me herself one rainy evening two days before I returned to college. I had half-complied with my father's request and was spending two nights with her, not at Goodney Hall but at Laurel Cottage. Upstairs Jamie was asleep in his newly decorated bedroom. Sometime during the night, Francis would return. To Vera's dismay and anger, he had taken advantage of her absence to have a honeymoon in her house with a girl she said was a barmaid he had picked up in Ipswich. The village shuddered with the scandal and disgrace of it. The girl had gone, and next day Francis too would depart, but she expected him back that night—in the small hours, doubtless.

"The doctor said Eden must go into hospital or he wouldn't be responsible for what happened," Vera said. She lowered her voice a little, glancing about her, as if the house were full of people who might hear her and be disgusted. "She was unable to pass water. She simply could not pass urine. The doctor said whatever it was had affected her kidneys. It's my belief it was the result of whatever it was they did to her when she lost the baby. Anyway, we don't want to talk about that. It's not the kind of thing I ought to talk about in front of you.

"They had an ambulance come for her. I phoned Tony at his father's and he said he'd come home straightaway. Jamie was at school. He'd just started school two weeks before. I didn't say anything to Mrs. King. I packed our cases, Jamie's and mine, we'd accumulated so much stuff, you wouldn't believe, and left them in the hall with a note for Mrs. King asking her to send them on. I walked down to the village and fetched Jamie from school and we just escaped together, it was really funny, we did laugh. It was such a *lark,* like a childhood prank. I kept thinking how cross Eden would be. And it's so nearly impossible getting from Goodney to Sindon without a car. We had to get three buses and it was eight before we got home. And then of course I found Francis here and the place in the most outrageous mess. I was exhausted but I didn't care. I put Jamie to bed in my bed and I crawled in with him an hour later and we just slept like that all night, it was such bliss."

Next day Tony came. He told Vera he couldn't understand why she hadn't just stayed on at Goodney Hall. Vera had laughed and told him she wasn't coming back and Jamie wasn't coming back and if he thought she was going to visit Eden in hospital, he could think again. She wasn't going out to give him the chance to come in and take Jamie from her. Tony must have been aghast, a conventional, rigid person like that. He didn't know what she meant, either, he really didn't then. Eden had told him nothing at that time except that she wanted to adopt Jamie. He had consented, to placate her, presumably.

Vera told me all this with glittering eyes, laughing sometimes at her own cleverness in outwitting Eden. I was unpleasantly convinced she was going mad. It was uncomfortable to be with her. But I had no idea then, no one had any idea, that she was herself responsible for making Eden ill. I thought I understood everything, that Eden had pressurized Vera into letting her adopt Jamie on the grounds that it would be in Jamie's own best interests, that Vera, though torn by her love for Jamie, had consented but later had had second thoughts and had seized her opportunity. What I never considered was the effect all this might have on the child. I was too young, I suppose.

Next day I encountered Francis. Most of the time he lived with his father and was about to do a postgraduate course at London University. The descent on Laurel Cottage had come about because Gerald would not have consented to his taking the girl home to sleep. Gerald's own relations with his new woman were circumspect and he would be fixing the evidence for his divorce with a girl he was hiring for the purpose. Francis I had not seen since Eden's wedding day, when I came upon him with Chad in the candlelit dark, and I felt embarrassment.

"She ought to be certified," Francis said. "She's doing the same to that kid as she did to me."

"Hardly," I said. "She seems to have pushed you out. She's doing her best to pull Jamie back."

"It's all symptomatic. She's a paranoid schizophrenic."

Jamie had come into the room. He was very quiet. I had noticed how extraordinarily quiet and "good" he had become. At night he slept from the time Vera put him to bed at six until quite late into the morning. This morning it had been after nine. He came in holding a small tractor with caterpillar rubber wheels and he proceeded to run this thing all the way round the room, over chair backs, bookshelves, windowsills, trundling it slowly, keeping up an apparently fierce concentration on what he was doing.

"So what?" said Francis. "I don't like the kid. Why shouldn't he suffer? That's not the point. She is sick in her mind, her mind is warped. I'd like to have the pleasure of putting her away. That would be a gothic thing to do, wouldn't it? Consigning one's own mother to a madhouse."

He no longer intimidated me. I didn't care what he thought of me either. Mine was a kind of indifferent repulsion.

"Why bother?" I said. "What's in it for you? You don't live here. It's not as if you cared about Jamie and his future."

"I'll tell you what his future will be. Eden will get better and come here and take him back and *she* won't have a leg to stand on. You'll see."

"I shan't. I shan't be here either. And you're wrong. Vera will never let him go back. She never lets him out of her sight for more than five minutes. She'll be in here in a minute keeping an eye on him."

He smiled, slowly shaking his head. He has hooded eyes, has my cousin Francis. The effect had become more pronounced as he entered his twenties, as if the eyeballs had protruded more and the eyelids stretched to cover them, taking on at the same time a purplish, bruised color like eye shadow. The hoods lowered and he smiled.

"I told you she hasn't a leg to stand on. Eden will come for him as soon as she gets out of hospital." He looked at the child. He looked at him penetratingly and Jamie continued running that tractor along the windowsill, up the architrave of the door. "I'd take him over to Goodney myself, only I wouldn't trust that fool Tony to hang on to him."

"You'd do that?"

"You are so naive," he said.

We all were. I came to believe that the family favored Eden's keeping Jamie because everyone openly or secretly thought Vera mentally unstable. This seemed unjust to me. She could not have been kinder to him, gentler, more caring. It wasn't till I was back at Cambridge and thinking about Vera and her problems one day, wondering what the outcome would be, that I realized Jamie had not been to school while I was staying at Laurel Cottage. True, I had been there only two days and two nights, but the village school's term had begun. Had not he been attending school at Goodney Parva for two weeks before Vera snatched him away? But perhaps it was only that Vera hadn't been able to get him into Sindon School.

While I was there I met Josie Cambus again. Anne was at teacher-training college in London and we had seen each other for a while the week before. She told me she had come to like her stepmother. I had never known Vera to have such a close friend. She and Mrs. Morrell, for instance, had always called each other Mrs. Hillyard and Mrs. Morrell, and as for Chad Hamner—he had extended his friendship with an ax to grind. But Josie and Vera saw each other almost every day. They confided in each other—though not absolutely, as I was later to learn. Josie was the only person Vera would entrust Jamie to. Intense in the few affections she had, Vera seemed to have transferred to Josie the love she once lavished on Eden. Of Josie and her achievements she was proud, at the same time denigrating poor Donald Cambus, whom she castigated as undeserving, ungrateful, totally unworthy of his second wife. Josie was an excellent cook, a Cordon Bleu cook according to Vera, she sang in the church choir, was no mean watercolorist, taught a yoga class before anyone had ever heard of yoga. Vera bragged about her unremittingly. What she saw in Vera I never knew, and though later on I had ample opportunity to ask, I never did. If I never came to love Josie as I loved Helen, I did like her very much. I got on with her. But with her I discussed

Vera only the once, and on that occasion my father was present. We had all—strange trio of drinking partners!—drunk too much by design so that we might without too much pain, too much shameful suffering, hear from the only witness what happened at the end.

Josie gave evidence at Vera's trial but I was not there, I read no newspapers at the time, and only now have seen the transcript.

She has been dead ten years. When I first knew her, she was about fifty, a tall, heavily built, dark woman whose hair only began to turn gray when she was in her seventies. Her voice was very beautiful—I mean her speaking voice, for I never heard her sing—and she was one of those people who are very calming to be with, very easy, so that you can relax in their company and never feel they have expectations of you that you can't fulfill. These two qualities her younger son has inherited, as well as her handsome Spanish looks, though he, as his mother was, is English through and through.

Josie, having her own car, offered to drive me to Stoke-by-Nayland the evening before Andrew and I were due to return. Vera, though Helen had invited her, refused to come with us. The road to Stoke, she said, passed through Goodney.

"All right, we won't go that way," Josie said. "We'll go the long way round."

The bypasses that have now made main roads out of lanes and left the villages in peace were not built by then. If you didn't go through Goodney you would have to go miles round through Langham and Higham.

Vera pointed this out. "I should see the signpost," she said, from which we were supposed to infer that even the printed names "Goodney Parva" would upset her. "You stay and have a cup of tea with Helen, though. I should like Helen to see you."

This was very Vera-ish. It was not that she wanted Josie to see Helen, but Helen to see Josie, just as in the past she had wanted to show off Eden and, more recently, Jamie.

In the car, why didn't we talk about Jamie and his future? We didn't, though he must have been uppermost in our minds. Perhaps Josie thought me too young. Not too young to discuss this, but too young to be interested. She asked me about my final year at college instead, about what I wanted to be. Only when we were at Walbrooks, in sight of Helen, who had come down the front steps to greet us when she heard the car, did Josie say:

"I would give a lot to hear that the Pearmains had decided to immigrate to South Africa after all."

"I didn't know they'd thought of it," I said.

"Oh yes, but not anymore, I'm afraid," and then she was saying how-do-you-do to Helen and shaking hands.

Just after Christmas my father had a letter from Vera asking his permission as owner of one-third of it to sell Laurel Cottage and move away. This letter doesn't survive and I remember nothing of it except the gist. He and my mother had spent a weekend with Vera during the autumn, and while there, had visited Eden in hospital. She was in hospital for weeks and weeks, months even, while they tried to work out what was wrong with her. I don't know what happened that weekend. Did Vera go with them on the hospital visit, for instance? Did they see Tony? Was anything discussed about Jamie's future? My mother wrote to me only that they had been, that they had stayed with Vera, that Eden would be in hospital at least another month, and that it had rained the whole weekend. Vera's letter put the cat among the pigeons. For a while my mother must have declared a truce in order to stay with Vera and visit Eden, but it was war again now.

"If that house is to be sold, we're taking our share out of it and she can buy a place for herself with the rest."

My father immediately demurred. "What could poor Vera possibly buy with a thousand pounds?"

"Let Eden make it up then. She's rolling in money. Why should you subsidize your sister when she's got a husband who is making good money in the army and a son who's old enough to support her, and I haven't even got a refrigerator?"

My father, in his way, also objected to Vera's moving. In this, at any rate, they were united. She had lived in Sindon all her life, he said, forgetting the India years, all her friends were there. By "all her friends" he meant Josie, and I did rather wonder how she would feel about leaving Josie behind.

"Why does she want to move?" he kept saying.

I was dreadfully afraid the answer might be to take Jamie out of Eden's reach. Eden was still in hospital, though she was better and expected to come out very soon. They had never found out what went wrong with her kidneys. They were back to normal now, for Eden was basically very strong and healthy. Once she was out and home again, would she do as Francis said she would, come to Laurel Cottage, perhaps with a supporting retinue of Mrs. King and June

Poole, and snatch Jamie back? It seemed unreal, a lawless, ante-diluvian thing comparable to rustling a neighbor's cattle. But when I was staying in Essex, someone had told me of a cattle-rustling inci-dent that had taken place on a nearby farm only just before the war. Why not a kidnapping?

"Why does she want to move?"

"Doesn't she say in the letter?" said my mother.

He had given up reading them aloud, finally conquered by her relentless sarcasm.

"She says she feels like a change."

Eden would have to be consulted. Hers was the third share in Lau-rel Cottage. She had a private room in the hospital and he could have phoned her but of course he wouldn't. He wrote instead, asking for her views. It was Tony who phoned us. Eden was home, he had fetched her home that afternoon. She was sitting beside him now, doing the *Daily Telegraph* crossword. In February he was going to take her to Majorca to convalesce. It sounds commonplace today, the place where everyone goes to if they can't afford better, but in 1950 Majorca was still an unspoilt, virtually unknown Mediterranean is-land. I had just about heard of it. They were going to Formentor, retreat of French film stars. Vera's house? Laurel Cottage, he should say? No, they hadn't heard a word about plans to sell it. Eden came on the line and started off by asking him for the answer to a clue. She didn't think Vera ought to sell. At least let her think it over. She should tell her to think it over, and when she, Eden, came back from Majorca, they could discuss it again.

"Doesn't want to trouble her pretty little head with her sister's affairs now she's rich," said my mother.

In a fury my father screwed up the letter and threw it in the fire, which is why it doesn't survive.

That phone call made me feel better about things. I mustn't give the impression I was constantly worried about Vera and Jamie, I wasn't that altruistic, but it used to nag at me sometimes. I didn't, among other things, want Francis to be right. And now it looked as if he wouldn't be. Eden wouldn't laze around at home, planning a holiday almost a month off, take that holiday, itself a good month long, if she meant to renew her demands to have Jamie. So I rea-soned. I had forgotten the hunter who leaves the blocked lair while he eats his leisurely lunch, the cat who sleeps stretched out across the mouse's only escape hole.

15

EVERY FEW WEEKS Helen and I go together to see Gerald. He is seven years younger than Helen but he is a poor, broken old man who slobbers and cannot hear in spite of his deaf aid and sits all day in a wheelchair while Helen darts into the room where he is, her movements still swift and graceful, her hearing still acute, only her eyes misted over so that she peers to identify you and last time we went talked for some moments to another old man, mistakenly taking him for her brother-in-law.

I hardly know why I go. I knew Gerald only remotely while he was married to my aunt. He never married the woman he wrote to her about, asking for a divorce. The hanging presumably was too much for her, the marrying Vera Hillyard's widower too much to contemplate. It was too much for all of us, driving me into a panic marriage, scaring off Patricia's lover, killing (according to Helen) the General, destroying what remained of my parents' marriage so that they became strangers who seldom spoke. But Helen never lost touch with Gerald. She, of course, had known him while he was a subaltern, long before he met Vera. Both alone and to some extent exiled, they used occasionally to meet in London. When he handed over the house he had bought in Highgate to Francis and moved into the Baron's Home for Retired Officers, she began visiting him there once a week. He chose the Baron's Home because it was in Baron's Court and not too far from Helen's Kensington flat. She goes there less often today because of her great age, and perhaps my reason for going with her is that I don't think it a good idea for someone of ninety to be traveling alone about London.

The house is Victorian, red brick with white facing, a noisy place in one of those one-way streets that support a stream of traffic going south to cross the river. The front is more thickly double-glazed than anywhere I have seen, but at the back is a big walled garden with magnificent fig trees growing along the walls that seem to like the dirt and the fumes. They are mostly men, the inmates, though not exclusively, which always surprises me. Of course, I know that there were women officers in the armed forces in the Second World War but I still find it odd that two of them should have ended up here among the Western Desert veterans and heroes of the Normandy landings. All of them sit for most of the day in a big drawing room with French windows onto the fig garden. The television is never switched off, though no one seems to watch it except very desultorily, but if you pass in front of it or attempt to alter a channel, there is a murmur of grumbling. Nothing in the room indicates that these people are old soldiers (old sailors, old airmen), not a map, picture, war book. No one wears a regimental tie, much less a medal. One of the old men has the VC but he is the smallest and shyest of them and once I saw him get up and creep away when *A Bridge Too Far* came on the television.

Gerald is still thin but very shrunken now, his skin wrinkled like hide that has been underwater for a long time. He is senile. He has forgotten everything, not merely recent things but long-past happenings too. It is probably just as well. According to the woman in charge of this place, he loves to see us, our visits are high spots in his life, but he gives us no indication that this is so. He never smiles. He keeps his eyes on the television all the time we are there. When we come in, when we are beside him and indeed standing over him, he turns his eyes once and says:

"Ah, Helen!"

Me he does not recognize. He never has. He takes me for a daughter of Helen's, not Patricia, one whose name he has forgotten. I used to try to talk to him but I have given that up. What he likes is for me to hold his hand. He lays his right hand palm uppermost in his lap, takes my hand in his other and places it in the palm, finally gripping it quite hard. We sit like this, hands clasped for the whole of our stay. We do not talk at all, for talking to each other seems unfeeling.

Gerald faces the television, often with his eyes closed. I stare out of the French windows at the tall brown backs of houses behind, the narrow canyons between them through which, occasionally, a red bus can be seen passing, the gardens where nothing grows but plants and trees ugly enough and tough enough to withstand lead and petrol fumes, dirt and dehydration. Halfway through our visit, tea comes for the residents and cups of tea for us, though, mysteriously, we are never offered a cake or a biscuit.

Yesterday, just as tea arrived and our cups had been handed to us, a wrapped sugar loaf in each saucer, a man came into the room and stood looking about him, looking for Gerald as it turned out, and not immediately realizing he was the occupant of the wheelchair between two women. When he did, he came over, as unsmiling as his father. It was Francis. It is twenty-five years since last I saw him. On that occasion I met him by chance with his wife and children, Giles and Elizabeth, at the open-air theater in Regents Park. I saw them again, Liz and her children, but not Francis, for soon after the Regents Park encounter he had left them and gone off to South America looking for bugs. Francis has published two popular science books about the ways of insects. I wrote to congratulate him on the success of one of these, which I had enjoyed reading, which seemed to me to have nothing of Francis in it, but he didn't reply.

He looks like Vera now. The Anthony Andrews look has faded, the Sebastian Flyte ambience gone. He is thin to emaciation—how could he be otherwise with those parents?—and perhaps because he is an entomologist the comparison that suggested itself to me was with a praying mantis. There is a dried-up, wizened, worn-out look to Francis, a bleached-to-grayness look like one of those trees that have died and the wood been stripped of bark and abraded by weather. I think I only recognized him because this visitor could not have been anyone else.

Helen shifted herself into a vacant armchair in order to give him the chair next to his father. He kissed her, holding his face against hers for a little longer than is usual for a merely formal kiss. I remembered he had always liked her. Francis is the sort of person who can greet one woman with a kiss and the other whom he knows equally well with a glance of indifference. He was wearing a gray velvet suit, very old and shabby, with an extremely expensive new-looking shirt, Per Spook (I guessed) tie, and shoes from Tricker's. He gives the impression of being prosperous, the suit a rich man's eccentricity.

Helen told me afterwards that he has remarried, this time the widow
of a millionaire MP assassinated in Ireland. Why hadn't she told me
before? I asked. She had forgotten, she said, and the new wife's name
and almost everything about her. Now, if I had asked for his first
wife's name and where they had married and when . . .

I said, "How are you, Francis?"

"I am well." I don't know why this should be an affectation, not
qualifying the "well" with a "very" or a "quite," but it is. If he ever
writes letters, Francis probably begins them with a name and no
"Dear." He didn't ask me how I was. He sat down next to his father,
and to my astonishment, took his other hand.

Does he always do this? Does Gerald always hold hands with whoever comes under the age of ninety? He never holds Helen's hand. Or
is it that Francis, who seemed to me incapable of love and to Chad
Hamner capable only of the love of evil, loves his father? People are a
mystery, an enigma. Gerald never changed his name. Hillyard was
his name, not hers, and he stuck to it, but Francis, who seemed to
care for the opinion of no one, who snapped his fingers at the world,
called himself Hills from the day of his mother's arrest, anticipating
the worst, as he would; and lecturing at his university, writing his
books, collecting his bugs, he is Professor Frank Loder Hills.

So we sat there, each of us holding hands with Gerald, with
Gerald gripping our hands, for he does grip, closing his hand more
and more tightly over the imprisoned fingers until increasing pain
directs the time to get up and leave. Gerald did not slacken his grip
on my hand when he also had Francis's to hold, but held it harder, so
that weak and feeble as he is, he nevertheless seemed to be bearing
down on our hands preparatory to taking a flying leap out of the
wheelchair. I thought of Vera and that curious gesture of hers, leaning forward, pressing, crushing, as if to keep the pain from pouring
out. Does Gerald ever think of her now? Does Francis, also fair and
lined and dehydrated, not remind him of her, his eyes that same clear
sky blue? Sometimes surely, even now, he must think of how she tried
to palm off on him someone else's child, a child as dark-skinned as its
Puerto Rican father. I had forgotten about the eyes, forgotten how,
when in my teens, I had tried to remember or find out what color
Gerald's eyes were. But when Daniel Stewart started on his book I
remembered, and on my next visit to Gerald, yesterday's visit,
looked. They are blue. They are darker than Francis's and are a deep
cornflower blue.

We left the Baron's Home for Retired Officers together, all three of us, Helen and I to take a taxi home, Francis to head for the nearest NCP where he had parked his car. He talked to Helen, not about the family, not about his father, but, of all things, about a Russian science-fiction film currently showing at our local cinema, the Paris-Pullman. Apparently it is his local cinema too now, he and his wife having bought a house in Cresswell Place.

Taking no part in this conversation, I was looking for a taxi. On the opposite side of the street I saw an old man standing in the doorway of a shop, the kind of shop that is not much frequented, this one displaying in its window ceramic tiles. He seemed to be looking intently at us, or rather, to be looking at Francis, who had thrown back his head and was laughing at something Helen had said. He was a smallish man, gray-headed, wearing an overlong, unbelted raincoat, a man with an unremarkable face, eyes that seemed even at that distance full of sadness. I had a clutching sensation in my chest. The echo was not yet faint then, the voice not yet mute. . . .

Francis said to me, "You've been assisting Stewart with this book of his, I hear."

"Yes."

"That sort of thing is so vulgar and uncalled-for."

"Vulgar it may be, but not uncalled-for. His publishers asked him to do it."

"If he uses my name, that is, if he identifies me, I shall sue him. You can tell him that."

"*I* tell him?"

"That's what I said. It would bring me into hatred, ridicule, and contempt, all three of the grounds for libel. That husband of yours is a lawyer, isn't he? You ask him."

"That's two tasks you've set me in the past five minutes, Francis or Frank or whatever you call yourself," I said. "Just as well we only meet once every twenty-five years."

A taxi came. As Francis was helping Helen into it, I looked once more across the street and saw that the man in the doorway had been joined by a woman, that he was kissing her, that, arms linked now, they were moving off in the direction of Blythe Road. What yearning in me for romantic dramas, even of the tragic kind, had led me for one moment to believe that this was Chad Hamner? There was no resemblance, there was no possibility even that the aging process could have made Chad look like that. I was positive if he had passed closely enough I would have seen earlobes as unlined as a child's.

And suddenly, though between the two realizations there was no connection, suddenly I knew for certain that the event which Francis was so wrathfully anticipating, which made his eyes dark with rage as he glared at me, would never take place.

"You needn't worry," I said. "Stewart won't write that book."

"What makes you say that?"

"By the time," I said, "I've finished assisting him, as you put it, he won't want to."

That time he brought the girl to Laurel Cottage in Vera's absence was the last visit he ever paid to Sindon. It seems strange to me that someone who became an entomologist should have shown not the faintest interest, as far as I ever saw, in insects while he was a child. He didn't even pull the wings off flies, which is what one might have expected of Francis. After he went off to Edinburgh University to do his postgraduate work, he turned his back forever on Sindon, leaving behind, I was later to hear, a great many possessions, some of which were quite valuable and included presents from Chad. And Chad himself, who (whatever innocence in this matter he might claim) had used Vera as cover and deceived a good many people into believing they were having a love affair, never again went to Laurel Cottage once Francis was gone. That New Year visit when Vera was taken ill was almost the last time. Francis went to Queen Mary College and Chad followed him as soon as he could, covering Townswomen's Guilds and church bazaars in Willesden and living in that room at the top of a house from which Francis threw him downstairs.

Vera was alone. But she had Josie. She had Jamie. Quite often she also had Helen. After Eden had gone to Formentor, my father went to Sindon and stayed overnight, the purpose of his visit being to attempt to discourage Vera from moving. Without his consent and Eden's, of course, she couldn't move, but my father wanted it to seem her choice. She told him rather sorrowfully that she had never really believed he and Eden would consent, indeed she knew Eden wouldn't. It was just a long shot, worth trying, she said.

This conversation was later repeated to my mother, who repeated it to me at some time between Vera's arrest and her trial. My father had asked Vera why she wanted to move but she would say no more than that she was fed up with Sindon. He knew she was concealing her real motives.

"She thought she could run away from Eden," my mother said. "She thought she could escape with Jamie. The ends of the earth wouldn't have been far enough, not with Eden having money on her side."

"And right, I suppose," I said.

Having failed with him and Eden as she had guessed she would, Vera tried to get Gerald to buy them out, to buy their shares in the house for her. This was what she told my father she would do and presumably she did attempt it. If he wanted a divorce, he must pay for it, she said. No buying out, no divorce. I think my father was shocked to hear one of his sisters, pearls of virtue and rectitude that he thought them, talk like this. That, at any rate, is what my mother said. But she would, wouldn't she?

He told her that if Gerald offered to buy his share, he would sell it to him, but he couldn't answer for Eden. "You must make her, you must make her," Vera cried, clutching his arm, but she turned away then, saying it would be too late, it was all too late. My mother said Vera said a mysterious thing to him that we thought later we understood, though he, of course, did not at the time.

"Why did I do it this way?" she said. "I could have done it myself at any time."

Eden and Tony stayed in Majorca much longer than anyone expected. They had planned on a month and stayed nearly three. I suppose the weather began to get warm and the island pretty just as they were due to leave, so they stayed on and on. We had postcards and Helen had postcards, but according to my mother—how could she know?—Vera had none. They came back in the middle of April while I was staying at Walbrooks. It was a Saturday when they returned, exhausted no doubt, having flown from Palma to Barcelona and come by train from Barcelona to Paris, Paris to Calais, boat to Dover, train to Victoria, across London to Liverpool Street, train to Colchester. But on the Monday morning, Eden was in Sindon, at Laurel Cottage, prepared to take Jamie away.

No warning of her coming had been given to Vera. She knew Eden and Tony were home only because Helen (in my hearing) had phoned and told her so, herself very surprised that Vera was in ignorance. She had had a whole day in which to prepare herself—well, she had

had months really. I have said Josie was the only person to whom she would entrust Jamie, but the truth was she scarcely ever left him. Josie had probably baby-sat with him once in the past year and a half and that was when Vera went to a Naughton relative's wedding.

Vera lied to Josie. She asked her to have Jamie because her solicitor was coming to see her about the divorce. Did Josie really believe this? Her own son was in practice by that time and she must have known solicitors don't usually travel miles out into the countryside to visit unimportant clients at nine in the morning. For it was as early as this that Vera expected Eden to come and by then she had already taken him to Josie. When I first heard this, I thought of Moses being hidden by his mother in the bulrushes and I looked up the story in Exodus and found it wasn't like that at all. She made him an ark *out of* bulrushes and hid it in the flags by the river's brink, flags presumably being irises. But Jamie's concealment wasn't much like any of this, he being five and not an infant. Though he was young for his age in his need for Vera. By midday he was crying and asking for her, and Josie, harassed by it, took him home. If there really had been a solicitor and he had come at nine, he would surely be gone by twelve.

Vera had miscalculated. The reason probably was that Eden got up late as a matter of course. She can't have had much to occupy her. Instead of nine, she arrived at eleven. Even today I don't like to think of what Vera's state of mind must have been during those two hours. At least Jamie wasn't there. It isn't hard to imagine the kind of thing Vera would have said, not if you knew her as I did.

"I've hidden him where you'll never find him!"

And then Josie came. She found Vera and Eden there alone, sitting facing each other in the living room, each of them with the air of sticking it out as if for a siege. Vera put out her arms to Jamie when she saw him and he ran into them. Eden gave a scornful sort of laugh. She said:

"I suppose you rehearsed this little bit of drama."

I know all this because Josie phoned Helen almost immediately after Eden had left. She was very angry and very upset and she poured some of it out to me—I answered the phone—before I handed her over to Helen. Eden had left at last without Jamie but not without promising to come back.

Vera, on seeing Josie, appealed to her to support her in physically repelling Eden's attempts to take Jamie. She seems to have seen everything in physical terms at this time, as if action and the expense of energy would save things, while argument and reason wouldn't. She had something there, I suppose.

"I'll hold Jamie while you make her go," was what Josie told us Vera said.

This shocked Josie. She told Vera she wouldn't dream of being a party to what she suggested. There must be no question of Eden taking Jamie from his mother. She had never heard of such a thing, she said. I daresay she hadn't. She asked Eden—very sternly and sharply, I understand—whatever made her think she had a right to take Jamie forcibly away from his mother and his home.

"He's not being properly looked after here," Eden said. "He's got no friends of his own age. He's kept isolated like a hermit. He's nearly six and the only time he's been to school is for two weeks while he was with me. She neglects him—look at his shoes!"

The facts were that Vera was poor, she received a very meager sum each week from Gerald, and had nothing else. What was amiss with Jamie's shoes I don't know but no more than that they were unsuitable for the time of year or had the wrong color laces in them, I am sure. Neglected he never was, rather the reverse, for leaving him to himself more would have done him good. Anyway, Josie took no notice of this. She said if Eden was going to adopt Jamie it would have to be decided by lawyers in courts, not fought over like this.

"Make her go," said Vera, holding Jamie in her arms.

"You hear what she says," Josie said. "You'd better go."

The hatred between them hung in the air like poison gas, she said to Helen. "Vibes" was what we called this sort of thing later on. It was terrible to see sisters so at loggerheads, she said. How would she have felt if she had seen them as they used to be, like I had?

"I'll go now but I'll be back," Eden said.

This was the first time Josie had met her. She was not in the least intimidated by her wealth and what Vera called her "power."

"If this happens again," she said, "I'll call the police."

Helen reacted by getting Andrew to drive her to Laurel Cottage and bringing Vera and Jamie back with her to Walbrooks. Once there she did her best to get an explanation of all of it out of Vera. We were all there. Things had become too serious to bother about appearances or excluding people on grounds of age.

Vera was calm by now, almost cool. I think she felt safe at Walbrooks, which must have made what happened subsequently all the worse for her. It was a beautiful day, very warm for April, and we sat in the big drawing room where Eden's wedding reception had been, with the French windows open onto the garden and the sun streaming in. The great lawn that reached to the lake was scattered all round its edges with drifts of daffodils, and up near the house were blue scyllas and those little scarlet specie tulips that are more beautiful than orchids.

"If you tell Eden firmly she has to forget all ideas about adopting Jamie, she will have to give it up," Helen said to Vera. "Perhaps you had better write to her, darling. Why don't we compose a letter now, an absolutely uncompromising one, and you can send it off. Faith and Andrew will walk up to the village and post it for you, won't you, darlings? And that way Eden will get it in the morning."

Vera didn't seem too keen on this. It would "do no good," she said. It would just be "making matters worse."

"But why would it, Vera?" Helen insisted. "Did you make Eden some sort of promise when you were ill that she could have Jamie and you're afraid to revoke now? Is that it? Because you shouldn't let that count with you at all, you'll have to forget that."

"Of course I didn't promise that," Vera said. "Would I promise that?"

The General hated Eden. He was all for going to law. "If I got hold of my solicitor," he said. "I know what he'd do. He'd take the lot of us along to a judge in chambers and get an injunction. He'd get an injunction to restrain that little harpy from ever coming within a mile of you and the boy again."

"Now, General," said Helen, "she's my sister too, you know."

"Only of the half-blood," he said, forgetting no doubt that this also applied to Vera.

However, nothing else happened that day or the next. Eden had become ill again. Not in the same way this time, not with her kidneys. The prosecution at Vera's trial said that Vera had made a second attempt to murder her by giving her some noxious substance in a cup of coffee at Laurel Cottage on the Monday morning. The two objections to that seem to me that this time Eden had sickness and diarrhea, which at any rate argues a different kind of poison, and second, that one simply cannot imagine Vera offering and Eden taking anything to eat or drink in those circumstances. She is waiting more or less in a state of siege for her sister to come and take away her child and at the same time brewing a welcoming cup of coffee?

We found out about Eden because Helen phoned up to "have a

straight talk with her." She didn't have any sort of talk at all. Mrs. King answered and said Eden was in bed and the doctor had been sent for. Vera laughed when Helen told her, and said in a mad kind of way that God was not mocked. She talked like this a lot, or in disjointed non sequiturs rather like Ophelia does. She stayed on at Walbrooks, alternating her behavior between an almost cataleptic calm and excited, frenetic bursts of energy. I was due to go home in a few days' time and Andrew was coming with me for the rest of our holiday. It was to be our last term and finals were looming. Now I felt for the first time I couldn't wait to get away from Walbrooks to London. One of the things Vera did during one of her energy peaks was offer to lengthen all the kitchen curtains for Helen. They had been badly washed and had shrunk. There are five windows in the kitchen at Walbrooks so it would be quite a task. Ever since then, the sight of a woman sewing on a large piece of work, the stuff spread tapestry-wise across her lap, her head bent and pursed fingers dipping back and forth, brings Vera back to me. Perhaps it is why I never sew, never dreamt of making curtains for my own homes.

On the Friday morning, Andrew and I went off to London in the fifth-hand car Andrew had bought, an old Morris Ten. Helen told us not to stay and wait for Vera. She and the General would take her home. She had a feeling, she said, that we had heard the last of Eden's claims on Jamie. It was all over, it had been a try-on. The General had probably hit the nail on the head when he talked of promises made when Vera was ill and feeble.

So we went, relieved but with no reason to feel relief. I told my father nothing about it and Andrew said nothing either, though we had made no prearrangement to avoid the subject. I think now that what we both felt, what we onlookers all felt, was that there was so much more to this than met the eye, so many submerged secrets contributing to it, things deliberately kept from us, that we should be making fools of ourselves if we expressed opinions and advised courses. Andrew and I didn't even discuss it with each other during those few days, but when we were in the train taking us back to Cambridge, alone in the carriage, he said to me suddenly, in the manner of a man making a confession:

"I haven't told you this, I didn't tell anyone, I didn't want to cause concern. It's been on my conscience, after all that talk of solicitors and injunctions. While we were at home, the day before we left, I saw June Poole at the top of our drift."

"Drift" is what they call a lane in that part of the country. This one led from the road down to the house, passing Walbrooks cottages on the way, passing a boarded-up house no one had lived in for twenty years, passing barns and the stables.

"She might have been to one of the cottages, you know. She could have a cousin or an aunt there. It always seems to me that everyone down there is related to everyone else."

Andrew said, "She had her back to me, she was walking away, but I had the feeling she had been standing just inside the hedge, waiting. And then she saw me."

I asked him how he could be absolutely sure it was she. How far away had she been?

He was glad to clutch at any straw. At least a hundred yards, maybe more. If it had been a matter of swearing to it—well, no, he couldn't have done that. He was never asked to, as it turned out, but he came closer to doing so than he could have dreamed of when he made that dramatic-seeming declaration. I didn't think he should tell his father then?

"What good would that do?" I said.

It reminds me now, all this, of Sunny Durham and the Kirby Theiston murder, though I hardly know why. There are few similarities. At the time I thought of Kathleen March, spirited away while in Vera's care and killed. Was it really June Poole that Andrew had seen, and had she been waiting in the hope of snatching Jamie?

I never saw Vera again. That Friday morning, I dutifully kissed her good-bye, or rather, we laid our cheeks in juxtaposition and kissed the air.

"Give my love to your father," she said. "I might come up to London and surprise him one of these fine days."

The last words she ever spoke to me apart from good-bye. Longleys never say "bye-bye"—did I mention that? There is a prohibition on it, strict as the ban on eating with one's right hand.

"Good-bye," said Vera, waving, standing beside Helen on the drift and waving. "Good-bye!" Jamie waved too, both hands up, pinching his fingers open and shut the way I once saw an American professor, while lecturing, demonstrate quotation marks. The last time I looked back, he and Vera were walking back to the house hand in hand.

The rest I know from Helen and Josie. The General drove Vera and Jamie home to Sindon in the afternoon, by now convinced that all was well and that a great deal of what had happened had been in Vera's, if not Josie's, imagination. He stayed half an hour and went off home. Helen rang Vera next day and found her cheerful and calm. She rang Eden. Eden was much better, was expecting six people to lunch, refused to discuss the future guardianship of Jamie. There was nothing to discuss, she said, it was all settled. Helen took this to mean Eden had given up and was being haughty in defeat.

Nothing happened on Sunday. I have sometimes tried to imagine a day in Vera's life and Jamie's together at this time. It is hard for me to do this, for I have never lived such a life myself, alone in a remote country village, with few friends, without a car, in genteel poverty. Vera couldn't afford to ask six people to lunch even if she had wanted to. What did they do? Got up early, I have no doubt, Vera to do housework, the dusting and polishing that were done every day while I stayed there, Jamie to play with his toys. Then, for Vera, the *Sunday Express,* a walk perhaps; lunch, always a piece of roast meat, a tiny minuscule piece, the whole week's ration in 1950, roast potatoes, Yorkshire pudding, a green vegetable, and jam tart or custard trifle to follow. Another walk afterwards? A sleep? The wireless? Sewing or knitting, of course. She would have read a story to him, perhaps several stories, talked to him and played with him. But still the imagination is defeated by the task of filling those long hours, especially when it was cold or wet or got dark early. Vera never read except for the children's books she read aloud. The bookcase in the living room was stocked with a nonreader's collection, school "set" books and surely unwelcome presents.

If I close my eyes I can see that bookcase now. I can see Jamie running his toy tank along the lower shelf and up the spines of the books. Was Bulletin No. 23, *Edible and Poisonous Fungi,* there at the time? I don't think it was. I can see what was there: *Precious Bane, Anthony Adverse, Sesame and Lilies* that had been a school prize, *Black Bartlemy's Treasure,* Frohawk's *Complete Book of British Butterflies* . . . So was I wrong in saying Francis showed no interest in entomology when young? Was this Francis's book? Was it possible, then, that the fungi book was also his and at that period was upstairs in the book-shelf in his room? *Wuthering Heights, The History of Mr. Polly, Lamb's Tales* . . . and is this dark green spine next to it perhaps Bulletin No. 23? It can't have been in two places at the same time. It may not even have been in the house at all then. But I know that once I saw it there, in that bookcase, in Vera's living room, dark green with the gold chanterelle on its cover and the fascinating mycological lore within.

That particular Sunday—I don't remember whether it was wet or fine. I was in Cambridge. At that particular time I was "growing out" of my family, and this by leaps and bounds, making decisions that as a soon-to-be independent person I would in future have no more to do with my father's sisters, regretfully contemplating, too, a breach with Helen, which would be inevitable if I gave Andrew up. Since I gave a good deal of thought to all this, I was probably thinking of it that Sunday in between rereading Spenser's *Faerie Queene* and meeting Andrew. I don't suppose, though, that I thought of Vera as a suffering person, drawn into the worst kind of the converging of human lots. Like the rest of us, I believed she and Eden had settled their differences. And fancying myself in those days as a sprightly feminist intellectual, I am afraid I probably also thought their petty squabbles beneath me.

For that I was to be punished. Murder reaches out through a family, stamping transfers of the Mark of Cain on a dozen foreheads, and though these grow pale in proportion to the distance of the kinship, they are there and they burn into the brain. A question, a chance word, will discover them, as invisible writing appears shimmeringly when exposed to fire. Only time bleaches them away and makes it possible to reach back into the past in a kind of tranquillity.

Monday came. Vera contemplated running away. Later in the day she told Josie she had thought of running away. She had even begun to pack a bag, to gather together Jamie's clothes and certain of his books and toys. As a refugee she saw herself—in the past years, however ignorant we may have been before, we had come to know what refugees were—fleeing ahead of an invading army, uncaring of what she left behind, taking with her the only precious thing she had. But where could she go and how would she live? She had no money and no means of earning any and nothing to sell.

At ten o'clock, Eden arrived with June Poole and Mrs. King. June was wearing the gray dress we had seen her in and a gray felt hat, requisite nanny's garb. Mrs. King had a box of Black Magic chocolates. Sweets were still rationed in the spring of 1950 (and were to be for years longer), so these chocolates would have been accounted a rare prize, if a rather unsuitable choice as bribe for a child of six. It was a sunny morning, quite warm, and they found Jamie playing in the back garden of Laurel Cottage in a sandpit Vera had made for him up near the house. In my childhood and Eden's, the sandpit had been down at the bottom of the garden near the hovel, now irrevocably associated in my mind with the loves of Chad and Francis—but this would have been too far away for Vera. She needed him within her sight.

She soon saw what was happening, for she was in the kitchen doing the washing. It was Monday, so Vera was doing the washing. It was to be the most terrible day of her life, and I think she knew it would be, but it was also Monday and therefore washing day. From the window she saw what was happening. June Poole, in her gray uniform, was squatting down on the edge of the sandpit with her arm round Jamie, and Mrs. King was bending over him, showing him the chocolates. How had Eden enlisted them in her private army? By convincing them, no doubt, of the rightness of her cause.

Vera didn't immediately see Eden. She ran out of the house with dripping hands, literally to be caught by Eden, who was standing on the path that went past the back door. Eden took her by the shoulders and said:

"Now, Vera, be sensible. You know you're going to have to give in, so why not do it now without a scene?"

Vera let out a scream, struggled, and ducked under Eden's arms. She ran to Jamie but June had picked Jamie up and was carrying him back the way they had come.

"That's the way, June," Eden said. "Just get him into the car as fast as you can and we'll be off."

It was at this point that Josie arrived, calling as she did most mornings to see if Vera wanted any shopping or merely for a chat and a cup of coffee. At first she couldn't believe what she saw. That is the way it is when we witness sensational acts that seem unreal in the context of a humdrum life. Josie thought: Someone is acting, it's a game. But these feelings lasted only seconds. She could see Vera hanging on to June, being dragged away by the combined efforts of Eden and Mrs. King, hear Vera screaming and crying. She shouted at Eden:

"What on earth do you think you're doing?"

Eden said, "Stay out of this, please, Mrs. Cambus. This is a matter between my sister and me."

"Don't let them take him, Josie!" Vera screamed. "Don't let them!"

By now Jamie was in the car. He also was screaming. Two or three of Vera's neighbors came out, though she had no very near neighbors, it was not like it would have been in a London street. Josie's first thought was for Vera, whom she tried to take in her arms, but Vera threw herself onto the car, beating her hands on the windows and shouting Jamie's name.

Eden jumped into the driving seat. Josie thought she was going to slam the door on Vera's hand. She just missed. She started the car with a roar, turned once to look at Josie. The awful thing, Josie said, was that tears were pouring down Eden's face. Mrs. King and June sat in the back, keeping hold of the by now nearly demented Jamie, who was thrashing about screaming, "Mummy, Mummy!"

Eden drove away and Vera would have been sent flying except that Josie caught her. With one arm round her, Vera's head buried in her shoulder, Josie led her back into the house.

16

———————————————◆

THIS MORNING'S POST has brought from Daniel Stewart part of the transcript of Vera's trial. Until now I have kept myself in ignorance of what went on at the Central Criminal Court during that week in the summer of 1950. My father, too, died in ignorance of it. What we had instead was a firsthand version of what took place that Monday at Goodney Hall from Josie herself. But an account of the evening Josie and my father and myself spent closeted in our living room, a stiff whiskey inside each of us and more to come, I shall postpone until a little later.

Stewart wants me "to add your own comments, please, Mrs. Severn." What comments can I have? I wasn't there. I was in Cambridge and that term I never read the papers. My father, in London, canceled the *Daily Telegraph* from the day of Vera's appearance in the magistrates' court until a week after her trial ended, and when he came back to it found the crossword too difficult, after this lapse of time, ever to complete again. I tried to banish Vera from my mind, to cut myself off from her, but for all that, I took a less good degree than was expected of me. That one paragraph I had read before I banned newspapers from my sight haunted me, coming often between my eyes and other, more literary printed pages.

Vera Ivy Hillyard, 43, of Bell Lane, Great Sindon, Essex, appeared today at Colchester Magistrates' Court charged with the murder of her sister, Edith Mary Pearmain. . . .

Andrew and I married in a panic, to keep it in the family. So many people knew Vera and Eden were our aunts. I imagined them gossiping, and their gossip putting out tentacles to reach out as far away as London, as Cambridge. My resolution to shake off my family, to leave it behind like the snake's worn-out, no-longer-useful skin, had to be given up. What they had done made that impossible. I was stuck with them, tumbled with the other siblings and cousins, niece and nephew, into a kind of ghetto. It seems to me now that I married Andrew to be saved in much the same manner as someone may marry for citizenship or to avoid being deported. Or perhaps it was as the blind marry the blind or the crippled the handicapped. Two years our marriage lasted before we parted by mutual consent.

Soon after our divorce he married someone else who quickly gave Helen a granddaughter. Helen was a widow by then and Walbrooks sold and Tony gone God knew where in the Far, having with the approval of higher authority planted Jamie in boarding school. Jamie had been made a ward of the court, being like Melchisadek, the Priest King, without father, without mother, and without descent.

More than anyone I ever heard of, in fact.

Next week I am going to see him. He is going to cook the promised meal for me and we shall sit in his garden in the warm Florentine dusk and . . . compare notes.

Meanwhile, am I going to read this transcript? Why give myself the scratch of pain, the inevitable wincing, it is bound to bring? If this were the 1940's and a fire burned in my grate, might I not do as my father did with the winter letters, and drop these sheets of paper in the fire? Ah, but, I remind myself, he always read them first, and often read them, considering from whom they came, many times.

So here goes, then. At least it isn't all here, only the vital bits, says Stewart. Josie was principal witness for the defense and this was part of her evidence. Counsel had asked her to describe what happened after Eden and her henchwomen took Jamie away:

> JOSEPHINE CAMBUS: I went back into the house with her. She was hysterical, screaming and crying. There was some brandy in the house and I gave her some in a glass with water. I said to her that I would phone the police but she told me that would be useless so I said I would speak to my son. He would know what to do.

MR. JUSTICE LAMBERT: Is your son a policeman?

MRS. CAMBUS: No, my lord, a solicitor.

COUNSEL: Did you speak to your son, Mrs. Cambus?

MRS. CAMBUS: I tried to. I had asked the operator for his number. Vera, Mrs. Hillyard, took the phone out of my hand. She said lawyers and policemen would be useless.

COUNSEL: Did you ask her why?

MRS. CAMBUS: She said only she and her sister knew the ins and outs of it. Those were her words. She said she would go to Goodney Hall and talk to her sister and her sister's husband. It was important, she said, to speak to her sister's husband, and she would wait there, on the doorstep if necessary, until he came home. She was quite calm by then. She seemed fatalistic. She seemed—

MR. JUSTICE LAMBERT: Never mind what she seemed, Mrs. Cambus. The jury will wish to know what you saw and heard, not what you surmised.

COUNSEL: Did Mrs. Hillyard then go to Goodney Hall and did you go with her?

COUNSEL FOR THE PROSECUTION: My lord, is not my learned friend leading the witness?

MR. JUSTICE LAMBERT: I think perhaps he is.

COUNSEL: I apologize, my lord. I will rephrase the question. What did Mrs. Hillyard then do, Mrs. Cambus?

MRS. CAMBUS: She put on her coat and fetched her handbag and said she would catch the bus to Bures and wait there for the bus to Goodney, unless I would take her there by car. I did not much want to go, I didn't want to be involved, but I agreed to take her, having some idea that I wouldn't go inside but would leave her there and return home. I went home and fetched my car and drove her to Goodney Hall. When we got there she begged me to go to the door on the grounds that if she went they wouldn't let her in.

COUNSEL: Did you in fact do as she asked?

MRS. CAMBUS: I refused at first, I didn't want to, but at last I did. Mr. Pearmain opened the door to me. He said—

COUNSEL: You must not tell us what Mr. Pearmain said to you unless Mrs. Hillyard was present. Was she present?

MRS. CAMBUS: No, she was in the car.

COUNSEL: Very well. As a result of what Mr. Pearmain said to you, what did you do?

MRS. CAMBUS: I went back to the car and fetched Mrs. Hillyard

and we both went into the house with Mr. Pearmain. There was
no one else present at that time. We went into a room I think
they call the drawing room. Mrs. Hillyard said she had something to say to Mr. Pearmain in private, something she wanted
him to know, and would I go outside for a moment? I said I
would go home, I had no reason to stay, but she begged me to
wait for her, just to go out of the room for a short time. Mr.
Pearmain said he thought he knew what she wished to say but
he knew already, his wife had told him a few days before. At
this point Mrs. Pearmain came into the room and said to Mrs.
Hillyard, "I have told him everything . . ."

I laid the transcript down. I had read this sort of thing before,
having been shown such by my husband and in *Notable British Trials*.
They are all much of a muchness, all have that air of unreality in
which people converse as if programmed in language confined exclusively to these particular surroundings. Yet I am told transcripts are
almost always faithful verbatim accounts of what was said.
Strange. . . . From this point, anyway, Josie had begun her own tale
to us in the quiet, intimate, rather breathless atmosphere of my parents' overheated living room. There she began by repeating to us the
actual words Eden had used on walking into the Etruscan drawing
room that April morning:

"You can't get your own way like that, Vera. I've told Tony everything. I've told him Jamie is my son."

We knew, of course. We knew by then. The bare facts had reached us
even though we chose to take ostrich attitudes to the trial. It was the
details we wanted from Josie, the subtleties that clothed the bare facts
in kind, veiling disguises. Leaning forward in her chair, not looking
at us, but looking into the fire, she said:

"Vera cried out. I've never been able to make up my mind
whether or not it was a denial. Tony—I never knew him as that but
that's what I'll call him—Tony looked grim. He looked miserable.
He stood there nodding, with his eyes almost closed. Your sister—I
mean Edith, Eden—she said, 'He's my child. Vera only brought him
up. She offered to do it, I admit that, it was generous of her, a wonderful thing to do, but there was never any question of her having
him for keeps.' 'You liar!' Vera said. Tony was terribly embarrassed.
I think he's the sort of man who would be embarrassed more than

anything else in a tragic situation. He said, 'Mrs. Cambus doesn't want to hear all this. This is a private matter, let's keep it so.' 'Oh no, we can't,' said Vera. 'Everyone's going to have to know. I'm not having you hush it up. I'll shout it from the housetops what she's been to me, a snake in the grass, a cruel tormentor. I want to see my boy,' she said. 'Where's my boy?' 'He's not your boy,' Eden said. 'He's mine. He'll be mine and Tony's. We're going to adopt him legally.' 'How can you adopt your own child?' Vera said, and that was the nearest she got to conceding anything to Eden. Though of course you can adopt your own child if he's illegitimate, I asked my son about that.

"Vera began to abuse Eden. I don't suppose you want to know what she said, the actual words, I mean?"

My father shook his head. "The gist," he said.

"Well, I suppose you'd call them aspersions on Eden's moral character. Eden hated it. Tony looked as if he were going to faint but Eden was utterly calm. She told us the whole thing, I mean me and Tony. I'm sure he hadn't heard any of the details before. He sat down and put his head in his hands."

The story that came out was that Eden had found herself pregnant in the autumn of 1943. By whom she made no attempt to say. It was Vera who interjected that she had been with half a dozen men, including a G.I., a private soldier who was a Puerto Rican out of Spanish Harlem, and who was the most beautiful thing in Londonderry at that time. Josie had the impression that this must have been told Vera when Eden made the first outpourings of confession. It was true that Jamie, though fair-haired, had eyes of a rich, southern brown and a pale olive skin the sun never burned. Eden herself had, it seemed, tried to make Vera believe (and Vera *had* believed at the time) she had been having a passionate love affair with an officer in the Royal Navy who died when the *Lagan* was torpedoed in the September of 1943. Who could forget another naval officer claimed as Eden's lover or would-be lover, he who was the subject of Francis's most spectacular tease, he who also went down with his ship? Vera and Eden, poor things, were snobs to the end.

She had told Francis before she told Vera, I am sure of that. It is exactly what she would have done, and Francis's cryptic utterances to me on the morning before the first kidnap attempt confirm it. Francis probably told her where she could get an abortion, it is the kind of thing he would have known. And he may have given her the money, or some of the money, to pay for it. Francis always had money. I think he prostituted himself. For some reason, then, she didn't have an abortion. Did she tell Vera and did Vera talk her out of it, Vera who wanted a child and had told Helen so but was herself unable to conceive? Eden must have left the Wrens months, years even, before any of the rest of us knew she had. She came to Laurel Cottage and hid herself there.

It is hard today for us to understand, even for people of my age, how terrible it still was in 1944 for a conventional middle-class girl to have an illegitimate child. And Eden had set herself up so, presented herself and been presented by the arch PR woman, her sister, as such a paragon. She could not have written to her brother and confessed this to him, explained it to her half-sister and her half-sister's husband, have it known in Sindon where she had been the sweet, grave adolescent, orphaned young. But if her sister, that older sister who had been a mother to her, would seem to be pregnant, would seem to give birth, would appear with a baby . . . ?

Not all of this is what Josie told us that winter's evening. Some of it I have pieced together with my own knowledge, with observations I made and could not then account for, from my imagination and from my knowledge of those two women, my aunts, my dead aunts, one murdered by the other.

Vera may have made her offer out of love of Eden, from sheer altruism and a desire to protect her reputation. She may have made it because she wanted a baby. Having failed so lamentably with Francis, she wanted to try again. Or, and this is most likely, it was both. She saw it as being to everyone's advantage. Who knows now what was said between them? Did Vera truly promise only to keep the child till Eden herself wanted him? Or did she take him over unconditionally, to be absolutely her own son? Yes, said Eden to the first. Vera said nothing, Josie said. She sat there transfixed, listening.

The child was born in a nursing home in Colchester, the one which was bombed in the following year and all its records destroyed. Eden went in as Mrs. Hillyard, she said. She had been to a doctor for antenatal examinations as Mrs. Hillyard. Vera went away while she was in the nursing home and stayed in a boardinghouse at Felixstowe. They arranged things this way: Eden left the nursing home in a taxi with the baby. Vera left Felixstowe and they met in Colchester in the lounge of the George Hotel, being driven home together, all three of them, in another hire car. Vera laughed derisively when Eden said this, as if no fiction could be more absurd.

"Eden went out of the room," Josie said, "and came back with a long envelope with something in it. It was a birth certificate, Jamie's birth certificate."

"Did you see it?" I asked her.

"Oh yes, I saw it. It was for James Longley, mother Edith Mary Longley, father unknown. Vera snatched it from me. She said it was a forgery. Then she said Eden had made a false declaration to the registrar and that was a serious offense punishable by years in prison. It was ridiculous, of course. There was the birth certificate with the facts on it plain to see. Vera herself had never seen it before. I think she was afraid to see it, ever to ask to see it. She knew only too well what was on it."

"But surely," I said, "if they'd made this arrangement, they must also have arranged that a false declaration *should* be made. Why didn't Vera herself, who was well, who hadn't got up from just having had a baby, why didn't she go to the registrar?"

Josie couldn't tell us that but I thought I knew the answer. I could imagine the way it was. Not so much Eden hedging her bets, making contingency plans just in case one day she would want Jamie, as simple fear at making a false declaration. The warnings against so doing are very stern in registrars' offices. Did she set out determined to register Jamie as the son of Vera Hillyard and Gerald Hillyard, yet when she got there, lose her nerve? But that doesn't answer the question: why didn't Vera go herself? Most likely because Eden simply got there first, went out alone a couple of days after they were back in Sindon and returned to present Vera with a *fait accompli*.

"Vera had it in her hands," said Josie, "and she tried to tear it up. Those things are made of reinforced paper and they're hard to tear but she tore a bit of it before Tony took it away from her. Not that it would have done any good, destroying it. A copy of it would have been there in the records at Somerset House."

So Vera took Jamie to be her own son and Eden went away to London to this job she had lined up as companion to old Lady Rogerson. How much easier things would have been for Vera if Jamie had been born just a month earlier! Gerald would never have accepted a ten-and-a-half-month child. If she had told him the truth, would he have refused to let her claim Jamie as her own? Perhaps. Perhaps, even, he would have told people Eden was Jamie's true mother. In a way, I think, once she had lost Gerald, Vera wasn't displeased at having people suspect Chad of being her lover and Jamie's father. It gave her identity, it gave her youth. And she had Jamie. She could never have foreseen how devotedly she would come to love him.

Eden hardly ever came near her. She didn't inquire after Jamie, she didn't want to know. There is a Jewish joke concerning the man who says of an enemy: Why does he hate me so? I never did him any good. Was that how Eden felt towards Vera now? Vera had done her too much good, had done her a supreme service. It was too much for her to handle, the guilt was too heavy, and she transposed it into dislike for Vera. And then she met Tony and became engaged to him. She would have more babies now, Vera must have thought. It was all right, safe, for she would never want a husband to know about Jamie. But when no babies came, when there was a miscarriage, the result of an ectopic pregnancy, and the chances of a safe pregnancy, a delivery at term, looked unlikely, what then? It was then that Vera began to be afraid. She might never have seen the birth certificate but she would guess its contents. If Eden made a claim on Jamie, she wouldn't, as Francis said to me, have a leg to stand on. Perhaps it was made worse for her by Eden's evident indifference to Jamie. That would not prevent her taking him for the sake of having a son, of having an heir for Tony and his shop empire.

"Vera jumped up quite suddenly," Josie said, "and ran out of the room. No one was expecting it, least of all Eden. Eden sat there victorious, you know, her marriage in ruins, her family alienated, but triumphant just the same, unassailable, if you know what I mean. That was the feeling I had, anyway. She got up quite slowly and said, 'I suppose she's gone to find him. I don't precisely know where he is.'

"We followed her. I have often wished I hadn't. What was it to me, anyway? I was just Vera's friend who had driven her to the house. I should have gone home and I don't know why I didn't. It wasn't unwholesome curiosity, I had had enough of revelations, soul-baring. I expect it was a feeling that I shouldn't desert Vera there in the house of her enemies—for they were all her enemies, weren't they? Down to June Poole, that minion of Eden's."

I could not look at my father nor he at me. In a curious, unwise way, he had made his idealization of Longley womanhood, embodied in his mother, then his sisters, a cornerstone of his life. It was all founded on illusion as idealization mostly is, and it was very foolish of

him to have sacrificed his marriage to it, to have made himself ridiculous by investing his sisters with qualities they not only did not have
but which were the antitheses of what they did have. But how dreadfully sorry one felt for him! He had little left now because his world
was altered. He even had to rethink his conception of his wife and
daughter because hitherto he had seen them through Longley specta-
cles, one lens being Vera, the other Eden. He had seen them only in
the light of comparison and contrast. I will say for my mother, much
to her credit, that from the time of the murder and Vera's arrest, she
uttered no word of disparagement of either of his sisters, and when
she did speak of them, it was always with pity. But, for all that, she
became a silent woman.

Josie told us the rest of it. She went on to the end and finished.
Jamie was upstairs in the nursery. He was old to be in a nursery, he
was old to *have* a nursery, but those two between them, in their different ways, had kept him a baby. The room was beautiful, Josie remembered. Of course she had never been there before, had never
seen it when it had the fairy wallpaper, the carpet with the ivy leaves.
The new carpet was pale blue and the furniture was white. Yachts
sailed in a frieze along the walls on pale blue wavelets and seagulls
flew above the sails. There was a print of the boyhood of Raleigh,
another of Stubbs horses, and one of the *Fighting Téméraire.*

It wasn't a cold day but it was still only April and there was a fire
with a fireguard in front of it. June Poole was at the far end of the
room, folding linen. Jamie stood on the blue-and-white rug in front
of the fire and Vera knelt in front of him. Josie had the impression he
had had no occupation, was doing nothing at all when Vera came in,
had just been standing or sitting there bewildered by the recent violent events. They burst into the room—Eden, Tony, Josie, and Mrs.
King, though why she had joined them and at what point, no one
seemed to know.

"Eden said, 'If you won't get out of here I will have you put out,'
and she looked at Mrs. King and June. Mrs. King did nothing but
June Poole put down the pillowcase she was holding and came to-
wards us, it seemed to me in rather a menacing way. Tony said,
'Eden, this has got to stop,' and Eden said, 'I quite agree with you.
I'm stopping it now,' and she put out her arms to pick Jamie up."

I shall quote from the transcript now. It is the official version, after
all, and what Josie said in court predates by six months what Josie
said to us.

COUNSEL: What happened then, Mrs. Cambus?

MRS. CAMBUS: Mrs. Hillyard had a knife in her hand.

COUNSEL: What do you mean, a knife in her hand? Did she pick the knife up from somewhere? Did she bring it with her?

MRS. CAMBUS: I suppose she must have done. She took it out of her handbag. It was a long kitchen knife.

(Mrs. Cambus was shown a knife, Exhibit B.)

COUNSEL: Is this the knife?

MRS. CAMBUS: It was like that, yes.

COUNSEL: Had you ever seen it before?

MRS. CAMBUS: Must I answer that?

MR. JUSTICE LAMBERT: Certainly you must answer Counsel.

MRS. CAMBUS: Well, yes, then, I had seen it.

COUNSEL: Where?

MRS. CAMBUS: In Mrs. Hillyard's kitchen. She used it for cutting vegetables. I have see her sharpen it with a stone.

COUNSEL: So Mrs. Hillyard took a knife from her bag. What happened?

MRS. CAMBUS: Mrs. Hillyard lunged at Mrs. Pearmain with the knife. Someone picked the boy up, Mrs. King I think it was, yes, it was Mrs. King. She picked the boy up and took him out of the room. Mr. Pearmain tried to get hold of Mrs. Hillyard. She stabbed him in the arm, the right arm. Then she attacked Mrs. Pearmain, wounding her in the neck and the chest. There was a lot of blood, blood everywhere. Mrs. Pearmain screamed and fell over, she fell onto all-fours, she was bleeding dreadfully.

The blood went over the white walls and the yachts and the wavelets and the seagulls. Eden vomited blood and died. She rolled over dead on the rug in front of the fire. Vera would have turned the knife on herself, almost did, but June Poole took her by the arms and tied her with the belt of her own dress.

17

INSTEAD OF VERA'S story, Daniel Stewart is to write an examination of the Kirby Theiston case, tying the murder of Sunny
Durham in with the disappearance of Kathleen March. This will be
a reappraisal in the light of the new evidence he found while research-
ing my family. And he will be able to use a great deal of what I have
told him when he writes of the part Vera played. I think he is happy
about it, quite excited even, and relieved to be free of Longley and
Hillyard complexities. So I was right—though not wholly confident at
the time—when I told Francis his mother's story would never be written.

The trial transcript I have destroyed after reading it twice. Morbid
temptation might draw me back to it on wet afternoons or evenings
when I am alone, and I don't care to be so directly reminded of poor
Vera's pain or, indirectly, of my own failures, my sad first marriage,
my poor degree, results of a dread that Vera's notoriety would dog
me for life. At twenty-two I was as lacking in foresight as Francis's
daughter, Elizabeth, lacks judgment, believing that in the 1980's the
name of Vera Hillyard would arouse more than indifference. Having
no fires or furnaces, I have given the transcript to my husband and
he has handed over this particularly exciting and exotic morsel of
food, to be devoured by the paper shredder in his office.

As the accused in a murder trial, Vera was not obliged to give evidence and she did not. Perhaps defending counsel persuaded her not to, knowing that anything she would say could only damn her further, or else Vera herself had no defense to offer and no arguments to put forward. Josie had told us of Vera's total apathy, how when she visited her in prison she had gone into a kind of fugue, retreating into herself and in a deep silence. I am sure she wanted to die. The alternative would have been years of imprisonment and during those years she would have had the daily torment of knowing Jamie was outside and in someone else's less-than-loving care. Counsel, of course, put up a defense. She had intended only to frighten, then only to wound, her sister. But frenzy had taken hold of her and she had struck again and again. . . .

Of this Stewart knows nothing. There is something else which has led to his abandonment of his project, the doubt at the heart of things, for if it is true that an element of mystery as to what really happened may enhance a work of this kind, the unanswered question is always one of who did it or how was it done. In Vera's case there is no doubt about that. The uncertainty hinges upon something quite different, upon a bizarre point of genesis, the kind of doubt rarely encountered in any family in any walk of life, and one to which no amount of research can supply a solution.

Memory is an imperfect function. We are resigned to not remembering things. It is the knowledge, imparted to us by unshakable outside authority, that an incident we remember never took place, which we find so hard to accept. Jamie told me, when we sat in his garden after dinner, that Eden's blood had flown at him that day, splashing onto his clothes. It was the only thing he could remember. But when he read the trial transcript he saw he had been mistaken. He remembered something that had never happened, for Mrs. King had carried him away before Vera struck out with her knife, seconds before. So the mannerism he has kept, the flicking at blood, is founded upon illusion.

Jamie has moved into a little house behind a high wall in the Orti Orcellari. There is a gate in this wall, one of those gates of wrought iron backed with iron, and on the portico, flanked by two urns that are linked by a stone garland of bay, and engraved these lines of Dante:

Ahi, quanto nella mente mi commossi,
quando mi volsi per veder Beatrice,

per non poter vedere; ben ch'io fossi
presso di lei, e nel mondo felice!

Has Jamie, too, been overthrown, his mind in a turmoil, through being shown once more what haunts him? Through seeing and not seeing? Without subscribing to specious psycho-therapeutic doctrines of the let-it-come-up-and-it-will-go-away school, he tells me he is glad he read the transcript. At least it has made him face it. Ceasing to be a bugbear, a chimera, a half-imagined thing, it has come out into the open, no worse than what he imagined and no better, but the thing itself, the real thing. To use the jargon of those doctrines, he has confronted it.

He was laughing as much as ever, flicking at his shoulder as much as ever—though now with an impatient shake of the head and a conscious staying of his hand in mid-air—and he cooked for me as he promised, wonderful dishes, *farfalle con asparagi, manzo per un dio biondo* (beef with grapes, "beef for a blond god," which puts one in mind of Francis), *crema d'arancia,* and *amaretti.* The sauce for the *manzo* he makes at the last minute, essential apparently for perfection, and while he stands at the stove I tell him that the pictures Francis gave those absurd titles to have disappeared from the Hotel Cavour. For we are staying there again, Louis and I, and I have looked into that bedroom and seen their places taken by innocuous and even pleasing aquarelles of Venice. Francis's and his new books lie side by side on the kitchen table, each newly published, each fresh from the binders and in glossy multicolored jackets: *Nymphs, Naiads, and Mayflies* and *Cucina Ben Riuscita.* And I have a sensation of peacefulness, of all things ultimately coming together for good.

Jamie's garden contains no flowers. Of course it doesn't, it is an Italian garden. Between the stone flags grow oxalis and *Arenaria* and these have their own tiny blossoms, yellow and white, but otherwise the garden is the dark moss color of evergreens and the weathered gray of stone. In urns that remind me of the ones that stood on the terrace at Goodney Hall grow plants that may be aspidistras and also the spike-leaved succulents called the mother-in-law's tongue that rise out of beds of trailing ivy. There is a little stagnant pool, full of lilies, free of fish, and up under the walls and behind the walls and in the stone and brick caverns are cats, the feral cats that are everywhere in the cities of Italy. We hear them sometimes, bodies slipping between a branch and a broken pillar, and as the dark comes, see their eyes. Jamie has put a lamp on the table, to which the moths come, and I remember Vera asking me to let her sit in the dusk for a while in peace, not to put the lights on and let the moths in.

"Tell me about my mother," he says to me, his manner calm, his voice steady.

It is a catch question, isn't it? I remember what he said to me in the English Cemetery, about his mother being a good cook. The proverb says that it's a wise child that knows its own father. I get my courage up and tell him it is less usual to be in doubt as to one's *maternity*.

"I'm not in doubt," he says. "Whatever the family may think, whatever the world may think, I know Vera Hillyard was my mother."

How can I argue with him? In a way it would be presumptuous of me to argue. I am not even sure if I want to. In the dusk, the dark now, with the moths around the lamp, I tell him about Vera, the nice things, carefully editing my memories: how much she loved him, her doting care, her selfless love of Eden, her housewifely skills, her dutiful life. She emerges from my descriptions as a perfect woman, nobly planned. Gone are the sharp tongue, the snobbery, the prejudice, the preoccupation with trivia, the coldness. I don't mention such rules as eating with the left hand, drinking with the right. I say nothing of her fear and dislike of Francis. And perhaps those virtues of Vera's did outweigh her faults and when I tell Jamie she was more sinned against than sinning, I am not far wrong.

"I'm glad Stewart has given up the idea," he says. "His book would have been written from the other point of view, of course, or at least he would have devoted his last chapter to pros and cons that don't really exist. I may write a book about her myself one of these days. Would you help me if I did?"

"No, Jamie," I say to him. "No, I don't think I would."

A fine golden moon is rising behind the dark trees in the gardens of the Orcellari. I tell Jamie it is time for me to go and we have a little argument, he insisting he will go with me to find a taxi on the rank up by Santa Maria Novella, I determined on walking back to the Via Cavour. This time we kiss good-bye and I have the sensation of a brown bear snuggling up to me. But the illusion vanishes fast as he steps back frenetically to sweep invisible blood from his shoulder. In the end, he does come with me as far as the top of the street. From there onwards, it is light and busy, crowds thronging the Piazza della

Stazione, and I persuaded him I shall be safe. It is the menu outside the Otello that distracts him. I look back once and see him still studying it, for all the world as if he were without cares and without a history.

My husband has said he will walk part of the way to meet me and there he is coming from the corner of the Via Nazionale. After all these years, the clutch at the heart which comes to me when we see each other and wave, is good to feel. His evening has been passed with a businessman, English but resident in Florence, bent on suing a newspaper for libel. Louis specializes in litigation, or rather, as he puts it, stopping people engaging in litigation. It was to him I went to be made free of Andrew, having chosen Josie's son because he was the only solicitor I knew of. I went to escape from one trap and immediately fell, though this time with a conviction never proved wrong of future happiness, into another. Out of the frying pan into the fire. How lucky I am that the fire still burns so brightly!

I take his arm. I tell him about Jamie and what Jamie has said.

"What do *you* think?" I ask him.

"As to whose child Jamie truly was? Edith Pearmain's, surely."

"For years," I say, "I didn't believe that, and then for years I thought so."

"The point," says Louis as we come to the hotel, "is that it wasn't really relevant to the case against your Aunt Vera. Or shall I say that it was wise of neither side to have anything to do with it. It was more *just.*"

"How can you say that!"

"Remember Edith Thompson in the twenties. She was certainly innocent of the murder of her husband. Bywaters stabbed him, and not at her instigation. But Bywaters was her lover, she was a married woman, and that was what executed her. Remember Ruth Ellis a few years after Vera Hillyard. The climate of feeling still hadn't changed. It has been said that Ruth Ellis was hanged not because she had shot her lover but because she *had* a lover. If the defense had insisted Jamie was in fact Vera's child—instead of allowing it to be assumed he was Edith's—it would also have had to be made clear he wasn't Gerald Hillyard's. Do you see now?"

"It made no difference in the end."

"No. There's no penalty worse than hanging. But it might have done, there was a chance." Louis looks at me, one eyebrow up. "He was Edith's—Eden's—wasn't he?"

"I don't know. No one will ever know now."

I don't know. And that is the heart of the mystery that has frustrated Daniel Stewart and let him down.

It is perhaps most likely that Eden was Jamie's mother, but there is a great deal against that, isn't there? Certainly she became pregnant sometime in the summer of 1943 and the first person she went to in her trouble was Francis. There had always been close, secret things between them, arcane things. But if Francis told her the name of an abortionist and gave her the money, or some of it, for an abortion, why didn't she have one? Because she was afraid, because Vera talked her out of it? A postmortem, according to Stewart, was carried out on Eden's body, but not in order to discover whether she had ever been pregnant—that is, carried a child to term and delivered it.

And there is a very good argument for her having, in fact, had that abortion. Eden miscarried in 1948 as the result of an ectopic pregnancy. One of the principal factors contributing to an ectopic pregnancy, or the implantation of the fetus in one of the fallopian tubes rather than in the uterus, is a previous abortion badly carried out and causing infection and the subsequent blocking of a tube. Of course other possibilities here are gonorrhea (as my mother scandalously hinted) and a previous, carelessly attended birth. Perhaps we can't quite dismiss the venereal disease but surely we can the carelessly handled delivery. The nursing home where Jamie was born, to whichever woman it was, was a reputable one. I never heard the staff there impugned for any sort of negligence.

So perhaps the baby whose father was some Londonderry G.I. Eden did have aborted—and later bitterly regretted her decision. For that autumn she heard that her sister, her much older sister, was expecting a child, and she almost envied her. It was not Gerald's, though, that much is evident. Did it happen as I had earlier believed? Did Vera encounter some old boyfriend home on leave and in her loneliness make love with him? Anne Cambus once told me (not apropos of any of this) that a Sindon family, the Warners, owed their dark coloring to the fact that the children's grandfather, an old seafaring man, still alive when I was a child, had married a wife he brought back with him from Agadir. Two of their sons were in the army during the war, both officers. Is this too farfetched? Am I being absurd? Perhaps.

Vera suckled Jamie, she fed him at her own breast. I saw it. I can't be mistaken here. And since then I have read accounts in newspapers and magazines—a whole book has been written on the subject, I believe—of women who, adopting or taking over other people's babies, have induced lactation. By the intensity of their love and by their determination, holding the child to the dry breast, persevering, they have done it. So why not Vera? She was exactly the sort of woman to achieve it, intense, conscientious, prone to obsessions, driven by a self-formulated notion of duty. Taking over Eden's child, she might very likely have held him to her breast, let him suck, seen one day a drop of milk exuded from the nipple, and then persevered for a variety of reasons: to make him more her own, to do what was best for him, to allay doubts in others that he was not her child.

But it is more probable, isn't it, that Jamie was her natural child and that lactation happened as it normally does from the action of the emptying of the womb? Vera was a prudish finicking woman who would have pulled a face and said "How disgusting!" if told of the book by the self-induced lactator. She had never breast-fed Francis, though she was very young when he was born and nursing a baby would have come more easily to her. She would never have attempted to breast-feed a child not her own, for the idea would never have occurred to her.

You will say that if Jamie was Vera's own son, why did she allow Eden to name herself his mother on his birth certificate? The answer may be that she didn't, that she knew nothing of it until it was too late. Or she may, of course, have approved this false declaration. In her own eyes, after all, she had done a terrible thing. She had had a child by a man not her husband. That was bad enough. Was she to compound her wrongdoing by telling her husband Jamie was his? She lacked the nerve to confess he was not. Just to be on the safe side, why not let Eden do as she had offered and register Jamie as her own son? Neither of them wanted him at that time, anyway, he was an encumbrance to both, but their mutual devotion was great. Eden would do this generous thing for her so that one day—when and if Gerald came back, if he doubted her, if the child looked very unlike him or very like someone else—she could show Gerald that birth certificate and explain she had adopted Jamie for Eden's sake. At the time of his birth she could not have foreseen how much she would come to love him or that Eden would ever want him herself.

So Jamie was Vera's son, as he himself believes, and her fears of losing him arose simply from a false declaration on a birth certificate.

Never once, in court or at the time of the murder or beforehand or to Helen or my father when they visited her in the prison, did she admit that Eden had been telling the truth and that Jamie was her son. Never once did Vera weaken over her claim to be Jamie's mother.

But all the same he must have been Eden's. Why, otherwise, would she have left the WRNS when she did, telling no one in the family she had done so, virtually disappearing from the autumn of 1943 until the summer of 1945? Would anyone in her right mind make a false declaration to a registrar, and that declaration a claim to be the unmarried mother of an illegitimate child, to save a sister from a possible future contretemps with her husband? She could not then have foreseen that she would one day want to adopt a child. And a husband, not then in sight, might be involved. She was afraid to take the risk of having an abortion, afraid not to have the child, afraid to lie to the registrar, while clinging to Vera as her lifeline, sister-mother-savior Vera who had offered to take the baby and bring him up as her own. Jamie was Eden's. She would never have said he was if he wasn't, prudent, hardheaded husband hunter that she was. Those were the days when men still wanted virgin brides, or the kind of men Eden fancied did. At any rate, they didn't want the mothers of illegitimate children.

So it goes on, round and round in perpetual motion without ever coming to rest on Eden's square or Vera's. During these long-past years I have come to know other people's beliefs as to the truth of it. They are all conflicting. Helen is for Eden. Jamie was Eden's son, she says, and believes this as firmly as Jamie himself takes the opposing view. Vera would never have been so afraid of Eden, she asserts, if she were truly Jamie's mother and the doubt rested solely on an error in a birth certificate. Gerald, however, once confided in Helen of his own certainty that Jamie was Vera's, for if he were Eden's and Vera in caring for him was merely doing her sister a service, she would not even have waited to tell him this when he came home, she would have written it to him at once. I wouldn't have guessed him capable of such subtlety in character analysis, but yes, he told Helen, Vera being what she was, she would have been more likely to tell him Jamie was Eden's when he was in fact her own than claim him as her own when he wasn't for the sake of protecting Eden. What she did in fact tell him was—nothing. She refused to speak of Jamie's paternity, and this, ultimately, was why he left her.

Francis told Chad (and Chad told Stewart) that he knows Jamie was Eden's child. She came to him in the autumn of 1943, saying she was pregnant and asking for the money for an abortion. He got her the money and gave it to her with the proviso that if she changed her mind he wanted it back. She had told him she knew she must have an abortion but she was terrified of it, she was afraid the abortionist would kill her or so damage her as to make it impossible for her to have children in the future. But he didn't see her again for more than a year and he never got the money back. Chad himself has never doubted Jamie was Vera's, for, like me, he came upon her with the baby at her breast. Josie, my mother-in-law, always said Jamie was Vera's on the grounds that during the long hours they spent together when Vera poured out her terrors, she would have admitted he was Eden's and not hers. Yet Tony was convinced Jamie was his wife's child, knew she would never have dared risk losing husband and home by such a confession unless it were true. And Anne Cambus can remember passing Laurel Cottage in the spring of 1944 and seeing Eden emerge for a moment from the front door, the equinoctial wind blowing her dress taut across her swollen body before she fled indoors. But Anne is not quite positive about this memory, she would not swear it was Eden she saw and not Vera, and she and I have wondered if like Jamie she has innocently distorted the past.

We are back from Italy and the usual mountain of post awaits us, as much for me this time as for Louis, for Daniel Stewart has sent me back all the letters and photographs. I postpone opening the three padded bags until next day, until I am alone. But this time there are no tears, only a feeling of rueful nostalgia, of folly and of waste.

Here is Eden's letter of reproach, admonishing my father for my rudeness, and here is Vera telling him of her intention to live in Laurel Cottage and make a home there for Eden. Vera, photographed with Francis on her knee, has a brown dappling on her hair, spots of my father's blood from the finger he cut when wrenching that picture from its frame. Soulful Eden in the photographer's studio in Londonderry lies between radiant Eden in her arum-lily wedding dress and Vera and Gerald with the dome and the banyan tree.

I go upstairs and fetch the box and put them all back, laying in last of all, placing on the top of the pile, the picture of us all in Vera's garden in summertime, a united family, wearing our innocent smiles, not yet imagining those births and marriages and deaths to come.